Mytholumina

Mytholumina

A Collection of Stories

Storm Constantine

IMMANION
PRESS
Stafford, England

Mytholumina
Storm Constantine
© 2009

Cover Art and Design: Lucas Swann
Interior Design and Layout: Storm Constantine

Set in Souvenir

IP0023

ISBN 978-1-904853-58-9

An Immanion Press Edition
http://www.immanion-press.com
info@immanion-press.com

Immanion Press
8 Rowley Grove
Stafford ST17 9BJ
UK

Books by Storm Constantine

The Wraeththu Chronicles
*The Enchantments of Flesh and Spirit
*The Bewitchments of Love and Hate
*The Fulfilments of Fate and Desire
*The Wraeththu Chronicles (omnibus of trilogy)

The Artemis Cycle
The Monstrous Regiment
Aleph

*Hermetech
Burying the Shadow
Sign for the Sacred
Calenture
Thin Air

The Grigori Books
*Stalking Tender Prey
*Scenting Hallowed Blood
*Stealing Sacred Fire

Silverheart (with Michael Moorcock)

The Magravandias Chronicles:
Sea Dragon Heir
Crown of Silence
The Way of Light

The Wraeththu Histories:
*The Wraiths of Will and Pleasure
*The Shades of Time and Memory
*The Ghosts of Blood and Innocence

Wraeththu Mythos
*The Hienama
*Student of Kyme

Short Story Collections:
The Thorn Boy and Other Dreams of Dark Desire
*Mythophidia
*Mythangelus
*available as Immanion Press editions

Contents

Introduction 7

Immaculate 13

The Pleasure Giver Taken 31

As it Flows to the Sea 65

The College Spirit 83

Last Come Assimilation 117

Time Beginning at Break of Day 139

Did You Ever See Oysters Walking Down the Stairs...? 151

The Vitreous Suzerain 183

The Rust Islands 201

Built on Blood 231

God Be With You 255

So What's Forever 273

The Germ of Life 289

Introduction

Mytholumina is the third volume in a series of books collecting all my published and unpublished short stories. I've loosely themed each collection – although a few were difficult to categorise, so were placed where they seemed most comfortably to sit. Most of the stories in this collection are science fiction, although there are a couple that could be term dark fantasy.

Immaculate

Of all my short stories, this was has been reprinted the most times, and in several different languages, but it first appeared in David Garnett's *New Worlds* anthology (VGSF 1991). It was written while I was working on the novel *Hermetech*, and reflects the mood of that book.

When I wrote *Immaculate* I'd just bought my first 'proper' computer after writing two novels on a basic Amstrad word processing machine. I wanted to write about this new technology I was experiencing, even though I didn't know much about it. However, as a writer, I could make assumptions and invent. *Immaculate* was also inspired by a news story concerning women who wanted children without the inconvenience of having sex with men. A woman had experienced a virgin birth, thanks to IVF treatment. My writer's ears immediately pricked up as I read this piece. There's no escaping the religious aspect of a virgin birth.

The Pleasure Giver Taken

This was the first story I sold, to David Garnett for his first

'Zenith' anthology (Sphere 1989). However, it was the second to be published, since GM Magazine slipped in quickly by printing 'God Be With You' before 'Zenith' got to the printers. 'The Pleasure Giver Taken' was written in the heady days when 'The Enchantments of Flesh and Spirit' had just come out, and I really thought the world had laid a golden carpet before me covered in jewels. Reality soon took over! The universe of this story has recurred through a variety of other short pieces, and also in the two novels 'The Monstrous Regiment' and 'Aleph'.

As with many of my short story characters, I wanted to write more about Tavrian Guilder, but just never got around to it.

As It Flows to the Sea

This story was written for the collection *Tarot Tales*, edited by Rachel Pollack and Caitlin Matthews (Legend, 1989). The idea behind the anthology was for each contributor to base their story on a selection of Tarot cards. I drew three at random, and came up with the idea for this science fiction story.

I think this piece reflects the mood in SF during the Eighties, which in itself reflected the mood of the world. In speculative fiction, the future was envisaged as corporate-mindedness gone mad, with huge intergalactic conglomerates, mostly sporting Japanese sounding names, filling the universe with their greedy, soulless pursuit of riches. This was yuppy sf, obsessed with technological gadgets and the ultimate in cool. It became a subgenre in sf, and was dubbed cyperpunk. Although I wouldn't call *As it Flows to the Sea* a cyberpunk story, it contains cyberpunky elements in the avaricious character Gustav Mealie and the ideas behind the plot.

The College Spirit

This story first appeared in the Midnight Rose project's *Temps* anthology, created by Neil Gaiman and Alex Stewart (Roc 1991). The premise behind this shared world collection was that superheroes, called paranorms, become real. An organisation called the DPR monitors these individuals. I can see now that in some ways the concept shares similarities with the X Men idea, since paranorms are treated with great suspicion in the world of the stories. I'm not particularly into superheroes, but because of the people involved in the project, and the ideas they had, I wanted to be part of it. *The College Spirit* is a lighthearted story, and I had great fun writing it.

Last Come Assimilation
This story first appeared in *Digital Dreams*, (New English Library, 1990), an anthology edited by David Barrett. It's loosely connected with *The Pleasure Giver Taken* (which appears in the *Mythanima* collection), as it's set in the same universe. It is the universe of my novels *The Monstrous Regiment* and *Aleph*, as well as several stories. Reading through it again, I can't help feeling the technology in it sounds a little dated – computers and other technologies have come on so much since the Eighties; the futuristic predictions that writers used to make about technology then now come over as rather quaint. Still, I find it a pleasing little tale, and despite its SF trappings, it examines the concept of secrecy and betrayal in apparently close friendships.

Time Beginning at Break of Day
Quite often stories evolve from real life weird events that happen to my friends, or friends of theirs. The core of this piece is based on a frightening night's lucid dreaming once experienced by a guy who used to lodge in my house, back in the Eighties. Happily, his real story was just dreams. What he tried to convey to me, as he told me about it, was the frightening sense of slipping away from consensual reality, his utter belief that the fabric of what was normal and solid was beginning to break down. In some ways, I suppose, you just had to be there, in order to appreciate the depth of his fears, but what is recorded here is the gist of his feelings.

I've never tried to sell this story, because it is really just a fragment, but I wanted to include it in this collection, because I felt it was too creepy just to sit forever on the hard disk of my computer.

Did you Ever See Oysters...

The next story appeared in Roz Kaveney's *More Tales of the Forbidden Planet* collection, published by Titan in 1990. The title refers to an unlikely event; it derives from an old folklore saying. One of my favourite obsessions is abandoned old houses, and I think it is one of nearly everyone's greatest fears to lose track of what is reality and what is not. This story, I think, follows on nicely from the above piece. It also examines what can happen when people's imaginations begin to work overtime. Quite often, there are prosaic explanations as to what appear to be weird events, but then again... maybe not.

The Vitreous Suzerain

This story first appeared in a short-lived sf magazine called *The Gate*, in 1991. It's quite an early piece and involves humankind trying to interact with an alien species. It's about trying to establish a point of communication. The story is set in the same universe I used for 'God Be With You' and the novel 'Aleph' and again reflects the mood of sf at the time. I think it handles, quite ingenuously, heavy concepts like racial misunderstandings and the human drive to homogenise.

The Rust Islands

First appearing in *Interzone* magazine, in March 97, this story to me has the same techno-hippy feel of my novel, 'Hermetech'. It's rare I dip into the realms of pure science fiction, but this was a story I particularly enjoyed working on.

Built on Blood

The story first appeared in *Interzone* magazine in 1992, accompanied by some great illustrations by Dave Horton, who also illustrated the chapter headings for my novel, *Sign for the Sacred*. It was written way back in the early 90s and it's quite amusing now to note the surname of the messiah type celebrity who appears in the story. Just for the record, this was obviously not intentional, and way predates recent governmental administration in the UK!

People's obsession with, and perhaps need for, celebrities has always fascinated me, and I've examined the idea many times in my work. The person they revere is never real; it's a construct. And why do they have to revere individuals in that way, making them bigger than life, like gods? There is a sinister side to it, when they can turn on the object of their affections. Or maybe that is a primal impulse associated with the phenomenon. The sacrifice of the Most Fair. This is my take on it.

God Be With You
A recurrent theme throughout my work is my distaste for organised religion and how fanatical beliefs can turn people into monsters. When this story first appeared in the gaming magazine, *GM*, back in 1990, there was a furore going on with fundamentalist Christians insisting that role-playing games were the work of the devil and should be stopped. *GM* got a regular pile of hate mail from these types, so it was often the topic of conversation when I had phone chats with Wayne, who was a friend and one of the editors of the magazine. When I was asked to submit a story, it seemed only natural to vent my disgust at what was going on in fiction form.

God Be With You is set in the science fiction universe that I visit often when writing in that genre. Because the piece was written for a gaming magazine, I felt I should include a game aspect in the story. This also goes for the story that follows, *So What's Forever.* These were written for a specific market, so I was only going to include them here for the sake of collecting all my stories in this series of anthologies. But re-reading *God Be With You* for the first time since it was written eighteen years ago, I was surprised at how much I liked it!

So What's Forever?

Lighter in theme than the previous story, this was another piece I wrote for GM Magazine, in 1988. Again, it was written for a specific market, so revolves around a role-playing game. In some ways, the piece was quite prophetic. When I wrote it, I had never played any games of this type and wasn't particularly drawn to them. Back then, role-playing took place in 'real life'; computers were still primitive. But over the past few years Jim and I have become involved in multi-player online games, so I can certainly appreciate the attraction more now. I've had many discussions with my fellow gamers – and you'd be surprised how many creative types you find in these virtual worlds – as to why the games and their worlds are so addictive. One friend said that when they are 'inworld', people can be who they want to be; they can set goals and achieve them. That's sometimes not so easy in real life. The fantasy worlds we can visit now on our computers are so far beyond those primitive, clunky games that initiated the genre that you can only wonder how far it will all go. Will it eventually become some Matrix-style para-reality? And if so, how difficult will it be for people to leave these virtual worlds then? As one friend once said to me, 'There is no real life, only AFK.'

The Germ of Life

This story was written to be submitted to one of David Garnett's *New World* anthologies, but it didn't make the grade. I can't remember now what the editor didn't like about it, but he was always a strong supporter of my work, so it must have been something serious! I did nothing with it thereafter, and only read it again while compiling this collection to see if it really was too bad to be included. Actually, I found it an enjoyable little read. It's probably not heavy enough on scientific facts for a hardcore SF story, but with a bit of tinkering I felt I rounded it up enough for its inclusion here. It is again set in the universe of some of the other stories in this collection.

Immaculate

Donna can feel computers dreaming; they reach out and touch her mind, or so she says. In the dark of her room, as the white noise tide of day goes out, and the sky rises dark and glowing, the machines begin to meditate, or so she says. It makes Reeb think of dogs twitching in their sleep, the tongues of slumbering cats licking at invisible bowls of milk; human signs.

'You always have to look for human signs in everything,' says Donna. She's a star, she's a nobody. She sells things.

Reeb is a director, a creative of sufficient reputation to currently work for Say! Play!, a company specialising in leisure software. This is the man who configured the footage that sold the product that juiced the data-suit that excited the customer who paid the cash that went into the accounts of Say! Play! He would not dare to call himself an artist, although his previous campaigns have done much to increase the sales of Say! Play!; his mind is the company's, he can find no other.

Donna is their hot package of the moment. In studio, she is a child, innocent and trusting. As a warming light image on your retina, a sound effect between your ears, a grind and stroke of vibro-fabric, she can be your unforbidden lover. Is there such a thing as the girl next door nowadays? Who lives next door, or next floor, another tuned-up commodity? Marketing-wise, Donna is perfection. How young is she: thirteen? Sixteen? Twenty? She also hears voices; there's a market for that, but is she the right product? She can hardly be termed normal. Once, she had a strange pain in her side and when the medics examined her, they found a tiny six-sided die in her liver. Donna was not surprised; she said the People had put it there. The People advise her often, although fortunately for everyone concerned they appear to have a fairly favourable view of her occupation. Neither does Donna punish herself. She has no conscience that Reeb can detect.

Today, she is pouting and blinking at the scanners, sighing softly in a provocative and exciting way. 'Oh! Oh!'

Reeb supervises laconically. Later, he will tinker with the footage and, combined with a graphics package, will produce some hard-core delight for the consumer. Donna doesn't have to be too explicit, not like it's the real thing. Reeb can shoot a few limb movements tomorrow, some dildonics the next day; the software overdubs stock effects. Donna puts her tiny hands on either side of her face and grimaces. It is not part of the script.

'What is it?' Reeb asks from the other side of the observation panel.

'Oh, they are speaking to me,' Donna says, putting shaking fingers to her forehead, where the skin is almost translucent and has a damp sheen to it. Today, that suggestion of delicacy repulses Reeb; on other days, it has seemed attractive. She is a child, in mind if not in flesh. Reeb has a desire to tweak her smug piety with a burst of power; he can do that, but he doesn't.

'Who is speaking to you?' He adjusts one of the scan controls, still shooting.

She shrugs, hand flopping into her lap. 'My People. They're gone now.'

'What did they say?'

'Something about an elevator.'

She's making this up; she has to be. 'What?'

'I don't remember.'

She can be convincing when she wants to be. That's why she's here in his studio. Dice and elevators, computers dreaming. Young lips wetted with the tip of a nervous tongue, wide eyes. Donna lives in another world.

If Donna has her aspects of freakishness, Reeb has his own too. Nearly two years ago, he lost half of his body. The accident itself was freakish, like getting hit by lightning. Relaxing in his data-suit at home, living out a hi-res dream, the suit had suddenly turned on him like a swarm of vicious insects, cooking his right side to a frazzle, eating away at his groin and gut. The prostheticians had been delighted by him. (We can redesign this man, they had announced proudly, and proceeded to do so. Reeb could see the humour in it now, but at the time, their eagerness had sickened him). Medics could not rebuild his apartment though or resurrect the other victim of the accident, his dog.

'You called it to you, that power,' Donna once said. He hated her the day she said that, the very first time he worked with her. For a while, after his therapy had proved so successful, he'd been a reluctant media star himself. Donna had recognised him instantly. 'Electricity is alive too; it's what makes the machines dream,' she told him. His prosthetics are more sensitive than his meat ever was, but there is still a seam, a sense of unreality, a sense that outsiders have moved into his body and might, one day, take over.

'The machines are alive,' Donna says, casting a meaningful glance at Reeb's right side. He puts his hand on his leg; squeezes. It feels like flesh, but slightly rubbery; perhaps like some kind of tough mollusc. This is his first commission since he came out of therapy.

Donna has been one of the company's products for six months; her face is burned into a million consumers' dreams. She might have been a little crazy for years and kept it quiet, only now she wants to tell people about her Voices and Visions, her People. She has mentioned them in interviews. People have conjectured whether her peculiarities are the result of how she was conceived. Donna was one of the first of the home-grown 'virgin births'. This fact must be significant, surely? Some people are not only prepared to believe it, but desperate to do so. These people are a cult the media tagged The Immaculates. To Reeb, they are a sad group of crazies that grew up around the virgin birth kick, desperate under-achievers trying to populate the steamed- up, fucked-up world with little messiahs. At the end of the twentieth century the Goddess of Love had tended to stride around with a scythe in her hand, more often than not, and the fear of fatal disease had not only launched the suddenly-respectable software porn industry, but had also estranged many people from the desire for human contact. Through artificial insemination, women gave birth who had never known a man's touch, or indeed a woman's. At first, it was just the single women, then the gay women; later, the cult of the Immaculates grew up. Men can be Immaculate too.

Reeb thinks the Immaculates should all be locked up, even though he knows the phenomenon is merely a reaction against the fear of death, the de-lustifying of sexuality. There's no need for that anymore, but the vein runs deep in human consensus. Too many died back then. The Immaculates were a fringe group wanting to turn it all into a religion. Mercifully, they had never progressed beyond a minority, but they still gushed warmly about Donna in their cult magazines.

The company have kept an eye on the media and now wonder whether this is an angle of Donna worth exploiting. After all, if the rumours circulating on the networks are true, Donna is not unique. Many people, whatever their background, are stepping forward to talk about Voices and Visions. Donna, being public property, could very easily be turned into a spearhead for this movement. Her family is totally devoid of fevered religion-mongers looking for a place to hang their beliefs, but she does have two mothers; hers was a conception of convenience rather than conviction. Alexis, the woman who carried her, is now her agent and manager. Alexis is probably the opposite of anyone's vision of a Madonna. It is doubtful whether her hands have ever met beneath her chin in prayer. She is an eternal teenager, lankily attractive with razor-cut hair and slept-in-look anti-fashion gear. That she could have spawned an angel like Donna is in itself, Reeb supposes, a kind of miracle. And, if your child really does look like an angel, and fulfils everybody's dreams, then you exploit it; in the best possible sense. Especially when your girlfriend is obsessed by graffiti art and the photographic medium; nobody's into anything less than 3D nowadays, so somebody has to see to the family income. Alexis brings Donna over to the studio four days a week, for Reeb to record her.

Reeb is also interviewing the girl about her Visions and Voices. Donna is pleased to comply, because she likes to talk. She is one of those pale, tiny people who sometimes become attractive under the right lighting, the right conditions of the mind. Sometimes Reeb likes her very much and is convinced she has a startling clear-sightedness. Sometimes, she irritates him and he thinks she's stupid. He used to feel the same way about his dog, when he had one.

Reeb went back to live with his mother after the accident. It was supposed to be a temporary arrangement - he's still paying rent on his own apartment - but somehow he doesn't have the will to move back home yet. He knows there could-n't be a smell of burning flesh there anymore, and the block domestics would have cleaned everything up but... His mother's apartment is spacious, she's never there, she never bothers him. He likes the view, and it's nearer to the studio than his old place. Occasionally, he thinks about ending his lease with the property agency, although it seems a little ungrateful, seeing as they compensated him so heavily for the accident.

Sometimes, he goes over to Alexis and Meriel's for dinner; he has become friendly with them since working with Donna. 'When are you going to let go of Mommy's apron strings,' Alexis says, smiling. They are worried about him.

Meriel points a camera at him. 'And when are you going to strip for me,' she says.

He's not sure whether that's an offer or a request.

He goes to the studio early. Alexis and Donna are late today.

The trains were down again.

'Someone died, I expect,' Alexis says when she finally arrives, scraping back her artfully ragged black hair. 'Jumpers! I hate 'em. Why do I have to be inconvenienced by their inadequacy? It's so selfish!' Her eyes skitter nervously away from Reeb's body as if she wonders whether she's touched on taboo. 'I can't bear to be held up!' she says.

In the office, after her mother has left, Donna leans against the desk-top demurely. Reeb cannot imagine her living with Alexis and Meriel; she is an anachronism, a time-child from years past. She wears a white dress, but that is part of her costume wardrobe. The primness exists in the fabric of the dress, but is it a part of Donna? Reeb doesn't know yet. Is she an example of her mothers' artistic experiments? He would not put it past them. They never talk about Donna to him, and neither is she ever present at the dim-lit, smoky evenings Reeb enjoys in their company. It is as if the women lock her away in a cupboard when she's not working. Once, he tried to talk to Alexis about Donna's problem.

'She's imaginative,' Alexis said. 'That's all. She makes things up.'

'She believes it,' Reeb said.

Alexis rolled her eyes. 'You think so?'

He hadn't meant the voices and visions; the problem, in his opinion, was that Donna had a reality all to herself. Her home, the studio, A to B, and anything in between, like other people, her parents, street bums, commuters, interviewers, even himself, seemed only to touch her awareness on a superficial level. Her only contact with the world outside her own was through performance. And in her room, what did she do in her room? Reeb cannot ask Alexis questions like that; she is clearly not maternal material. The procedure was all the rage back then, of course. New legislation meant women could claim it as a right. Perhaps all Alexis' friends were having children that way. A public statement about her chosen way of life, her chosen lover.

Over the past two weeks, Reeb has been studying the

phenomenon that is Donna. There has to be a new angle on her as a product, something the company can use; that's his brief. Has she always heard the voices, had these experiences, and not spoken about them, or are they a more recent phenomenon? Donna cannot remember. She wrinkles her nose, pulls a face. 'One night Merry's laptop dreamed to me,' she says, 'but I don't remember when.'

And what does a computer's dream look like?

She doesn't have the words to describe it; she has grown up that much. 'I could think it to you,' she says, 'but that's all.'

He would dismiss it as fantasy, if it wasn't for the die. The slap-marks which had appeared instantaneously on her arm one day could be explained away as being psychologically self-induced. At the time, when it happened, Donna had told him one of the People had got angry with her.

'So, what are you going to do with this material?' Alexis asks him, through the cloud of marihuana smoke she has just exhaled. He is over for dinner again, but has only Alexis' company because Meriel's been called out; a rare offer of work, she can't refuse. Alexis never talks to Reeb about his work with Donna, so he is surprised she wants to discuss it now. Usually, she talks to him about himself.

'Donna is not unique,' he says, 'there are others like her, increasing all the time. They make a market. Understand?'

'A market for what?' Alexis swings her booted feet up on the table, kicking a plate out of the way.

'I'm supposed to be thinking that one up.' He considers the next question before he speaks. 'Aren't you worried about her?'

'She's quite happy,' Alexis says. 'She's always been happy. Completely alien to me, of course, but always happy. I think she gets on better with Merry.' She pulls a face and hands him her joint.

'I tried to be specific about what kind of donor I wanted when she was conceived. I think they lied to me, don't you?' She grins. 'Sometimes I wonder whether anything of mine went into her at all.' If she feels wistful about that, she hides it.

'Where is Donna?' Reeb asks. 'She's never around when I call.'

'She's in her playroom. All the things she likes are in there.'

Reeb thinks Donna is too old to have a playroom. She should be hanging out with kids her own age, learning to live. Is that discouraged? He can't believe so. Alex and Merry wouldn't be that into Donna fooling around with guys, he thinks, but they would never force their lifestyle on someone else, not even if that someone was their daughter.

'What's she get up to in there, anyway?' Reeb asks, jerking his head in the direction of the closed door that is Donna's.

Alexis shrugs. 'Who knows? She doesn't like us going in there, so we don't. We all respect each other's privacy.'

Reeb frowns at the door. Hasn't Donna any friends at all?

'Donna will be OK,' Alexis says. 'Don't you worry about her; she's a survivor. Now you -' She stabs a finger in his direction. '- you, I worry about.'

She hardly knows him. He's been working with Donna for maybe six weeks and hadn't met Alexis before then. He ought to be annoyed at her interference, and would be, if he didn't enjoy it so much. Is that what he wants, motherly concern? Becka, his own mother, doesn't know how to deal with emotional crises; she organised his life and then butted out to leave him with the burned-out mess of his self-image and feelings. Perhaps that's why he hardly ever sees her. She isn't busy exactly; just busy avoiding him.

'I ought to find myself a place,' he says.

'What's wrong with the one you've got?'

'It's my mother's. I cramp her style.'

'I meant the one you pay for, stupid. Are you never going to go back there?'

He shrugs.

'What reason is there not to?' Alexis demands. 'Your

body probably performs now better than it ever did...' She drops her eyes, actually blushes. 'Oh, I'm sorry...'

More than an arm and leg had been burned away. But they can fix that. They can fix everything. He didn't believe it.

'It's o.k.,' he says. 'You're right. I just feel... I don't know. It's as if someone died in there.'

'You had a dog, didn't you?'

'I didn't mean him. Someone else.'

'Oh.' Alexis shrugs awkwardly. 'I think I understand that. It's terrible.' She brightens and pours him another glass of wine. 'Tell you what. We'll look for a new apartment for you this week, shall we? Somewhere near here, so we can keep an eye on you.'

Reeb is glad he has met these women. He is happy to lean on them. 'Yeah. Fine.'

'I heard you talking to Alexis last night,' Donna says, when she arrives at Reeb's studio the following day.

'Oh?' Reeb tries to recall what he said, what Alexis might have said. But Donna isn't interested in what she might have heard about herself.

'You've *never* been back to your apartment?' she asks, round-eyed.

Reeb is taken aback. He smiles, laughs unconvincingly. 'Not yet.'

'What are you afraid of?'

'Nothing. Just, well, bad memories.' *I lost half my life there*, he thinks, half *myself, perhaps more than half.* A bad thing in the walls had swarmed into his data-suit and sucked away his juice. He feels the place is haunted, perhaps by himself.

'Your dog died there,' Donna says.

'Yeah. Now, tell me what you've been experiencing since I last spoke with you.'

Donna reaches out and puts a delicate hand on his arm, the right arm. 'I want to experience your old apartment,' she says.

'Why? What for?'

She smiles an adult smile. 'The People want me to.'

'And what do they want to do that for?' He smiles back at her, although he feels nervous. He is thinking about the place, his collection of old books, his wall paintings, the way the morning light comes into the main living space, the colour of the floor. He sees himself standing in the kitchenette, mixing an old-style Martini for a shadowy ghost sitting on the couch, out by the hearth. The whole apartment is lit by the flicker of holographic flames. He can hear a body shifting impatiently. The air is full of perfume. The owner of these shadows, these subtle noises, this perfume was, in Reeb's memory, nothing but a human template. Later, he recreated this person as Elna, creature of dreams, modified to his taste. Elna never had to go home, live its own life, but the dream had existed only in the artificial world of recreation and had burned out along with his datasuit.

Donna's small, pale fingers dig into his artificial flesh. He winces a little, brought back to the present. 'When are you going to confront this problem, Reeb?' she asks, in a voice very much like Meriel's. 'Until you confront the dark things inside you, they make you helpless. They are your weaknesses.' She stands up straight, arms folded, and, for a moment, she is a young woman wearing a child's dress. 'Please, take me there.'

He doesn't want to go, even though he's sure the place will be cleaned up. He doesn't want to see that place again and yet, at the same time, he does. Some of his life is still there.

Donna seems to sense his indecision. She doesn't argue with him as Alexis would. She simply breathes some words at him. 'Please, oh pleeeese, Reeb. I have to go there. I have to see. Let me help you. I can do that. Really I can. Take me there.'

The door is familiar yet strange. He puts his lock-card in the slot and, as if he's never been away, the door opens. Donna steps past, steps inside. He stands on the threshold staring, his right side tingling, his heart beating quickly. He can't go in. He can't. It stinks too much. The smell comes out in a wave of sharp remembrance. Blinking, he watches as Donna goes to the far side of the living room and raises the blind, opens the window. The city comes inside; noise below. The only smell is of disuse, a kind of staleness, harbouring memories, but not reeking.

The girl turns round, a silhouette against the light. 'I like it,' she says.

The walls have been repainted in a creamy colour. The sofa has been replaced, an inoffensive yet nondescript piece of furniture. Reeb would not have chosen it himself, but he can see Becka hurriedly and distastefully ordering it from the mail order channel. As he looks at it, a memory resurfaces: frantic barking, teeth closing on the fabric of his suit, pulling desperately, the deadly current passed on. He looks away quickly. Everything else is just the same. His equipment, surprisingly, doesn't even look slightly damaged, although the data-suit has gone. Most of it was burned into him; the medics removed it along with his ruined flesh. Reeb feels sick, yet detached.

Donna crosses the room on light feet and puts her child-like hands on his arms. 'You must come inside,' she says.

'I don't think I...'

She pulls him over the threshold. 'You think it's haunted here?' she says, breathlessly.

He doesn't answer. Now he's here, he might as well pack some of his stuff together. The kid can poke around if she wants to. He can see into the small bedroom, the disarray which was caused by his mother throwing things around, looking for the items he asked her to bring him. It isn't too bad for him here. He should have come before. He feels he's been trying to spray plastic skin over a rotten wound. He might as well face reality.

Donna stands in the middle of the room with her eyes closed, humming to herself. One hand is held out towards the far wall, against which the couch rests. Her face is frowning in concentration.

Reeb shakes his head and goes into his bedroom. This is where the ghosts would lie, not back in the other room, or splayed out on the floor, but here, healthy and whole. He looks at himself in the smoky mirror behind the bed, pulls down the collar of his shirt, scrapes back his hair. It is impossible to see the join between what is human and what is not human. The two materials have meshed invisibly. He has been told by the medics that his synthetic cells are no less part of him than the cells he had before; if anything, the new ones are more efficient and durable. There is no reason why he shouldn't simply forget half of him is synthetic. He wishes he could. Turning away from the mirror, he opens a wall cupboard, but finds it difficult to summon any interest for his possessions inside. Perhaps he should throw everything away. Begin again.

'Reeb?' Donna is standing in the doorway. 'You're still in the wires.' She looks small, hugging herself.

Her words make his spine crawl with unease. Why did he let her talk him into bringing her here? What was the point? There's nothing left for him here. 'Let's go, then.'

She shakes her head. 'No. You need that part of yourself. You need to connect with it again.'

Alexis and Meriel should have done something about her a long time ago. Computers dreaming? She's out of her mind.

'Don't look at me like that,' she says. 'I know what you're thinking, but it's true. Part of you is in the wires here.'

'We're going, Donna,' he says. 'Come on. Don't scare yourself.'

'I'm not scared.' She submits passively as he tries to lead her out of the apartment. Before they reach the door, she says, 'You were in a dark red room, like a womb. The light was red. Someone was with you. They were very dark. Their hair felt like feathers under your hands. They were like a shell-fish, like a cat, like a bird. The name was Elna.'

Reeb drops the girl's arm as if it has burned him. A hi-res

dream, a ghost's dream. How can she know the last thing that was playing in his mind before the swarm came down the line?

Donna looks troubled. 'I don't want to invade you,' she says, 'but I have to make you see I know what I'm talking about. I'm not mad.'

'How do you know that?'

She shrugs. 'It's in the walls, your leisure-station, the heating ducts. It's all there, and the People thought it all to me.'

'What *are* the people, Donna?' He wonders whether they could actually be real. Has she been telling the truth?

Donna turns away from him. 'Oh, the People are only parts of me, that's all. I call them People because I want it to be like a movie, or, like having friends. I'm friends with all the parts of myself, and they speak to me. Some are smarter than others.' She holds out her hands to him, as if she wants to touch him. 'Your data-suit's been replaced, Reeb. It's in the drawer under the monitor. You can take back what you lost, if you want to.'

'I can't take back the flesh,' he says sharply.

'That is replaceable, it doesn't matter about that,' Donna replies. 'You've left stuff behind though that does matter. Feedback.'

He feels awkward putting the suit on in front of Donna, he feels vulnerable. She is quite familiar with the equipment, which surprises him. 'I have stuff like this in my room at home,' she says.

Is that all? Reeb hadn't imagined her secret playthings would be anything as mundane as data-suits.

'There are two suits here,' she says.

'There shouldn't be.'

Donna pulls a face and shakes out the wired fabric. 'But here it is. For me. I need it, so here it is.' She smiles. 'You see?'

It's only further compensation, Reeb thinks. Two suits left

in the apartment to replace the one that fried him. Most people would never think of putting one of the damn things on again. If the suits are a gift from the property agency, it's in the worst taste.

'Ready?' says Donna. For a moment, Reeb wonders whether he is afraid. Not of being hurt again, but of Donna herself. There's something too eager about her. The hood goes over his eyes.

'Relax,' Donna murmurs. 'You're on your way.'

He feels claustrophobic for a few seconds until Donna connects him. At first, it is all fuzzy; black and white static, noise-sight. He is hooked into nothing but the main power system. The program they are running is the day-time purr of appliances ticking over, the nowhere hiss of mindless, directionless, formless energy. This is crazy. The girl is crazy. There's nothing here. Nothing.

Then, out of nowhen, he is aware but dreaming, jacking into a tactile visualisation. The light is red around him. His body throbs in anticipation and there are feathers beneath his hand. For the first time since the accident, he senses a feeling of desire, his body is waking up, but this is only a dream, isn't it? He is in a dark place, surrounded by a sense of breathing, perhaps his own. There is also a feeling of confinement. Reeb flexes his arms, his fingers, breathes in through his nose. He does not know where he is.

'In the wires,' says Donna, close by, yet far away.

This is not real, Reeb thinks and attempts to extend his awareness. He feels the presence of Elna, his animal-human companion, but cannot see it. Part of him can sense the touch, but it is incomplete. There is no sound, no chirrup of welcome, no sensuous brush of fur. Red light pulses swiftly round him, and for an instant, he is back fully in the old dream; that of feathers and sex, warmth and envelopment. He sees Elna's slanted slitted eyes, open mouth, small, pointed teeth. The eyes blink in greeting, the velvety throat purrs. Then, it has flashed past him, just a fragment, like an echo of a cry.

'Come to *me*,' Donna says.

'Where are you?' Reeb gropes blindly, fighting vertigo, nausea. He has never experienced anything like this before. He is nowhere. What if he can't return? That is ridiculous. All he has to do is disconnect, press the stud in his arm, which in reality will end the program run. But there is no program. He's hooked into nothing.

'Here!'

He blinks and Donna is standing beside him. 'How did you get in here?' he asks. A stupid question. Donna knows what she is doing. He is aware of that.

She holds out her hand. 'Come to my room,' she says. 'My playroom. All my things are there, the things that I like.'

Ahead of them is a plain white door. It could be any door, but Reeb knows it is the one that leads to Donna's playroom. As they approach it, it swings open and a strong light pours out.

'Here we are,' Donna says, gripping Reeb's hand. 'Home again.'

The room is full of things. Things and people. Creatures like automatons, beautiful dolls. Puppets hang from the ceiling, which is a blue sky, the impossible blue of childhood memories. The puppets swing on invisible strings. They are objects of human desire; cars, gleaming household goods, jewellery, expensive consumables, silk and real leather, but at the same time they are effigies of people. There are no walls to this room, only a ceaseless rush of colour and visual noise; scenes flashing by. Reeb sees dark forests, beaches, city-scapes, alien lands, the interiors of immense houses.

'Look,' Donna says, pulling on his hand, jerking him out of a stunned stasis. 'I have something of yours here too.'

They push their way through the dangling feet of the puppets and Reeb sees two yellow eyes glowing from the darkness of a forest. There is a throaty purr and a sinuous shape slinks towards him, dragging its landscape with it.

'Elna,' he says. 'You reconstructed her.'

Donna shakes her head. 'Oh no,' she says. 'No need to. I

have the dreams of all the machines here, the computer dreams. I collect them. I bring them through.'

Elna drops to its belly in front of them.

'Part of you,' Donna says. 'Take it back now.'

Reeb has to fight to escape Donna's tight-fingered grip. His hand is damp. So real. It feels so real in here. He could almost believe she's somehow flipped them out of his apartment into her own surreal world. He never doubted it wasn't real for her. Is it possible to share a dream?

'Open the door.' Donna's voice has become hard. She is holding to her breast the hand that Reeb wrenched himself away from, as if he has hurt her. 'Open the door, and you'll find Merry and Alex getting stoned, as usual. You doubt me, don't you?' She smiles at him and walks towards the door, which is closed.

'Don't open it,' he says. 'Donna, get me out of here. It's too crazy. Take me back.'

'You are back,' she says. 'Stupid. I let you into my world and you're too stupid to believe it.'

He knows, if she opens the door, and he steps out into reality as she described it, he will go mad. If he walks out into Merry and Alex's apartment, the shock could kill him, because it wouldn't be possible. It isn't possible. Why even be afraid that might happen? Even if it did, it couldn't be true reality, but only be further evidence of Donna's virtuosity in programming leisure software. She's always been on the wrong side of the camera, he realises, but perhaps this is all too weird for public consumption, too detailed to be comfortable. Elna has curled a fingered paw around his ankle. Instinctively, he extends a hand to caress the feathered head. Elna has never felt so real to him before.

'Do I open the door or not?' Donna asks.

He shakes his head. 'No, I believe you.'

She relaxes, folds her arms. 'Good. Now, fuck your animal-person. Do you mind if I watch?'

'Donna!'

'Oh, you're not shy are you? It's easy. I can do it, so can

you. I only want to help you, Reeb. Take back what you lost. Be a man again.'

'I'm not into this, Donna.' He feels for the disconnect stud, the bump on his non-real arm that corresponds to the button on the data-suit, back in the apartment. He tries to concentrate on the fact that he never left there; this is just an illusion. No need to be worried.

'Don't bother doing that,' Donna says. 'It won't work. I brought you here, down the wires. To my playroom. I collect the dreams of machines here. I collected the dreams of your machines. Aren't you pleased? You thought Elna was dead, didn't you?'

Reeb puts his hands against his eyes, shakes his head. Donna makes a sound of distress and hurries towards him on her tiny feet. 'Oh, I've scared you. I'm sorry. I was showing off. Silly. Like a kid. I'm not that, I don't want you to think I'm that. Look, the animal has gone. I made it go. But there's me. There's me!' She leans against him, a Reeb that is not real, that cannot be flesh and blood, a dream icon. He closes his eyes and she puts her arms around him. She feels warm and solid against his body.

'Whatever is given to you here can be taken back to reality,' she says, and kisses him. 'I promise.'

Child-woman, dream lover of a multitude of leisure sleepers, at home in her true medium; the non-real, the fantastic. There are no feathers beneath his hands.

Donna can feel computers dreaming, or so she says. She collects the dreams of machines, or so she thinks. The dreams of people are in the machines, a planet network of active imaginations hooked into their made-up, make-believe worlds. Artificial reality is taking over; it has its own children. Donna feels the dreams of people. There are others like her. She is not unique.

The Pleasure Giver Taken

I am not by nature vindictive; neither am I particularly vengeful. If the slight is slight, I am prepared to overlook it. Not for me the grinding anguish of damp, dark nights nursing an over-ripe grievance. I have seen the unnecessary consequences of such behaviour and decided long ago that the boredom of it is superseded only by its utter pointlessness. Me, I can turn my back and walk away. Anytime. Well, nearly anytime. Naturally, the exception proves the rule, otherwise there wouldn't be a story to tell and far be it from me to tire you with a fruitless paean to my self-restraint.

At the time I had just successfully walked away with pride intact from the kind of insult that normally severs all philanthropic feeling between mind and soul forever. I walked away laughing. I didn't want to live with the woman. For God's sake, I'd made that clear from the start, but they never quite believe you even when you spell it out in words of single syllables. When you try to exercise your prerogative of escaping their nerveless clutches, they have the effrontery to complain, and then, if they feel the occasion merits it, they try to destroy you. I didn't want to get involved in that kind of mess, so Lenora Sabling had been left screaming at her mirror, claw marks visible only on my credit statements. I knew her tactics would never work. The plans lacked decisiveness, and the killer instinct was completely absent.

She was a fool; I could have taught her so much. During those months I spent being a woman for the job on Leda 217B, I never disgraced myself by histrionic displays. I can't understand why other people can't live up to my standards or why they have to deliberately misconstrue my intentions. I'm neither dishonest nor hampered by outmoded concepts of morality; a combination of traits that once very nearly broke my heart. I try not to think about it nowadays. Lenora, by contrast, feasted on my income rather than my affections. She began to bore me with tedious possessive inclinations that were dangerously near to getting out of hand. It wasn't just a self-preservation measure to leave the planet; I had work elsewhere. Goodbye, Lenora. It was nice knowing you.

Asher Tantine is a small, solitary world, circling its angry sun devoid of companions. I'd been offered the position there some months earlier but, even though there'd been veiled hints of enormous payment, the vagueness of the commission had put me off following it up. After the incident with Lenora, which had effectively rendered me fundless, I decided to accept the job and trust that the lack of detail didn't conceal something unpleasant.

I am a professional and my talents are nested in an interstellar reputation of excellence. There used to be a time when I leapt upon any job that came my way with dog-like enthusiasm and a desperate desire to please. Now, I'm older, more experienced and can afford to be choosy. Discerning clients make offers designed not to offend my dignity and, thus, I choose them. And what is my profession? Well, that is the beginning and end of most of my problems. It is why I've learned to be strong and unassailable. I am a Pleasure Giver. Pleasure in all its forms, however dark, is available from my fingers, eyes and body. I began my life as a white-skinned male but, over the years, have found that several adjustments to my pigmentation and physical form improved the appearance not only of myself but also my bank balance. I was apprenticed to a veritable master of the craft, Eeging Lampeter, who is sadly now unavailable for commission. He trained me well. For many years I couldn't afford sophisticated equipment to aid me in my work and relied wholly upon what the gods had given me, plus whatever hardware can be obtained from an average kitchen. Sexual gratification is not the only form of pleasure in this universe. It is one of them, certainly, and one at which I am exceptionally gifted, but there are many others, some explicable only in the language of their planet of origin. Suffice to say, I know my stuff.

On arrival at one of the two spaceports on Asher Tantine I was feeling alert, invigorated and looking forward to serious employment. The evening air was very sweet on that world, almost like a thick liqueur in the lungs. The sun was sinking behind the grotesque, skeletal forms of slumbering space-yachts, cargo vessels and those sleek, nippy cruisers that burn out after only a couple of years. This spoke of affluence. The population might have been small, but it was moneyed. There were a few weary moments at the customs kiosk, during which I had to endure comments from the officials that weren't very clever and didn't inspire hilarity within me at all. Naturally, I have become inured to the effect my papers have on insects of such nature. It occurs with depressing regularity on each world I visit and has long since lost any entertainment value.

'Ah, a *pleasure giver!*' they say, winking roguishly.

'Yes,' I sigh. 'That is correct. Is everything in order?'

Why such words should be viewed as a double entendre is a mystery to me, but they are inevitably followed by sniggers and further winking. Only by refusing to become involved in any repartee do I escape without wasting my precious time. If it gives them pleasure to imply things about my private life, then they should be paying for it.

Asher Tantine was no exception; the ritual was enacted and my silence guaranteed the return of my papers. I left the spaceport and faced the town. Having already taken the precaution of having my equipment and luggage forwarded to the Hotel Evening, I found I had a few minutes to survey my new terrain. It is considerably helpful to sniff around the environment before commencing work. All worlds are different and I've found it beneficial to observe local habits and customs so as not to appear completely alien to my employers. In this case, it was a Mrs. Amberny – a quaint and old-fashioned way of addressing oneself, as titles had more or less become obsolete once gender changes became so prevalent. I've always been just plain Tavrian Guilder, whatever my sex.

Mrs. Amberny had sent orders that had been oblique in the extreme. It wasn't very often that I arrived for a job completely unprepared, but the veiled and cautious nature of all communication I'd had with Mrs. Amberny meant that I had no idea what was expected of me. For the last job, I'd been required to take a skin pigment of viridian hue, which had also affected my eyes and hair. I saw no reason to change that; there'd been no special requirements from Mrs. Amberny on this score. Only once have I refused a request of this nature and that was when some fat person had asked me to put on several stone in weight. I starved for nearly a week after turning the job down, but I didn't regret one agonising moment of it. I have my principles and though some might criticise me for being vain, I am not ashamed to admit I take great pride in my appearance. I may have mutilated other people's bodies in my time, but it causes me untold grief if I as much as break a fingernail. Now I have a perennially youthful appearance, a body as svelte and slim as a whisker and luxurious waist-caressing hair – currently the same colour as tarnished copper but with a better shine.

Violet Way, which I understood to be the largest town on this sparsely populated world, was an urban complex of modest size. Its industries are primarily tourism, because the planet is beautiful and unspoiled, and crystal-growing, because the planet sprouts the things like weeds. Kids in the street can scoop up handsful of pyratitanite or shellamine; on Asher Tantine such gems are two a penny. Not so upon other worlds, of course, where a single splinter of pyratitanite will sell for more than a fleet of night-cruisers with luxury trim.

What a happy circumstance it would be if the traveller could pop such street-littering treasures into his pocket before taking his leave of the place. Unfortunately, this is impossible and we can thank the same technology that prolongs my youth for that. No one gets a toe out of Asher Tantine's atmosphere in possession of a single stone. They have ways of detecting them and heavy corporations from larger worlds who have a commercial interest in Asher Tantine supply effective weaponry to act as a deterrent. I must admit it's discreet. I never saw a single sign of surveillance the whole time I was in Violet Way.

Walking through the brightly lit streets, past noisy casinos thronged with glittering catamites and women of the blight, I found my thoughts straying to the subject of Lenora Sabling. It had been a mistake to let her get involved with me. Why I should still be thinking about her was an enigma. Only on reflection did I realise it was a portent. She was a hairdresser; that alone should have warned me. I disliked her personality at once, but if she kept her mouth shut she looked mysterious and vampiric. We looked good together. She complemented my appearance like my hair, my jewellery, my brindled hounds. Out of those items, all I'd got away from her with was my hair. As far as I knew she was still in triumphant possession of the jewellery and hounds. Ah well, no use sighing. I'd earn more than enough from the Amberny woman to replace my lost belongings.

I checked into the Hotel Evening, a delightful palace of subdued lighting and crystal encrustations that looked like plants. The receptionist stared at me rather rudely. Obviously, Asher Tantine was quite a provincial place on the planetary scale. I doubt whether many Pleasure Givers award the Hotel Evening their custom.

I dialled Mrs. Amberny as soon as I was installed in my suite. The screen displayed, as usual, an inoffensive graphic design instead of the face of the person I was speaking to. Mrs. Amberny was very cagey. I recognised her breathy yet clipped tones. 'Tavrian Guilder,' she said. 'How relieved I am to hear your voice. You sound so close.'

'I am, Mrs. Amberny. I'm at the Hotel Evening,' I replied.

'Good, good!' She laughed, which sounded like an exhalation of tension. What did this woman want of me? I was quite intrigued. 'Come to my house tomorrow before lunch,' she said. 'The hotel should be able to provide you with transport.'

'I'll be there, Mrs. Amberny.' I paused a moment to indicate that what followed was slightly distasteful to me. 'Perhaps we could broach the subject of remuneration at this point?'

Mrs. Amberny laughed nervously. 'No need for concern, Mr. Guilder. You will be recompensed beyond your expectations if your work proves... satisfactory. Perhaps we can discuss this further, once I've briefed you on what will be involved.'

'Very well, Mrs. Amberny. I look forward to doing business with you.'

'Yes.' She laughed again. 'Goodbye.' The screen fuzzed and whined. I broke the connection.

In sunlight, the following day, I discovered that the streets of Violet Way are not quite so glitzy as they appear at night. Crystal trees lining the pavements looked dusty and chipped and I could see that all the buildings were crusted with a grey scale of encroaching unpolished grisacite. I sat in an open-topped hovercar and the inhabitants of the town stared at my unusual colouring. Perhaps they thought I was a new strain of crystal. Anything is possible nowadays. My driver took me to the outskirts of the town, where large residences squatted amid brittle, crystal-scoured trees of gem-like hues. Beyond these manses, I could make out the shimmer of fertile crystal-fields crawling up the sides of gentle hills; above them a cloudless sky of lilac blue. The landscape of this world was beautiful, even if somehow sharp and unwelcoming. That day the air seemed full of salts and minerals that left a metallic taste on the back of the tongue; a contrast to the prior night's balm. I presumed it not to be toxic.

Just as I could see the gates of Mrs. Amberny's house, Violet Way Villa, the road was blocked by a group of people holding banners, milling their way towards the town centre. I leaned forward to speak to the driver. 'What is this nuisance? I'm expected at Mrs. Amberny's before lunch.'

'I apologise Mr. Guilder,' the driver replied. 'It's the church, you see.'

'*Church?* What do you mean church?' I was irritated and decided not to hide it.

'The New Church of Infant Jesus.'

'Oh, for God's sake! What are they doing?'

'Singing, Mr. Guilder. They like to sing about sin.'

'As do we all, driver. Is there no way we can get the car through them?'

'Not without injuring them, sir, and I advise against that because the Church of the Infant Jesus has considerable voice on Violet Way Council and it might be looked on as an offence if we mow them down.'

'Perhaps it might be quicker to take a detour.'

'As you wish, sir.' The car purred and rose and swung around. I caught a last glimpse of ecstatic, smiling faces in full tongue. It was not a sight conducive to a healthy appetite. There was a banner that proclaimed, 'Denounce the spawn of Satan in our midst'. Perhaps it was a welcoming committee for me, I thought.

So, by necessity, I arrived at the back gate to the Amberny estate. This caused confusion with the servants, who had all been looking out of the front. The car swept grandly up the rear drive. As I alighted from the vehicle, a fussing gang of white-gloved retainers swooped on me and ushered me towards window-doors that led into a sun-lounge at the rear of the house. My driver was shooed away. The gardens were splendid. Long lawns of furry verdaline threads were groomed by huge, white birds wearing collars. Fountains tinkled and plants grew in strained formation over trellises. A woman came hurrying out onto the terrace holding a tall glass clinking with ice. She was tall and skinny, wearing a spare but concealing lilac gown. 'I'm Mrs. Amberny,' she said, but I'd guessed that already.

'Tavrian Guilder at your service,' I said and extended my hand.

She looked at it quizzically before taking it in her own, which was cold and damp from holding the glass. She was a mature and elegant creature, with coils of upswept red hair and exquisite make-up, but was clearly a stranger to the processes of holding age at bay. 'Won't you come into the house,' she said, directing the way with a graceful hand.

I walked beside her.

She took a deep breath. 'Forgive me, Mr. Guilder, but you aren't quite as... well, you don't look as *masculine* as I thought you would.'

'Forgive me, Mrs. Amberny, but I don't remember you stating any preference as to my appearance.'

She shrugged. 'No matter. You *are* male, aren't you?'

'In a universe of shifting ambience, I am as male as I can be, Mrs. Amberny. What exactly do you require of me?' We were now in the lounge.

'Do take a seat,' she said. 'Have you eaten? No? Splendid. Lunch will be served shortly. I hope you like Asher Tantine cuisine.'

I made some polite remark and sat down on a low couch, brushing aside the fronds of a prodigious fern that stood on a table next to it.

Mrs. Amberny took a stance against a high, white fireplace, where no fire burned. She leaned on the mantelpiece and lit a cigarette; an old-fashioned addiction. At her gesture, a servant flicked to my side and mumbled a list of drinks available for my consumption. I expressed my preference and he glided away.

'What do I require of you?' Mrs. Amberny took a long draw off her cigarette, squinting into the smoke she exhaled on the next breath. She spoke without taking another. 'It is difficult for me, Mr. Guilder, because of certain... *circumstances*. Of course, I appreciate that in your profession you must come across many unusual requests.'

I nodded with a smile. 'If you are afraid of embarrassing me, don't be.'

She smiled back. 'That isn't what I'm afraid of, Mr. Guilder. What I want you to do is, well, I regret that it is against the law in Violet Way.'

'Really? How intriguing. What is it?'

She sighed and folded her arms. The servant returned with my drink on a tray. Mrs. Amberny kept one eyebrow raised until he had left the room. 'What is it? Well, first I had better explain some of the background to the legal situation. You are aware of our *Church of the Infant Jesus?*' There are few people who have the knack of speaking in italics. Mrs. Amberny was one of those privileged with the talent.

'Yes. Some of its devotees were singing in the street outside. We had to take a detour.'

Mrs. Amberny nodded. 'Mmm. Quite. Their founder Matthew Breed came to Violet Way about a year and a half ago. He came here to *Spread the Word.*' She raised her arms and rolled her eyes. 'A cursed day, one might say.' Then she paused suddenly, her arms drooping. 'I hope I'm not offending you, Mr. Guilder. Do you have any religious beliefs?'

'That depends on whether it's necessary for the job or not.'

She smiled. 'Then I'll continue over lunch. This way please.'

A servant had come to hover in the doorway and preceded us to another room. It was entirely white, the dining table an astounding piece of furniture cut from a single gigantic crystal. The only colour was provided by the steaming tureens of vegetables and meat standing in the middle of the table. We sat down and the servant began to spoon helpings of the fragrant food onto our plates. Mrs. Amberny smiled appreciatively as I complimented her on the meal. In truth, I found it rather bitter.

Mrs. Amberny took a glass of wine and twirled the stem

in her hands. 'As you no doubt realise, Asher Tantine is not a heavily populated little world and Violet Way is not a large town. We need tourists to survive.'

'I would have thought the crystal farms brought in more than enough revenue,' I said, taking a large mouthful of wine to help cope with the food.

'Of course they do, but they virtually run themselves. There is no need for manual labour and the farm owners jealously guard their land. I should know; I'm one of them. Thus we have a population of people whose families have lived here for hundreds of years with very little to do. Tourism is their livelihood. We sell them crystal stock at a cheap rate (inferior quality naturally) and they produce curios for off-worlders to purchase. On top of that, we have the hotels, the wilderness package firms, the casinos, and a host of other trades that support the industry.'

'I don't understand what you're getting at, Mrs. Amberny. Where do I come in?'

She tapped her wineglass with long, lacquered nails. As yet, she'd made no move to begin eating. 'I told you this request might be *unusual.* You'll have to bear with me, Mr. Guilder.'

I made a contrite gesture. 'I apologise for the interruption.'

'Matthew Breed is a dangerous man,' she said acidly and lit another cigarette, before taking a small forkful of food. Perhaps nicotine improved the taste. 'He comes here with his talk of sin and salvation, his resurrected religion and his unbelievable, unshakeable charisma. He talks to our young folk. He infects them and fills their heads with his sanctimonious claptrap! He reviles the evils of drinking, gambling, whoring and dancing. He rants and they listen. It's astounding. At first, he had a following that consisted only of all our subnormal degenerates. They hadn't a hope in the world till he took an interest in them. Now he commands hundreds of our people. An army! Terrifying! The man is an absolute pest! A threat to the livelihood of Violet Way. Of course, as an elder of the town, I've had parents coming to me begging for help, but what can I do? The wretched man nicey-niced his way into the town council. At least a third of the councillors are enchanted by him! Now there's talk of setting up religious retreats on Asher Tantine, of closing the casinos and clubs.'

'But Mrs. Amberny,' I just had to interrupt, 'why haven't you had him seen to? It's not a Pleasure Giver you need, it's an Annihilator.'

Mrs. Amberny made an irritated gesture. 'You don't understand, Mr. Guilder. He has too many followers for that. If we had him removed tomorrow, it would only increase the zeal and determination of his devotees. Then you'd be talking about civil strife rather than a potential threat of inconvenience.'

'I still don't understand what you expect me to do. Seduce him?'

Mrs. Amberny gave a bitter laugh. 'Don't be ridiculous, Mr. Guilder. I doubt that even you, with all your reputed talents, could lower the trousers of Matthew Breed. He is above reproach. Don't think we haven't looked into the possibility of trying to discredit him. We have. But there's nothing. He's left a trail of happy Christians right across the galaxy. That might be fine on other worlds, but Asher Tantine is just not big enough to take it. Violet Way certainly isn't. Mr. Guilder, it is said that every known form of depravity is an accomplishment with you...'

'I'm flattered, Mrs. Amberny.

'You must help us. There is only one way. I could think of no one other than a Pleasure Giver who is sufficiently discreet to perform this service.'

'Which is?'

She squashed out the cigarette on a side-plate, her eyes taking on an eerie, girlish glitter. 'Witchcraft,' she said.

'Witchcraft,' I repeated, to play for time.

'Yes. We must fight fire with fire, or in this case, cult with occult.'

I was sufficiently perturbed to throw down my fork. 'Mrs. Amberny, I'm not a witch. And if anyone has said I am, it is doubtless because of some petty offence...'

'Be *quiet*, Mr. Guilder. I know what you are. In this universe the only person who can be trusted to utter silence is a Pleasure Giver; their income, their life depends on their discretion. As you yourself said, the only other alternative is some sordid kind of hired killer and you've heard my views on that.'

'Perhaps a real witch might be discreet, Mrs. Amberny.'

She shrugged. 'Perhaps so, but I was advised against it. Discretion cannot be guaranteed in any profession but yours. I trust no one. If Breed found out about what I'm planning, he'd ruin me. I'd be thrown off the council. Frenzied acolytes of the Baby Jesus would tear my crystal fields to shreds with their bare hands. Only witchcraft can remove his allure, and of course, the first policy he instituted on the council was to outlaw all alternative religions. You must do it, Mr. Guilder, even if you know nothing about the occult at all.'

'I wouldn't go so far as to say that, Mrs. Amberny,' I said, making further investigation of the meal, even though the plate did not appear to be getting any emptier. 'I know a little, obviously, for as you said my work takes me upon unusual paths, but I don't know enough to bewitch someone – if that is what you're implying you want.' My mouth was apparently getting used to the unusual flavours. I discovered that eating was becoming less of a trial.

Mrs. Amberny still had not taken more than a mouthful. 'Mr. Guilder,' she took another breath, 'your name came to me from a very reliable source. I can't say more than that. I know of your reputation; no other Pleasure Giver's can rival it. I trust your ingenuity and wit. After lunch, I would like you to return to your hotel to ponder upon the problem. I will see you again tomorrow.'

I rubbed my face with a cautious hand. 'This might seem indelicate, Mrs. Amberny, but you did say we could discuss it. How much can I expect to earn if I complete this task?'

She smiled widely. 'How much? Oh, you saw the cruisers at the spaceport, no doubt? Well, you could buy all of those and a freighter to transport them on. Is that enough?'

'I'm already working on a solution to your problem, Mrs. Amberny.'

'Good boy.'

'One more thing, and it's merely curiosity, why were you so concerned that I should be male?'

'I would have thought that was obvious. You say you know a little about the occult? Well, I am female and need to work magic with a male. You will be my High Priest, Mr. Guilder, and you will teach me what I need to know.'

I thanked the Infant Baby Jesus I'd shelved the idea of having an additional female orifice implanted before coming here. I raised my glass. 'To our success,' I said and drank. Mrs. Amberny smiled.

Riding back to the Hotel Evening in Mrs. Amberny's own silver hover-car complete with female chauffeur who had eyes with slit pupils like a cat, I was already considering a certain course of action that could be of immense assistance. Several times, my well-trained brain tried to skirt the idea; the sensation of wincing was quite alien to me, but there seemed no alternative. I was under no illusions as to the state of Mrs. Amberny's mental health – her solution to the problem was wild and emotional and highly impractical when looked at with an objective eye. However, it was what she wanted and I was in no position to question it. Neither did I want to, because it gave me an excuse to make a particular holoscreen call that I'd needed an excuse to make for years. This was what was causing the wincing.

I was shamefully aware of how my spirits had leapt when she'd mentioned the fateful word: witchcraft. How absurd it sounded in this age of space cruisers and gender implants and black hole bistros. Witchcraft. A dark word that draws one inexorably into the dim, haunted past of our race, to a time when people lay in the mud of Mother Earth and worshipped the sun and the moon. Did anybody nowadays adhere to that ancient religion and wield the ways of the elements? Yes, they did. I'm sure of it because there is a name in my address file beside which I have inscribed the legend, 'Sneaky, snaky WITCH'. It was a bitter time when I wrote that, the extent of the bitterness illustrated by the fact that I've never scrubbed it out. What Mrs. Amberny didn't realise was that witches were extremely reluctant to actually harm people, despite popular myth, and especially so in the case of my acquaintance. There was no one else I knew who could help me with this job, and I did need assistance, because my knowledge in this field was slim to say the least. On the one hand, I shied from getting involved with this person again, on the other hand, no matter how hard I tried to deny it, I was overjoyed.

I suppose there are two popular images of witches. The first is the raddled hag armed with various parts of batrachian anatomy, and the second is the lissom seductress against whom all men are witless. Pharaoh Hallender was neither of these. Half of all available witches are male. Pharaoh was born male. The last time we'd met he hadn't changed sex at all, but that had been some time ago. Knowing him as I did, however, he probably had some deep-seated principle about interfering with one's external expression of polarity. I expected him still to be a 'he', although I knew for a fact that his principles didn't extend to refusing rejuvenation. We'd been friends for a while, on a far world that in my memory is a paradise of summer evenings and slow-moving water and shady trees. I can still see his house, dim lights through a veil of fern trees and I can smell the heady incense that smouldered in a dish of ashes on the porch. Our friendship ended with a misunderstanding on his part that left me powerless against a barrier of protection he cast about his house to keep me away. No amount of pleading, contrition, gifts, rage or avowals of love would affect his decision never to speak to me again. It was a long time ago, and I never let anyone get to me like that again, as Lenora Sabling would no doubt have been able to tell you. I only hoped that enough time had passed for his anger to have cooled. He might even be speaking to his sister again by now. They were both beautiful. Was it my fault I couldn't make up my mind?

I paced my bedroom for half an hour back at the Hotel Evening. I kept looking through the door to the sitting room, eyeing the holoscreen with aversion and longing. Eventually, I found myself quite suddenly sitting in front of it and speaking his code to the long-distance operator. It must be an old system they have on Esher Belling. There was a discernible delay before my call clicked through. And then with a shiver and a brief, whining purr, the screen gave me a picture, and the face of Pharaoh Hallender was before me, enchanting as a dream, exactly the same as the last time I'd laid eyes on it. He wasn't looking into the screen but was leaning down to fiddle with something on the floor, holding a towel unsuccessfully to a tumbling mop of wet, black hair. I could see the room behind him. That, unlike him, had changed. The shawls on the wall looked more expensive than I remembered. Clearly, fortune-telling was an expanding business. 'Yes, who is this?' he said, now peering into the screen. Perhaps they had bad reception at his end.

'An old friend,' I said confidently.

He looked blank. 'Who is this?'

'Tavrian Guilder.' I tried to control a desperate note in my voice.

'Tavrian Guilder?' He stared at the screen suspiciously. '*The* Tavrian Guilder?'

'Of course.'

He looked bewildered and my heart gave a helpless leap. 'What do you want?'

'I wondered whether you'd give me some assistance on a contract I have.'

'Are you still a Pleasure Giver?' he sneered.

'Yes. Are you interested? It's just your kind of job.'

'Tavrian, it is painful to remind you that we haven't spoken for years, even more painful to remind you why. I suppose there is a kind of charm in you calling me up like this with such an insulting suggestion. It's almost childlike. I really don't think anything that comes within the line of your profession could ever be termed "just my kind of job".'

'You don't know what it is yet.'

'This is true. Neither do I expect to in the near future.'

'Your words are bleak, but I am encouraged by the fact that you haven't broken the transmission.'

'You have green skin, Tavrian.'

'I know. This woman wants to work some spell or another. I can't talk about it now, but it's beyond my abilities. I thought...'

'Tavrian, you have green hair.'

'I know. Are you listening? There's a lot of money to be earned here.'

An interstellar sigh travelled all the way from his world to Asher Tantine. 'All right; tell me.'

'I can't really. It's not a rat promise, Pharaoh, I need you. It's genuine, it's lucrative.'

'And where is it?'

'Asher Tantine.'

'Asher who? Is that near Gulfride?'

'Sort of. More near Ilthante.'

Pharaoh closed his eyes and shook his head. 'Are you asking me to come there, Tavrian?' he asked in a low, dangerous kind of voice that I knew of old.

My finger was poised over the recall button. 'It will be worth it.'

'Do you know how much it will cost me? Is the job that lucrative? Can it possibly be worth it?'

'Yes.'

He sighed. 'Give me directions.' There was a fatalistic note in this.

I experienced a thrill of victory. Patience had won. I always knew I'd get the better of him. I wanted to get up and dance around the room. I'd won – after all this time. He couldn't resist me. He was coming. My elation was bordering on hysteria. Send me packing would you, you little witch? Ha, I'll show you!

'How is the charming Raifina?' I enquired, after delivering the information on where I was.

Pharaoh did not flicker. 'Fine. Goodbye, Tavrian.'

Even on the fastest transport available, Pharaoh would not reach Asher Tantine for three weeks or so. Mankind might have conquered the concept of space and its traversal, but was still struggling with the concepts of timetables and connections. I used this time to cast a wary eye over the antics and cavortions of the New Church of Infant Jesus. I went to listen to Matthew Breed speak, but could only stomach it once. There was a newly built church in the middle of town, its walls crystal-scum-free and adorned with framed representations of the man himself. He was a very prominent figure in the town and death was clearly not a spectre he left the light on for. Any enterprising annihilator could have disposed of him neatly a hundred times a day, so lax was the security around him. His appearance was much as you'd expect; clean cut, shaved raw, eager. His eyes, as is the custom with his type, were exceedingly pale. All men of god tend to look at the world through eyes like oysters, I've found. Matthew Breed was, of course, a very rich man.

Mrs. Amberny began to twitch when I told her about Pharaoh Hallender. The woman is paranoid to the point of delusion. I heaped assurances upon her as to Pharaoh's irreproachable discretion. She was only half convinced. More than the downfall of Matthew Breed, she looked forward to being able to wield some kind of power herself. The slap in the face, the appeasing knife thrust, the silver bullet, were denied her because Matthew Breed was too popular to be harmed. In the place of such delights, she longed to gather dark power to her breast and throw it in his direction. Not murder but the curse of ill luck. Matthew Breed must lose his allure. His sincerity must become questioned by even the most stupid of his followers.

Pharaoh Hallender arrived on the evening flight and I went to the Violet Way spaceport to meet him. The customs officials were almost as delighted by his papers bearing the occupation 'occultist' as they had been with mine. Standing beyond the doors, I could see Pharaoh smiling and joking with them, as is his way. His tolerance of other humans was one of the few things I disliked about him. When I saw one of the officials extend his hand for Pharaoh to read the palm, I decided I must interrupt. Mrs. Amberny was meeting us for dinner at a fashionable restaurant in town and I did not want to be late.

'Pharaoh,' I said, 'it's me, Tavrian. We have a dinner appointment.' I indicated the door.

The customs official looked downhearted.

Pharaoh followed me out into the sharp fragrance of an Asher Tantine evening. Hire cars hovered hopefully around the entrance to the spaceport. I hailed one and we climbed inside. Pharaoh is the kind of person with whom people are irresistibly tempted to fall desperately in love. Not just because of his beauty, which is unique in itself, but because he brims with childish wonder and vivacity, that is healing and infectious at the same time. I was not surprised when he told me of his success as an occultist. Even if his predictions were completely made up, which they weren't, people would pay vast amounts of cash just to be soothed by him and listened to. I sat leaning against the door of the car, discreetly appraising him. He was looking out of the window taking in the harsh, splendid sights of Asher Tantine. I still couldn't believe he'd agreed to come. 'I'm pleased to see you, Pharaoh,' I said.

He turned and smiled wanly at me. 'Weird kind of place this, isn't it?'

Mrs. Amberny fell under the Hallender spell as soon as he swanned into her line of sight, which I considered to be quite an achievement on Pharaoh's part. She was quite a hard nut. The restaurant was furnished in dark, midnight blue and startling white. Crystal chandeliers shone dimly from tented fabric. Mrs. Amberny was sitting smoking at a table set on a dais at the back of the room, in front of windows through which the nightlife of the town could be seen emerging for another evening's rampage. The white cloth of her table was littered with ash; her glass of wine stood half empty. I admired her svelte body in its white gown; she was really quite a stunning creature. Pharaoh and I took our places beside her and she summoned a waiter. By now I was thoroughly acquainted with the local cuisine and ordered our meals with calm expertise. Then I had to sit and listen to Mrs. Amberny pouring out her heart to Pharaoh. She heaped scorn upon the New Church at which Pharaoh twitched uncomfortably. I did not dare look up to witness his response.

'Forgive me, Mrs. Amberny,' he said, his voice full of gentle censure, 'but although I can understand your grievance, it would not be appropriate to cast a malison over this Mr. Breed. Everyone has a right to their own beliefs, even if they do happen to conflict with your own.'

'You are right,' Mrs. Amberny said, at which I just had to look up. 'And if it was just a case of that, I'd do nothing. But as I explained to your colleague, Matthew Breed will destroy the livelihood of this town, indeed this planet, if he's allowed to continue in his fanaticism. I cannot believe that religious retreats can earn half as much as a single, decent nightclub.'

'Clearly, you are unfamiliar with the Church's reputation in this galaxy,' Pharaoh said dryly. 'I really don't think you have anything to worry about if it's only the financial aspect that concerns you.'

Mrs. Amberny shook her head. 'It's not just that,' she said. 'How can it be right for this parasite to come here and inflict his ways upon our society? It smells of conquest to me. It is empire building, and I, for one, will fight most vehemently against subjection.'

Pharaoh considered her words. 'There is a happy solution to every problem in this universe, Mrs. Amberny. I shall just have to find the one for yours.'

After the meal, we rode back to the hotel in silence. The journey took longer than expected because of another detour we had to make around a group of yelling Breed converts. I didn't mind. I was just happy to sit there thinking that only a few weeks before I would never have dreamed it possible that

I'd be in the presence of Pharaoh Hallender again, never mind working with him. Another, more rational, part of my brain was flashing warning signals that I was entering a dark and dangerous place, which I ignored. The moment was too sweet.

Back at Hotel Evening, I asked Pharaoh to come for a drink in my suite. He said no, he was tired. Then I suggested that he come for a drink and then sleep.

His face assumed a hard expression. 'Tavrian Guilder, if you as much as think about getting within touching distance of me, I will remove your throat with a blunt instrument. Is that clear? I came here to work. Although I've forgiven you for the past, which is purely the fault of genetic abnormalities on your part, I have not forgotten. You are a trail of slime across the gateway to hell, Tavrian. You are as hollow as a rotten mag-fruit. You are as sincere as a starving man who says he is a vegetarian. In short, I despise you.'

'I suppose sex is out of the question then?'

He didn't answer.

The next evening, a car arrived to take us to Mrs. Amberny's estate. Pharaoh had been locked in his room at the hotel all day, emerging at sundown looking tired. By the time we reached the Violet Way Villa he was full of energy again. I guessed he'd found a solution to Mrs. Amberny's problem, although he was reluctant to tell me what it was.

In olden times, a witch would stand and summon up the elements with the power of her own voice; not so in our wondrous golden age of technological miracles. Pharaoh had a set of resonating machines, which were housed in four, hand-sized silver boxes, inscribed for effect with runic symbols. When activated, these machines produced sounds that conjured up within seconds the elemental forces necessary for any occult work. It took years of training for a human being to achieve such an effect.

Mrs. Amberny had cleared a room for us. It overlooked the lawns and was floored in spotless, white marbeline. Pharaoh paced the room, sniffing, and then set up his machines around the edge. Next, at each compass point he set out long, white candles which were lit from a glowing taper. Mrs. Amberny turned off the lights and the room became a temple; dim-lit, mysterious, the air hushed.

'Will this... *spell* take effect straight away?' Mrs. Amberny asked anxiously in a low voice. 'How many times will we have to do this?'

'It will only have to be done once,' Pharaoh replied, setting up his portable altar and draping it with a dark cloth.

'Just once?'

'Trust me, Mrs. Amberny. I assure you I know what I'm doing.' He laid out his magical tools on the altar and produced some self-igniting incense from a packet of silver foil. 'I prefer to work naked, Mrs. Amberny, though you and Tavrian may wear robes if you prefer. You'll find some in that bag over there. One of them is bound to fit you.'

Mrs. Amberny's eyes went quite round as Pharaoh wriggled without affectation from his clothes to reveal a body that looked scrubbed and clean and which I knew would taste of salt. I led our hostess over to the bag. She looked at me once and her eyes said, 'Such hair, such a face, such perfect flesh.' Poor woman.

'Remember, you wanted magic,' I said.

She smiled vaguely and took the robe I put into her hands.

The sun had disappeared beneath the horizon of Esher Tantine. In the white room of Violet Way Villa, we stood within the circle of silver boxes and candle-light, Mrs. Amberny and myself clad in sombre black, Pharaoh white and naked as a laser. He turned on the machines and went to sing to each in turn. In the east, he sang of air, in the south, he sang of fire, in the west, water and in the north, earth.

'Hear me, oh shining beings of the air...'

The machines sang back to him and began to emit a glowing blue-white radiance. Above each box hung a spectral five-pointed star sketched in beams of light, each the size of a man. They were connected by a trembling, glowing cord which formed the circle itself. The candle flames flickered and danced and a faint but rushing breeze brushed Mrs. Amberny's red hair back from her face. She stared straight ahead, mouth open.

Pharaoh never needs a High Priestess because of the incredible control he has over his own polarities. When he needs to be female, he thinks 'female' and he is; it's as simple as that. However, as a concession to Mrs. Amberny, and because she was paying us, once he'd cast the circle, he beckoned her to his side. She gingerly stepped forward, timorous as a woman half her age. Already, she was in love with him. He must find his attractiveness quite an inconvenience at times. From his lips feel beautiful poetry, which Mrs. Amberny repeated breathlessly at his side.

I closed my eyes and allowed myself the luxury of letting their words drift over me, drinking them in, helping to make them real. I doubted whether Mrs. Amberny could understand what we were asking for exactly, because I certainly didn't. The invocation had a weird effect though; I felt quite light-headed. I also experienced a peculiar tickle in the back of my head, the sort that cannot be scratched. Pharaoh's voice rose in timbre, Mrs. Amberny's leaping gamely behind. Their words described the mystery of the universal fabric. For a while, I stood entranced, only half conscious.

A half-heard sound summoned me to open my eyes. The room seemed different, the atmosphere almost strained. Pharaoh threw back his head, and at that very moment the door to the room opened and slammed against the wall with a resounding crack.

Mrs. Amberny squeaked, distracted from the invocation. Pharaoh ignored it. I looked at the door. What I saw there removed the middle section of my courage with one easy slice. How? How the devil?

That she'd possessed the ingenuity to follow my trail was astounding enough, but why in this universe, did she want to? Surely no one could bear such a grudge that it was worth the time and money of interstellar travel. There in the doorway stood Lenora Sabling, looking as devilish and powerful as if Pharaoh had conjured her up himself. A brief panic turned my veins to wood. Had he? No, surely not. She was looking right at me, black eyes round and wild, black hair sticking up in a crazy halo, red lips smiling. In her hands she held a shiny black gun which was pointed right at me. I recognised it instantly as one from my collection of antique weapons; another thing I had lost in my flight from the sordid relationship.

'Lenora!' I said in surprise.

She did not appear to hear me or even notice me at that point, but walked forward a few paces, eyeing the glowing blue circle nervously.

Pharaoh had come out of his trance and was looking at her with interest. He did not appear to view this event as unexpected.

Mrs. Amberny had one hand to her throat, no doubt thinking that this was part of the spell.

Lenora turned around sluggishly and saw me. She lifted the gun and I instinctively put up my hands to shoulder height. 'Tavrian Guilder,' she said. 'I'm going to kill you.'

'Don't be hysterical, Lenora,' I said, trying to be reasonable.

'Just a minute, young lady,' Mrs. Amberny butted in. 'You can't kill him. He hasn't finished his job yet.'

'Be quiet!' Lenora ordered. She looked drunk. Never in her life had she enjoyed such power, I'm sure. 'Don't look so scared, old woman. It's not your blood I want, it's his! Now Tavrian, perhaps you think this is a selfish gesture on my part. It isn't. You are paid to give pleasure; that's fine. The only problem is, you're so mean, you can only give it when you *are* paid. Perhaps your work sickens you. Perhaps you find relaxation by giving pain; I don't know. All I know is that you wrecked my life, destroyed my self-respect and broke my heart.'

'Ah, you'll overlook ruining your best carpet then.'

She wailed in an undignified manner and waved the gun

dangerously.

'All right, all right,' I said, hands aloft once more. 'Let me remind you, my dear, you have my hounds, my jewellery, my collections, my cars. Sell them. Then you'll be able to buy a new self-image and a new carpet.'

Now she made an angry, spitting noise. 'Vermin! Get on your knees. Go on: down! I want to see you grovel before you die. No one will ever be destroyed by you again. This is the end, Tavrian. Let your life, such as it is, flash before your eyes. See all those broken lives that have your name burned into the flesh.'

Naturally I would not kneel to her. Who did she think she was? I made a mental calculation about how much bullet damage I'd have to receive before death was inevitable and how much damage I could afford to get repaired afterwards. From the way her hands were shaking, I even doubted whether she could score a direct hit. I stepped forward slowly, intending to take the gun from her.

'No!' Pharaoh leapt upwards. 'Don't break the circle!' he cried and went to throw himself against me.

I can only presume Lenora panicked. There was a shot and then, in an arc of blood, Pharaoh Hallender's body flew backwards from my arms, hit the south pentacle and was swallowed in the blue light, disappearing with a short hiss and a curl of pale smoke. I stared aghast at the South. Of Pharaoh, all that remained was a streak of dark red upon the floor. Mrs. Amberny had gone utterly stiff with shock and said nothing. Lenora was looking round the room as if unsure of how she had got there or what she had done. She had also begun to cry. As I thought: she had no killer instinct. Heedless of whether I was breaking the circle or not, I charged through the ring of light and knocked the gun from her hands. She looked up at me, imploring, helpless.

'Tavrian, Tavrian,' she murmured.

It was a nice touch that she died with my name on her lips. I broke her neck.

Mrs. Amberny stood, drooping, within the circle. Now

the ring of light spluttered and faded in places, pulses of power running through it. Mrs. Amberny was a ghost in its centre. She seemed dazed.

Now that the blood lust had been spent, I was reluctant to cross the glowing threshold again. I stared at the South, at the stripe of dark upon the marbeline floor. He was gone. He was really gone. For a while I sat on the floor, truly stunned. I'd been given a chance to make amends; Pharaoh had come to Asher Tantine at my summons. Now he was dead, and at the hands of another of my self-pitying ex-lovers. What a shitter. Why had I been cruel to Lenora and made her hate me so much? Why indeed had I ever seduced Pharaoh's sister Raifina all those years ago? Must I forever blight my own future with vomit-pools of my past?

Lenora was just a dark huddle on the floor behind me. The gun lay a few feet away, shining blue with reflected light. Mrs. Amberny didn't move. The machines hummed and spat. Then a breath of night-air came into the room and a tall, dark figure was drifting past me, bowed and stumbling as if walking in its sleep. It paused, wagging its head from side to side and then passed through the blue light; the current surged and rippled as if it was water. Mrs. Amberny raised her head. I scrambled to my feet.

Matthew Breed was standing within the circle, facing her. In the vague light, I could see he appeared disorientated, frightened, confused. His clothing was dusty and runkled, his hair in disarray.

'Mr.... Mr. Breed,' Mrs. Amberny said. 'What are you doing here?' In an instant she had recovered all of her poise. Her voice came right from the back of her nose.

Matthew Breed shook his head. 'I don't know. At least...' He looked around the room, seeing nothing. 'Mrs. Amberny, I've been meaning to speak to you for some time. At least, I think I have. I'm a lonely man, Mrs. Amberny. I admire strength in a woman...' He spoke as if reciting a set of well-rehearsed lines.

Mrs. Amberny was clearly aghast.

I just began to laugh. Pharaoh had found a solution all right and it would harm no one. Admittedly, it was rather more manipulative than he usually felt happy with, but it had worked. Now Matthew Breed was desperately, irretrievably, helplessly captivated by the allure of Mrs. Amberny. He loved her, would do anything for her, would worship at her feet until the day he died. The Church of Infant Jesus would mean nothing to him unless the woman he loved was by his side. Naturally, the woman he loved could then more or less dictate what form that church would take. Even in my shocked state, I couldn't help thinking of holy whores, gospel nightclubs and religious holiday gambling events. Ingenious. Even though my face was wet with tears, I couldn't help but laugh. Ingenious!
Order came home to Violet Way Villa. Mrs. Amberny discarded Pharaoh's robe and smoothed her creaseless dress. She called for her manservant and murmured something into his ear, briefly waving a hand in the direction of Lenora Sabling's remains. The manservant did not even change his expression of bland servility. He nodded and left the room, perhaps to find a spade. With a commanding hand, Mrs. Amberny led the confused Matthew Breed into another room. By the time he came to his senses he would have forgotten what he'd seen; the body, the blue light, the blood upon the floor.

I stood for a moment, staring at the fading circuit. Now only four balls of vague light glowed above each box as the resonance died. I would not touch the blood upon the floor. As I turned to leave the room, something tapped my shoulder. I looked back. Behind me was clustered a group of shining beings, tall and spectral, glowing with brilliant, shifting colours and emitting strange, half-familiar odours.

'What about us?' one of them said.

'Excuse me? Who are you?' I backed carefully towards the door.

'You summoned us. Now we must be dismissed.'

'And how do I do that exactly?

The elementals shrugged en masse. 'We don't know;

that's your job. But we can't leave until we're dismissed.' I could tell they didn't want to stay, but how do you dismiss an elemental? The only person who knew had disappeared in a vapour of his own ichor through the south quarter. Sighing, I pushed through the eerie throng and began turning off the machines. I didn't know whether that would work, but even as I watched the creatures vanished with a slow, vibrating hiss. I went into the next room.

Mrs. Amberny didn't want to discuss what had happened. She wrote me a banker's order, gave me instructions on how to cash it at her bank in Violet Way, and then handed me four bags of crystals. 'Thank you for your help, Mr. Guilder,' she said, tight-lipped.

I wanted to smack her face. Pharaoh had died because of her. It made me sick. 'What are these?' I asked her, looking into the bags.

'A fitting payment,' she said dryly. 'They are elemental stones, pyratitanite, aqualine, egrecite, cave-diamond. They're worth a fortune. Your business seems risky, Mr. Guilder. If I were you, I'd use the revenue from these stones to retire. Here is the declaration certificate; you'll need it to get them off Asher Tantine. It was... *interesting* doing business with you, Mr. Guilder.'

Thus, I was dismissed.

I went back to Hotel Evening and ordered a bottle of liquor to drink in my room. Lying in darkness, I thought about what had happened, glancing occasionally at the four bags of crystals sitting on the bedside table. Pharaoh Hallender was dead because of me; that fact was inescapable. There was no way I could blame Mrs. Amberny really. Now I would have to contact Raifina and tell her. She would be distraught, alone, in need of comfort. A slow, grin curled across my face. I leaned over to turn on the light and a cold hand gripped my wrist. From nowhere a sylph had materialised by my side. This was a creature of the element of air, tall and gaunt and robed in grey-blue. Its touch was icy, a breathless wind raised its long, tawny hair from its back. 'You did not dismiss us,

Tavrian Guilder,' it said menacingly. 'We are still here and we want to go home. You must dismiss us.'

'How?' I cried. 'The witch who summoned you is dead! It's nothing to do with me! Pester Mrs. Amberny instead.'

The sylph looked at my bedside table. 'You have the crystals,' it said.

'Yes.'

It folded its arms. 'They have the power to return us to our lovely realms. Give them to me and we may leave.'

'And if I don't?'

'We shall be with you always and we shall be very unhappy. Have you ever been in the company of an elemental who's very unhappy?'

'No, I can't say I have.'

'Not many people can. They don't last long enough to tell anybody about it.'

'Take the crystals,' I said and held out the bag of egrecite, the air stones.

With a puffing sound, both elemental and bag were gone. I lay back on the bed and sighed, wiping a mist of perspiration from my brow. Had the others returned to their realms as well, or was I going to have to give away all my crystals before I was safe? This job had gone thoroughly sour on me. Mrs. Amberny's suggestion seemed attractive. Retirement, if only as a temporary condition. But without the crystals, I wouldn't have enough to finance such a plan. Saving had never been one of my strong points. Easy come, easy go. I felt as if I wanted to turn my back on the whole human race. None of them was fit to receive pleasure, no matter how much they paid for it. I wanted out.

About an hour later, an undine pooled itself into existence on my bedroom floor. This was a water elemental, naked and beautiful and quite without qualms about taking my crystals. The aqualine had to go. Tomorrow I would leave this world, crystals or no crystals.

By dawn I thought I was safe, but was accosted by a gnome in the hotel corridor, a dark, brown-robed entity of

Earth, who smelled of rich, carrion-fed soil and who rudely demanded my cave diamonds, even as a hovercar waited outside to take me to the spaceport.

Carrying only a bag of pyratitanite, I boarded the cruiser that would take me to Ganymede East. I knew it to be a quiet, tranquil place. I needed time for reflection; anywhere else would just be too damned fast.

Asher Tantine receded beneath me. I watched it from a window in the cruiser's cocktail lounge; a small, revolving jewel, mother gem, fertile in her own bristly, spiky way. In my pocket the bag of pyratitanite remained intact. I sat down on a sofa and picked up a newspaper, another anachronism of the quaint world I was leaving. The journal informed me that already Mrs. Amberny and Matthew Breed had announced their nuptuals. Some people, at least, were happy then. I put the paper down on a nearby table.

Although no longer as rich as I could have been, the pyratitanite would secure me a modest future. If I was careful, and invested it wisely, there would be no need for me to work again. On top of that, I had Mrs. Amberny's money. As soon as I reached civilisation I would have it changed into standard credits. It could grow, as long as I wasn't stupid with it. I didn't want to lower my standard of living, which was disproportionately high, but neither had I the stomach for work at the moment. Perhaps this would change. Perhaps not. After half an hour, I decided to go to my cabin and contact Raifina Hallender.

The cabin was in darkness. I fumbled for the light, passing my hand back and forth over the heat sensitive panel that should have turned it on as I entered. Nothing happened. Grumbling, I backed out with the intention of finding a steward to complain to.

'Wait,' a voice hissed. This voice smelled of sulphur and ashes. The door slammed shut behind me and I pressed my back against it. 'You did not dismiss us, Mr. Guilder.'

'Oh no, not again,' I whimpered.

A salamander is not a cute little lizard as you might

expect. It is an eight-foot flaming warrior who doesn't take any shit off anybody. Now there was one in my cabin holding out its hand. Goodbye retirement. 'The crystals...' I began.

'However,' the salamander interrupted, 'because of the arrival of a certain Pharaoh Hallender in our laps, it was not necessary in our case, anyway.'

I breathed a sigh of relief and then said, 'Why are you here then?'

The salamander folded its arms, drops of liquid flame from its hair causing unusual holes in the fire-resistant bed spread. 'Well, we thought you ought to be offered a choice. After all, Pharaoh Hallender is known to us. We have worked with him many times. My brothers thought you might want to give us the crystals instead.' It extended a glowing hand and illuminated the bed. Now I could see that upon it lay the body of Pharaoh Hallender, his breast rising and falling gently, his black mane covering the pillows, his shoulders, the sheets. His colour was healthy; there seemed no sign of injury. 'You can keep him or the crystals,' the salamander said. 'It's really up to you. Mrs. Amberny gave you the stones. Pharaoh cannot give them to us.'

'And what will happen to him if I keep the crystals?' I asked.

The salamander shrugged. 'It is doubtful whether he'd survive long in the realm of fire, at least not in this form.'

I walked over to the bed and looked down.

'Take your time,' the salamander said sarcastically.

Beautiful Pharaoh. Forever a boy, full of love and life and laughter. He also hated me. I was everything he despised and loathed, and it took an awful lot for him to despise and loathe anything, however foul it was. I realised that once the salamander had gone, it would be quite possible that Pharaoh Hallender would still hate me just as much. On the other hand, if I let the fire elementals keep him, I could retire and get him out of my system altogether by forgetting about him. If only I could know now what he'd be like when he woke up.

The salamander cleared its throat. 'The crystals or the

witch, Mr. Guilder?'

Too bad. I turned my back and said, 'Take him.'

Or at least I thought I did. It was like someone else was in my body saying, 'Take the crystals. And go.'

The salamander whipped the bag from my hand with an air of glee. Pharaoh stirred and writhed upon the bed. Had I really said that? No, of course I hadn't.

'You have just ruined me,' I said.

He sat up and brushed the hair from his eyes. 'Where are we?'

'Aboard a cruiser on its way to Ganymede East.'

'The spell worked?'

'Yes, with your own inimical mark upon it.'

'A sticky moment. I was nearly lost.'

I threw up my hands in disgust. 'Pharaoh, I have just saved your life! All I've earned from this venture is enough to keep me well-fed for three weeks!'

'On the contrary. You have also learned a very important lesson. But it wasn't you who saved my life, Tavrian. If I hadn't been so resourceful, at this very moment you would be speaking to my sister Raifina and doubtlessly arranging to meet her somewhere.'

'Don't you trust me?' I asked acidly, aware that an unfamiliar tinge of real anger was colouring my voice.

He rolled his eyes. 'As I said; childlike.' He hopped from the bed. 'I'll have to use some of your clothes for the time being, Tavrian.'

I sat down on a chair, dejected, as he rummaged through my bags. A thought was hammering through my brain; I'd disobeyed my own, first commandment. *Walk away, always walk away.* For Pharaoh, I'd turned back. What lesson had I learned from this other than to trust my own instincts? I should have told Mrs. Amberny I didn't want the job, couldn't do the job. But no. I just had to use it as a means to lay eyes on the incomparable Pharaoh Hallender once more, thinking I could turn the tables. Now I was a wreck, defenceless, bleeding, directionless.

'Why aren't you dead?' I asked, dully.

He carried on rummaging. 'What? Oh, I always take precautions. Only a fool wouldn't, and I'm certainly not that.'

'So it's back to where we were, is it, when you first arrived on Asher Tantine?'

Pharaoh turned and smiled at me sweetly. 'Not exactly,' he said. 'I never bear a grudge. You obviously like me, Tavrian, so I'm prepared to let bygones be bygones.'

I stood up and held out my arms in premature relief.

He raised a cautionary finger. 'However, I feel it's only fair to warn you that should you attempt any course of action that may cause me harm or grief, I shall have to put your new psychological implant into play.'

'What do you mean?'

He came and kissed me briefly on the lips. 'Tavrian, two spells were worked in Mrs. Amberny's house. The bewitchment of Matthew Breed was child's play, and took me barely a minute. The potential for his affair with Mrs. Amberny was there already; I soon worked that out. So it required hardly any effort at all to remove the obstacles, namely the more unsavoury aspects of his moral character. The other work took more time, but I am happy to say that it too was successful. Tavrian, I can govern your words. I can make you say anything I want to. I can govern your actions too. As you can no doubt predict, this could cause you considerable embarrassment should I wish to exercise it.'

'You monster,' I croaked. 'I'll fight you! I...'

Pharaoh shook his head and smiled. 'No, no, no, Tavrian, you can't. If you need an illustration of the effectiveness of this technique, cast your mind back to how Lenora Sabling answered my call.'

'What?' My croak had degenerated into an undignified squeak.

Pharaoh shrugged carelessly. 'Naturally, I had you investigated Tavrian. Did you really think I'd come to Asher Tantine unarmed?'

'I could have been killed!'

Another shrug. 'I doubt it. Did you see the way her hands were shaking? Anyway, I wouldn't have let her. That wasn't part of my plan. Foolish of you to try and break out of the circle. Foolish of me not to have protected myself more thoroughly; an oversight. Still the salamanders burned me into health again. It's fortunate that I have such an excellent relationship with them, isn't it. Perhaps the injury was karmic punishment for my display of pride, but I'm afraid I couldn't resist it. I have no excuse. You've tasted the extent of my power, Tavrian. It has grown considerably since we last met. I haven't been idle these past few years. You humiliated me in the past, before my family and friends. It's bad for you to get away with things like that and I looked upon it as my duty to make sure you don't in the future. You thought you were so clever, calling me to help you, didn't you? I expect you thought it an easy way to squirm yourself back into my bed.' He laughed delicately, which stung as much as a slap across the face. 'It was me who arranged for Mrs. Amberny to be given your name, Tavrian. It was me all the time. I wove a web and drew you to its centre. You came like a child; a role that suits you incidentally. Your brutishness does have a strange, infant quality.'

I could not speak. The inhuman enormity of his plan appalled me. He touched my cheek. 'Don't look so downhearted, Tavrian. Some of your qualities disgust me, but you are still beautiful, witty and proficient in the arts of pleasure. I loved you once; perhaps I can learn to do so again. We shall have a long and happy life together now. You earn a fortune as a pleasure giver, don't you? All you needed was a manager to stop you wasting your commissions. Coupled with the fact that I've removed the claws that used to lead you astray, I think you're now the ideal mate.'

My body had become icy cold.

'Poor Lenora,' Pharaoh said, shaking his head. 'I hope she can organise the threads of her life again. I wanted to see to her before we left but... well. You didn't hurt her, did you? How is she?'

'Oh, she's all right,' I managed to say. He didn't know everything and things were bad enough for me as it was.

'What she said was right, you know,' Pharaoh said. 'You did destroy people with your heartlessness, but it certainly won't happen again. Now, I'm hungry. Is there a good restaurant on this boat?'

I'm not naturally a vindictive person...

As it Flows to the Sea

Sabriel Leaves left the club by a back door. *I have lost before,* he thought, shrugging himself further into his coat. *It is nothing. People have lost more than I did.* He found that such reassurances meant very little in the face of the enormous financial squashing he'd just received. What made it worse was that the grin he'd had to face across the table belonged to his erstwhile partner, Gustav Mealie. The rings on Mealie's fingers had glittered with appalling smugness as he'd scooped the credit shards over to his already handsome pile of winnings. Outside, the air was humid and thick, the town lit by the glow of an immense, vapid moon. Sabriel Leaves decided he disliked this world, a revelation made all the more depressing since he now owned no funds with which to leave it.

Cambium Delta should never have been colonised, he decided. It appeared to offer very little; its fields and forests were grey and ragged, unpleasant to all five senses, and its animal life was colourless and hairless and invariably toxic. The planet's only attribute was its situation in the galaxy; men had turned it into a sprawling space-port of several, linked townships. When he'd arrived, Sabriel had thought the stark, industrial buildings had possessed a weird kind of beauty, now he saw them as temporary, off-centre, heartless.

That evening, he'd been under the impression that he was meeting with his partner, Mealie, to discuss business - they owned a thriving, inter-planetary export company, dealing in cheap, local trinkets that could be sold for scandalous amounts once shipped half-way across the galaxy.

Mealie had given no intimation of what was to come. Sabriel had walked into the crowded, low-ceilinged bar, smiled and sauntered to the table where he could see Gustav Mealie sitting with a couple of tarnished-looking females. It was only after two bottles of liquor and the first game of fayning that Mealie had announced he was breaking the partnership up. Sabriel had been careless; he hadn't covered himself. He'd let Gustav handle all the financial side of the operation and had no way of proving whether Mealie's claims that the last shipment had gone down in flames over Tatarka was true or not. Mealie had said they were ruined, although his smile and his jewellery spoke otherwise.

'So what do I do?' Sabriel had asked, a question which served as a dessert to a host of others, which had begun with, 'What money do we have left?'

'Do, my friend?' Mealie's large, handsome face had shrunk back from a toothy smile. 'Why, you have half of what was left in our account. A modest amount, but sufficient for an enterprising soul. Start anew - as I shall.'

Sabriel had demanded why Mealie wanted to end their partnership. After all, it had worked very well; he doing the planet-hopping searching for merchandise, while Gustav sat on Croon Cree looking after the administration side. Sabriel could not see why Mealie should want to change that.

Mealie's eyes had swivelled away from Sabriel's as he answered. He'd spoken vaguely of new interests, new fields, a desire for independence.

In truth, Sabriel had thought, he must have had a better offer from somewhere.

'We might as well enjoy ourselves while we're here,' Mealie had added, shuffling fayn discs with unsettling, professional ease.

The liquor had numbed Sabriel's common sense. He agreed - and lost, crushingly.

How could I have been so stupid? he wondered, rhetorically, as he scuffed along the metallic streets. Mealie knew Sabriel's weaknesses and had efficiently exploited them.

It had been a blend of pride and defiance that had kept him playing, round after round. He remembered the feverish certainty that he would win soon; after half of his funds had slipped towards Mealie's pile, there was no going back. His half of the 'modest' amount that was left him had now evaporated.

Of course, the situation was not as bad as it seemed. Sabriel still had reserves in private accounts on Croon Cree and Zanzibar Cloud, which meant that once he was home he could survive until he'd sorted himself out, but that did not answer the immediate problem of how to get home. He'd trusted Mealie too much and had neglected to memorise his private credit codes. He'd never really needed them, other than when he was at home and making deposits into the accounts. Apart from that, Mealie had always handled everything to do with finance. Sabriel had never even booked his own cruiser seats. At best, he could only work here in Euterpiax until he had enough to place an interplanetary call so that his friends on Croon Cree could forward him a ticket home or the funds to purchase one.

Sabriel crept into the flimsy hostelry where Mealie had booked him a room for the night; it was a gaudy and unwelcoming place. He felt as if destitution was a word printed indelibly all over him and shied from the furtive vision that greeted him from mirrors on the wall in the reception area. He looked like a kicked rodent and the receptionist raised her eyebrows at him in distaste. *Damn the guts of Gustav Mealie!* he thought as he scurried to his room.

Inside, an intense and pungent humidity hung in the air. Sabriel dimmed the lights as best he could, tore off his clothes and took a shower. Over the hiss of water, he could hear forlorn sounds coming from the town centre; honkings, mechanical groans and the sighs of listless craft sweeping drunkenly into the dark sky.

Still wet, he lay on the bed trying to ignore his reflection in the mirrored ceiling. He looked as if he had just been brought back from the dead. Memories of happier days on far worlds flitted provocatively through his mind. He dismissed them with colourful curses. If he'd had any sense he'd have made provisions to gain access to the business account, he would have salted money away as insurance against a situation such as this. Gustav Mealie had come out on top. He'd discarded Sabriel without a thought. No doubt he was moving onto better things in which Sabriel had no place. Sabriel guessed there was a lot more to Mealie than he knew about.

Burdened with a depressive gloom by such thoughts, Sabriel Leaves writhed and grunted into a shallow sleep, only to be roused abruptly several hours later by the piercing whine of the hostel's intercom system. He waved his hand in front of the answer panel next to the bed and mumbled, 'Yes?'

'There is somebody in reception to see you, Mr. Mealie,' a nasal, female voice replied.

Sabriel paused. He choked off the retort that he was not Mr. Mealie. 'Ask them to come up in a few minutes, will you?'

'Of course.' The connection was broken.

Sabriel heaved himself off the bed and rubbed his face briskly. A visitor for Gustav? Here? Obviously, when the room had been booked, Mealie's assistant must have used the wrong name. A happy oversight. For reasons unknown, Sabriel felt an inexplicable elation at the event.

Shortly, a small, elegantly attired gentleman named Caspar Soames presented himself at Sabriel's door. Sabriel had activated the air freshening system in the room, dressed himself in clean clothes and had slicked back his dark hair with water. Now, he felt more capable of dealing with the situation. Caspar Soames strutted into the room, making genuflections of greeting that hailed from some little-known culture. Sabriel responded languidly.

'I had problems locating you, Mr. Mealie,' Soames said in a reedy voice. 'I seem to recall you were to leave a message as to your whereabouts at Spaceport Delph.'

'I regret the inconvenience,' Sabriel replied. 'Still, you are here now.' His mind was tumbling over itself wondering how to conduct this interview. Clearly Soames had not met Gustav in the flesh before. Was this the new business partner? It seemed likely. Sabriel thought it too good an opportunity to miss.

'I had to ask information to look for your name on the hostel reservation lists,' Soames was saying. 'They weren't too happy about it. It was costly.'

Lucky that this place was fortunately placed alphabetically, Sabriel thought, otherwise Mr. Soames might have gone straight to Gustav. 'My office will reimburse your expenses,' he said. 'Take a seat. Would you like a drink?'

The small man pursed his lips and shook his head. 'I anticipate only staying here a moment or two. I have little time to spare, as I'm sure you appreciate... in my line of business.' He grinned in a particularly unpleasant, fleshless way.

Sabriel inclined his head. 'Naturally.' He hoped that Soames would introduce the subject of the meeting and played for time by mixing himself a complicated cocktail from the room's portabar.

'All I require from you at this stage is the deposit we talked about,' Soames said, sniffing.

'My office will arrange it.'

Soames made an exasperated sound. 'Have you forgotten, already? I stipulated cash for this venture.'

Sabriel was glad he had his back to the man. Cash? What an outmoded concept. He smiled. What on earth was Gustav getting mixed up in?

'Forgive me,' he said. 'I've been working too hard recently. Facts escape me. A keepsake from a childhood illness, the symptoms of which included a fever to the brain.'

Mr. Soames clutched his throat with one hand. 'How unfortunate.' He looked suspicious. 'I hope this disability will not affect our transactions.'

Sabriel shook his head. 'Unlikely. You have proof as to my success. Surely that reassures you.'

Soames shrugged. 'You have a partner,' he said. 'Even

though my investigations as to your financial position produced sound results, it is still possible that Mr. Leaves was the mastermind behind your schemes. I'm still perplexed as to why you wish to exclude him from this business. He seems trustworthy.'

'You do not know him,' Sabriel replied, which he felt was how Gustav would have responded to such a remark.

'True. Anyway, I have the sample you requested. Do you wish to try it now?'

'Er...'

'It is fine quality psychedrine, refined by the thought processes and essential juices of Tellagoona maidens, pounded with piquant oils and sieved by the white hands of exquisite, blind eunuchs of Shar C'mui...'

Sabriel turned his back again while his features wrestled with expressions of shock, disbelief and, regrettably, sheer fright. Psychedrine was possibly one of the few narcotics that various authorities still tried to ban the use of. Therefore, it was an extremely desirable and costly item. It wasn't so much that the effects of psychedrine were dangerous or addictive, but rather that the method of refining it was questionable to say the least. Its components included the essences Soames had mentioned - that alone meant natives of Tellagoona had to be farmed and butchered to obtain them - and there were also the rumoured elements of live foetus marrow and animal remains. Only a fanatical enthusiast of unexplored experiences could possibly wish to try such a drug. Sabriel was sure it would even taste of blood and suffering. He'd always suspected Gustav of being totally amoral as well as hard, selfish and cunning. Now his suspicions had been confirmed. The penalties for being discovered possessing psychedrine were so harsh, anyone caught doing so could expect never to see the light of day again. The benefits of dealing it successfully were similarly extreme. Gustav could look forward to lifelong affluence on the strength of a single deal, Sabriel was sure.

'Well, Mr. Mealie?' Soames' voice compelled Sabriel to

turn around. He took the small, silver box which Soames offered him and opened it. A delicious scent invaded the room as he did so, casting back the curtains of Cambium Delta stink. It smelled of breathing flowers, erotic dreams and half-glimpsed visions of unimaginable, heart-breaking beauty. Sabriel quickly closed the box. The temptation was great.

Caspar Soames raised an eyebrow, his lips curled into a smirk. 'Take it, Mr. Mealie. Lie down upon your bed and drop a single pinch upon each open eye. You haven't tried it before, I can tell. Anyone who has would never hesitate.'

'Rather early in the day for such delights, isn't it?'

Soames laughed. 'As you wish. It doesn't matter. All I'm doing is selling the stuff. What you do with it after that is your business.' He stood up. 'Now, the thirty thousand standard credits, if you please, then we may discuss how to conclude our business.'

'We shall have to meet later,' Sabriel said quickly. 'There are certain details that have to be finalised.'

Soames made an irritated sound. 'I object to having my time wasted. How much later? I had hoped to be off this charmless chunk of rock by tonight.'

'I will meet you for lunch in the Dry Dog. It's a quaint establishment not far from here. Allow me to apologise for this inconvenience, but I'm afraid it's unavoidable.'

'Very well, but I shan't wait long.'

'Thank you. May I keep the sample?'

Soames was already at the door. 'Of course.' He nodded abruptly and left.

Sabriel sat down on the bed, holding the psychedrine box in his hands and stared at it unblinkingly. What now? Several courses of action presented themselves. By now, Gustav Mealie must be wondering where Caspar Soames had got to and very shortly would no doubt begin investigations of his own as to his whereabouts. It was a tricky situation.

Sabriel called reception and asked them to put a call through to Gustav Mealie at his hostel. 'Tell him that a Mr. Soames will be meeting him for lunch at the Dry Dog after being unavoidably detained elsewhere,' he said, and then lay back on the bed to think. After a while, he got up and left the hostel. Within half an hour he was knocking on Gustav Mealie's door.

Mealie did not look overjoyed to see him. 'Yes, what is it?' he said irritably, his face foamy with depilatory cream. 'I thought we'd concluded our business last night.'

'Last night, you filled me with drink, delivered the news you hoped would destroy me and cheated me of my half of our earnings.'

'My dear Sabriel,' Gustav blustered. 'I most certainly did not cheat you. As I recall, you have never been a particularly adept fayning player.' He grinned in a manner intended to placate. 'Come now, we all need to diversify occasionally. I enjoyed our partnership, Sabriel, but feel that I've gained all I can from it.' He batted Sabriel's arm with a comradely fist. 'How about I reimburse you what you lost at fayning last night?'

Sabriel took a step back. 'Forgive me for saying this, Gustav, but I can't help suspecting that I'm owed rather more than what you took from me last night.'

'What can you possibly mean by that?'

'Don't bother to look aghast, Gustav. I expect I've been used and deserve to have been simply because of my own ingenuous stupidity. However, I think it's only fair that you allow me to examine the ledgers back on Croon Cree so that I may be assured of your honesty.'

Gustav Mealie gave a flippant shrug. 'If it will mean anything to you, Sabriel, go ahead. I assure you I spoke the truth last night. Nearly all we had was wrapped up in that root carving delivery from Pazhin. I was as shocked as you were.'

Sabriel's heart sank. Gustav's relaxed pose obviously meant the ledgers were works of fiction and all funds were distributed into different areas. So much for that plan. He sighed. 'Very well, I accept your offer of returning what I lost last night. It grieves me to sink so low but I have little desire to stay here for much longer.'

Mealie laughed heartily. 'That's my lad, Sabriel. Take things in good grace. Here!' He tossed a couple of credit tokens at Sabriel which were taken from a heap of such tokens on the bedside table. Sabriel pocketed them and then hesitated. 'Was there something else?' Mealie asked, impatience beginning to tinge his voice again.

'I can't think of anything.'

'Good. Please excuse me, Sabriel. I have a luncheon appointment.'

Sabriel left the room, feeling he'd missed some opportunity, but couldn't work out what or why. His fingers ran over the smooth edges of the silver box in his jacket pocket.

Disconsolately, he roamed the streets of Euterpiax. Perhaps something would come to him. He believed in the power of coincidence, that same power which had brought Caspar Soames to his hostel room. He was continually conscious of the box in his pocket, aware of a faint but insistent aroma that escaped the confines of the silver seal. Far from hinting at luscious visions, it only reminded Sabriel of news reports he'd heard about atrocities glimpsed on Tellagoona; the coppery clouds above the psychedrine plants, the corrals of listless, hopeless essence donors for whom salvation could only ever be the kiss of the draining spikes, the inevitable dark. Sabriel could not decide how to utilise the knowledge he now possessed. Gustav Mealie deserved a slap from the hand of Justice, but Sabriel was unsure of the manner in which it should be delivered. Above him, a grim, metallic sky boiled above the saurian outline of the town. He felt dwarfed by the looming buildings pressing down on either side of the black street. People hurried past, all busy, all engaged upon pressing tasks of their own. Not many folk were penniless in Euterpiax; it was a waterhole for the affluent, on their way to more picturesque worlds at the rim of the galaxy. Sabriel sighed. Now he wandered down a bleak, cornerless lane named, incongruously, Shadow's Curl. On either side identical doorways, flanked by single, scratched plastic windows, offered access to the booths within. An alley of alchemists, lank-witches and scryers. Sabriel gazed half-heartedly into the bescarved, betasselled and beribboned windows. Perhaps he should seek the advice of one of the diviners to be found within. An advertisement in one of the windows wiped the sardonic smile from his lips.

'Learn the Secrets of the Universe's Poisons' it declaimed boldly, and underneath, 'For a mere dinkin, step within and Clytie Tredway will teach a Secret'.

Sabriel smiled again. How quaint. What had really caught his eye, however, was the legend beneath this information: 'Psychedrine - learn how the dreams become nightmares with no waking; Loquatim - nervousness banished to the point of complete insensitivity,' and so on. Apparently Clytie Tredway knew how to mutate benign or harmless substances into lethal or debilitating toxins; interesting.

Sabriel Leaves lifted aside the door curtain and stepped within. He found a gaunt, dishevelled creature sitting at a velvet-draped table on which stood a box of coins, a murky glass half-filled with tea-coloured liquid, and a much-thumbed pamphlet. The woman looked up and said, 'What's your business, mister? A faithless lover, a brutish parent, careless friends...'

Sabriel sat down opposite her. 'None of those. A fiendish business partner.' He removed the silver box from his pocket, opened it, and put it on the table between them. 'This is psychedrine,' he said.

Clytie Tredway shut her mouth with a snap. Her eyes narrowed as the unmistakable, seductive scent of psychedrine investigated the sordid corners of her booth. 'Well sir...'

'Tell me what you can do with that.'

'It is a rare thing, mister, a rare thing. I've never handled it.' She could not keep her eyes off the box.

Sabriel winced at the hungry gleam she could not conceal. 'Oddly enough,' he said, 'you claim to have knowledge of its transmutations, or perhaps you didn't write your own sign out there?'

Clytie Tredway pulled herself together. 'My predecessor had worked with the stuff a couple of times,' she said, with a sniff, and began to thumb through the pamphlet. 'Ah, yes... well, this is interesting.'

'How interesting?'

'Well, according to the words of Dame Merdice, president of our guild, psychedrine has only to be immersed in the simple beverage, ermola, to become an intoxicant of the most alarming nature.'

'Please explain.'

'I hardly can. Cavortions, madness, euphoria, manic glee, occasional violence, delusions, speaking in tongues - these are only a few of the possible symptoms. All the more sinister because whatever peculiarities manifest in the victim take at least twelve hours to develop, so that a poisoner can be off and away before he.. or she... is suspected of crime. The effects are irreversible.'

'I see. Are these widely-known facts?'

'Psychedrine itself is hardly a widely-known fact, sir. I admit that the sole reason for it being mentioned on my placard is to whet people's interests. Psychedrine is a legend, a dream drug. I had never expected to come across it.' She eyed the box once more with a furtive, half-guilty, glance.

'How much of the stuff is needed to...'

Clytie Tredway obviously did not care to hear whatever indelicacies Sabriel might come out with. She essayed to maintain a certain dignity about her work. 'Two good-sized pinches, according to Dame Merdice's pamphlet. You have enough pyschedrine there to send a good portion of Euterpiax insane.'

'That is not my intention,' Sabriel said drily. 'Madam Tredway, I have no dinkins - only credit tokens of disproportionately high amounts. Will you accept half of this psychedrine in payment for what you've told me?'

She shrugged. 'You must be mad, but I am definitely sane. Of course, I accept it.'

Sabriel hovered cautiously around the entrance to the Dry Dog for at least half an hour. He investigated several shops in the area, emerging each time to eye the unimposing facade of the place where Gustav Mealie and Caspar Soames were destined to meet. He wondered if they would actually make contact successfully, still unsure of whatever action he would take himself. Eventually, he saw Mealie striding purposefully down the street, his air that of a man about to be offered vast wealth. Sabriel ground his teeth. He experienced irritation, anger and then calmed himself to a steely resolve. Sabriel waited five minutes before following Mealie into the inn. Mealie went directly to the bar, swaggering and preening at the bored woman serving behind it. Sabriel waited until he'd bought himself a drink and settled himself comfortably in a window-seat, before sauntering casually to the bar himself. Mealie must have noticed him instantly. A quick glance over his shoulder assured Sabriel of the poisonous, dark, rodent expression he had expected to find.

'What do you want of me now?' Mealie asked Sabriel as he sat down.

'Do I understand I am not welcome?' Sabriel shook his head and smiled ruefully.

'I'm expecting someone. I have business to conduct; important business.'

'Don't worry, I'll be gone before your new partner arrives. Can't we share a last drink together?'

Mealie rolled his eyes. 'Sabriel, you sound like a spurned female. Have I misunderstood the nature of our partnership all these years?'

'I don't mean to sound bitter. You are right. I went to have my fortune read today and was told it was time my circumstances underwent a drastic change. Perhaps you have done me a good turn, Gustav.'

Mealie made an irritated sound. He looked uncomfortable. Sabriel took some moments to savour the situation, sipping from his glass and gazing carelessly round the bar.

Small bursts of fidgeting began to escape Mealie's suave restraints. Eventually he said, 'Sabriel, did you follow me here?'

'Perhaps.'

Mealie rolled his eyes. 'Oh, for God's sake! What do you want? Can't you leave me alone? I don't need haunting. Your behaviour is most unhealthy!'

'I had a visitor earlier today.'

'Really!' Mealie turned to look out of the window, craning his neck to peer up and down the street.

'Yes. It was somebody who expected to find you. A Mr. Soames.' Sabriel put his glass down on the table carefully.

Mealie gently eased himself back against the seat and narrowed his eyes. For once, he appeared quite at a loss for what to say.

'I didn't enlighten him as to my identity and the poor man spent several minutes trying to extract a rather large sum of money out of me.'

'Sabriel, enough of this clever word-play. If you have a point to make, make it.'

'I suppose you think I will try to blackmail you.'

'By that, I expect you are intimating you know something of the nature of my business with Soames.'

'I know that it is a risky, immoral but highly lucrative venture. How much do you know about what you're becoming involved in?'

Mealie sighed. 'Sabriel, it is not your affair. Our partnership is dissolved. If you have some wild plan concerning betraying me to certain authorities...'

Sabriel interrupted. 'I am offended. Do you really think I would do that?'

Mealie took a nervous sip of his drink. 'Many people might, even those you were not feeling hard done by, bearing in mind the nature of the commodity. I am not a fool, Sabriel.'

'If all goes well, you will be a very rich man, Gustav.'

Mealie waved this aside. 'What did you say to Soames?'

'He is under the impression that he will be meeting me here so that I may give him the money for the deposit on the merchandise.'

'And I presume you want to stay here to keep your appointment, only using my income and my goodwill to conclude your business? Am I to understand that you are forcing me to continue our partnership, Sabriel?'

'You give in easily, Gustav.'

Mealie smiled and made a careless gesture with his hand. 'You have outwitted me, Sabriel.' His eyes did not smile. Sabriel could see his own death waiting in that blank gaze. He was not deceived. Mealie laughed loudly. 'Young scamp!' he said.

Sabriel visualised briefly a damp, dark alley, a hired assassin, a tidy extinction. 'We are still partners, then?' he asked.

'How could I ever think of losing such a resourceful fellow?'

'How indeed? Allow me to purchase us some refreshment. I owe you that at least.'

'Thank you.'

Some minutes later, Sabriel returned from the bar. Mealie still grinned at him in a manner designed to be comradely but which appeared almost insane; a veritable rictus of a grin.

'Isn't that Mr. Soames coming in at the door?' Sabriel said. 'We shall have to tell him of my little deception. Let's just call it a wise precaution, shall we?'

'As you wish, Sabriel. You'd better beckon him over; it's your face he'll recognise.'

Sabriel nodded. He raised the china cup he held in his hand. 'To our success, Gustav! Finish your ermola. Perhaps Mr. Soames can be persuaded to furnish us with something stronger.'

Mealie smiled and drained the cup. Sabriel observed him with a kind of bashful incredulity. He watched Mealie's throat work as the liquid slipped down. It was gone. Within twelve hours, Gustav Mealie would be a twitching, gibbering, possibly dangerous, heap of human remains. Sabriel wondered what he, himself, would be doing within twelve hours.

Caspar Soames, far from being offended by Sabriel's deception, seemed to regard it as normal business practice. Sabriel was sure he detected a hint of respect behind Soames' high-pitched titter of amusement. Conversation kept away from the subject of psychedrine. There was an atmosphere of impendence and a glitter of relish in Caspar Soames' pale eyes. After maybe an hour, Soames cleared his throat to introduce a more business-like mien. 'Well gentlemen,' he said, 'we have only to conclude our affairs. You have the funds, Mr. Mealie?'

Mealie nodded. 'Naturally. And the product?'

'Ah, well, you'll understand when I tell you that it is in a safe place.'

'Here in Euterpiax?' Sabriel asked.

Caspar Soames shook his head, smiling. 'Of course not. However, it's only a short journey away.'

'You make it sound as if we are going to have to make this journey ourselves,' Gustav Mealie said drily.

'Come, come, gentlemen,' responded Mr. Soames, grinning waggishly. 'You must agree you are getting a bargain here! A swift jaunt, nothing more. Don't you trust me? As I recall, at present I am merely in possession of a small deposit and am prepared to wait for the retention until your good selves are satisfied. One of my company cruisers is waiting.' He stood up. 'You'll only be away a couple of days.'

'A couple of days,' said Sabriel in a wooden voice.

'A couple of days?!' spluttered Gustav Mealie in annoyance. 'I have other business to attend to! I am a busy man!'

'Gentlemen, gentlemen,' Mr. Soames said placatingly, rolling his eyes. 'You have stepped into the ante-chamber of the biggest, most lucrative narcotics temple in the universe. Is it unreasonable that you should sacrifice a little of your time upon its altar? After all, once your destination has been reached, you will both be very, very rich men.'

'Will you be coming with us?' Sabriel asked nervously.

'No - the boat is quite capable of transporting you and seeing to your needs. She has the character of an odalisque and the common-sense of a school-mistress.'

'A robotic ship... no crew... no-one else on board at all...'

'Mr. Leaves, you've gone quite white!' Soames exclaimed. 'Surely you don't suffer from space-sickness.'

'No... I...' He flicked an agonised glance at Mealie who was looking quite puzzled by Sabriel's reaction. 'Is it really necessary for us both to go?'

Mealie made a noise of annoyance. 'For God's sake, Sabriel! We might not be the best of friends, but a journey of over twenty-four hours is too short to be passed under induced sleep and too long to be spent alone. Don't be such a ninny! Of course, you're coming. What's the matter? Are you afraid I'll bite you?' He laughed. 'You wanted in, Sabriel,' he added menacingly.

Sabriel leaned back in his chair. He had the horrible feeling that, even under normal circumstances, Gustav Mealie would probably try to dispose of him in some way once they were alone in space. In just under eleven hours, Mealie would change into something unpleasant that nobody could give the exact characteristics of. Sabriel would be alone, on a flimsy mote in a vastness beyond comprehension with a lunatic whose rage would at best be murderous. Already he could hear frenzied howls echoing down gleaming corridors, his own footsteps running ahead of them. Could the doors be locked on a robotic space-cruiser? What if Mealie damaged the ship in some way...?

Tortured by such thoughts, Sabriel allowed himself to be led into the street. He could not run.

Mealie had him firmly by the arm. 'Sabriel, don't look so damned scared!' he hissed in Sabriel's ear. 'We're partners, right. You don't have to be scared of me.' Mealie squeezed his arm encouragingly. 'Believe me, kid. God, I'd have missed you anyway. Let's just forget all that happened, OK?'

Sabriel could not speak. Ahead of them, he could see the high, wired gates of the spaceport. *I'm dead*, he thought. *I'm dead.*

'One thing you need to learn is how to be strong,' said Gustav Mealie with a smile.

The College Spirit

Julianne Farr did not want to be paranormal. She wanted to be a competent secretary and, perhaps later, somebody's wife. Her ambitions were small, on a cosmic scale.

Her powers had simmered quietly away inside her until she reached puberty, when they had rudely come to a boil. Only a strong instinct for self-preservation and a good deal of common sense had prevented an early public exposure of her condition. It had begun with a tingling in the fingers, nothing more, which she attributed to having gone to the library without her gloves; it had been an especially chilly day. Later, she had become aware of an unpleasant metallic taste in her mouth, and her toes had gone numb, so her mother had wisely bundled her off to bed and consequently turned out the bathroom cabinet in search of cold remedies.

Lying beneath the duvet, in a ginger murk of orange-flowered curtains drawn against the drab afternoon, Julianne listened, with mounting unease, to the inner rhythm of her juices. She now regretted having gone round to a friend's house the previous evening to watch a horror film. It had been a particularly lurid movie, which had portrayed, in gleeful detail, the possession of a teenage girl by devils. Julianne was normally far too sensible a creature to believe anything like that could happen in real life, but couldn't help wondering, given the puissant pressure of the sensations she was experiencing, whether the sub-aural groaning in her fibres presaged the imminence of something supernaturally nasty.

She had a fever; her mother dosed her with remedies.

That night, tossing and turning in a bed too hot for comfort, she directed her rage at the enveloping quilt. When it then flew off the bed and landed, in a clatter of deodorant and cleansing cream bottles, on the dressing table, she assumed she'd physically thrown it. That was the first manifestation of her Talent, but she did not recognise it as such.

Steven Rider quite liked the idea of being paranormal. His Talent had emerged in the crib, as it were, although *from* the crib might be a more accurate description. Luckily, or unluckily depending on viewpoint, his mother attributed the first vision she received in the baby's room to the product of an unhappy combination of two tranquilliser pills and a furtive slug from the vodka bottle she kept hidden among the cereal packets in the pantry. It cured the woman's tendency for drug abuse, although, as further manifestations presented themselves, she had to revise their cause.

Baby Steven had Dream Fingers. He could waggle his fat little fists and fill the room with illusions of whatever took his fancy. During the weaning period, some of these illusions were quite alarming. Nannies came and went from the Rider house with the frequency of trainees on government training programmes. Steven's father came and went, usurped by the miracle child in his wife's affections. Some people thought Steven was bewitched.

Mother eventually took matters into her own hands, dismissed the hired help and, steeling herself to the unsavoury task, administered corporal punishment whenever Steven became ectoplasmic. By the time nursery school became due, the boy had been imprinted with several mother-fixated behaviour patterns for good. He had also learned the survival lesson of concealing his Talent from others. For quite a long time, he thought he had a lot to thank his mother for.

Leslie Carter simply accepted without argument that she was paranormal, being a prime specimen of the Archetypal Victim persona. Her tendency to shrink from more assertive children, developed gradually into the ability to fade – with romantic grace, if only anyone had noticed – into a mere wisp of a phantom.

She discovered her Talent while witnessing a particularly aggressive classroom brawl. As other children shrieked and goaded the opponents into greater depredations upon each other, Leslie, overcome by nausea and a desire to flee the horrid sight of bloody noses, poured herself away through the floor. Nobody noticed. Finding herself in the school basement, she sat for a moment or two, quite disorientated. Always an imaginative child, and possessed of a parentally-repressed visionary personality, she calmly experimented amid the gruntings of the school boiler with her newfound Talent.

Leslie knew from the moment of its manifestation that her Talent made her very different. She, like Steven and Julianne, also managed to hide it exceptionally well. Its secret was a strength that sustained her through many a childhood humiliation. In private, she was a ghost and had visited the deepest caves of the earth. In public, she was a non-entity and, as such people generally are, was often on the receiving end of cruel taunts. She had no friends, but saw things of immense wonder that compensated for that lack.

Julianne's power grew from modest beginnings. She could not remember when she actually became aware of it as a distinctly unusual part of herself, but knew that the absolute confirmation of her Talent had been the time when Zoe Bradley flounced past her in the art room at school, aglow with the smugness of having recently claimed Julianne's boyfriend for herself. Blind with humiliation and, she regretted to admit, jealousy, Julianne had quite unconsciously directed the beam of her thoughts at a precarious bronze sculpture – the pride of the art teacher, though lacking in aesthetic merit of any sort. Everyone had been astounded at the way the thing flew through the air like a burnt-out, crash-landing satellite. Julianne had known, with no doubt whatsoever, that she had been responsible for its flight, although, luckily, nobody else had the wit to realise it. She had not been proud of that victory. It had been the voiceless and anguished cry of a female deeply hurt. She had not meant to hit an artery.

Julianne Farr could move objects, seemingly *any* object, by the power of her will alone. For a while, she had nurtured this secret power, considering herself possessed of an innately female talent. Her mother had a bookcase full of distinctly suspect New Age literature, which seemed to confirm Julianne's beliefs. She knew she must not divulge her secret to anyone. Then, the Department of Paranormal Resources had gone public, and it had been brought to society's awareness that a sub-species of humanity lurked within their midst – the paranormals, people possessed of unusual powers.

For a long time, Julianne deluded herself that she was not one of these people. She was not a freak. Later, as womanhood led a developing insight into her life, she realised the truth. Then, the Talent she had loved, and which had given her secret pleasure, became a thing to deny, to purge from her being. No more making cups of tea from the other side of the room so that her viewing of the portable kitchen TV didn't have to be interrupted. No more putting her feet up while her mother was out and directing the Hoover and duster to clean the house themselves. No more watering the hanging baskets without having to balance on the rickety stool. If she wanted to be normal, she must hang on to it fiercely. If she denied the power, then it could not exist. It was still useful when cutting her toenails in the privacy of her room, however.

Steven Rider and Leslie Carter were also faced with this dilemma when they realised they were not, as they had believed themselves to be, unique, but part of something rather more common. Paranormals were not as abundant as the media liked to make out, of course, and neither Steven nor Leslie ever came across someone else who had a Talent. Steven's mother actually discussed it with her son at the time the news broke.

'It was the tranquillisers,' she said. 'When I was carrying you. It must have *affected* you, in some way. You are definitely not one of *those* people.'

Steven knew she was wrong, but did not contradict her.

All paranormals were expected to make themselves known to the DPR, and were, in fact, required by law to register their Talent. Steven's mother would not allow him to do any such thing and, as he himself considered there had to be sinister implications in registering himself anywhere, was happy to abide by her decree. He and his mother spent many a happy hour as he entertained her with the delights he could spin from his fingers.

Sometimes, he was forced to use his Talent to protect himself from assailants; his fey delicacy had inflamed many a bully's attack circuit. One night, after school, he had systematically driven a fat bully insane, and had watched the dismantling of his enemy's mind with the cool detachment of a scientist. He had the ability to discern exactly what would scare a person witless, and could provide an illusion to fulfil their worst nightmares with ease.

Leslie, of course, had no aggressive slant to her Talent. Privacy was important to her, which was the only reason why she never presented herself to the DPR. Everyone knew that paranormals were expected to work for the government. Leslie knew her nerves would never be able to cope with that. Anything that smelled even faintly official sent her into a dumb trance of fear, and the thought she might be forced to use her Talent for something dangerous like spying was intolerable. The sight of blood had her in a dead faint even before the first drop hit the ground, and spies had to shoot people, didn't they? Leslie considered that paranormals could not provide any service other than those connected with espionage. She imagined that most Talents would be very similar to her own.

Her other secret was a shameless adoration of an American paranormal named Kid Spectrum. Americans, naturally, were not discreet in any way concerning paranormality, and to most people's eyes, the States were infested with posturing super-heroes who had little regard for decorum and absolutely no good taste in dress. Leslie, however, had been entranced by the scrubbed, youthful exuberance of Kid Spectrum when he'd been interviewed on TV during an exchange visit. In her dreams, she evanesced into his affections like a winsome film star. It was a worship quite at odds with the rest of her personality, although devoutly pure.

As Julianne's life progressed and school was left behind, she prided herself on her self-discipline. She enjoyed her course at the local secretarial college and, because computer keyboards required so little physical effort to use, she had no real use for her Talent there, anyway. It shamed her that the occasional lapse was almost always generated by negative feelings towards her fellow students. She was careful, but it was noted by her peers that those who fell foul of Julianne often suffered accidents and mishaps of one form or another. She endured terrible guilt about this and went out of her way to make it up to the injured parties. Her friends joked that she must have an exceedingly efficient guardian angel, or something. *Or something.* In every other respect, Julianne Farr was an unsurpassably typical girl and this, more than all her precautions, probably preserved her secret.

Steven's mother told him he was artistic and packed him off to art college as soon as he left school. Steven would rather have become a psychiatrist, or something similar, as he was very interested in conditions such as schizophrenia, but his mother wouldn't hear of it. He managed to amuse himself through college by spinning the odd illusion at the expense of various tutors he especially disliked or other students whom he felt deserved shaking up a little.

Once, after he was supposed to have produced an analytical drawing of a chrysanthemum and hadn't, he conjured the illusion of a beautiful piece of work, which he presented to his tutor, only to snatch it back, fake an artistic frenzy, weep, tear it up and cry, 'It's not good enough! Not good enough!'

The tutor concerned, a woman who strained for empathy with her students, comforted him for an hour and then awarded him a high mark for his work. It was a shame he couldn't use that trick more than once.

Romantically, he tortured women, for he was an exquisitely attractive creature. Even after he discovered, with no surprise given his upbringing, that his romantic interests lay in a decidedly alternative direction, he did not abandon his adoring females. He needed them for developing his Talent. It took practice to create the illusion of a phone ringing from considerable distance away.

After leaving college, he coolly abandoned his mother (who had since descended into such an alcoholic oblivion his departure registered only slightly in her consciousness) and moved to a new town. The brilliance of his portfolio – he only had to implement his Talent a small amount in this respect – secured him a position with the first design company he applied to. Thereafter, he applied himself to devastating any female hearts he found himself sitting near to and seducing happily married men. His job was attended to, with deft panache, in his spare time.

Leslie Carter graduated from shunned child to wall-flower till girl, drooping behind one of many conveyor belts and electronic pricing scanners in a cavernous hypermarket. She was a pale little waif, not ugly by any standard, but deliberately plain. Her mouth turned down at the corners and was too thin. In the staff-room, she drank her tea from a special mug she'd brought from home and became quite agitated if her refreshment break rituals were ever disrupted by newcomers insensitive to her requirements. She was affably tolerated by other members of the staff and, to some degree, protected. Leslie was a person who brought out the maternal instinct in full, although people with the best intentions usually tired of trying to help her live what they considered to be a normal life, after all their efforts to improve her appearance and social graces were ignored.

Leslie *never*, under any circumstances, used her Talent in the presence of others. She was not an unhappy person, for she had her own flat, with plenty of small rooms so she could drift between the walls to her heart's content, and was fulfilled by simple pleasures such as an orderly walk on Sundays and a supply of good books.

If ever anyone at work was crass enough to mention boyfriends to her, she never even blushed or simpered, but said, with firmness, 'None of that for me. I like my life the way it is, with just me in it.' It was the simple truth. She never craved company. Every night, before she drifted off to sleep, she spent a pleasant half hour conducting an imaginary affair with Kid Spectrum. This consummated her romantic inclinations to capacity, even though they had still not got beyond the meaningful glances stage of their relationship.

Julianne never really developed any relationships with men either, although she did sometimes wonder whether using her powers somehow drained her in that respect. Well, there'd be plenty of time for that later. She had decided that the age twenty-six would be a good time to get married. If difficulties presented themselves when the time came, maybe she could use her ability to nudge events along in her favour. Saving someone's life, for example, might well sway their affections, and it would be no problem organising a convenient accident. After that, she promised herself she would stop using the power for good, devote herself to a fulfilling relationship, and raise children. She would not even use it to help her with the housework. She would not use it at all. Well, not unless her husband was unfaithful, or something.

Steven Rider's powers were unmasked when he was only twenty-one. He killed a man, but only by accident. How was he to know the illusion of a slavering Doberman would drive the fool into the path of a speeding car? Stupid. Steven had no regrets about this – the man had been an unfaithful lover, after all – but was furious with himself that the shock of seeing the accident caused him first to evaporate the dog in front of over a dozen onlookers and then quite visibly to spray out a selection of quasi-illusions as a reflex action. He had been bundled into a police car even before the ambulance arrived.

Knowing he had been discovered evoked a dark god from Steven's soul. His police cell resembled the seventh circle of hell by the time the man from the DPR arrived to interview him.

'I think you need some help,' said the man.

Steven merely sneered in response, in a distinctly Mephistophelean way.

'You can't frighten me,' said the man, unperturbed. 'Maybe you should put away the horns and fangs now.'

'You can't kill me,' Steven said, restored to angelic beauty.

The man sighed. 'My dear boy, I have no desire to. You are far more useful to us alive. My name is Mr Sharpe. Now, if you would be so kind as to answer a few questions...'

Leslie Carter presented herself to a local DPR office when she was twenty-five. She quite surprised herself in doing so. One night, she'd been sitting in her flat, drinking a mug of cocoa, her cat on her knee, while watching the late news on TV. Bad news followed bad news. The world was in such a mess: killings here, deceptions there, depredations to the fair planet everywhere. She had turned off the TV and sat in deep thought for several hours.

Like everyone else, she always felt so powerless in the face of global destruction and yet, perhaps she was mistaken to feel that way. For too long, she had hidden herself from the world, concealed her unique Talent. Perhaps she had been put here for a purpose. Perhaps she could actually *do* something. *Leslie, what's come over you, girl?* she said to herself, although her heart had begun to flutter with the enormity of her decision. She knew that she was going to offer herself to the world. She was going to stand up and be counted; tomorrow, she was going to make herself known to the DPR!

It was as if the path of her life had suddenly divided before her and, from somewhere, she had found the strength to take the more difficult road. Deliriously, she spun through the rooms of her flat, a shining phantom of random particles. In her peak moments, Leslie was an awesome sight.

Perhaps a certain over-confidence was responsible for the eventual unveiling of Julianne's Talent. She had worked her way up the bureaucratic ladder, her path eased by discreet administration of her powers. She was acclaimed for her efficiency. Eventually, she secured a position as personal assistant to a high-flying executive, for a company that manufactured metal tubes. It was here the truth of her condition came to light.

As if the victim of monstrous bad luck, Julianne was caught out on one or two occasions by her colleagues. Once, a clerk had walked into her office to find her gliding round the room, watering plants, while speaking into the telephone which floated alongside her ear. When her door opened unexpectedly, Julianne had turned round quickly and, but for a startled moment of mutual staring, managed to hunch up her shoulder against the phone, and smile brightly. The clerk looked confused, but made no comment. Julianne wondered whether she should cover her tracks in some way, in some permanent way, but decided against it. The girl concerned was considered stupid by the majority of the staff, so her word would be doubted anyway.

Then came the time when, up to her ears in paperwork, she had again been caught on the phone, but this time with a document hovering in mid-air before her nose. It had prompted an alarmed exclamation from her colleague, at which Julianne yelped and shouted, 'Shut the door, will you!

Look what you've done!' The paper floated innocently to the desk, but Julianne suspected her excuse would not be believed.

It was unfortunate that there'd been considerable coverage in the news recently concerning the activities of the DPR, and also an embarrassed documentary on a TV late slot. Suddenly, everyone was exposing their friends and neighbours as being paranormal, although it was almost certain the majority of these identifications were erroneous. Still, it was causing a lot of trouble. Paranormals were required by law to be registered. Failure to do so incurred severe disapproval, and also suspicion about the way the individual concerned might be using their Talent. There had been one or two outrageous crimes where paranormals, who were undoubtedly psychotic, had donned ridiculous costumes, in the manner of Americans, and used their powers in a reprehensible fashion. The public feared for their safety and immense pressure was placed on the DPR to control these freaks of humanity, before they held all decent, normal people to ransom.

Julianne's colleagues had begun to talk. Rumours were exchanged, conclusions reached. One morning, she had a visitor, who was nervously shown in to her office by her secretary. From the way her stomach instinctively churned, Julianne knew instantly just what the arrival of this suave, black-suited stranger presaged.

She stood up, held out her hand. 'How can I help you?' She was impeccably groomed, her perfume expensively tart, her manner cool and confident. Inside, she was boiling jelly, but she steeled her exterior to conceal this.

The man shook her hand briefly and she gestured for him to sit, raising her brows in enquiry.

'My name is Mr Sharpe,' said the man. He held out a laminated card. 'I'm with the Department of Paranormal Resources.'

'Of course you are,' Julianne responded coolly, idly twisting a gold pen in her fingers. 'And what can I do for you?'

Sharpe smiled in a pained manner. 'I think you know the answer to that, Ms Farr.' He bent down and opened his briefcase, withdrawing a folder, thinly new and unthumbed. 'Could I have a few minutes of your time? I need to ask a few questions.'

'If you must,' Julianne replied.

'How long have you been aware of your Talent?' Sharpe asked, a ballpoint pen poised above a form.

Julianne threw back her head and uttered an unconvincing laugh. This gave her the briefest time to consider her answer. Should she try and deny it or should she be honest? As she lowered her head, she appraised the unflinching, metallic stare of Mr Sharpe. He was, of course, Talented himself.

'How long have you been a telepath, Mr Sharpe?'

He grinned fiercely. 'Please answer my question.'

'I feel there's little point.'

He shrugged. 'This is a formality, you understand.'

Julianne sighed. 'Very well, but before we begin I want to know how this is going to affect my... well, my life.'

'That is really up to you, Ms Farr.'

It was a poignant moment. Julianne felt as if a comfortable cocoon of fluffy cotton had suddenly fallen away from her body. Within it, as it drifted into oblivion, were the seeds of her hopes and dreams; husband, home, child. Years later, she would recognise this wistful feeling as being one of relief, but at the time she felt only a weary resignation. Zoe Bradley's face flashed across her inner eye, grinning horribly.

'I suppose I have been aware since my early teens of my... difference,' she said.

'And the description of your Talent?'

She shrugged. 'It must have a name, of course, but I just look upon it as being able to move things with my mind.'

Sharpe ticked a box on the form. 'Telekinesis,' he said. 'Anything else?'

Julianne frowned. 'No, just that.'

'Hmm. And you are in the habit of using your Talent regularly?'

Julianne paused, feeling cornered by the question.

Sharpe's expression softened. 'We are all in this together, Ms Farr. Please don't be afraid to answer my questions. No one is judging you. If anything, I am here to help. It is not easy to live a normal life possessed of an unusual ability. Now, if you would tell me...'

'Yes, of course I use it!' Julianne said. 'There's nothing shameful about it. I've only used it to help me with my work! Where's the harm in that?'

Sharpe laid down his pen and slowly raised his hands, palms towards her. 'Please, Ms Farr, there is no need for defensiveness. I only want the facts. For the record, you understand.'

Julianne nodded irritably. 'Alright. It's just rather a... shock to be... discovered, so to speak.'

'An inevitability, Ms Farr. You really should have contacted the DPR a long time ago, but I can understand your reluctance.'

'I just wanted to be normal,' Julianne said.

Sharpe smiled, but not harshly. 'Really! And yet you still used your Talent.'

Julianne blushed. 'I just want to live my own life.'

'Naturally, and I'm not condemning you for your actions. Your Talent should be used, but for the good of society. You are a gifted young woman, Ms Farr, and you must accept that you have responsibilities. Now, if you could tell me in your own words, the exact history of your Talent.'

Numbly, Julianne related the facts, although she attempted to skirt the issue of the unwanted vengeful face of her power. Sharpe made no comment, but she knew, given his own ability, he must have seen the guilty thoughts emblazoned across her mind. She felt exhausted by the time she'd finished speaking and, although her throat was dry, she could not face summoning the secretary to provide coffee.

'You need a drink,' Sharpe said, placing his folder back

in his briefcase. 'Might I ask your assistant in the next room to furnish us with refreshment?'

Julianne nodded weakly. Her whole body was shaking. What would happen to her now? For a few moments, she sat blinking at the windows, her mind utterly empty.

Sharpe came back into the room and sat down. 'I am sorry to have distressed you,' he said.

'What happens next?' Julianne asked. 'Will I lose my job?'

'Your personnel record suggests you are an exemplary employee, Ms Farr. If your employers feel that such a radical step is necessary, then it will be to their detriment. The Talented are generally well thought of by corporate bodies. You never know, my visit may even presage promotion.'

Julianne laughed bleakly. 'Somehow, I can't believe that. If I was so well thought of, then surely my boss would have spoken to me first, before running to the DPR. That is what happened, isn't it?'

'You must understand that the un-Talented are often nervous of our kind, Ms Farr. Do not judge them too harshly. I'm sure my presence will quell their fears.'

'Is that it, then? I just become a statistic on your files? You go away and leave me alone?'

Sharpe blinked, but did not avert his eyes from her demanding stare. 'Part of my job, I confess, is to encourage you to join the ranks of the DPR, Ms Farr. There will be benefits if you co-operate.'

'And if I don't?'

'I'm sure that will not be the case,' Sharpe answered smoothly. 'You strike me as a responsible young woman. As you know, you will be required, at the very least, to attend a brief training course at one of our establishments.' He burrowed once again in his briefcase and produced a handful of brochures. 'Employers are required to allow paid leave for this, so it will be no hardship. The DPR feels this is necessary, because having a Talent can mean you need help in how to control it. It would be irresponsible of us to permit untrained individuals to run around the country. Sometimes, having a Talent can cause untold psychological problems. Our training establishments can ease all this.'

'It sounds like a sentence to me,' Julianne said, picking up one of the brochures. There were high-colour photographs of an imposing country house, and several pictures of smiling groups of people, dressed in tracksuits, running through the grounds, using a gymnasium, eating in the restaurant. It reminded her of a health farm.

'Should you decide to sign on to our register, you will have several options. If you wish to continue in your present occupation, you need only work for us as and when a suitable contract presents itself, on a temporary basis. Again, your employers are required to give you leave for this, but the financial arrangements are something you must discuss with them yourself. Naturally, the DPR will pay you a salary comparable to your current earnings, during the time you are in their employment.'

'And what sort of work will I be expected to undertake?' Julianne asked.

Sharpe shrugged. 'Well, it could be anything, but certainly nothing beyond the scope of your abilities.'

'You are very vague on this point, Mr Sharpe.'

'It is something that can be decided only after you have completed a training course, I'm afraid. I'm not trying to deceive you, Ms Farr. Dispersal of contracts is not my department. I'm only recruitment.'

On a crisp autumn morning, Julianne drove to the DPR training establishment, Tintern House. She had chosen a facility some distance away from her home town and had had to start out very early in the morning in order to reach the place by nine o'clock. Her hands were slippery on the wheel as she pulled up outside the gates and presented her introductory documents, provided by Mr Sharpe, to the security officer on duty. She had been prepared for military formality, but the uniformed, middle-aged man smiled at her benignly, made a joke about the weather, which she forgot instantly because of its utter inanity, and then patted her car's roof and opened the gates. Giving him a tight smile and a wave, Julianne accelerated up the drive.

Tintern House was a beautiful Elizabethan manor, set in a rolling estate of wide lawns, gravelled paths and stately, elderly trees. Julianne could see people taking leisurely morning strolls, some in groups, the occasional loner, obviously walking off a recent breakfast. It all seemed very relaxed, and some of her inner tension eased. She parked her car in front of the main steps and marched briskly through the open front doors, carrying only a small case. Inside, she found a magnificently appointed hall where a young female receptionist sat behind a highly polished table.

'Good morning, Julianne,' said the receptionist. 'I'm so glad your journey was pleasant.'

Another telepath, obviously, Julianne thought, extending a hand.

'Now, if you could just sign in, someone will show you to the morning room. There are three newcomers today, and you're the first to arrive. I'll have someone bring your coffee into you.'

'I'd prefer tea,' Julianne said, perversely.

The receptionist frowned prettily. 'Oh... well, of course.' She brightened. 'Ah, Roger's coming!'

Julianne nearly dropped her case as a man floated into the hall and hovered in front of her.

'Roger!' the receptionist admonished. He landed nimbly and shook Julianne's hand.

'Roger Mint,' he said, winking at her roguishly. 'I like to sweep a woman off her feet!'

'Julianne Farr,' she replied dryly. 'I move heavy objects.'

Steven Rider was the last to arrive. Shown into a pleasant drawing room where the morning sunlight fell flatteringly onto the smart, young brunette sitting by the window, he rid himself of the invertebrate presence of Roger Mint with a timely illusion of having fangs. One smile was enough to send the corpulent Mint bobbing from the room. Steven advanced to assess his peers. The prim spinster was dismissed almost instantly from his attention; thin as a stick with a personality, no doubt, resembling weak tea. The other appeared more interesting. She thought herself to be a cool customer and her trappings oozed the perfume of money. He wondered what her Talent could be and found himself thinking of black widow spiders.

Julianne had afforded Steven one glance, so covert he didn't even notice it. 'He looks like a serial killer,' she thought and resumed her inspection of the magazine on her knee. She and Leslie had exchanged tight smiles and brief hellos. Julianne, scorning the whole concept of *training*, imagined all other paranormals to be freakish in personality. So far, given the evidence before her, she assumed this belief to be correct.

Shortly after Steven's arrival, a grim, towering, middle-aged woman presented herself as their Counsellor. Her name was Emily Band. She explained, without embarrassment, what her own Talent consisted of, and then demonstrated it. Emily had the ability to appear any age; crone or child or anywhere in between. At first, all three newcomers were puzzled as to why she chose late middle-age as her habitual form. Only when they saw an example of Emily in the full flower of youth did they understand. Not a beauty at any age, she was certainly a creature whose looks improved with maturity. Once the demonstration was over, Emily settled herself into a chair and said, 'Now, perhaps you can introduce yourselves to each other, and give examples of your own Talents.'

All three exchanged shy glances, although Steven's glance was perhaps less shy than those of the women. Both Leslie and Julianne confessed to feeling inhibited about giving a public display. 'It is always something I've done in private,' Leslie said, her face crimson.

'You're not being asked to take your clothes off,' Steven said in an airy voice, 'or, forgive me, is that part of your show?'

'Steven,' Emily Band said patiently, 'I think we'll all get along much better with a little team spirit, don't you?' She grinned, showing a lot of teeth, at the cringing Leslie. 'Don't worry, my dear, there's a first time for everyone. You'll soon get over your shyness.'

'Want me to go first?' Steven asked.

Julianne sighed noisily. 'Seeing as you seem to be the one with the least problem with this, I don't think so. I'll go first.' Without further preamble, her magazine flew off her lap, flapped across the room like an origami bat, and hit Steven in the face. Julianne smiled sweetly and shrugged. 'Sorry. Nerves.'

Steven treated her to a wicked smile and transformed himself, in the eyes of all present, to something horribly wet and undead. Julianne blanched and gagged; he'd even managed to mimic the smell. Leslie uttered a dismal cry of terror and sank into the floor. Emily smartly clapped her hands together.

'Team! Team!' she said sternly.

Steven evaporated the illusion and shrugged, looking sheepish.

'Come back, Leslie,' Emily said, 'it's all over.' She glowered at Steven. 'Can we please be professional about this? Time is the DPR's money; we have little to waste.'

For the remainder of the morning, there was a kind of group counselling session, where Emily Band had encouraged them to talk about themselves. Julianne and Steven had enjoyed cat-fighting their way through that, although, to Emily's chagrin, Leslie had refused to join in, sitting with arms folded and disapproving, lipless mouth.

During the afternoon, they had been shown videos that educated them about the enormous scope of paranormal Talents. Some of the examples they saw paled their own Talents into comparative insignificance, while other abilities seemed unremarkable in the extreme, even laughable, in some instances. How, for example, could the ability of being able to detach all of your teeth from your mouth ever be put to practical use? Steven immediately dubbed the wielder of this Talent the Tooth Fairy and consequently suggested one way, at least, in which he would use the ability should he be fortunate enough to possess it. Julianne glanced at him sharply and he grinned back quite openly.

At dinner that evening, the newcomers met the all the other trainees in residence, and the rest of the staff. There were roughly two dozen individuals currently undergoing Department training at Tintern House, with a staff of nine to supervise them. The proprietor of the establishment, a Mr Derek Valiant, made a late entrance to dinner, which Julianne suspected was in order to impress the newcomers. She whispered to Steven, 'And what is his Talent do you think?' No mention of this had been made, although it seemed likely that the person in charge should have one.

Steven shrugged. 'Imitating human life, perhaps?' It was obvious he hadn't liked what he'd seen in Mr Valiant.

'It must be pretty... well... *big*, though, mustn't it?'

Derek Valiant was tall and well-built with an almost American glamour.

'I would have changed my name, if I were him,' Steven said.

As Julianne ate, she inspected the people sitting round the table. They seemed utterly normal, the sort of people who worked in supermarkets, petrol stations or insurance offices. One or two of them self-consciously used their Talents during the meal, with self-effacing grins, flicking glances at the statuesque Derek Valiant to see whether he'd noticed and approved. Consequently, condiments sets whizzed up and down the table, wine poured itself, entertainments were provided. The Tooth Fairy carefully removed all her teeth after the meat course and cleaned them individually with a napkin before replacing them.

'Yuck!' Julianne said. She herself felt no desire to exhibit her own ability, and certainly not to court the favour of Mr Valiant.

Another person, whom Steven dubbed Present Arms!, grew an extra limb from his arm-pit, fringed by tentacles, and proceeded to tickle a coy, flouncy sort of woman further up the table, who cried black tears of joy in response.

The newcomers were all given individual bedrooms, although, after dinner, the three of them congregated in Julianne's room. None of them felt like joining the community downstairs to watch TV for the evening. All three confessed to feeling uneasy in the presence of the other paranormals. Perhaps this would pass.

Julianne reflected what an odd group they were. In everyday life, their paths would never have crossed. Even if they had met, they would never have been compelled to forge friendships.

'This is a bit like being in hospital, isn't it?' Steven said. He produced a large bottle of wine from his luggage and, in the manner of hotel guests consuming illicit liquor, they drank it from tooth glasses.

Leslie, who had never been in hospital, shrugged.

'A psychiatric hospital,' Julianne agreed. 'Surrounded by loonies. God, I just thought of something! Is it going to affect our own minds being cooped up with these creeps? It happens that way in mental homes, doesn't it?'

Steven grinned. 'We shall just have to make sure, my dear, that it doesn't.'

Next morning, after breakfast, Emily Band escorted her charges to an orientation lecture, to be delivered by none other than Derek Valiant himself. The newcomers had been required to dress in the House uniform of tracksuit and training shoes, and Julianne felt quite ridiculous sitting there in the spacious auditorium, appearing as if she was about to go to an aerobics class. It was all unpleasantly institutional.

Valiant wore his tracksuit top open to mid-chest to reveal a bush of manly hair, which Julianne thought lacked only a large medallion to complete his image. She cringed as this larger-than-life individual bounced around the podium, trying to instil them with a sense of team spirit. She had never been a person to visit holiday camps. Valiant clasped his hands and stared above their heads with moist eyes as he extolled the virtues of their country, ending his sentimental speech with the entreaty that they grasp their Talents in their hands and offer them up to the welfare of their fellow men and women.

Julianne caught Steven's eye; he was smiling tightly, and the smile was edged with distaste. 'Do you suppose they have a bar in this place?' she whispered.

Valiant noticed her speaking. 'You have a question, Ms Farr?' he asked.

She shook her head, withering beneath the lambent stare.

'You are all possessed of a mighty destiny,' Valiant said. 'And it is vital you live up to it.'

Emily Band nodded vigorously at the end of the row.

'God, I hope so,' Steven whispered back to Julianne, in response to her question.

After the lecture, it was time for fitness classes. Julianne's heart sank; she had expected as much. 'I hate exercise,' she told Steven.

On the way to the gym, they were intercepted by an individual who, Emily explained, was practising his charisma. It was considered good manners to assist one's colleagues at all times, so the four of them had to stand there while the man, dressed in a black cloak, postured before them.

'Hello,' Steven said, introducing himself. 'Who are you?'

'I...' said the man, flashing his eyes and raising his hands, 'am *Darkness*!'

Whereupon, he enveloped the surprised spectators in a net of utter blackness. Julianne winced. She could smell fly killer.

'And I,' came a voice beside her – Steven's, 'am Hallucinato, the Master of Pernicious Deceptions!' Steven manifested light from his fingertips, and Darkness retreated with a harrowing hiss.

'Kevin has yet to tone down the more flamboyant tendencies associated with his Talent,' Emily Band explained, dryly. 'Come along, straighten yourself up, Steven. Fun's over.'

The Physical Fitness instructor was disappointed by the newcomers. A few aerobic exercises caused virtual collapse. 'You haven't looked after yourselves, have you?' the instructor said, in a hurt voice.

'He's taking it so *personally*,' Steven whispered to Julianne. 'Does he have a Talent, do you think? What Talent would a Physical Fitness teacher require? Hmm. I know! An ability to deceive the world he does, in fact, have a brain rather more advanced than that of a walnut. It works too, doesn't it? I mean, there's real intelligence in those eyes!'

Julianne smothered a laugh.

'Being fit can save your life in times of crisis,' the instructor said, directing an owlish glance at Steven. 'Are you feeling alright now, Leslie? Perhaps we can get on with ten minutes of jogging on the spot. We can't stand around. I have another class in an hour.'

Julianne groaned and Leslie looked as if she was about to descend into hysterical sobbing. An hour? They would be dead before then!

'Relax, girls,' Steven said, slinging a casual, reptilian arm around each female shoulder. 'Just relax. Sit back and enjoy the show.'

Both Emily Band and the instructor paid attention to the illusion Steven had constructed in front of them; that of three newcomers diligently being put through their paces. In reality, they had sat down at the back of the gym to do as Steven suggested; relax and watch the show.

'Hey, I'm really glad you came here at the same time as me,' Julianne said to him.

He winked. 'Early days yet, my love.'

Steven was summoned to the office of Derek Valiant later that day. It had to be because of something important, as he was plucked from one of Emily Band's proficiency sessions, where she encouraged the fledging paranormals to stretch their powers.

Valiant had a thick, pale cream jumper slung around his neck, the arms tied insouciantly over his chest. He paced the room, while Steven sat demurely in front of his desk. Steven examined the walls, which were covered in framed photographs of Valiant smiling at the camera with wilting paranormals in track-suits clutched under his arms.

'You've had... problems, haven't you?' Valiant said.

'No more than anyone else,' Steven lied.

'I've read the report.'

'Oh.'

Valiant nodded. 'Yes. I am aware of how your Talent came to light.'

'Well, I had expected that.'

'And, as such, realise you might need *special treatment*, gentle handling. I do sympathise with your condition, Steven.'

'Do you?'

'Of course. That is why I'm in charge of this establishment. I'm here to help. But I do expect co-operation. It will cause *difficulties* if you play up, Steven. High spirits are all very well, and there'll be plenty of time for those, but you must put a curb on them during your classes.'

'I'm afraid I don't know what you mean.'

Derek Valiant sighed, sauntered behind his desk and flicked a switch. Monitor screens were unveiled as sections of the wall glided aside. On one screen, Steven could see a class in the gym, all on their backs, riding imaginary bicycles; on another, he could see Julianne and Leslie with Emily Band, Leslie just in the middle of de-materialising. He raised his eyebrows and gave Derek Valiant a look of enquiry.

'So?'

Derek Valiant blinked slowly. 'My talent, Mr Rider, is that no other paranormal's ability has an effect on me. Now, do you see why I am the ideal candidate for the position I hold?'

Steven nodded, his expression thoughtful. He felt embarrassed, and Steven Rider hated feeling embarrassed. 'It seems you've caught me out.'

'Completely. You have a powerful Talent, Steven. Wise up, grow up, and don't abuse it. OK?'

Steven raised his hands. 'Your worries may rest, Mr Valiant.'

'I'm glad. Now, run along to your class. Oh, and one more thing. Now you've settled in, I think you and the girls should socialise with the rest of us tonight, don't you?'

'See you later, then.'

Steven was so furious that, on the way back to Emily Band's class, he could not contain the illusion he'd turned into a roaring, blood-soaked werewolf. It projected exactly how he was feeling. Other trainees and unfortunate members of the domestic staff who came across him cringed from his path. How dare that pompous, coiffured imbecile humiliate him! He would have to pay!

Both Julianne and Leslie could tell Steven was seriously upset when he returned to the class, but there was no opportunity to speak to him about it in private until the end of the day. Steven went to Julianne's room as she was getting changed for dinner and began to tell her what had happened.

'Shut up!' she said.

He looked surprised. 'What? Well, thanks a lot for the support!'

'Be sensible, this place is crawling with telepaths!'

'I see your point...' For a moment, he looked utterly defeated. 'This is a prison, isn't it? I don't care who hears, it's true. We're prisoners.'

'It's only for eight weeks, Steven!'

'Yeah, and what will we be at the end of that time? Have you thought of that? What will walk out of here? Zombies? Robots?'

'I think you're over-dramatising the situation. You just hate authority. We'll simply have to play it their way, I'm afraid.'

'You've thought about this, haven't you?'

'Yes,' Julianne replied, busying herself with the

application of lipstick in her mirror and trying to ignore the reflection of the dejected figure sitting on the bed behind her. 'Emily gave us a dressing down over the gym episode. I realised then we were wasting our time trying to be anarchic. There are too many paranorms here. Even our thoughts aren't our own.'

Julianne hated having to speak to Steven like this, but in the light of what Emily had told her that afternoon, she realised the DPR were paying special attention to him. She would not be doing him a favour by encouraging him to misbehave. She had also realised her first impression of him had been almost correct. He had devilish charm, of course, but she knew now his fooling around concealed something rather more dangerous. Emily hadn't wanted to tell her and Leslie about it, the information was highly confidential, but it was the bond of womanhood that had forced her to speak. Steven Rider destroyed women. He hated them. He was not to be trusted.

'You look really nice,' he said.

She steeled herself and held out a hand. 'Well, escort me to dinner, then.'

Steven was surprised to find he was quite hurt by the way Julianne distanced herself from him that evening, dragging the malleable Leslie with her. He had thought they were on the same wavelength. True, Leslie had directed a couple of mournful glances at him, but had bonelessly allowed Julianne to lead her into a boisterous group of paranorms in the TV room. Steven followed them, somewhat wistfully, although it was clear his company was not required. So Ms Farr wanted to be a good girl, did she? He couldn't summon the energy to be angry about it. It was all too pointless. His vague depression was made more tangible when a furtive Kevin Darkness had sidled up to him and brayed in a soft voice how impressed he had been with the earlier defeat he had suffered at Steven's hands.

'Go away,' Steven answered in a toneless voice. 'You are

physically repellent and conversationally coma-inducing.'

Darkness had drifted away as a mortified black cloud. It momentarily extinguished the light in every soul in the room. Steven noticed this, for he was an observant person and had long been able to see into the core of people's hearts. For the rest of the evening, he essayed one or two covert experiments. It lifted his spirits considerably.

Julianne herself felt a little guilty about shunning Steven, but Emily had been quite emphatic about him. 'Between you and me, girls, he doesn't really belong here. He's trouble. Mr Valiant tried to argue against his placement at Tintern House, but was overruled. He knew there'd be difficulties.'

Still mulling these words over in her mind as she readied herself for sleep, Julianne thought to herself, *Well, here I am. This is it. Make the most of it. Head down. No trouble. Get home.* She climbed into bed and turned off the light. *Goodnight, Steven.*

She was woken into darkness by two cold hands on her wrists. Instinctively, she directed her Talent at her assailant, but it was like fighting a mist. 'Leslie? she said. 'Leslie! What are you doing?'

The room filled with a dull blue glow and there was Leslie hovering above her, phantom face inches from her own. She was a nightmare succubus, all floating, sparkling hair and funeral night-gown. Her incorporeal fingers bit like the kiss of frost into Julianne's crawling skin. She shook her ghost's head and the hair floated on the air like ferny weed beneath water. She did not, or could not, speak. Just shook her head.

And lifted.

Julianne let out a feeble cry, as she was drawn, bodily from the bed. Her flesh tingled as if a thousand minute sparks dusted her skin. Then her whole body went numb. Her lips were frozen shut; she could make no sound at all. Leslie's phantom robe swirled around her like a ragged cloud. She was enveloped by the presence of Leslie; at one with presence of Leslie. And then the air was midnight cold against her flesh. She shivered inside her thin nightclothes. *Where am I?* Far below, the dark roof of Tintern House surveyed the thin beams of light thrown out on to the gravel drive from long windows. Julianne could see her own car, spot-lighted. *Leslie?*

'The only way,' Leslie replied. 'The only way. They cannot hear us up here.'

'Why?' Julianne asked, breaking into a hysterical giggle. She was floating effortlessly in Leslie's Talented embrace. It was exhilarating and deliciously scary too.

Leslie manifested a chill, spectral wind. It signified displeasure. 'They lied,' she said. 'They lied to us.'

'What do you mean?'

'About Steven. It was lies. I know.'

'Don't be silly. Why would they do that?'

Leslie hissed meaningfully. 'Because they are afraid of him.'

'Then maybe we should be, too.'

'No,' Leslie sighed. 'No.'

'Look, I really think we should go back. I don't care about Steven Rider... Leslie, I want to go back'

'You are back.' Leslie replied. 'You never left.'

Julianne wiggled her toes experimentally. They felt real enough. 'You are more Talented than they think, aren't you?' she said.

'Steven showed me how,' Leslie replied.

On her way to breakfast, Julianne marched into Steven's room without knocking. She pulled back the covers on his bed and hit him across the head with her open hand. He screamed and covered his head with his arms.

'You bastard!' Julianne said. 'What have you done?' She hit him again. 'Come on, tell me!'

Steven cowered away from her female rage. He knew how devastating that could be and also the pointlessness of illusion-spinning when faced with such a creature. Normally, the only action he took with furious women was swift retreat. He scrabbled into a sitting position.

'Come on, Steven, out with it. What did you do to Leslie?'

'Nothing!'

Julianne raised her hand menacingly.

'Honestly! I just – well – fulfilled a little dream she has, that's all. I didn't touch her.'

'She told you what Emily Band said, of course.'

He shrugged. 'Yes.'

'I'd really like to hear you deny that accusation, Steven. I really would.'

'It's exaggerated. These people are paranoid.'

Julianne narrowed her eyes. 'I'm beginning to learn something here. There is more to you than illusions. Much more.'

Steven scratched the back of his neck. 'Well, there's something I've only recently discovered, as it happens. Perhaps all that group therapy brought it out, I don't know.' He smiled tentatively. 'I was going to tell you about it today.'

'In unforgettable fashion, I suppose.'

'Don't be a bitch. I've been thinking. About this set-up. It's not the right way to train paranormals.'

'No?'

'No. Want to know what is? Want to know the future, Ms Farr?'

Julianne sighed and sat down on the bed, intrigued in spite of herself. 'Astound me,' she said. 'Please.'

'Some people say that reality is an illusion,' he began.

Julianne shrugged and folded her arms.

'Illusion is my Talent, therefore, I alter reality. Perhaps even create reality.'

'I don't think so,' Julianne replied. 'For example, if you made people think you had a gun in your hand, and shot them, no bullet would actually enter their skin. It couldn't kill them.'

Steven shook his head. 'Don't be naive. If they believed they had been shot, they might well manifest an injury. It's the power of the mind.'

'You've tried it, then.'

'Not exactly. But I discovered something by accident.' He leaned towards Julianne earnestly. 'Tell me, how much do you want to go back to your metal-tube executive life, how much *really?*'

Julianne didn't like the sound of that question. 'Very much so. I love my job; I have a great amount of responsibility.'

'Where everyone now knows you're paranormal...'

'What are you trying to say, Steven?'

He leaned back among his pillows, arms behind his head. 'What I'm saying is, all those organizational skills you have, your excellent business head – wouldn't they be just as useful in another bureaucratic set-up?'

'That goes without saying, I suppose...'

'Like here?'

Leslie Carter had become a glittering mist which filled her whole room. She could not regain corporeality, and did not even want to. Her joy dictated she must expand to her limits. Flesh would only make her ache. She had kissed Kid Spectrum. He had held her in his arms, and it had transcended all her desperate imaginings. Oh, she knew it had really been Steven, but for a few moments, she had lived her dream. And he had given her such strength, such strength.

Coalescing into a kind of solidity she regarded herself in the mirror for a few moments. Now, even in flesh, she appeared transparent. Her eyes were virgin's eyes, but the containment had become power. She had become prophet, angel, saint, all from a short embrace. She had come alive. *Steven, Steven, you waited at the end of my difficult path. You were there with open arms.* Oh, yes, and she had taken the out-stretched hand willingly. Soon, everything would be different.

'Your lessons are really quite instructive, Mr Valiant,' Steven said.

'I don't remember you having an appointment.' Derek Valiant was perturbed to find this nuisance in his office at such an early hour. After the previous interview with Steven Rider, he had immediately contacted the DPR and repeated his misgivings about having such a potentially destructive presence under his roof. His complaints were being sent to committee. As if that did any good! The whole place could be in chaos before anything was done, and Derek Valiant was quite sure that something would have to be done. *Weevil,* he thought, looking at the smug smile opposite.

'Actually, I don't have an appointment,' Steven said, affably. 'I assumed yours was an open door.'

'What do you want? Please be brief. I'm very busy today.'

'Well, I have a small problem.'

Valiant grunted. 'You should go to Emily Band with problems. That's what she's here for. I'm very busy.

'Well, I would have, but as the problem I have is you, I thought I'd better be more discreet.'

'What?'

'Well, I wouldn't want to embarrass you.'

'I think you'd better explain, Mr Rider.'

Steven leaned back in his chair. 'My Talent is more... *interesting* than I thought. But then, I suppose, given that you know everything, you're already aware of that.'

'Don't try to play with me. Say what you have to say.'

Steven stood up and sauntered, hands in pockets, round the desk. He relished the moment as Derek Valiant flinched. 'Well, your Talent enables you to run this establishment without mishap, without fear of deceit or cunning. Am I right? Now, tell me, if you discovered a paranorm who could somehow, through manipulating your mind, emphasize that Talent, what would happen?'

Valiant laughed, scudding backwards a few inches on his wheeled executive chair. 'You tell me.'

'Well, to be honest, I'm not quite sure. I do know that for a person who can turn themselves into a phantom, it means they magically find the confidence to extend that ability, to be able to turn other people into phantoms too, or at least draw the essence out of their bodies. How it would affect a person with an already impressive Talent for telekinesis I've yet to find out, but ... well, it's just a hunch, but surely for a person whose Talent is the ability to be unaffected by other people's Talents, expanding that ability would mean they'd also be unaffected by their own Talent, too, wouldn't it?'

Derek' Valiant made one or two flustered noises. 'Your idea is preposterous!'

'It sounds so, I agree, but it is possible. Be so kind as to activate the monitoring device you have in Leslie Carter's room.'

'We don't monitor the trainees in their rooms!' Valiant said.

Steven shook his head. 'Please, it will save us having to walk up there.'

Valiant activated the screen. Leslie's room had been transformed into a whirling maelstrom of coruscating light. 'She is happy,' Steven said, 'very happy, but I must point out that, until last night, her Talent was nowhere near as powerful as that.'

'This is one of your illusions, then.'

'No, all I did was give her a belief in herself. That is the beauty of my Talent, Mr Valiant. I can change reality for people, and thus give them the confidence to reach out further than they ever have before. It is all a question of belief.'

Derek Valiant tapped his lips with his fingers. He looked thoughtful. 'I have to admit I'm impressed – if what you say is true.'

'It is. But this raises another issue. Your methods of training paranormals involve imposing disciplines, definitions – boundaries. I envisage a new training programme, where trainees are encouraged to strive beyond the limits they have imposed on themselves.'

Valiant laughed. 'Far too dangerous. Ambitious, yes, but...'

'No, not dangerous at all. It depends on how you define danger, of course. Anyway, I intend to implement this myself.'

'Out of the question.'

Steven sighed. 'May I remind you of how my Talent could affect you, Mr Valiant?' He laughed. 'Your way is history, I assure you. The DPR are going to be very interested in my ideas. Now, would you be so kind as to make a telephone call for me?'

'We are living in strange and wonderful times,' said Mr Sharpe, snapping his briefcase shut. 'As yet, it is a time of discovery, one of daring and gambling, too.'

'The sky's the limit, then,' Steven said, putting his feet up on the desk that used to carry the nameplate of Derek Valiant.

'Oh, far beyond that, Mr Rider. Far beyond that.'

'You are greedy people,' Julianne Farr said. She sat on the window-sill, composed in killer business suit, each nail perfectly filed to a point. 'You are sucking from us, aren't you?'

Mr Sharpe directed a hurt glance at her, faultlessly performed. 'We need the best,' he said. 'That's all. As I said, we are constantly learning.' He smiled at Steven. 'You have been given a chance, Mr Rider, don't abuse it. We want the best from the Talented, the utmost, and you can help us achieve that. Don't let us down.' He stood up. 'Well, that's all for now. I'll leave you to it. The administration of Tintern House has been officially passed to you and Ms Farr.' He smiled benignly at Julianne. 'Your responsibility, I feel, is to keep this young man's enthusiasm under control, and to groom his ideas into workable programmes. I also leave the staffing of this establishment in your hands, Ms Farr.'

As Julianne escorted him to the door, they passed a pretty waif of a girl who nodded to them as she drifted into Steven's office. For a moment or two, her identity quite escaped Mr Sharpe, despite having recently been shown a video of her Talent by Steven and Julianne. Then he realized:

the prototype. Steven had also described how he intended to implement her Talent into his training courses; out-of-body-experience classes would be fitted into the curriculum alongside fitness training.

Leslie closed the door behind her. Her heart was aflutter with the enormity of her decision. 'Kid Spectrum,' she said. 'Show me your most serious colours. Show me.'

Somewhere outside, a phone began to ring.

Last Come Assimilation

'Ola, can you never wait for anything?' Con Redley punched flamboyantly his terminal exit pads and swung around in his body-cupping seat.

Ola was impatiently drumming her fingers against the wall, wearing an exaggerated expression of irritation.

'It will be your downfall, Ola!'

'Some of us have work to do tonight, Redley. If you'd spent less time wagging your jaw today, you might be ready to leave on time.'

'Ah, my little Ola,' he said, jumping up and brushing her swiftly retreating cheek with casual fingers. 'Don't complain. I left the seat warm for you.'

Ola grimaced and slid fussily into the formacurl chair, her fingers reaching greedily for the micro-pad as if she'd been away from it too long. She knew Con Redley was aware she didn't enjoy having to share her 'place' with anyone. Ola's brusque impatience was one of the many standing jokes around the Centre and had given rise to the expression 'Uh oh, I can feel an Ola Embeleny coming on!' to signify irritation at some system hold-up or another. Ola was mildly amused by this; she was conscientious but far from easily offended.

The daytime shift gradually left the building, chatting together in groups, shrugging themselves into fleecy jackets, speaking of rendezvous in local bars. Ola listened with satisfaction to their fading voices before settling comfortably into her chair and leaning back for a moment's relaxation. She breathed in deeply, taking in the smoky sweetness of

Incoce's vaporous exhalations far above her head. Recess 920, a vast chamber other than its name implied, seemed to breathe a sigh of relief also, as if welcoming the quiet and solitude of night. One by one, the overhead lights dimmed to blackness, allowing the more pellucid gleam of low-glow nightlights to bloom around Ola's terminal; the only one still on-line at this hour.

Ola stretched and hopped up to fetch herself a coffee from the dispenser by the door. Sipping, she leaned over her chair and stroked her Initiate pad.

How can I help you? Incoce asked; its usual polite greeting. Beneath this, it shyly offered the options of 'Interrogate', 'Check' or 'Fill.'

'Hi there, Inc. What kind of a day have you had, eh?'

The computer terminal blinked its soft blue lights as if in perplexity.

Ola slid back into her seat and tapped in her response. 'Check, please, Inc. Let's see what the data-shovels have fed you today, huh?'

Swiftly, as if greeting an old friend, Incoce asked for her authorisation code, which she supplied with one hand, still sipping the hot, sweet, vaguely synthetic tasting liquid from her cup. As Overnight Shift Recess Supervisor, Ola had to check the day's input for obvious errors before beginning her own work each night. It wasn't much of a chore; Incoce knew enough by now to recognise most mistakes itself. In fact, Ola was sure it seemed to take a certain pleasure in displaying them to her: *Look what I've found. Aren't I good?*

Wriggling blue lines played across her face as Incoce skipped through the day's text. Ola twisted a few strands of hair between her fingers, not really looking that hard. A niggling anxiety had slipped back into her mind, which she'd been trying to dismiss since waking up that afternoon. She sighed through her teeth and murmured, 'Lancy, Lancy,' before abruptly leaning forward, stroking a pause pad and switching to vocal command. Often she forgot to do that, taking it for granted the machine heard and understood her anyway. If it did, it was cunning enough not to let on – ever. 'What was that, Incoce, back a bit.' The wriggling lines wriggled backwards. 'Asshole!' The screen flared brighter for a moment at her outburst. She had found an error. Timely. It conveniently pushed from her attention the problem of Lancy Lefarr, and it would be at least another day before Ola found time to think about it again.

Incoce – an abbreviation of Information Collection Centre – was an impressive sleek bulk possessed of massive memory banks. The machine had been diverted far from its original purpose, and expanded and improved because of that, even if a lot of people thought it a rather gross and outmoded model. Its home was the small, congenial world of Brickman, named for the Senior Administrator, Osmund Brickman, who'd headed the team first arriving on the planet. Now centuries dead, Brickman's name and his machine lived on, if not the scheme towards which he had dedicated himself and whose collapse had been partially, if not wholly, responsible for his own.

Incoce had originally been designed as the thinking mind, administration centre and personnel department behind OFEX Project, a grand plan to mine fliridium from the dozen or so worlds circulating Rover's Star. Back then, the mineral had been newly discovered and had engendered enormous excitement owing to the fact that it appeared to be a powerful energy source of limitless life and without any radioactive strings attached. Initial excitement, glee and vast financial outlay had withered to craven embarrassment when other, unexpected side products of fliridium had emerged. It wasn't radioactivity exactly, but it still rendered all living creatures sterile, plants included, before inflicting a particularly horrid death that few journals kept a record of nowadays.

The money and the mega-corporations flitted off to the further reaches of the galaxy in search of more verdant mineral pastures, leaving a rather shame-faced, if not redundant, settlement of colonists on Brickman. The

Governmental Station two stars away had declined Osmund Brickman's request for the transferral of his people. The Administrators there were reluctant to decolonise a world so supremely amenable to human habitation as Brickman's was. It would surely come in handy one day, when perhaps other purposes could be thought of for its dozen sister worlds and yes, they surely did have a use for the great mind of Incoce.

These days, Brickman existed as a vast information collection agency, documenting the history and human achievement of the galaxy. Its huge, inimitable source of knowledge was used by academics, sales companies and students from as far away as could be imagined. Incoce, in fact, was an encyclopaedia, directory and dictionary to end them all. And the machine seemed very happy about that, too. Of course, it cost people to use the facility and this kept the population of Brickman, most of whom worked with Incoce, comfortably, if not well, endowed with financial incentive.

Ola called up on screen from the comms store the material it was her task to sift through before directing it to the relevant files of Incoce's memory. Throughout the vast complex centre, hundreds of other Recess supervisors would be embarking upon the same employment, but to Ola, it felt as if she was the only person awake in the whole complex every night. Occasionally, one or two of the nightshift data clerks – there was a skeleton crew of those – would pop in to ask her advice or simply to pass a few congenial words, but on the whole Ola was left alone.

This suited her fine. The only time she felt she could truly relax was at work. She also had a great affinity for the machine itself, conscious of a quirky if evanescent personality coming through her screen now and again. Less imaginative operatives would scoff benignly at such fancies; to them Incoce was a yawning mouth, ever hungry for the food of knowledge, never satisfied, whose supplies never ran dry. Data sorting was not the most stretching of jobs if one did not have an interest in the data itself. Ola considered herself lucky. She at least worked in a Recess that dealt solely with planetary flora and fauna, to her an absorbing and fascinating subject. She reflected that she could have been allocated a statistics or governmental procedures terminal; life might not have been so enjoyable then.

All Incoce employees spent nine hours a day at work during days that lasted only twenty hours. Admittedly, three out of every seven days were free, but often Ola would work overtime then. Learning about the exotic and far-flung worlds newly discovered by intrepid exploratory teams was of far more interest to her than passing on the latest of trivial gossip in one of the local bars. Not even the holovids on show at the Movie Palace were as intriguing as the real fantasticals with which she communed every day. 'Oh,' Ola would sigh, 'if only I'd been born in a place where I could be on one of the teams sending the information back instead of stuck behind a bloody terminal! Sorry, Inc, I know, at least I have mobility, not like you, stuck here forever, even if I don't have the funds to make more use of it!'

Lancy didn't show up for dinner on Ola's next day off. This annoyed Ola intensely. She had spent three hours preparing a relatively sumptuous repast and was also unaccustomed to her best friend standing her up. Uncharitably thinking that some new man must have glided over the horizon and into Lancy's range, Ola sat regarding the congealing sum of her efforts for nearly an hour before she called up Anton Givesey, one of her more senior colleagues but a long-standing friend, to come and help her eat it.

Anton didn't seem to mind the food being a little cooler, its texture a little more unsupple, than it should have been. Like Ola he lived alone, but unlike Ola he didn't have the particular knack for culinary arts. He thoughtfully brought along a carton of wine, which lubricated the food nicely and broke the ice of Ola's frosty temper. 'I don't know what's up with Lancy these days,' Ola said, after her third helping of wine. She generally refrained from discussing other people on principle, which often made it difficult for anyone to hold a conversation with her.

Anton shrugged. He'd never cared for Lancy Lefarr anyway, thinking her a shallow person and rather an unlikely comrade for the astute and industrious Ola. Perhaps it was true that opposites attracted, although what the two talked about when they were together he could not imagine.

'I mean she's just started not being where she should be, or arriving when she shouldn't or...' Ola shook her head. 'I know she can be a flittery creature, Anton, but I've known her since we were kids and she's never been like this before.'

'Perhaps it's love or something like that,' Anton offered.

Ola pulled a face. 'I'd thought of that, yes, but I've heard nothing and you know how everybody hears everything around here. Anyway, Lancy would tell me. We've never kept secrets like that from each other.' Ola thought briefly of all the affairs in her life that had ever fallen apart and how Lancy had been there, a far from fragile support, to see her through all of them. Could Lancy be going through something now that she could not share with her friend? Surely not. It hurt Ola to think Lancy would keep her distance if she was in trouble or in love.

As soon as she reported for her next duty, Ola made a point of calling Lancy's personal mail-file. It had until recently been the custom most days for she and Lancy to leave little messages for each other, but Lancy had been unusually silent for over a week now. She had not materialised at all during Ola's rest period and attempts to call her apartment had been met only with an answering machine. Ola had even gone round there in person on one occasion, but no one had come to the door. Barely giving Incoce time for its usual greeting, Ola punched in Lancy's mail code, squinting at the screen.

Con Redley hadn't yet left the complex. He eyed Ola's evident worry with speculation. 'What is it?' he asked her, looking over her shoulder. Incoce appeared to be giving a theatrical display of colours.

'What is this?' Ola barked in reply, gesturing at the nonsensical information on her screen. 'Has the terminal been acting up today?'

'No. Been fine.' Con reached over and stroked a few keys. 'Little more patience, eh?' he said smugly as the chaotic lines settled down.

'I don't understand this,' Ola said. Incoce had ignored her request for access to Lancy's mail-file. She made a swift interrogation only to be presented with the more concise message: *Authorisation Code does not match request. Please abandon transaction.* She turned to Con Redley. 'Do you get this, Con?'

'What are you trying to do?'

'Oh, something terribly classified – reach Lancy Lefarr's mail-file!'

'Has she been upgraded?'

'Not that I know of.'

Con Redley shrugged and finished wrapping himself in his coat. 'Must be some kind of error, then. Want me to give Lancy a message if I see her?'

'Are you likely to?'

Con shrugged again. 'Don't know. She shows up sometimes in Blitza's.'

'If you see her, tell her to get in touch, that's all.'

'OK.' Con wandered from the Recess, leaving Ola alone. She was aware of her heart beating faster than usual, her body becoming instinctively aware of her next course of action before her conscious mind.

She waited until she was sure there would be no immediate interruptions, until the last echoing footsteps had faded down the corridor outside, the last farewell called out for the night. She waited until the lights began to dim, but there was no atmosphere of tranquillity in Recess 920 that night. Perhaps it was in her own head, but Ola sensed a tightness in the air, a watchfulness.

'Incoce, can I trust you?' she muttered. With damp fingers she activated vocal command; there was less chance of records being kept of her transactions that way. At least she hoped so. There was no real way of telling just how much Incoce kept in its memory, or even how much it was prepared to divulge if requested. The machine had been innovatory back in the days of Osmund Brickman, one of the new computers whose intelligence was contained in charged fluid rather than microchips. Because it was a prototype, Incoce had enormous vats and pipes running all over the place; nowadays its younger brothers were more compact. Because of this huge, rambling mind, half of the workings of which its creators hadn't fully understood, it was suspected that Incoce operatives did not have access to all parts of the machine. The comparison with the human brain had to be made then. Did Incoce have consciousness, or more to the point in Ola's case, did it have a conscience? If Lancy's file had become inaccessible, it would at the very least be frowned upon for Ola to try and break into it. If it was just a fault, surely she was entitled...?

Steeling herself, Ola made one or two brief preliminary enquiries. Incoce replied that Lancy's security code had been changed and unfortunately Ola did not possess enough security clearance to breach it. 'We'll see about that,' Ola muttered, tapping keys.

It took her nearly an hour; one long hour of swerving and dodging, playing strange, convoluted games with the system's logic, but eventually, Ola found a way through. She'd been careful to hide her tracks, as much as possible, and now the familiar logo of Lancy's mail-file was on screen before her. Releasing a breath that had been held for considerable time, Ola tapped in a simple message: 'Where the hell are you? Are you dead? Are we conducting a silence I'm not aware of? Get in touch, Lancy. Now. As soon as you read this. Ola.'

Rubbing her face, Ola stroked keys to file the message and was unprepared for the sudden blast of colour, accompanied by a previously unheard of whine, which swept across the screen. As if the machine had gone mad, text poured over the page, too fast for Ola to understand it. She frantically hissed a few commands, stroking keys simultaneously, and for a few moments the text wobbled and then became more or less static, if leaning rather drunkenly to the left.

Ola's mouth dropped silently open in surprise. She read quickly, voicelessly forming the words as she read. Other messages had been left in the file. Normally, these wouldn't be displayed to a new caller, but for some reason, probably because of her meddling, the entire store was on screen. 'Lefarr: access genetic data, operative level 23, class OO47. Results by 04:09:378.' 'Operative 23/0048/cgH2059 unsuitable for conversion; hereditary disorder. Please amend record.' 'Operative 23/0048/oeS3001; report accepted. Personality update required, including psychological analysis. Immediate response.'

Other, even more cryptic messages followed, esoteric, Ola reasoned, because perhaps parts of them were not displayed. Acting on instinct, she immediately erased her own chatty little missive from the end of the file. 'Make that a certain, Incoce,' she said. 'Wipe it. Kill it.' She considered making a hard copy of what was left, but thought it too risky. Best to get out. *Now.*

Already suppositions were forming in her mind, not least because one of the messages bore her own code, telling her the report had been accepted and that they, whoever 'they' were, would be investigating her psychological state.

Ola fled from Incoce's mind. She sat staring at the blank screen. What was Lancy involved in? She wasn't even a supervisor, just a simple data clerk of low security clearance, junior salary grade and working on the most routine medical records; no classified stuff at all. Most of the information Lancy's crew handled was out of date by the time it reached Incoce. It was just history. But this? How was Ola involved? Why were they investigating her and what for? It was creepy.

Ola's voice sounded small in the huge, crepuscular dimness of Recess 920. 'Incoce, can you tell me?' she whispered. The machine only blinked slowly, revealing nothing. Ola sighed, shudderingly. 'Put me on Check, Inc,' she said, and began her night's work.

Ola was almost overcome by superstitious paranoia when Lancy called around the next day. She woke Ola early, finger pressed unrelentingly on access buzzer, until Ola came, dishevelled, to the door. Ola couldn't repress the suspicious 'What do you want?' that slipped from her lips as soon as she saw who'd come visiting.

Lancy swept into the apartment, to all appearances acting as if nothing unusual had been going on. 'Con Redley said you'd been trying to reach me,' she said, peeling off long gloves and touching up her long, red hair before dropping fluidly into a chair.

Ola shuffled into her kitchen to fumble with the coffee dispenser, uncomfortably conscious of her messy appearance, trying to pat her haystack hair into shape without success. She needed a few moments to wake up properly. 'Yeah, I thought you'd disappeared for good!' she called out.

'Sorry, Ola, I've been that busy!' Lancy said cheerfully. 'I was going to call you soon, honest.'

Ola brought two drinks into the room. She didn't sit down. 'I tried to leave a message in your mail-file,' she said. 'Couldn't get through.'

Lancy didn't even blink. 'I know. It's been acting up recently.'

Ola had to turn her face away from such a blatant lie. She wanted to interrogate her friend, while aware such action would be fruitless. She wanted Lancy to go. She wanted to shout. She wanted to remind Lancy Lefarr they'd been friends for fifteen years, and didn't that imply they should have mutual trust and loyalty? 'So what's been keeping you so busy, then?' she said, her outrage under constraint.

'Oh, this and that. We had a huge workload come in from some distant speck or another. We've all been on overtime. I've been too bushed to call anyone at nights.'

Ola stared at her friend hard, only prudence concerning her own safety preventing the hundred questions bursting to be voiced. Lancy stared back without wavering, but Ola could sense the barrier between them as if it had been constructed in brick. 'There's a rumour you've been upgraded,' Ola said carefully.

An alert flash passed over Lancy's face.

Did you really think I was that stupid? Ola wondered.

'You know what rumours are,' Lancy said lamely.

'Why are you giving me this bullshit?' Ola asked, caution giving way to outrage.

Lancy dropped her eyes then. 'I'm not going to say "I don't know what you mean," Ola, but I can't answer, OK. Just drop it.'

'Lancy, we're an information collection centre; bibliographers, encyclopaedia compilers. What the hell is going on that suddenly there's the scent of conspiracy all over the place?'

'There isn't. It's just you. You think too much, imagine things.'

Like I imagined the messages in your mail-file, Ola thought, but of course she could not say that. 'Suit yourself, but I'm not pleased you don't trust me, Lancy. Not pleased at all. You were like a sister to me, more than that.' She got up stiffly and took the coffee cups back into the kitchen. Behind her, she heard Lancy sigh. Soon after, neither of them able to overcome a static discomfort, Lancy made excuses and left.

Con Redley was surprised by Ola's uncharacteristic desire to have him hang around the Recess and chat that evening. Usually, she couldn't wait to get rid of him. 'You saw Lancy, then?' he asked.

'Yes, she called around today. Thanks.'

'Everything OK?'

'Everything's fine. It's all sorted out.'

'Good. Seems to have put your mind at rest anyway. Any

more trouble with the terminal last night?'

'No. Lancy said she'd been having trouble with her mail-file. It's probably been fixed by now.'

'Yeah. Fine.' He picked up his coat. 'I'll be off, then.'

'OK. Have a good time.' Ola sat down and made a few preliminary keystrokes.

Con Redley stared at her for a moment. 'Lennering's been sniffing around today,' he said. Mr. Lennering was their head of department.

'The man's a prat! What did he want?'

'Asked me how you were.'

Ola laughed nervously. 'He hardly knows me!'

'Yeah, I know...'

'I'm honoured, then. Hope you said I was fine.'

'Naturally.'

'Great. Well, don't let me keep you.' Ola waved him away but he paused at the door, causing it to hover half-shut, confused.

'Ola, are you OK?'

'Yes. Of course I am. See you.'

Ola was conscious of holding her breath until he'd gone. She hoped he hadn't picked up her eagerness to get down to what she'd decided to do. Had she been unconvincing? Oh well, she thought, too late to worry about that now. It's just another night's work, nothing more. Stop panicking.

She fetched herself a cup of coffee and watched the ceiling lights dim. Incoce blinked expectantly in front of her. She glanced to either side at the rows of blank screens, each terminal personalised in some way by its operator; stickers, mascots, slogans. She no longer felt part of that.

Anton Givesey was a personnel supervisor, grade 2. He had access to all personnel files and Ola, a long time ago and for a completely innocent purpose, had memorised his authorisation code. It had been a favour for Anton; he'd been sick. She'd completed a small job he should have finished the day before. Anton trusted her. Now, she hesitantly tapped his code into the machine and soon after, requested access to

Lancy Lefarr's file. It was only a simple request. The personnel staff worked on these files every day. There was no need to feel so nervous.

Startlingly, Incoce flashed up the message: '*Classified. Please access WX/3000/05 for authorisation.*' Should she do that? Anton would have to give reasons why he wanted to consult that file. Probably, he'd just be asked to enter his request and wait for a reply without being granted direct access. Ola hesitated. What could she ask that Anton would possibly want to know that would help her in any way?

To hell with it: take risks. She compiled an innocent query regarding Lancy's insurance code. At least that would show whether she'd been upgraded. As she'd expected, she had to wait for a reply without being given access to the file. Incoce displayed Lancy's code. It was unchanged. So why the hell was her file classified? Ola did all she could again to cover her tracks, hoping no record of the query would be sustained.
Her hopes were short-lived. The next day, Anton Givesey was requested to attend the Law Enforcement Office to assist enquiries into illegal activities concerning data store. Ola found this out as soon as she got to work. Everyone was full of it.

Con Redley didn't even wait until she'd got her jacket off to tell her the news. 'What's happening?' he asked, a rhetorical question. What could Ola know that he didn't? 'Illegal activities? How? Nothing we do is remotely interesting is it?'

'I'm sure we don't know about everything that gets stored in Inoce,' Ola answered, rather stiffly.

Con Redley shrugged. 'You're right, I suppose, but I can't think what. They have other centres for that sort of thing, don't they?'

Now, people were beginning to get jumpy. Nothing like this had ever happened before. Incoce was only a big book, after all. Ola sat down before her terminal, heart thumping. She felt as if something were closing in on her. Extreme measures of self-preservation were called for. There was no denying it; she had every reason to feel afraid. It would not take long for the authorities to discover, by process of elimination, given they possessed knowledge of the times and location of the 'aberrations', who might be responsible for them. Ola knew she would have to act fast. If she could find out what was going on, at least she'd have some kind of armour, find out what she was up against. It might be nothing. *Oh, don't fool yourself, girl,* she thought.

For nearly two years, Ola had been working on a programme for Incoce for her own use. Although she hadn't kept this a secret, she hadn't exactly divulged what it was. Many Incoce operatives possessed personal programmes, usually recreational software, which they'd slip in to the appropriate terminals whenever they got the chance for a little entertainment. Ola supposed her employers were indulgent enough to let sporadic game-playing go on if it didn't get out of hand. Perhaps the information gained from it was even useful to Incoce. Ola's programme, however, was not a game.

Everything relied on privacy. Ola went softly to the door, trying to hear the murmur of voices from other Recesses nearby. Silence did not necessarily mean safety. She was aware of how anyone who was quietly working at this moment might decide to walk over at any time to ask her a question. 'Get a hold of yourself,' she said under her breath.

Apart from the regular terminals, there was one designed to take software, further up the Recess. It was not used very often, so the screen was one of the older types of lesser quality. It did possess the facility for a neural link, however. Ola approached it with a feeling close to dread. She picked up the sensor unit, slipping it over her head even before she sat down. Might as well be as quick as possible. *This had better work!* she thought.

Because she'd always felt such an affinity for Incoce, Ola had been working on the idea that, through a neural link, she could attempt to communicate direct with the machine. It had only been an idle interest up till now, something to ponder over and fiddle about with. She had realised she'd have to make pretty well sure the use of such a programme was undetectable, for she had a feeling her employers would not approve. Such a move might be regarded as the unhealthy practice of machine/man link. Scientists had proved it possible for computer and human brains to interact in complete accord, but it was felt being able to effectively turn living beings into half-machines was morally wrong. Mankind, through its own ingenious and galloping intrusion into the world of technology had everything it needed to survive and expand. There was no real need to tamper with the body and mind's original layout. A religious revival in the forty-eighth cycle, spearheaded by top figures in the galactic authorities, had made this premise law, more or less. Naturally, humanity being the curious, meddling thing that it is, numerous illegal and black market enterprises along these lines still continued, but it was certainly not legitimate practice for corporate bodies. The rules were stringent but somewhat vague around the edges. Ola was not really sure whether her programme was illegal or not, but what the hell; it was her only chance. Now, she had to try it.

Ola sat down at the console. Fumbling in her trouser pocket, she pulled out the programme software, a sac of bio-conductive fluid, still warm from contact with her skin. Sighing through her nose, she inserted it into the machine. 'Incoce, don't fail me,' she said as the screen before her sprang to life. As she stroked keys, Ola's mind was more concerned with the threat of interruption than with what she was actually doing. What hit her was met entirely without preparation of any kind.

First it was a blinding headache sweeping chaotic migraine colours through her head. This stunned her so much, more because of its instantaneous assault than for what it really was, that Ola was virtually flung back in her chair. Then it was sound, a high-pitched scraping. Ola's instinct was to writhe, twist and bleat in pain, but some mercifully rational part of her brain ordered her to attempt to take control. She should have known something like this would happen. Regulating her breathing, Ola calmed herself. Gradually the pain subsided to a dull, heavy ache and behind her closed lids acid green and blue pools floated lazily across her vision. The sound had become virtually inaudible.

'Incoce, this is operative Ola Embeleny,' she thought, clearly. The silence was infinite. She was conscious of a hugeness inside her head as if she was floating in space, a starless space. Timeless seconds seemed stretched into hours as Ola waited for a response. The sensation of limitless emptiness was getting to her. She was beginning to experience a tremendous vertigo that nauseated her. It was very similar to massive over-indulgence in alcohol, only worse. Just as she was about to pull out, she became aware of a dim rosy glow beginning to swell behind her. She could see it even though it felt as if she faced the opposite way.

'Incoce...' She wasn't sure what was manifesting before her; it looked absurdly like a gigantic jellyfish, all transparent veins and trailing, glowing fronds, with a central dark core. Was this Incoce's vision of itself? The thing circled Ola a few times, even stretching out the occasional tasselled thread as if to feel her. She was not aware of being touched. Then, without warning, the creature bunched itself up and shot off into the darkness. Ola began to make a sound, but it was swept away from her. Without volition she was dragged along in the creature's wake. Being sucked away from corporeality, farther and farther, into the liquid depths of Incoce's mind. *No! Stop!* All Ola's thought commands were impotent. The darkness was so dense, so dense...

Smack. Wetly, she landed upon something grainy and shifting. It felt like sand. Ola opened her eyes, not to the familiar sight of Recess 920 but to some bizarre, unrecognisable landscape. Breathing deeply for a moment or two, she took stock of her surroundings. Her body felt solid enough. Odd. *Where the hell am I?*

She stood up and had to brush grains from her clothes.

Real grains of sand, a dull grey-blue in colour. Ola rubbed it between her fingers. It jolted a memory. Of course! This was the iron beach of Meeble Trench, on planet Gardra 10. She'd been cataloguing it only last night at work. Further along, the beach melded gently into what she now recognised as the feather sands of Eli's Reach, catalogue work from a week before. To her left, dunes of multi-coloured sands led to a chaotic arrangement of topographical features. Mountains from one world, plains from another, all carefully seamed together. To her right stretched a slowly shifting ocean, metallic, and with a horizon so far away it seemed to curve up towards the lilac-coloured sky. Around her sprouted a multitude of shoreline plants from as many diverse worlds. Had she emerged into Incoce's private den, where the machine had made an environment for itself from all the things it catalogued? Ola stood up. The air was good, clean and temperate.

'So what shall I do?' she said aloud.

There was no sign of the jellyfish thing, or indeed of any other animal. The sunless sky above her glowed as if with dawn. Water heaved gently onto the shore. Ola went to investigate one of the plants. It felt real enough and exuded a pleasant, sharp smell when she pressed its leaves. All of her senses were being stimulated; it was incredible. Ola took a few moments to assess how she felt; no fear, no discomfort. If anything she felt lighter and healthier than she had for months.

Almost stumbling with a sense of wonder, she advanced up the beach. Ola wished she had some way of recording what she was experiencing. Surely, even if it meant she would face imprisonment for a hundred years, she must not keep this quiet. People should know. It was a miracle!

'No miracle, but your information,' said a voice.

Ola wheeled around, but there was nothing there. 'Incoce?' she whispered. 'Is that you?

'Is this me? Are you joking? What else could it be?'

Ola laughed. 'Then show yourself. Can you do that?'

'OK.'

Ola squinted at the shimmering air. What would Incoce manifest itself as? Nothing seemed to be becoming solid. She took a few steps forward.

'Here!'

She turned around. Behind her stood a mirror image of herself. Ola yelped and backed away. The other Ola sighed and rubbed its face. Ola was swept by cold; it was a gesture she knew so well. 'What do you expect?' Incoce asked. It gestured at the surroundings. 'All this is your input. I thought you'd like it here.'

'It's... it's fine,' Ola said carefully. She didn't want to get too near to Incoce; the image unnerved her.

'Good. I must say this is an interesting experience, so much more stimulating than just being fed the facts. Just a taste of what's to come, I suppose. I appreciate the gesture, Ola Embeleny.'

Ola couldn't speak. What Incoce was saying wasn't wholly reassuring. What did it mean? The figure gestured for Ola to follow it up the beach and she did so, at a distance. 'Don't go thinking I'm lonely,' it said. 'I'm perfectly content. I expect you think you're the first to do this?'

'Well...' Ola didn't know.

'Of course the others are far more cautious than you, so I suppose in a way, you are the first. Everyone else just hangs around on the threshold being nervous. I should have known you'd be the best choice.'

'I'm not sure I understand your implications,' Ola said. Strange how it now seemed so natural to be walking up what could only be an imaginary beach talking to a vision that looked like herself.

'Well, that's why you're here, isn't it?'

'What's why I'm here?'

'Because you want to know what they're going to do with you.'

'Well, yes...'

Incoce paused. 'Basically, this is it,' it said, gesturing once more.

'I'm sorry?'

'This. They want you to become part of me. Not just you, but many others.'

'What?'

Incoce shook its head. 'They think it would be more productive for me to have actual parts of myself out gathering information than having the data transmitted to Brickman.'

'*Parts* of yourself? Me? Others? What do you mean?'

Incoce sighed. It seemed impatient with Ola's inability to grasp immediately what it meant. 'Assimilation; myself and humanity, or bits of it. I don't want to use crude terms like cyborg; they're far too emotive, but I'm sure you get what I mean.'

'But that's illegal!' Ola cried.

'Well, that point is being debated, but it is envisaged that all the problems should be ironed out by the time my operatives are properly prepared.'

'It's inhuman!'

'Only partly.'

Ola stopped walking. Lancy's face had suddenly popped into her mind. She had to face the fact that somebody she had long regarded as a close friend knew about all this. Lancy knew what they had planned for her and hadn't told her. Ola found that harder to believe than the plan itself. 'What if I refuse?' she said belligerently.

Incoce looked perplexed. 'Why should you want to do that? I know you're fed up with just being stuck on Brickman. You've told me yourself many times, remember? All that, "Oh I wish I was out there etc. etc."?'

'What about my independence?'

'Oh, you think you have that, do you?'

Ola disliked the irony in Incoce's tone. 'What about my mind?'

'Don't be so precious about it. It's not that special. We'd be working together, Ola. You wouldn't be a mindless slave. Do you really think the authorities would stand for that?'

'I'm not sure of anything.'

'Come here. Look at this.' Incoce pointed to what appeared to be a VDU screen standing on a plinth a few yards away. Ola shook her head and went to look at it. 'See,' Incoce said. 'This is the centre they've been preparing for the necessary surgery, and alteration. Oh, I know that sounds unpleasant, but it isn't. Look, it's all automatic, just waiting to go, really.'

'Just looks like an incubator,' Ola said. It was like peering through a window into a room.

'I suppose it is rather like that. We'll have good times, Ola. What do you think? We could go anywhere. Not only would you experience all the far worlds you dream of, but I could too, through you.' Incoce extended a tentative hand and touched Ola's shoulder. It felt just like the touch of a real woman.

'I'll have to think about it,' Ola said. 'Can I go back now?'

Incoce rolled its eyes. 'You don't have to ask! Just go. Don't take too long to think. It's only wasting time.'

Then, with an Ola smile, a smart wave of its hand, the image of Incoce was no longer there.

Ola opened her eyes, and the bright whiteness, even though dimly-lit, of Recess 920 made her blink. She was back. Quickly, she disentangled herself from the headset and threw it down beside the console. For a few moments she just slumped, half-dazed, in her chair.

Her first coherent thought was one of revenge. *Damn Lancy! What an unbelievable bitch.* Ola considered whether she should call her so-called friend and bawl her out. There was little point in trying to keep what she knew secret. It seemed she was fenced in, anyway. She got up, stretched and walked stiffly back to her own terminal. An unfamiliar logo was on the screen. 'What the hell's happening now?' she muttered.

'All the information you'll need,' Incoce wrote in soothing blue.

This was it: the file. 'Incoce Mobilisation Project.'

'OK, I'll look at it. Can't promise any more, but I'll look at it,' Ola said.

The following morning Ola was waiting for her head of department in his office. It was a normal day. All the sounds around the building were those of routines beginning, work getting started. Mr. Lennering took off his jacket, grunted, shrugged his shoulders a few times and went to take his seat. What followed was the most splendid double-take Ola had ever seen. Mr. Lennering jumped back with an audible 'Yip!'

Ola stood up. Mr. Lennering's chair squeaked softly as she did so. Ola laughed. Her eyes were silver eyes. Apart from that, there were very little external signs of note, but even to someone who didn't know her, Ola was somehow larger and certainly stranger.

'What do you want, Ms. Embeleny?' Mr. Lennering asked, prepared to act as if nothing was out of the ordinary. He looked at her as if he thought she was merely intoxicated in some way.

'I know about the mobilisation project,' she said, smiling.

'I have no idea what you mean. Go home, Ms. Embeleny. I believe your shift is over.'

'I most certainly will not,' she answered.

Mr. Lennering craftily reached for his intercom but was unprepared for the swiftness of Ola's response and also the firmness of Ola's grip on his arm. This was not the grip of a human woman.

'I know about it, Mr. Lennering. I know what you're planning. Incoce told me. Incoce showed me.'

'Let me go! You've broken every rule of the company! I'll...'

'Shut up, Mr. Lennering,' Ola interrupted. 'There's no need for this. I've gone along without you, can't you see?' She realised that not only was the man stupid, but he also knew very little about the project. Certainly not enough to understand what he was looking at. 'Incoce and I decided to bring the date forward for modification,' she said. 'What you are looking at is a successful assimilation of human mind and machine. Aren't you pleased it works?'

Mr. Lennering spluttered helplessly. He must think she was mad. No matter. Ola dropped him. She activated his intercom and spoke to his secretary. 'Mr. Lennering would like you to have Lancy Lefarr come over to his office.' She touched Mr. Lennering's arm. 'You're going to do something unprecedented,' she said. 'You're going to fire Lancy Lefarr.'

'What?' Incoce operatives were never fired. There had never been any need. The machine was their life.

'I won't explain,' Ola said, 'other than to say I have a gut need for retaliation. It's the only stipulated condition in return for my co-operation. You have to admit, I could have been difficult. In fact, if you think about it, there are many ways I could cause difficulties for you even now.'

'You'll never get away with this,' Mr. Lennering said impotently.

Ola laughed politely. She really didn't care what he thought. She was the company's prime tool now; a success. He was nothing; a clerk.

'Just you wait,' Mr. Lennering was continuing to babble, 'you wait until...'

Ola interrupted him again, still smiling. 'Oh come now,' she said gently. 'Don't you know my reputation? I can never wait around for anything.'

Lancy Lefarr could hear Ola's delighted laughter even before she opened the door.

Time Beginning at Break of Day

A dismembered limb arced gracefully across the television screen. Gavin drew up his knees with a squeak, hiding his face in Dawn's shoulder.

'For God's sake, Gavin, what's the matter with you?' she demanded, wriggling further up the sofa. The lounge was in darkness, but for the glimmering screen and the faint glow from the street outside coming through the curtains.

'I was nearly asleep,' he answered.

'So are Tim and Shona.' Dawn gave one of their friends a sharp prod with her toe; they were curled up on the floor. 'Wake up, Tim. God, what a riveting film! Whose idea was it to get this one?'

'Not mine,' Shona said, stretching. 'What time is it?'

'Half one.'

'Not that late, then,' said Gavin. Thankfully, the credits were beginning to roll across the screen in front of them. 'Want to watch another one? We've still got *Visceral Terror in L.A.* here.'

'Is that the one where the girl gets turned inside out?' Tim asked.

'No, that's *Giblets Freak Out the Possessed Child*,' Gavin answered mock-knowledgeably. 'You know, and all those gerbils grow giant fangs and start reciting from the Book of Revelations.'

'Shut up, Gavin. Make a coffee.' Dawn turned on the

lights, thus successfully bringing another evening's entertainment to a close. She started gathering beer cans, heaping them into an already full waste bin.

Gavin shuffled, yawning, into the kitchen. The neon light burned dimly, fizzing to itself.

Dawn came to lean in the doorway, six feet of shapely Amazon. 'I've forgotten the last time I was frightened by a good film,' she said.

Gavin was heaping coffee into mugs; a cat twined round his legs, mewing furiously. 'Real life's more scary,' he said.

'Yeah, the supermarket at tea-time on Friday.'

'The Post Office queue on pension day.'

They both laughed.

'Want a hand with those coffees?' Dawn asked.

Gavin Arnold had been a moderately successful musician for nearly a year, and had lived with the sultry Dawn Banning for two years. Now they aspired to an upwardly mobile contentment. Their cats and their furnishings, if not their taste in films, were expensive. Gavin was a highly imaginative creature, creatively inclined, easy-going and prone to outbursts of weird and witty behaviour. At these times, Dawn called him childish and retreated behind a cool and stylish reserve. She considered herself, rightly, to be the guiding force and common sense behind their relationship.

Tim and Shona were staying the night. The four of them sat together, the TV busy with static before them. They sipped coffee and discussed various other video victories they'd experienced. 'What is the ultimate in horror?' Tim asked.

'Isn't it different for everybody?' Dawn said thoughtfully. 'I'm not scared of spiders, but most people are. See what I mean?'

'OK, what *does* scare you?'

Dawn shrugged. 'I think it varies from day to day. What you think, Gavin?'

'If someone threatened to push me into a meat-mincer, I

think it would worry me.'

Dawn rolled her eyes, gesturing with one arm. 'Yet another immortal Arnold utterance to be engraved on stone!'

Gavin made a placatory gesture. He was tired. 'OK, what scares me? Losing control, being unable to differentiate between fantasy and reality. Fantasy becoming reality. Total weirdness.'

Tim laughed. 'That's your mis-spent youth showing through, matey!'

Gavin shrugged. 'Well, you did ask.'

'Know what scares me at the moment?' Dawn said. 'The thought of spending the rest of my life with this maniac!'

Everybody laughed and Gavin gibbered and leered obligingly.

Gavin and Dawn had a room at the back of the house for their bedroom. Dawn maintained it was the best one as it caught the sun for the better part of the day – and who wanted sunlight when you were getting up for work in the morning anyway? You'd only be stuck in the office unable to take advantage of it, so why be tortured by what you'd be missing? After installing their friends in the spare room, Gavin shambled into the bedroom, kicking off his shoes as he went.

'Gavin, are you making a mess?' Dawn called from the bathroom.

Gavin didn't answer.

Dawn appeared, a ghostly apparition swaddled in thick, white cream from neck to hairline, her abundant black hair tied up for sleep.

'I feel a bit achey,' Gavin said.

'You deserve to, the amount of beer you've consumed tonight!'

'No. Perhaps it was the curry you made...'

Dawn only sniffed in response. Together they peeled the bed and wrapped themselves in the thick quilt. There was no further communication.

Gavin woke up, suddenly. What had roused him? He could remember nothing. A dream? He felt cold, disorientated.

'Dawn?'

The girl shifted and mumbled in sleep beside him.

'Dawn?'

'What is it?' Her voice was muffled

'I feel weird.'

He heard her sigh. 'In what way, *weird?*'

'I don't know...'

'Can you push the cat off my neck?' she asked in a sleepy voice.

'There's no cat on your neck. She's on my feet.'

'Gavin!'

'She's on my feet, I said. And I feel weird!'

'Want a cigarette?' Dawn reached out and turned on the bedside lamp, filling the room with a comforting glow. The cat slept peacefully at the bottom of the bed. Gavin lay on his back, staring at the ceiling.

Dawn handed him a lit cigarette. 'Are you OK now? Is it your stomach?'

'Maybe. Yeah.' Gavin took a draw off the cigarette. 'I just felt so strange.'

'How?'

'Hard to explain really. I just opened my eyes and felt kind of confused, as if something had happened that I couldn't remember... or was *about to happen*.

Dawn stared at him for a moment. 'Did you have your hand on my neck?'

'When? Before we woke up?'

'Yes. Did you?'

Gavin laughed.

'You did, didn't you!' Dawn accused.

'No, no, I didn't.'

'Looks like we've both been dreaming, then.'

They finished their cigarettes and Dawn turned off the light. Gavin curled into her arms. 'Must have been your curry,' he said.

Landscapes shifted behind his eyes; the province of the released dark self, journeying through the brief freedom of night. Comfortable, daytime symbols became alarming extravaganzas, artfully twisted by the true mind that did not care to lie.

Gavin gasped into the darkness; thick, almost unbreathable darkness. He'd been asleep, yes. Awake again now. Had he woken up before? (A dream.) Why did he feel so strange, so unsafe? An echo from sleep, a cry from the past, fleeting, fading, forgotten; perhaps part of the first dream.

Feeling absurdly shaken, he grabbed Dawn's shoulder. She seemed frighteningly far away on the other side of the bed. Woken so abruptly, she jumped in surprise and made a small, startled sound.

'What were we talking about?' Gavin asked her.

'What? Gavin, what's the matter? Let go, you're hurting me!'

He shook her. 'What were we talking about before? When I woke up and there was a cat on your neck, only there wasn't?'

She pulled away from him. 'I don't know what you're talking about! You must have been dreaming. Go back to sleep.'

'Did I wake up before?'

'No, be quiet. You're scaring me.' She drew the quilt further round her neck, turning her back on him. 'Want the light on?' he heard her say.

'No, no. It's all right.' He closed his eyes, making an effort to regulate his breathing. *What a strange dream,* he thought. *So real.* And yet so banal, hardly terrifying. Perhaps it was the reality of it that frightened him. *Perhaps I'm going to be ill.* Gavin turned over and relaxed.

He woke up, screaming. As he reared up in the bed, flailing coverings, Dawn rose up eerily beside him, echoing his cry. They sat for a moment, breathing hard.

'Why the hell did you scream like that?' Gavin said at last.

'You could have killed me with shock!'

'What? You just yelled out. It woke me! Christ, Gavin!'

'I yelled out? No, it was you. You woke me.'

'No, I didn't.'

Gavin rubbed his cold arms with clammy hands. 'I've had a nightmare. I feel ill.'

'Lie down.' Dawn was conscious of the impenetrable night around them. In daylight, Gavin's scream would just have seemed part of his ordinary clownishness. But beyond their walls, the world slept; she felt alone. The wild look in Gavin's eyes frightened her. Was he ill? She stroked his face. 'Tell me about the dream.'

He screwed up his eyes. 'I dreamed I woke, that's all. Twice. And each time...' He turned and looked at her in the vague light that came through the curtains, his face pale upon the pillow. 'It was so real, Dawn. So weird.'

'But not really that scary,' she concluded lightly, clearly trying to hide her own night-fear. 'I've often had dreams like that, lucid dreams. Usually when I have an interview or a dental appointment in the morning. Don't you have them? You know, waking up, getting dressed, going out, being late, getting lost, and then waking up in bed?'

'Yes, I know what you mean, but it wasn't like that.'

'How was it, then?'

'It was the waking...' He shook his head. 'I can't explain.'

Dawn smiled at him encouragingly, a smile reserved for small children or imbeciles. 'Come on, let's sleep. It was just a dream.'

'Perhaps this is, too.'

'Gavin, it isn't. Just go to sleep, OK?'

'OK.'

He lay thinking about what had happened. He could remember waking up the first time so clearly. It couldn't have been a dream, and yet Dawn said he'd been asleep all the time.

Was she lying? Why should she? It wasn't in her nature to play tricks like that. The conversation before going to bed had done it, obviously. His worst fear; reality slipping. Becoming unsure of comfortable things. Becoming unsure of your own mind, your own senses.

No, don't think about it. Just sleep. Think of nice things. Sing a song in your head. How does it go? No, not like that. That's not quite right; that's weird.

He heard the echo of his own song, newly conceived that weekend, sweeping faintly round his brain. Off key.

Sing something else. A safe song. A top-ten throwaway. That gave him the image of black discs sailing through the air, cutting through it, gleaming at the edges like knives.

No, not that. Try breathing. Deep breaths. Concentrate on warmth and light. Try to relax. You're winding yourself up, Gavin. Am I asleep, now? Am I really here?

The thought was small, but startlingly clear. Space receded swiftly. He curled into a ball and pulled the quilt over his head.

His eyes opened to darkness, a stretched kind of darkness. *I've woken up again.* He thought it slowly, in single words, breathing in cool air, feeling it circulate inside him. *Did I wake up before? Of course I did. I can remember it.* But there was an insidious apprehension creeping over him that he hadn't. *I'm becoming afraid of the fear*, he thought. *I'm becoming obsessed.*

'You spoke your fear,' an inner voice admonished waspishly. 'You spoke it and made it happen.'

No, this time's real. I can feel it.

He gripped his own flesh, pinching hard. The pain was reassuring, made the blackness less black.

I'll wake Dawn. I'll ask her. He felt in control, knowing he could do that. But, said a sly voice inside him, will she tell the truth?

'Dawn!'

She groaned. He could hear her mouth chewing as she surfaced to wakefulness. 'Mmm?'

'Have I been awake before, tonight?'

'What time is it?' Her voice was croaky.

'Just answer me. Have we woken up before? Did we talk?'

He heard her scratch her head. 'I can't remember doing so,' she said.

'Are you just trying to freak me out? Is that it?'

'Gavin, it's the middle of the bloody night? What's this interrogation? We came up to bed. We fell asleep, and now you're yelling at me. A load of tripe, as usual!'

'I won't have this!' Gavin said, in a low, determined voice.

Dawn grumbled as he scrambled over her, groping for the light switch. She shielded her eyes as he stood rigid in the middle of the room. Then, he began pacing.

She sat up slowly. 'Are you all right?' she asked, clearly unsure. Her mouth dropped open as he held out his arm and pinched the flesh fiercely.

'Am I awake now, Dawn?'

'Of course you are. Stop being stupid! Get back into bed. This light's too bright.'

'No, I'm not getting back into bed. I'm going to prove that I'm awake.'

Dawn groaned and pulled the quilt over her head. He heard her say, 'You're mad, and I'm tired.'

Am I mad?

He found himself scrabbling in the drawer where he kept his pens and notepaper. *I'll write myself something,* he thought. *I'll write myself a note and, in the morning, if it's still there, I'll know I was awake.*

He took up a pen and the reluctance to begin writing was like an external force.

I must begin, he thought. *It started downstairs, after the film. The conversation with Tim and Shona. I don't remember coming upstairs. Did I come upstairs? Oh God!*

He looked around the room quickly, which was silent and watching, the light of the lamp as unilluminating as if it was held in a fist.

The light's not really here. I'm in darkness. No, I can see.
I can see. Write the note. Are we still downstairs? Are they
looking at me? What am I doing? Am I imagining this? Go
back to the first dream. No, it's one dream. Get out of the
room!

The command seemed to come from outside of himself.

Yes, go downstairs. Check. Then everything will be all
right. But what if I'm still down there?

He shuddered.

Pull yourself together, he ordered himself. *Make a noise.*
Write. Wake up from the first dream. Become real. No. Yes.
Write.

'Whenever I go one stage back in the dream,' he wrote,
'I'm never sure if the other stages (in my mind, that is), have
even happened, or if they were all a dream of the first dream.
I fear that if I go downstairs, I might find that I've been down
there all the time, and just woken up in the armchair. Not
been up to bed yet.'

He threw down the pen. It was gibberish, but there in
black and white. Indisputable. (*Unless you're dreaming this.*)
He hated that voice. The voice didn't want him to write, have
proof. He picked up the pen and wrote, 'Some force
(predestined future) is trying to stop me from writing this
down.'

There. That caught it. He'd made it actual.

Then go downstairs.

No. I don't feel real.

Dawn, is she here? Is that really Dawn?

Where's the morning?

He went and looked out of the window, at the street
beyond, grey with the faintest of dawn light. It didn't make
him feel safer. He knew he would have to go back to sleep to
wake up from this. There would be no hope of return
otherwise. *Perhaps this is the true reality,* he thought, *this*
half-world.

He stared at the scrawled note he'd written for a
moment, and then carefully climbed over Dawn and got into

bed. She hadn't gone back to sleep. She said, 'You really are scared, aren't you?'

'Something's not right. Can you feel it?'

She considered, one hand over her eyes. 'Yes, I think so. Maybe I'm picking it up from you.'

'How does it feel?'

She looked at him. 'Like a sense of confusion.'

Gavin nodded, and they both looked around the room. Their cat was still asleep, oblivious, but even its innocent stillness seemed pregnant with sinister import. The furniture seemed squeezed tight, as if vibrating at a higher rate, as if a sound too high for them to hear was filling the house.

'Gavin, you're crazy,' Dawn declared, 'and your crazy ideas have got to me! We'd better do something normal, otherwise we'll both be gibbering idiots by morning.'

'Can you remember coming to bed?' Gavin asked her.

'Yes,' she said, although he noticed it was without any real conviction, and that her habitual poise and confidence were not quite as genuine as they ought to be.

'Do you think we ought to go downstairs?' he suggested.

'For a drink?'

'Yes. For a coffee. I can't sleep anyway.' He couldn't tell her the real reason; that he wanted to open the lounge door and check that they weren't still in there.

They put on their bathrobes and walked together, very closely, out of the door, along the silent landing, lit by streetlights from outside, down the stairs, throat-like in the dimness. They were both nervous, but aware that speaking of it would transform that nervousness to fear. By the living room door, Gavin took Dawn's hand in his own. They paused, looking at one another. He wasn't sure if she was thinking the same thing he was.

The door opened. It was dark inside. The TV was off, and there was a lingering smell of beer and tobacco smoke, but it was clearly empty of people, real or imagined. Gavin had been holding his breath. Now he gasped. *I've been frightening myself,* he thought. *Thank God. That's all it was.*

In the kitchen, the strip light seemed faint. 'Needs a new tube,' Dawn said, sitting on a high stool.

Gavin filled the kettle and turned it on. 'God, that was so weird up there,' he said, shaking his head.

'What *were* you so scared about?'

'You won't believe it! I had these crazy dreams about waking up, and I wasn't sure what was real and what wasn't... I think I was even doubting my own existence. I wrote myself a note. Can you believe it?'

Dawn laughed. 'A note?'

'Yeah, to prove I was there! I thought I was stuck in this other reality, and that I was really sitting downstairs with you and the others, and that I hadn't gone to bed at all!' He laughed again. The kettle was making comfortable, gurgling sounds. He could smell the aroma of the coffee as he twisted open the jar. 'Jesus, it could make you too scared to sleep again!'

Dawn shivered. 'Don't say that, Gavin!'

'It's almost morning.' He poured hot water into their cups. 'What the hell did you put in that curry?'

'Nothing peculiar, honest. Must be your digestion.'

'Or Tim's cheap beer!'

'Don't be ungrateful! It was free.'

Gavin smiled. 'Yeah, I know. Come here.' He put his arms around her, breathing in her familiar smell of night-cream and a lingering whiff of coconut oil...

And woke up to her white, white face next to his on the pillow, her mouth stretched wide in a cavernous, black grimace. Her voice was a harridan's coarse squawk. She no longer smelt clean.

'Get that cat off my neck!' she roared. 'Get that cat off my neck!'

Gavin could hear his own voice, screaming, screaming, and the air was full of swirling slivers of paper, proclaiming his own reality.

Did You Ever See Oysters Walking Down the Stairs...?

What a hell of a day that was. Rain like you've never seen before, pink lightning... Yes, pink lightning. Tara said it was an omen for strangeness and, looking back, I know she was right. Simon and Dominic moved in that day. They were taking the top floor and Tara and I were all eyes watching their delectable male behinds struggling up the stairs with a less than delectable sofa. Becky was off work sick (she had the other, smaller, middle floor with her boyfriend Al), so she joined us, sniffling, on the stairs to watch the scenery. 'Funny coloured light out there, isn't it,' she said to the boys. They made one or two smart remarks which we all laughed at. I don't remember what they were.

Tara suggested the six of us have dinner together that night, a sort of getting to know each other party. Of course she was overjoyed at the prospect of having two unattached, attractive males around. As our flat was the largest in the building, we would play host. All afternoon, I was shifting junk into the studio from the living room, where a lot of our tools and sketches and even half-finished pots had strayed to. Tara was looking forward to telling Simon and Dominic about how we were successful businesswomen. Successful? Well, we kept our heads above water, that's about it, but we had a good life.

Both of us adore freedom and working for a big pottery would have stifled that forever.

I shook out the coloured shawls that covered the sofas and Tara dragged a duster round the place. We shoved a mixture of mince and vegetables and spices into a pot, called it bolognaise, and hey presto, we were nearly ready.

Eight o'clock and everybody was banging on our door. Thank God they'd had the presence of mind to bring wine; we'd forgotten completely. Becky, by daylight a decent sort, had turned into the clinging, whining limpet she usually was when Al was home. Tara and I made faces, recognising the signs straight away.

'Al, why didn't you get Riesling? You know I hate this one!'

Al this, Al that. All we could do was roll our eyes and watch her smother him. He was a nice guy though, thin like a hunter, dark and lissom, so we used to put up with night-time Becky because of that. He was a systems analyst, which I thought sounded like some kind of cyber-punk psychotherapist. Computers are not my line really, so it was a relief Al was not the kind of guy to rabbit on about the things outside of work.

Tara and I swapped glances across the room when Simon and Dominic arrived. I reckoned we'd both made the assessment of ten out of ten, although I didn't go for Simon's slogan T-shirt too much. Dominic, altogether lither and darker, impressed me more with his designer-rips, although Tara remarked to me in the kitchen as we prised meat from the saucepan, she thought that was a little passé; she was more interested in peroxide Simon.

The boys hovered around looking awkward for a while, until we sat down to eat, and then praised the meal beyond all reasonable requirements; it was pretty foul after all. Tara and I eat to carry on living, not for any particular pleasure in the act. After the meal, Dominic produced a bottle of Jack Daniels, the sly beast, and we all proceeded to dilute the soggy spaghetti in our guts with good liquor.

Tara, with her usual gift for diplomacy, soon managed to scrape out the information that neither Simon nor Dominic was romantically attached at present. They were both students and, oh joy, Simon was a poet too. Perhaps that was what first made my hackles rise about him. I've had many bitter experiences of men who thought they were poets, and many subsequent embarrassing experiences of learning how much they certainly weren't any such thing, generally while they were expecting favourable critiques of their earnest outpourings. I actually cringed when Tara cooed about how much she'd like to see some of his work.

Dominic must have been psychic. He said, "Fraid I don't write,' to which I nearly responded, 'Oh good,' but caught myself in time and said, 'No, me neither.'

'Do you like poetry, Al?' Simon drawled, leaning back on the green sofa.

Luckily, it was not the one with three legs. Al looked positively cornered, poor thing. I began praying Simon wouldn't offer to nip upstairs and fetch some of his efforts down for us.

'Um,' Al replied. 'Well, I – er – read it at school.' He shrugged. 'You know.'

'Yes, well I think you'll find styles have changed since then,' Simon said.

His tone was quite sarcastic. I couldn't understand why on earth he'd want to get at Al, who was such a pussycat.

'You prefer horror books, don't you, Al,' Becky put in, quite courageously I thought, although I doubt whether the put-down was intentional.

Simon sniffed. A *horror book* had clearly never sullied his shelves. He decided to change the subject. 'This is a great house. I love it! It was so lucky we got a place here!'

'Yeah, we like it too, but I wish we had it all to ourselves,' Tara said, 'I keep hassling Mrs. Cryer to let us use the ground floor as a studio. It's full of junk down there, but she won't have it. This must have been one hell of a place when it was all one house.'

'I like old houses,' Becky said.

'Well, there are hundreds of them around here,' I said. 'This must have been quite a hoity-toity area at one time. Now, people like us live here.'

'Who lives in that green place down the road?' Simon asked. 'Looks pretty run down. More students, by any chance?'

'Don't think anybody lives there,' Tara told him. 'Last we heard, it was going to be knocked down and they were going to build pretend houses there. You know, the ones that are all red brick and patio and last about twenty years before the cardboard goes soggy between the rooms. The ones that sell for risible amounts to young executives.'

'What a waste! It's enormous. And the silly bits on it – it looks like a Victorian wedding cake!'

Tara sighed. 'Ah, that's progress you see. Destroy the country's heritage and smother it with disposable eyesores.'

'Is it haunted, do you think?' Al asked, rolling his eyes and making ghoulish faces.

Tara laughed. 'Honey, any house that big and old is haunted! At least, I bet anyone going in there will be scared shitless whether it is or not. It must have seen so much, so many lives...'

I recognised the warning signals that Tara was about to become philosophical; a state of mind unsatisfied unless it provoked arguments. One glance at the nearly empty Jack Daniels bottle confirmed my fears.

'Why don't we go and see?' I said, brightly. They all looked at me; sprawling around, stuffed, lazy and warm. Nobody wanted to move. It would be cold outside. 'Oh, come on!' I cajoled. 'We could do with some exercise. I can hardly move.'

'Neither can I, nor do I want to,' Tara said.

Becky pressed closer to her beloved Al, pouting prettily for the benefit of the attendant males and mimicking the shivers.

'I'd like to,' Simon said.

At that point, I had to concede he was certainly the better looking of the two and I saw Tara and Becky stir themselves towards him like sun-glutted lizards. Suddenly house exploration seemed like a good idea.

It was cold outside and damp too; streets all wet and shining. Tara took hold of Simon's arm, marching into the lead. Dominic and I looked at each other assessively for a moment before deciding we'd forego the bodily contact. He hunched into his leather jacket, I hunched into mine and we walked behind the others, some distance apart. 'I can't believe we're doing this,' he said. 'It's like something out of a cheapskate horror movie.'

'No, it's not,' I replied, rather stiffly. 'Everyone goes in that place, I'm sure. It's fuck-city. Nobody has ever disappeared or even been scared in there, to my knowledge.'

'Have you been there before, then?' A double-edged question, I felt.

'No.' I fixed him with a gorgon stare. 'Always meant to. I was curious but never got round to it.'

He stared back speculatively, wondering whether all that was a double entendre or not.

While this sparkling repartee was going on, we'd arrived in front of the empty house. Becky started going on about how she wished she was rich and could afford to buy such a place etc. The front gates, gowned in dead convolvulus and rust, were padlocked, so we all had to scramble over the wall. Tara and I went first and headed off up the drive. We knew what eruptions could be expected from Becky playing helpless female and didn't have to say a word to each other about wanting to avoid it; we just vacated the area swiftly.

Lamp House, it was called. Lamp House. Why? It had a rakish look to it; knew it was past it, didn't give a shit. This is me, it said, uncompromising. Half of the external woodwork had gone. It would have cost several fortunes to restore the place.

Simon and Dominic came scampering up behind us; further back Becky was complaining to Al about some ravagement to her tights.

'We could be in the middle of nowhere,' Simon said, clearly impressed.

A fat, waxing moon illuminated the scene but we had still been organised enough to bring torches. The grounds to Lamp House were flat and, if once lawns and borders and all that business, now only weak scrub. Trees formed a thick border round the edge but grew nowhere else. Clearly, the garden had never been landscaped properly. Soon it would all be cheerful estate populated by middle executives and their cosmetic families. I experienced a deep, resonating pang of sad frustration, sharing Becky's desire to be rich, to be the saviour of this grand old folly. Behind us, I could still hear her going on about what she'd do with it, if she had the money.

The blistered front door was impenetrable and the lower windows all boarded up against the soulless attentions of the local youth. Naturally, such obstacles had been overcome some time ago by determined explorers and we found a back door that was open a few inches. It was a gap just wide enough to squeeze through; the door wouldn't move a fraction either way. Simon went in first and switched on his torch, the rest of us piling in behind rather tentatively.

It had crossed my mind that Lamp House might be regularly occupied at night by characters I wouldn't want to stumble over, and I don't mean supernatural ones. We were in the first of a series of rooms that had probably been domestic-staff territory in Lamp House's days of glory. The presence of illicit occupants, either present or past, was evidenced by the fact that all the woodwork had been ripped away, even the floorboards here and there. We guessed it had all been used as fuel by tramps, junkies, or lovers seeking warmth.

In single file, we ventured further into the house. Wounds upon the passage walls, revealing gouged plaster, showed where the panelling had been torn away. We had to be careful where we walked because of the vandalised floors. It made me think about how it wouldn't be easy to make a fast getaway from Lamp House. I wasn't scared though; it was all rather depressing. I'm sure no ghosts could have stomached such a raped and ransacked environment. The place was dead.

We gathered in the front hall and shone our torches around. Cleaner patches on the yellow walls showed where furniture and paintings had once lived. The tiled floor was mostly intact, surprisingly, but the banisters had gone, the stairs leading up into a predictable, sepulchral gloom.

Tara came and took hold of my arm. 'God, it makes me want to cry,' she said. 'Just imagine if the guy who'd built this place could see it now!'

'Bloody kids and vagrants!' Becky exclaimed.

'No, antique dealers, dear,' Tara said dryly, and went to stand at the foot of the stairs, looking up. 'The panelling and banisters alone must have been worth a bit.'

We took a look around the ground floor rooms. It wasn't mentioned aloud, but no one felt like going upstairs. What had promised to be an adventure back at the flat now felt as if we were examining a vandalised family mausoleum. All that was missing were the blackened bones kicked carelessly around the floor so that whoever had come for profit could get at the mahogany coffins. I wanted to go home. This wasn't fun at all. We were a sensitive lot; we all cared about poor old Lamp House.

'Now I wonder why no one took this,' Simon said. We were in a room at the front of the house with French windows at the far end. There was a huge, black, empty hole in the wall where a posh fireplace had once stood. It must have been beautiful at one time, perhaps a dining room, for there was a fairly large table standing in the middle of it on what remained of a carpet. Even to me, and I know nothing about furniture, it seemed an interesting piece; carved legs, sturdily built. Hopelessly mauled, of course, and covered with the detritus of previous visitors; yellowed newspapers, remains of crisp packets and beer cans, various lumps of unrecognisable material and an undeniable dried dollop of faeces that looked uncomfortably human. Al wandered over to take a look, shining his torch up and down the room, while Tara, Dominic and I hovered near the doorway. Becky was still poking about in the hall.

'Think this is worth something?' Simon asked Al.

'How should I know?' Al replied touchily.

I thought, 'Ah, he's not that impressed with boy wonder either,' and immediately felt justified about my slight antipathy towards Simon.

'Doesn't everyone recognise something worthwhile when they see it?' Simon continued, undaunted.

At that point, Becky came noisily through the door. When she saw the table, she gave a twitter of delight and danced over to it, like some disarmingly gauche heroine out of an American teenage movie. 'Al, look!' she squealed. 'It's divine. It's unique!'

'It's still here,' Tara said to me, and her look was more cynical than usual in the light of the torches.

Al, brightening up with his usual goofy, self-effacing humour (the life-saving trait which Tara and I were sure was responsible for him being able to put up with Becky), started cracking jokes about how it was a crap table. Ha, ha. From Becky's enthusiastic noises, it seemed logical to conclude the dizzy bitch wanted to take it home with her somehow. Simon, Dominic, Tara and I had unconsciously started to back towards the door.

'It's just what I want,' Becky said, 'and we can't afford to buy one. Those second-hand stores are such rip-offs! We could put it under the window, you know. Al. Al!'

'Beck, it's filthy!' Al pointed out to her. 'And how could we get it out of here anyway? The only open door's stuck and everywhere else is boarded up.'

'Don't be such a wimp!' Becky replied and shouted over to us, 'Come on, you lot, give me a hand.' Nobody moved.

'Al's right, Becky,' Tara said. 'And not only do we have a door problem, but the gate is padlocked too, remember? I don't fancy hauling this thing over the wall. Anyway, people would see us and I suppose it's a kind of stealing, isn't it?'

'From who?'

'Property developers?'

'It's been left here,' Becky insisted. 'Probably isn't worth much to a dealer or anyone, but it's just fine for me. Oh, come on, help me, please?' She can be charming when she wants to be. Sighing, Dominic and Simon went over, rubbing their hands. Tara and I went into the hall.

'She's mad,' I observed. We could already hear her calling out instructions and the rattle, rustle and crash of garbage sliding to the floor.

'They won't get it out of here,' Tara said. 'Come on. Let's leave them to it. Let's go home.'

We went back and put the coffeepot on. Tara lay down on the best sofa and described what she'd like to do with Simon if given the opportunity. I cleared the plates from the room and put milk into mugs, deliberately refraining from comment on that score. 'I wonder where they are? It's nearly half past one.'

'Probably trying to explain to a policeman why they're nicking firewood,' Tara replied. 'If they got that table over the wall at all, I doubt it's still in one piece. Must have weighed a ton. Christ, they could be at the hospital for all we know!'

'That girl is an asshole.'

Tara sat up, grinning. 'Don't be stupid. Nice young ladies like that don't have assholes.'

'Unless you count Al.'

'True, but he's more of a masochist with a self-image problem than an asshole!'

With such banter, we started to drink the coffee, adopting one of our favourite late night topics; what Al saw in Becky and why.

At two o'clock, Becky swept triumphantly into our front room and announced, 'Well, we got it.'

They certainly had.

It had taken the men an hour to haul the damn thing out

of the house, force the back door open wide, stagger down the drive and drag the table over the wall. Luckily, it was not as heavy as it looked and in the unflattering light of our downstairs hall, did not appear to be very much of an antique at all, but a recent copy of something older. The surface was stained and scratched, all the polish gone, bits of the carving were missing and it didn't smell too sweet either. Becky seemed oblivious to its shortcomings. In the morning, she planned to have another day off from her job and start work on restoring it. After examining her haul, the rest of us retired back upstairs for a quick coffee before bed. Much to Tara's displeasure, Simon and Dominic didn't stay for long and Simon made no intimation at all about wanting to get to know Tara better. The evening ended on rather a sour note.

The next morning our landlady, Mrs. Cryer, turned up. She's a decent sort; rich, old, a bit scatty, but generous. She has agents to handle the property and rent collection but likes to drop in from time to time to see how the old place is getting on and to have a chat. We gathered her family used to live here. I was in the front room, working on a new design with the door open, because Tara had just popped out for some supplies, when I heard Mrs. Cryer's unmistakeable fluty voice come wavering up the stairs. 'Tara, Jo!' She always shouts out to us when she arrives. Tara says it's a trait left over from when her people used to have servants or something.
 I called out a hello, but her voice came back more urgently, 'Tara! Jo! Please!'
 I thought she'd hurt herself and came hurtling out of the flat still clutching pencil and rubber. I leaned over the banister. 'You alright, Mrs. C?' I could see her wrinkly, powdered face looking up at me all confused.
 'Jo, hello darling! There's something horrid down here in the hall!'
 'Something horrid? Hold on a min, Mrs. C. I'll be right down.'
 The horrid something turned out to be Becky's table. I did a quick explaining job. 'She's going to clean it up today,

don't worry. I'll get them to move it upstairs.'

'But what does she want it for and where did she get it?' Mrs. Cryer was still puzzled.

'She thinks it's unusual. It came from Lamp House, the old green place down the road.'

Mrs. Cryer made a strange dismissive, half-disgusted, half-disinterested noise. 'I've better tables than this in my attic,' she said scornfully. 'Rebecca could have had one of those if she'd asked.'

'I don't think she knew she wanted one until she saw it,' I said. 'But if you've got any spare, we could do with another table.'

'Of course, dear. I've a lovely old piece with little lion feet. A bit marked, but you could put a runner on it.'

Feeling pleased with myself, and not a little smug, I invited Mrs. Cryer up for a coffee. She sat down vaguely on the rickety sofa, so I had to move her, wondering whether I ought to enquire whether her attic stock ran to sofas as well as tables.

It didn't look right, Mrs. Cryer sitting there, gripping a big, thick mug in her dainty, papery hand, but we haven't any fancier crockery. She didn't appear to notice though, still holding out her little finger and asking, with a roguish, naughty-girl glint in her eye, if I'd mind if she smoked. Shaking my head and even accepting one of her black, Russian, horribly vile but posy, cigarettes, I asked her about Lamp House.

'Family went under,' she said in a condescending tone, nodding and winking. 'They were never people to know, the Ruttickers. When I was a girl, the daughter, what was her name... oh, Celia, was always trying to get in, but we'd have none of it, of course.'

'Why was that, Mrs. C.?' I hoped that wasn't an indelicate question.

'Suspect background,' she answered darkly.

Tara came in then. There was a flutter of greetings, more table talk, and Mrs. Cryer said, 'I'm not sure if I approve of

Rutticker furniture in my property,' but from the way she said it, we knew it was a bit of a joke.

'Tell us about the scandals, then,' Tara said.

'Scandals, dear?'

'Well, there must be some.'

'We never talk about that family,' Mrs. Cryer said firmly. 'The last Rutticker left Lamp House about forty years ago.'

'It's been left to decay since then?'

'I think it was rented out for a while. It's been empty for a long time, though.'

We couldn't get much more out of her than that. She wanted to tell us about the latest antics of her neighbours, an ongoing soap opera. We felt we knew them as well as she did, although we'd never met the people. Before she left, she made us promise to get Becky to move the table from the hall as soon as possible.

Tara went straight over and knocked on Becky's door. Somehow, she was roped into helping clean the relic up and I spent the rest of the day in glorious peace, lost in the euphoria of a creative surge.

Two weeks later, Becky and Al invited the rest of us in for a meal, to be eaten off the Rutticker table and to celebrate Becky's success in restoring it. When we arrived, we found it had been pulled into the middle of the room, where it gleamed seductively beneath the light of a dozen candles. 'Wow!' I said, genuinely impressed. 'You've done a great job on it, Beck!'

'All thanks to my help,' Tara added, breezily, and swept into the kitchen to open a bottle of wine.

'She didn't do that much!' Becky said sharply, and with a touch of venom that was most unlike her. I wondered if she and Tara had quarrelled. It happened occasionally, mainly because Tara took a sadistic pleasure in flirting with Al, knowing how it wound Becky up into a frenzied ball. Becky was an irritant and, I thought, rather stupid, but she wasn't spiteful at all. Tonight, she wore a definitely mean look. Perhaps not Tara, then. Perhaps Al had done something we'd all be praying for – been unfaithful or answered her back. Miracles might happen.

So: Simon and Dom arriving and then down to the meal. Bare arms in the candlelight and soft, witty conversation drifting across the glossy surface? Hardly. For a start, Becky whinged and bickered at Al all evening and hardly spoke to Dominic and Simon, so the atmosphere wasn't exactly congenial, until everyone had drunk enough to ignore her. The meal wasn't that great either. Perhaps eaten off knees in front of Al and Beck's TV as per our usual habits, it wouldn't have tasted so boring. Perhaps we should only have eaten venison and consommé off Becky's elegant restored furniture; I don't know. Anyway, Tara, never one to mince words, pushed back her plate half-finished and said, 'Not up to the usual standard, chef.'

Normally, Becky would come back with the nearest she could manage to a smart remark. This time, she merely glowered at her plate. Her face went bright red, but she said nothing. Tara didn't notice. She was up to her usual trick of trying to allure Simon.

It seem Al had changed his mind about Simon. Now, he was almost as bad as Tara, sucking up to the insufferable jerk as if he was Apollo incarnate. Heaven forbid, he'd even been reading some of Simon's work, which certainly put one over on Tara, who hadn't been offered the privilege. 'And is he a genius, Al?' she asked.

Al shrugged. 'I'm not an expert.' He smiled into his wine. 'But I can honestly say it doesn't make me cringe.'

'What more splendid praise could an artist hope for?' Simon cried, throwing arms all over the place.

Tara giggled, batting her eyelashes like the rollers on a car wash.

'Simon is going to be famous one day,' Dominic told me in mock serious tone.

'Don't be such a Philistine, Dom,' Simon said smoothly. He looked at me, which didn't happen very often. 'This boy reads nothing but comics. Sometimes I worry about him, although I have it on good authority it's merely part of his image.'

'You talk to me about image?' Dom cried, but I could tell there was never any real bad blood between these two.

Becky made an odd, grumbling noise and stood up to gather the plates, which were still half full of food. Seeing as nobody else was going to offer, I helped her carry the remains out to the kitchen and junked it into the bin. Even Becky's cat didn't stir itself to come and investigate. Becky looked tired so I asked her if she was OK, a perfunctory query. Personally, I'd found her moodiness rather tedious. 'I'm not a cook,' she said.

'Oh hell, Beck!' I exclaimed. 'Don't take it to heart! Since when have you or Al been able to finish one of our efforts anyway?'

'But I wanted it to be a good evening. It all looked so nice, didn't it?'

An alcoholic, emotional surge took me over. It happens. *Poor, forlorn little thing*, I thought. What could be bugging her? She was normally such a frothy girl. 'It *has* been good, you idiot!' I said and, overwhelmed by this brief wave of sympathy, not to mention several glasses of wine, I went and put my arm around her.

She started to cry. 'Why, when I try so hard do things go wrong?' she asked.

I was stumped for an answer. I had no idea Becky thought that way, or that deeply, come to think of it. 'Oh, come on, who's complaining?' I said, shaking her a bit. 'We've had a laugh, a performance from dear Simon, and plenty of good wine. Cheer up, love, it's not that important.'

'No, I don't suppose it is,' she answered and wriggled away from me, slamming plates into the sink.

And that was the beginning of Rebecca Jane Olson's decline. Her personality changed so dramatically that, to begin with, we wondered whether she was putting it on. She became unapproachable, no longer dropping into our flat all the time for a gossip, and once even avoided me in the street. Tara caught her hanging about on the landing one night and she almost jumped a mile when Tara asked what she was doing. There was some excuse about hearing noises on the stairs, but Tara was unconvinced. Al, on the other hand, seemed unaware of Becky's afflictions. We had to admit we'd rarely seen him so cheerful.

After several sessions of deep discussion of the matter, and because Tara and I are artistic, imaginative people, it didn't take long for us to confess a mutual suspicion. Could Becky's marked change in behaviour be something to do with the imposing, shiny mass of the Rutticker table? It became quite an obsession with us really, as Becky's sunny personality sank progressively deeper into an irritable moodiness. Some nights we could hear her whining at Al, and his exasperated responses. We concluded that the main problem was an increasing decline in self-confidence on her part; introspections that the dizzy Becky of old wouldn't have had time for.

After only a week, Tara told me she thought we should tell Al what we suspected and that he should get rid of the table. 'It must be that,' she said.

I couldn't imagine being greeted with a favourable response coming out with such an idea, however, so Tara suggested that we mention it to Simon and Dom first to see what they thought.

'Not Dominic!' I said quickly, because I cared enough about my friendship with him not to want to look stupid in his eyes. Maybe he hadn't come anywhere near declaring his raging lust for me, and OK, we'd never even touched each other, but I was growing to like him and despite his penchant for fantasy comics, he didn't strike me as an impressionable sort. On the other hand, I felt sure the poetically inclined Simon would love our theory, even if it did sound like something out of one of Al's tacky horror books.

Tara bounded up the stairs straight away (any excuse) dragging a rather bewildered Simon back down with her to hear our suspicions.

'What's all this cloak and dagger stuff?' he asked. 'What can't you tell Dominic?'

'Just listen!' Tara told him, pushing him into a chair.

He brushed that glorious, gold hair off his face with a gesture that seemed almost nervous. Tara began to explain in great detail what Mrs. Cryer had said but he interrupted her story-telling with, 'So who's haunting the table then? This Celia person?'

To be fair, he didn't sound utterly sceptical or even that amused, but there was a light in his eyes that showed a certain amount of reserve. He was sounding us out.

'Seems likely, doesn't it?' Tara replied, who'd concocted romantic theories about the socially spurned Celia Rutticker cutting her wrists over the table or something.

'Perhaps you'd better find out a little more about these people first,' Simon said. 'For all you know they might have gutted a local child on that table.' He snickered at his own joke.

Tara pulled a face. 'OK, don't take it seriously, but you have to agree Becky has changed dramatically for the worse and it started happening since she got that table.'

'Do things like that happen in real life, though?' Simon asked.

Something about his posture was irritating me like mad; a certain smugness, his awful tolerance. It reminded me of a teacher I used to have. I wondered again why Tara found him so attractive. OK, he was positively beautiful, but also undeniably furtive and calculating. I took a swig of wine. Perhaps I too was being affected by the vibes in the house.

That night I dreamed of Becky, duster in hand, leaning over her beloved table and polishing and polishing. Her movements were sinuous, her face creased into a frown of despair. I woke up thinking, *That table has got to go*, terrified things could get worse.

I intended to start investigating seriously. The situation had gone beyond the analytical discussion point. We had a huge order on that week, so really neither Tara nor I had the time to drop work, but I couldn't let the matter rest. I scraped a breakfast together and went to telephone Mrs. Cryer. She sounded overjoyed to hear from me and began to relate a tale concerning her neighbour's teenage son. Carefully, I wheedled my way in to her monologue and asked if she'd mind popping round that day. There was a silence. Never, in the two years or so that we'd lived there, had we ever asked our landlady round before. She smelled trouble and began to fire questions at me. No, we hadn't had a fire. No, the windows were fine. I managed to calm her. 'Look, Becky's not too well and I really need to talk to you,' I said. She said she'd pop in around lunchtime.

I went across the hall and knocked on Becky's door but there was no answer. She must have gone to work, although she'd had a lot of time off recently. I'd tried talking to her several times, but she hadn't wanted to know. Each time I'd asked her how she was, she'd flown off hysterically at a tangent, as if desperate to avoid talking about herself. I'd said to Al, 'Becky's not looking too grand, is she?' and he'd shrugged.

'She's going through a phase,' he'd said. 'Tough time at work, you know? Personality clashes or something. She'll work it out. She always does.'

I'd sensed a brush-off and had backed off, bowing. Why couldn't they confide in us? Wasn't that what friends were for? I'd been a bit put out, and Tara had said they obviously thought I was just being nosy.

'They know I'm not like that,' I'd said, all wounded dignity.

'Oh, come on, everybody's like that to a degree,' Tara had replied.

Mrs. Cryer arrived just as Tara and I were taking a break, which was good timing. We offered the usual coffee and settling down talk and I said, 'Mrs. C., would you tell us about the Ruttickers, please? It's very important.'

She gave a little laugh. 'You look so earnest, Joanna. Have they come back from the dead to sit around their table or something?' Whether that was intuition or coincidence, we'll never know.

'Mrs. C., we think there's something... not quite right about that table. Becky's not been the same since she got it.'

'So we were wondering whether there's anything we ought to know about the previous owners,' Tara put in, 'to help us work out what might be bugging her.'

Mrs. Cryer gave a little shrug. 'I think it'll disappoint you, but there's not that much to tell, really. The Ruttickers were an ill-bred bunch, rather coarse, though they pretended to airs and graces. I think the parents were disappointed that they were never accepted around here. They must have moved in, hoping to become acquainted with their influential neighbours. That was how they were, you see; social climbers.' She sneered delicately. 'They moved out when the father bought a country estate further north. Happy as pigs in muck then, of course! I really can't see them leaving any... *psychic* mark on their furniture. They weren't those type of people; totally insensitive. Anyway, the table might have belonged to someone who rented the property off them after they left.'

'Does the family still own it?' Tara asked.

Mrs. Cryer took a sip of coffee. 'As far as I know. They've let the place run down, which is sinful and probably deliberate. Ruttickers have cold business heads on their shoulders. They'd know that land would be worth a fortune for development one day and must just have been waiting until they needed the money for something else to sell it. That would be just like them!'

Tara leaned back against the sofa, sighing. 'Well, it wouldn't seem as if the spirit of a despairing Celia Rutticker is haunting the table, would it?'

Mrs. Cryer spluttered. 'I should think not! She married very well in the north and as far as I know, now has grandchildren training to be nuclear physicists and God knows what else, and a successful dress-shop chain of her own. She's not even dead!'

'No, but her youth is,' Tara said, which made me shiver.

'Do you know who lived in Lamp House after the Ruttickers, Mrs. C.?' I asked quickly, thinking Tara's remark might have offended her. She was no virgin girl herself, after all.

'Can't remember, I'm afraid,' she answered. 'Nobody memorable.' She frowned. 'I have a feeling the son stayed on for a while.' She shook her head. 'No, he was a bad sort. Ended up in jail, which caused an awful stink for a while. I'll wager the old man turned purple over that!' She laughed with delight at the image.

'Aha!' Tara said, raising a finger. 'So there *was* scandal!'

I clapped my hands with pleasure. 'Mrs. C., *do* tell!'

She shook her head, smiling in a strange manner. 'No, what happened wasn't anything to cause a haunting, and it's over now. An ugly business at the time, but people look at things differently now.' She came back into the present. 'Now, if you want to know about who lived there after the Ruttickers, you might try Capt. Lonsdale who lives at no. 6, supposing you can get any sense out of him. I believe he's rather... past it, now.'

Tara and I exchange a glance. Capt. Lonsdale was a local character, completely batty, who sometimes walked the streets with his flies undone. He lived on the ground floor of his old house and rented the rest of it to students. He was a typical old-timer, who liked to talk to everyone he met and tell them about the war and things. He was also a filthy old goat who stared at your tits and your arse and occasionally was brave enough to invite you in for tea. Nobody ever accepted.

After Mrs. Cryer had gone – we'd had to assure her it would be no help if she had a word with Becky herself– Tara paced the room, tapping her lips with a pencil and frowning.

'Are we going to beard the ancient perv in his den, then?' I asked.

'I still think it's something to do with the Ruttickers,' Tara replied.

'Really? Why? You heard what Mrs. C. said.'

'She's biased, Jo. Remember the social gulf. I still think poor old Celia with her less than blue blood sat at that table sometimes, wondering what the hell she'd done wrong and why nobody wanted to know her. It makes sense. That's what Becky's like now. She feels totally inadequate. People don't have to be dead to leave feelings around, especially if they were strong feelings. Maybe Celia's parents tried to make her think it was her own fault she had no friends around here. Perhaps she ended up blaming herself.'

'Well, it didn't appear to leave an indelible scar!' I said. 'She's a successful woman now.'

'We don't know her,' Tara insisted. 'How can we tell what she's like? I don't trust Mrs. Cryer's judgement for a start. No, Celia's the answer, I can feel it.'

'What about that business with the brother? Shouldn't we investigate that? I wonder what it was.'

Tara wrinkled her nose, unwilling to let anything sway us away from her convictions. 'Oh, it was probably some financial shenanigans. That's generally the sort of thing that offends people like Mrs. C. She did say it was nothing that could have caused a haunting, didn't she?'

It seemed plausible. 'So what do we do?'

'Tell Becky, of course. Make her see what's happening. She'll have to fight it.'

I had to laugh. 'Tell Becky? Are you serious? She'll think we're mad! She hasn't an imaginative bone in her body!'

'So what do you suggest, smart arse?'

I shrugged. 'Perhaps you're right.'

'Shall we tell the boys?'

'Do we have to?'

'Faint heart!' Tara sneered. 'I like people thinking I'm weird!'

That evening, before Simon and Dominic came down to see us, there was a commotion across the hall. Tara and I leapt to our feet and struggled through the door at the same time. Outside, Becky was crouched against the banisters, screaming, really screaming. Her nose was bleeding.

'Becky! What the fuck's happened? Becky!' Tara's voice was high with panic.

Simon and Dominic came belting down the stairs.

Becky wriggled round and yelled at them, 'Hate it! Hate it!' She tried to get away from Tara, stumbling, hitting out, making for the stairs. She had no shoes on, no coat, her hair was wet with blood and tears. When the boys tried to help us calm her, restrain her, she went wild.

'Where's Al?' I cried, to no one in particular, running into Becky's flat. It was empty. He wasn't home.

Tara managed to drag Becky into our flat and the boys lingered on the landing. Their presence clearly made Becky worse. I thought she'd flipped completely.

'We have to find Al,' I said. 'This is going too far.'

'She's nuts!' Simon said.

'Yeah?' His smug voice made me so angry I couldn't think of anything to say.

'So call a doctor, Joanna. Get involved if you want to.' Simon went back upstairs.

'Perhaps I should,' I said. 'But we still have to find Al.'

Dominic was hovering. I was bored with the pair of them and turned to go. 'He's upstairs,' Dominic said, just as I was about to shut the door on him. 'Al's upstairs.'

I wondered what profound meaning he was trying to inject into those words, hopping around on my threshold. 'Do you know something, Dom?' I asked, not meaning to sound quite so sarcastic.

Dominic closed up like a fist. He shrugged. 'I think Al's had enough of that relationship, that's all. He's had enough.'

Had enough? I was dumbstruck. His girlfriend was having a complete breakdown on the stairs and poor old Al's had enough! So much for responsibility. I went to tell Tara. She would probably be up to going up and bawling the spineless cretin out. I couldn't face it.

Tara had forced a glass of vodka down Becky. Neither of us was sure whether that was a good idea, but we were desperate to calm her somehow. I was afraid that Al had beaten her up or something, but she burbled out something about falling over. Neither Tara nor I could really see Al being violent, anyway. We left Becky lying limply on our sofa, weeping softly to herself and went into the kitchen for a conflab.

'That's it,' Tara said vehemently, 'we have to do something. I'd rather take that wretched table outside myself, chop it up and risk not having Becky speak to me again than let this crazy stuff continue.'

I told her about Al.

'He's a pussycat, Jo,' Tara said. 'We know that. He can't handle this, so we must. Let's try and talk some sense into Becky and then we'll get Simon and Dom to help us lug that table downstairs.'

Becky was sitting up on the sofa when we went back in to her; hunched up, hair hanging in strings, looking thin and pathetic. She wasn't crying anymore and had tried to rub the blood from her face. Tara sat down next to her with a circling arm. 'OK honey, tell us about it,' she said in a professionally kind voice.

Becky looked at her with mistrust.

'Look, we've an idea what's going on,' I said.

Shock wiped the misery from Becky's face for an instant. 'Do you?' she said, truly surprised. I was relieved to see how well she'd pulled herself together. Or appeared to have done.

'Yes,' I said.

'It's the table,' Tara said.

'The table?' Becky's voice was bewildered. She obviously didn't know what we were talking about.

'Yes, we've done a little research,' Tara said, and told her what we knew.

Becky listened with a thoughtful expression on her face, not looking at us, not interrupting at all.

'So you see,' Tara concluded, 'we reckon some nasty vibe is hanging around that table and it's kind of infecting you.'

'Causing delusions...' Becky whispered and then more

urgently. 'Could that happen? Delusions? Even hallucinations and things?'

'Well, yes,' Tara said, backing off an inch, clearly surprised by Becky's seemingly ready acceptance of our theory. 'I suppose it could. What you've been experiencing recently haven't been your feelings but Celia Rutticker's... probably.'

Becky sighed deeply. 'Oh, of course, of course,' she said, and the relief in her voice was heart-wrenching. 'I didn't think for one moment that it might be me!' She looked at us desperately. 'And now I know, the... feelings will stop?'

Tara glanced at me. 'I should think so,' she said. 'But anyway, we're here across the hall. We'll help you.'

Becky set her face in a determined expression. 'I think I should get rid of the table,' she said. 'It might seem like cowardice, but I don't care. It's going, whether we need one or not.'

'Hey, you can have the one Mrs. C. gave us,' I said, not daring to look at Tara in case she disagreed. 'We didn't really need another one. Everything's fine.'

Becky sighed again. 'I did such a lot of work on it,' she said. 'And this is how it repays me. With tricks, with lies. I hate it. I want to burn it.'

'Then let's do it. Probably do you good.'

Becky nodded. 'I have to apologise to Al,' she said.

Tara went upstairs to fetch the men. It all seemed like a happy ending. I thought I'd go over to Becky's and clean up. She was perfectly OK now. She'd been given answers. In the flat, I dumped papers, Becky's sewing and a few mugs off the table and left them on the floor. The table gleamed beautifully; its surface almost like a mirror. What a shame, I thought. All that work. What a shame. Becky must have gone a little wild before she burst out onto the landing. The place was pretty well messed up, things thrown around, so I started tidying. On the fleece rug by the hearth I found Al's little strongbox, the one he kept his birth certificate, kiddy photos and exam results in. Becky must have broken it open. The rug was strewn with the black flakes of burned photographs.

Almost like a religious ritual, the table was ceremoniously carried downstairs and into the back yard. Muffled in scarves and gloves, we beat the thing to bits and then set fire to its hacked-up body.

Becky and Al stood close together, but with a definite barrier between them. Becky stared into the flames and her eyes were saying, 'Burn you bastard, burn!'

I was feeling strangely annoyed with Dominic and reacted badly when he came over and whispered, 'Why the hell are you doing this?' in my ear.

'It's symbolic, that's all!' I hissed, not prepared to explain further. Obviously, nobody else had told him.

By ten o'clock it was all over, just a mess of smouldering charcoal, and we went upstairs to hit the vodka.

God, how naive we were! What wonderland did we inhabit where ghostly emotions could live on in a piece of furniture? Some wonderland, surely, for we just accepted that it could happen. In stories, in our story, the haunted table can be burned, burned and destroyed. A tidy ending. What we'd forgotten was that lives were involved; those complex things, beyond straight lines or analysis.

The house was on tenterhooks for a few days, testing the water, sniffing around, but nothing happened. Quiet prevailed in the flat across the hall and all we heard at night was the whir of Becky's sewing machine. Al still spent a lot of time upstairs, though. Whenever Tara or I called in to see Simon or Dom, Al was there with them, either curled over a chess board or else tapping his feet, listening to examples of Simon's infinite collection of cacophonous jazz records. It was true he always looked more relaxed away from Becky, hanging bonelessly over Simon and Dom's furniture and flashing his wonderful, dark eyes far more than he usually dared to. We half suspected he hadn't noticed that much going on.

Dominic, in fact, began to spend more time down at our place (perhaps he didn't like the jazz either), offering to help out with our orders, which both Tara and I appreciated. He was no artist, but at least he could keep our coffee mugs topped up and offer encouraging remarks. One night he told me I looked nice which pleased me immensely. I revised all the suspicions I'd had about him being gay, and wondered whether he was just shy.

A couple of nights a week, Simon would come down too and the four of us would get drunk and set the world to rights until 2 a.m. Sometimes Becky and Al would join us and we'd all stroll off to see a movie or go to a nightclub. Becky certainly seemed like her old self, but perhaps it was only me who saw the real ghost, the real phantom; Becky's smile, Becky's laugh. I realised she hadn't forgotten whatever illusions the table had shown her but, because I truly wanted it to be over, I didn't even talk about this with Tara. I just watched and, God help me, I know I waited.

One afternoon, I was in by myself toying with an idea for a new line of dinner plates and Becky came over for a chat. It was a weekend, and Tara had gone shopping with the upstairs boys. We'd planned to spend the evening in with liquor and a couple of new videos. Becky prowled round our front room until I told her she was making me dizzy and to sit down. She perched on the edge of the sofa and pushed back her hair. God, she'd lost so much weight, to the point where it was past becoming. 'Want a sandwich?' I asked.

She said, 'OK,' in a tired voice and followed me into the kitchen, leaning on the sink, looking like a schoolgirl. I cut cheese and slapped margarine around, uncomfortable and edgy. Becky never used to be such a looming presence

'What do you think Celia Rutticker used to worry about?' she blurted out.

'No, Becky,' I said, 'don't.' But it was for my benefit, not hers.

'Tell me. You asked Mrs. Cryer. You know all about it, so tell me.'

I blathered on, repeating Tara's theories about social rejection, inadequacy, self-blame, etc. etc.

'So you don't think it was to do with... a boyfriend, or anything?'

I furiously cut bread. 'How the hell can we know that, Beck? Most of it is guesses. How can we know what Celia used to think about?'

She shrugged. 'Just wondered. Whether Mrs. C. said anything about that or not. Do you think I should get in touch with Celia Rutticker?'

'Good God, no!' I cried, excruciating visions rushing before my eyes; the results of such a suggestion. 'At best she'll think you're insane, at worst, dangerous and call the police. Leave it, Beck, it's over. You must forget it.'

'It's cosy for you to think that, isn't it,' Becky said quietly. She took the plate of sandwiches from my hand and went into the living room again.

I took the slap in the face and thought about it for a few seconds. She was right. I went after her. 'You're still bothered then?'

She nodded. 'I am. It seemed so convenient to blame it all on what you said. I'm still not right, Jo. I'm scared.'

'So what's wrong?' I sat down next to her. She was nibbling on a sandwich.

'I get these crazy ideas, really crazy. Sick too. I'm not sure what's me anymore. If I'm going mad or not.'

'What ideas?'

She looked at me gravely and shook her head. 'No, I can't tell you that, Jo. I really can't. Not that I don't trust you. I just don't want to hear them aloud, not ever.' She took another bite. 'I am fighting it, and I know I can be naturally paranoid over... certain things, so I am fighting it.'

We were silent for a while.

'I've been wondering whether I should get away for a day or so,' she said eventually, 'but I know I can't do that because the fears, the sickness will just feed on that, making it worse when I get back. My head will be full of the things. I can't leave, but I don't want to stay. What can I do?'

I put on a blank face. 'Have you thought of seeing your

doctor?'

She gave a small, bitter laugh. 'Weeks ago, Joanna dear. The magic pills he gave me have kept me quiet these past few weeks.'

'I'm sorry, I...' I shrugged helplessly.

'I've been happy for years,' she said. 'That's what makes me keep on thinking it's all to do with that damn table. It has to be, otherwise...' She shook her head.

'What does Al think?' I asked.

'I don't tell him. He goes upstairs to drink beer and play board games and listen to music. I don't want to bother him.' She avoided my eyes. 'I'd better go. I'm interrupting your work.'

'No, no,' I said.

'I don't want to stay,' she replied and walked out.

If only she'd told me what was going on in her head. She didn't. She didn't tell anyone until it was too late. A week later, Becky tried to commit suicide, cutting her wrists, inexpertly, on the floor of her living room while Al was upstairs with Simon. We only found her in time because Dominic was down with Tara and me, helping us with a rush order and we ran out of milk. Becky and Al always leave their door unlocked when they're in. Perhaps she wanted someone to find her. Perhaps she'd have locked it otherwise. Tara went over to scrounge milk and we heard her yelling and rushed across the hall to a scene from a horror movie. Becky had managed to spray a hell of a lot of blood around. There were ambulances and police and noise and panic and rushing about, Al wringing his hands in the doorway, Tara blaming herself for whatever reasons and Becky saying to me in a weak voice as they patched her up before the journey to hospital, 'There were no faces in the picture, but I knew Jo. I just knew.'

She never came back to live in our house, never. Her mother came and I helped her pack up Becky's things.

'It's best if she came home for a while,' Mrs. Olson said.

Post script. About a month later, Simon moved out of the upstairs flat and in with Al. We guessed Al needed the company; he'd gone white and withdrawn, understandably. After a lot of self-denial and flirting disguised as sparring, Dominic and I realised we'd fallen in love with each other somewhere along the way.

All that time I'd been thinking he didn't fancy me and he thought I wasn't the kind of girl who wanted proper commitment in a relationship. We'd both been wrong. I also decided that he was far more beautiful than Simon, and one night told him so. He laughed ruefully. 'Simon sends people up, you know. He's not that bad a person.'

I shrugged and rolled onto the other side of the bed, wondering at the same time, why those words made me feel edgy. 'I don't like him,' I said, relishing being able to say that out loud at last.

'I know. You hide it well, though. That's a talent you both have.'

'What do you mean?' I did not like being compared with Simon.

'Hiding what you feel. Simon comes on like a hard-hearted bastard. It's a defence mechanism.'

'You don't have to defend your friend to me!' I said, angrily.

Dominic sneered and laughed and grossly misinterpreted my words, which as usual, I'd uttered in all innocence. 'Oh, I see! You thought...' He laughed again. 'Is that why you hate him so much? I suppose I'm flattered. Shows you care. I like possessiveness in my lovers.' He sidled up and nuzzled me, while my brain did a few somersaults.

'Hold on, dear,' I said, fending him off. 'Can you just elaborate a bit on that, please?'

'Simon and I have never been lovers,' he said matter-of-factly.

I spluttered a little.

'Does it make you feel better to hear that? Will you stop hating him now? Of course, you must still feel bad about your friend, but... well, I heard all the other side of it, I suppose. I know it's hard, but try to understand. He did try to talk with her about it, you know, but it was so difficult, she was so... well, straight, I guess.'

I sat up in bed. 'Dom, what are you telling me?'

There was a huge silence. He lay there, looking up at me, his mouth half open. 'You don't mean... Christ, Jo, don't tell me you don't know!' He slapped his head. 'Jesus! What have I said?'

Well, naturally, I made him tell me the rest. He said that Al and Simon had been having an affair from virtually right when the boys had moved in upstairs. The biggest jigsaw piece ever. I felt giddy when I heard that, not just because it was such a shock to discover that Al had gay proclivities never suspected before, but because it made me realise that us, with our stupid table theories, had probably fucked up Becky's life, if not forever, then for a long time to come.

Everything became all too clear; the suspicions Becky must have had, the change in behaviour, paranoid prowling of the stairs, feelings of inadequacy. She'd known, of course she'd known, but hadn't wanted to accept such a horrifying truth. She and Al had been together for nine years, for God's sake! And we, little know-all occult sleuths, we'd taught her not to trust her instincts. We'd let her lie to herself, encouraged her to, until the overwhelming wave of evidence against her safety must have swamped her.

Why the hell hadn't one of us had the sense to see what was going on? The start of Becky's trouble coincided not just with acquiring the table but when Simon had arrived too. Simon the seducer. It was obvious now the way he'd taken Al over, getting him upstairs away from Becky who was quietly going mad beneath them. But we'd ignored the signs; too fond of the mysterious, I suppose. We'd just made it easier for them. If possession exists, it's surely a human manipulation.

'If you'd told me about your crackpot theories, I could have enlightened you!' Dominic said in a bristly way. 'I just thought you knew. I thought Becky would have confided in you...'

'I think she tried to,' I said, 'and we kept insisting it was the table! God, were we fools!'

'It's not your fault, Jo.' Dominic soothed. 'Like I said, Simon's good at hiding things.'

'And you did pretty well too,' I said coldly.

'I never gossip about him. We've been friends for years. I'm sorry. What else can I say?'

Well, he said plenty, and I forgave him eventually, but it still made me feel sick about the way dear Simon must have watched Becky disintegrate. If he'd been decent, he'd have confided in Tara or something. He'd had the perfect opportunity that night we'd called him down to tell him our suspicions. How he must have laughed at us. I'm not as generous as Dominic. I think there's a pretty hard heart beating in Simon's beautifully tanned chest, whatever my lover thinks.

Tara and I don't have much to do with Simon and Al now. In her most generous, philosophical moments, Tara says this is because we feel piqued because we weren't in on what was going on. Perhaps she's right. Neither she nor I ever really liked Becky that much. I wonder. Are we all cold, cruel creatures under the skin? One thing still had me foxed though, and that was how Simon had managed to seduce Al of all people. That is, until...

Yesterday, I met Capt. Lonsdale in the street. For whatever reason, maybe because the sun was shining and it was a beautiful day, or I was just in a good mood, I stopped to listen to him. An idea struck me. 'Tell me about Lamp House,' I said. 'Our landlady thinks you knew the people who lived there after the Rutticker family left.'

He chewed his beard and rolled his eyes a bit. 'Knew, young lady? Hardly.' He leaned forward. 'Knew *of*, of course.' A roguish wink. 'But knew, never!'

'Really?' I prompted. 'Why?'

He lowered his voice to a confidential level and came so close I could smell the whisky he'd had for breakfast. 'Queers, you know,' he said. 'That Rutticker boy. He stayed on at the house after his people went to the country. Had some kid living there with him. Perverts! The police got 'em! Bloody good job too! Locked 'em up good and fast, but there was a hell of a mess.' He grabbed my arm, which had frozen, despite the warm weather. 'Young lad tried to kill himself, you know. Cut his wrists or something. Rutticker was done for it. It's like attempted murder when you think about it, isn't it?'

Tara and I are amateur researchers of the supernatural. I don't think we'll bother again.

The Vitreous Suzerain

The days were entirely disorientating to the new Suzerain of Leeleefam. They were of a new length to him, of course and he suspected that length was bizarrely variable. They told him he had been in residence in the squat palace for three weeks now, yet it seemed like months.

'Guldron, this planet makes me dizzy,' he would say to his withdrawn, long-fingered principal aide. Guldron was not a native either, but Claude envied her adaptability. Perhaps it signified only a lack of imagination.

Suzerain Claude Enquito also craved company. Back in the governmental office on Abbey Five, he had enjoyed his work; the social life being perhaps more fulfilling than his job, but here on Sheller's Brake in the province of Leeleefam, he felt alone, surrounded by people who would obey his every word but whom he could never call friends. It was almost as if this new position, which in financial terms was certainly a promotion, was really some kind of punishment for misdemeanour - a banishment. He'd often thought about this, wondering whether he'd unwittingly offended some high-ranking person on Abbey Five, but could think of nothing. He'd always been a popular man and it had been for this reason he'd been offered the suzerainship of Leeleefam, or so his superiors had told him. There had been warnings of course. Working on a world where there was a subdued native culture was never a straightforward operation.

Leeleefam had been a nonchalant host to humankind for about three years now. Sheller's Brake was a planet rich in ores and Seven Worlds Enterprises had lost no time in staking a claim there when it had first been discovered; a moon-ringed radiant ball hanging at the edge of Wineburst Star's planetary system. Whatever lofty notions humankind had started out with when it had acquired enough knowledge to traverse the infinity of space, had degenerated locally into the usual commercial power struggles. Naturally, 'locally' now meant something rather greater than the distance comfortably travelled in an hour or so; it referred somewhat carelessly to entire solar systems and star clusters. Gulfs of culture wider than anyone from the past could ever imagine had divided the human race into a multitude of diverse races; each seemed to adapt psychologically to the environment it found itself in. Great empires had never been realised; the universe was too vast for that. Claude Enquito belonged to a society of assorted ethnic origins that had control of a handful of planets. They were industrialists not tyrants. The fact that Sheller's Brake had indigenous life of its own had not been regarded as a cue for conquest but merely as an inconvenience. It necessitated being very careful; civilised humans went to great pains not to interfere with or upset native cultures less advanced than their own. It did not prevent, however, the use of local labour for less than princely salaries.

It was mid-day and a colliding scrum of vague moons were already advancing above the horizon. Claude Enquito looked up from the screen where figures and glyphs proclaimed a stultifying mass of information about local minerals. He tried not to be downhearted about his position, being wise enough to realise that with time, familiarity might plane the edges from his feeling of alienation. People had to get used to him as much as he had to get used to them - and their location. However, there were times in the day when he would have liked to sit back, sip something hot and sweet in the company of like minds and gossip about inconsequential things. None of the human population of Leeleefam seemed disposed to idle chatter. They had evolved their own identity here, for which the first suzerain could probably claim responsibility, and it seemed a sombre and joyless one to Claude, who was used to the frivolity of Abbey Five. He regarded through narrow eyes the small glass ornament which sat on his desktop; a gift from his new colleagues. Rather like he found them, he thought it a singularly cold and uninteresting thing. Its novelty was in the fact that had been donated by the local Leelees, the natives (a term all employees of Seven Worlds Enterprises were discouraged from implementing in daily speech). Claude had accepted it with forced gratitude on the day of his arrival and it had sat, gathering dust, beside his console ever since; an uninspiring and shapeless lump. What it was supposed to represent, he could not tell. However, something about its shape disturbed him if he looked at it too long; an aversion which Claude thought merely mirrored his current discontent.

Ively Guldron swept into the office, disturbing Claude's reverie, trailing domestic staff guiding a floating trolley of food. 'I would like to join you for lunch,' Guldron said, which Claude wearily thought was the price to pay for yearning company.

'By all means. Put your feet up,' he said and Guldron sniffed the slightest of sniffs before perching on the edge of a seat. The food, like the people of this complex, was dull and did little to stimulate the senses, concentrating more on the no-nonsense business of correct nutrition. Claude knew that Guldron wouldn't have joined him if there wasn't something on her mind. He had the feeling that a meal interrupting the flow of a day's work could never be consumed with pleasure by the woman. He was right. She had barely taken one careful nibble of food before coming to the point.

'The Leelees have requested an audience with you,' she said. He stared, dumbly, unsure of what reaction to exhibit.

She chewed, swallowed and shook her head briefly, creasing her brows. 'Oh, don't worry, it's quite in order. Usually, they don't want to come near us, apart from on salary day, but it seems to be some kind of custom with them to make a formal welcome to a new suzerain. Bizarre title, I'm sure you'll agree, but we had to have something they'd like and it's the only word in human language having approximately the same meaning to each of us.'

'Manager would be rather mundane, I agree,' Claude said.

'You don't understand. It's nothing to do with the sound of the word, but the way your face works when you say it. These people are aliens, Claude, and I mean, aliens. It's no use trying to anthropomorphise them. It simply won't work. You probably have more in common with a dog.'

He wondered whether the implied metaphor was deliberate, but her mind seemed on other things. 'So, when do I see them?'

'Oh, I arranged it for this afternoon. Might as well get the whole thing out of the way, because we have work to do for the ores shipment next week. You have robes, you know. You'd better put them on. Leelees like that kind of thing and we aim to please them whenever possible. They were always trying to badger your predecessor. He learned the knack of dealing with them quickly.'

Hint or criticism? Claude wondered.

'I suppose we must be like gods to them or something,' Guldron continued.

Claude couldn't repress an inward wince. She smiled smugly. 'However, they're good workers and not much trouble, so we indulge them occasionally.'

That was her summary of an entire culture; alien as she had mentioned and doubtless richer in strangeness and possible new lessons for the human race than could be imagined. The representatives of S.W.E. kept the natives happy with the least possible inconvenience to themselves, and regarded them as exotic animals, albeit a rare species to be preserved and, undeniably, rather useful.

Claude Enquito waited to receive his visitors in a skylit room, decorated with exuberant examples of local flora. He was nervous. Guldron came to wait with him, sighing and tapping her foot to show that she had more pressing business awaiting her elsewhere. 'I've not had much experience of this kind of thing,' Claude said.

Ively Guldron shrugged as if to say there was nothing to it. She was looking out of the window. 'Ah, wonderful, at last. Here they come.'

Claude went to stand beside her. A troupe of perhaps twenty Leelees was being escorted up the paved walkway to the palace. As most intelligent species that humanity had fallen across in its travels, superficially the Leelees appeared very manlike, having similar facial features, four limbs and a vertical spine. They were chatting animatedly together, their hands and faces writhing and flitting and flickering so fast, they became a blur. As a contrast, the escorting humans bore the countenances of statues.

'See the big eartha?' Guldron asked Claude. 'That's Zozozo, whom we presume to be the leader of the local community. An impressive lump, eh?'

Claude was surprised at Ively's attempt at humour, the first he'd experienced here. He had to agree with her though. The leading Leelee was striding purposefully ahead of the others, well over six feet high, heavy-limbed, wide, and sporting a wild costume of artful rags that fluttered behind like sails. Leelees were comprised of three sexes, of which the earthas were the nearest to female, being the bearers of young. The rest of Zozozo's group was comprised of energetic wafts, biologically the intermediary between the seed-bearing flyers and the mammoth, fertile earthas. Claude had only seen Leelees from a distance before.

Zozozo was not terrifying to look at. She was awesome yes, simply because of her size, but on the whole she resembled nothing other than a large, fat woman. Claude, however, was terribly afraid. There are no words to convey the primal fear brought forth in the human psyche by having to face a creature essentially un-human. Having lived a far from cosmopolitan life in the cosy little governmental complex on Abbey Five, Claude had not had direct contact with a nonhuman before. As he quailed, Guldron swept briskly forward, smiling and nodding, saying, 'Hello, hello, hello.'

'Hello, hello, hello,' intoned Zozozo gravely. She executed a series of alarming grimaces, then bent primly from the waist in a formal bow.

Claude was wondering whether he would faint. Bright waftish eyes surveyed him with interest, faces peeking round the imposing bulk of their queen, all blinking, twitching and wrenching their features into impossible expressions. Zozozo had queerly grey skin, which appeared smooth, perhaps finely furred. Behind her, the wafts had flushed a deep buttercup colour with excitement.

'Zozozo, may I present Claude Enquito, the new suzerain of our establishment here in Leeleefam,' Guldron said, enunciating carefully.

The Leelee queen emitted a sound which may have been laughter and waved her arms swiftly in a series of meaningful gestures. 'Zoozoorain, yes, gooood!' she exclaimed, exposing her teeth until it seemed her lips were inside out. The teeth themselves were alarming; spadelike and irregular as if used to tearing fibres completely different from those familiar to human mouths.

Guldron threw Claude a private glance.

'Pleased to meet you,' he said.

The Leelees appeared to consider his words, then Zozozo threw up an arm with the half-intelligible remark, 'Too steef, too steef, skeen too night night. Feel go eenside!' She thumped her chest and roared with delight. 'Out heer! Out heer!'

Claude realised she had been addressing him. He peered at Guldron in mute appeal.

'Zozozo feels the colour of your skin is caused by a stiffness of emotion boiling inside you. She advises you to let it out.'

'Satan's teeth!' Claude responded, weakly.

Zozozo had shuffled forward and, leaning towards Claude, muttered confidentially, her face juggling a chaotic multitude of expressions, 'Special special for you. Heeer.' She gestured behind her and, amidst a buzz of twittering, the wafts ejected a seemingly protesting figure from their ranks. 'Say hello, hello, hello!' Zozozo commanded and with a motherly thrust, propelled the unfortunate waft in the direction of the self-consciously contained human beings before her.

'Hello, hello, hello,' said the waft.

'Happeee!' cried the Leelee queen and, uttering another bellow, arranged her troupe about her and marched out without another word.

Silence surged in to fill the space left by the Leelees. Claude leaned weakly on a table.

Guldron stood stiffly to attention, arms straight by her sides, fists clenched, nostrils flaring. 'Never before!' she said.

The waft looked from one to the other of them; its skin colour had faded to a tentative cream. It was impossible to read the expression on its face. Several untranslateable flickers convulsed its features but, other than that, it remained silent.

'Guldron, would you tell me what the hell has just happened please?' Claude said. 'I feel like I've been standing face-first into a hurricane.'

Guldron had repossessed herself. Claude could see her temperature gauge sweeping sleekly back to normal. 'What has just happened, Claude, is that Zozozo has presented you with a... with a gift. This waft.'

Both humans stared at the gift in a moment of mutual dissatisfaction.

'Naturally, our language caused them a bit of a problem at first,' Ively Guldron said. 'Took them a year or so to get the hang of the basics. We arranged to have teachers sent in, linguists from Wipple College.' Taking control, Guldron had seen to it that the waft had been taken off somewhere and entertained until they could decide what to do with it.

Claude was still feeling shaken. 'Pity you couldn't instil a little diplomacy along with the lingo!'

Guldron laughed. 'My dear suzerain - that *was* diplomacy. At least, diplomacy Leelee-style. They always speak their minds. Artifice is unknown to them. Likewise, tact! Zozozo couldn't comprehend in a million years the social graces of human culture and even if she could, she'd think it ridiculous. These people wear their hearts on their faces, so to speak. In a word, they are honest.'

'That, more than anything, proclaims them truly alien!' Claude decided and went to pour himself a large drink.

'Perhaps you can understand now why we discourage intercourse with the Leelees,' Guldron said, an image of correct behaviour.

'And conversation too, I trust!'

Guldron didn't even twitch. 'We can't risk offending Zozozo. Well, not offending, exactly, that's not the word, because I don't believe you can offend a Leelee. They are susceptible to disappointment, however, and that affects their work. We have that big order coming up...' She shook her head, bared her teeth and tapped them with a bony finger. 'You'll have to play the game a while, Claude.'

'Meaning what exactly?'

'Let the Leelee hang around. They don't generally get in the way, but they're rather curious, like children. Give it a few toys and it'll be happy for weeks. OK?'

'Guldron, I won't feel comfortable with that weird thing hanging round me.'

Guldron smothered exasperation. 'Look, Claude, it is a kind of honour, after all. Zozozo is concerned for you. The Leelees change colouring all the time; it exhibits moods in them. She doesn't understand we don't do that. They've never seen a human as dark as you before; therefore, she thinks you're worried.

'Wonderful. She's right. At this moment, I am worried.'

That evening Ively Guldron invited Claude over for dinner. When he got there the waft had been placed on display ready for him, perched on a stool by the glass-topped table. It was chattering away, grimacing, apparently to itself; a thin, waif-like creature, pale lemon of skin, with thick golden hair, strangely streaked with black. Claude thought that it looked like an abused infant and recoiled at the door, which had already slid shut behind him. The waft turned its heart-shaped face towards him, which for several seconds became unusually void of expression.

'Well, come in,' Guldron said. She was relaxing on an air-filled lounger, drink in hand, keeping an eye on her staff as they set the table for the meal. Claude had never met with Ively Guldron out of work hours before, and was surprised by what appeared to be a relaxed mien. He edged towards her, unable to take his eyes off the waft. Like Zozozo the creature emanated a profoundly disturbing aura.

'Perhaps the Leelees think it's time we understood them a little better,' Guldron said. 'Is that so, Vava?'

The waft flicked its glance away from Claude, its skin deepening a shade, and said to her, 'You understand us. We don't understand you.'

'Good command of our language, eh, Claude?'

'Your faces never say anything,' said the waft. 'You are disabled in that way.' With that observation, it resumed concentration on its own fingers, which were conversing to each other rapidly and silently.

Ively appeared to dismiss the creature from her attention, producing a sheaf of print-outs. 'Fetch the suzerain something to drink,' she instructed one of her maids. 'Claude, come here. There's something we should discuss.'

So much for the social evening, Claude thought. He stared blindly at the papers Guldron was stabbing at with urgent fingers. Her words didn't penetrate his mind. The drink he'd been offered was low on alcohol and unpleasantly sweet. Out of the corner of his eye, he could see the waft watching them intently.

'So you see,' Guldron was concluding. 'We have to be ready for the next phase in three days at the latest, otherwise the whole procedure could be held up for weeks. What do you think?'

'Er...'

'He thinks he would rather be at home now with something stronger in his glass,' the waft announced.

There was a moment's icy silence.

'Perhaps we should eat,' Guldron said.

The meal was usual Leeleefam fare. Claude didn't have much of an appetite. He was beginning to think seriously about applying for a transfer. Promotion or not, he'd be happier going back to Abbey Five with less status, less money but blissful normality around him.

Guldron continued to talk about shipments, thinking out loud more than trying to have a discussion.

'This food's not right,' the waft said, breaking into Guldron's diatribe; its skin now displayed a distinctly mustardy shade.

'What's wrong with it?' Guldron asked sharply, impatiently.

'It's just not interesting. It doesn't taste of anything. Can I have something else?'

'It's all we have. This is what humans eat, Vava, and it certainly won't poison you, and so unless you want to feel hungry in the night, I suggest you eat it too.'

The waft exhibited an array of private grimaces and then picked at the food.

Claude experienced an unmistakeable warming towards the little creature. It was childlike; small and ingenuous. Perhaps if he just looked on it as a rather odd child, he wouldn't feel so discomforted.

'Why did Zozozo leave you with us?' he asked it.

'To make you glow. You people never do, but you must be worse than the others.'

'Why?'

The creature wriggled, which Claude interpreted as the equivalent of a shrug. 'Zozozo thinks so. She's always right.'

Guldron was staring at Claude over the table, her look implying what ridiculous creatures these Leelees were. Claude couldn't wait to leave.

Claude walked back home through the soft multiple moonlight with the waft zipping this way and that across the lawn in front of him. Ively Guldron had insisted he take it with him. After an evening in Vava's company, Claude didn't feel quite so alarmed about it. In fact he was beginning to think he had more in common with the waft than he did with Guldron. Soft, mournful cries, the night-song of the flyers, came to his ears from beyond the complex. Of all the Leelees, the flyers were the most peculiar to behold, and the least seen. Pale and limber, they kept to their tree-top villages, never flying exactly, as they had no wings, but leaping gracefully from branch to branch in an almost simian way. The waft uttered fluting sounds back occasionally, but was clearly far from interested in answering the calls.

After a short walk through the low colonnades of the outer palace structure, they reached Claude's own apartments. Soft lights blossomed about the eaves when their mechanisms sensed his approach. There was nobody else about; security was not a problem in Leeleefam.

Once inside, Claude went straight to his drinks cabinet to satisfy the craving he'd suffered all evening.

The waft walked round his living-room, looking with interest at his possessions.

'Are you tired? Do you people sleep?' Claude asked.

'Yes. Doesn't everything?' The waft jumped up and down in front of him, spinning, chittering, its skin an astounding shade of daffodil yellow.

Claude turned his back. 'Let's get one thing straight, Vava. You can't make me glow, whatever that is. My skin's not darker than Guldron's because I'm unhappier than she is. Humans are all different colours, but we can't change the one we're born with, at least not naturally. Understand?'

Vava stopped jumping. 'No. Neither do you. Can I have some of that?' It pointed to his drink.

'I don't think so. I'm going to sleep now. What do you

want to do?'

'Sit and listen for a while. I'll sleep here later. Goodnight.' It skipped to the sofa and sat with its forearms on the plump backrest, staring out of the window at the moonlight.

Claude sighed and went into his bedroom.

In the morning, Claude tried to persuade the waft to stay in his living quarters. Vava didn't seem to understand what he was saying, which Claude found suspicious in view of the little creature's astounding grasp of human speech the previous night. He wondered if the Leelees were as honest as Guldron thought.

'Stay here!' Claude commanded as he backed towards the door that led to his offices.

Vava sped past him emitting a series of squeaks, which to Claude's ears sounded ominously jubilant.

By mid-morning, the vivacity of the Leelee had caused his head to spin. Unable to concentrate on his work because of the antics of his guest, he stabbed a few pause buttons and sat back to have a hot drink. The waft was at his side in an instant, the writhings of its features resembling the palsy of some terrible disease. Claude grimaced and turned away.

'Why?' the waft asked.

Claude looked back and found his expression parodied repeatedly. 'Stop it!'

The waft looked perplexed. 'But why?' it said and tentatively mimicked the expression one more time.

Claude caught on. 'Your conversation makes me dizzy,' he said.

Before the Leelee could make a response the comm buzzer sounded on Claude's desk. He tapped out the reply code. 'Yes?'

'Iveley Guldron wonders if you have a few minutes to spare,' the tinny voice of his secretary replied; a creature possibly even less entertaining than Guldron.

Claude silently groaned and rubbed his face. 'I'm sorry, you'll have to tell her I'm up to my neck in it until this afternoon,' he said, averting his gaze from the silent screen in front of him, the empty correspondence racks. 'After lunch, OK?'

'Very well, suzerain Enquito.' The connection was broken.

Claude shook his head.

'You have gone darker!' the waft accused.

Before he could stop himself, Claude's glance flicked down to his hands, where, naturally, he could see no difference at all. 'No, Vava, I haven't. Be useful and get me a top-up from that machine over there. Have one yourself if you like.'

The waft took his cup, but its gaze never left his face. 'You spoke mistakenly,' it said. 'You deliberately spoke mistakenly.' There was a kind of wonder in its voice and its features writhed in slow, folding gestures.

Claude realised it was referring to how he had put Guldron off seeing him that morning. 'Clearly, you haven't spent much time with humans,' he said with a smile, a smile that, undeniably, covered an insidious twinge of shame caused by the open expression of innocent shock on the waft's face.

'Why didn't you say what she couldn't see? That she damps your glow and makes your head sleepy?'

Claude had to laugh. 'I don't think Guldron would appreciate that, Vava.'

'What do you mean?'

Claude sighed. He remembered what Guldron had told him about the Leelee inability to dissemble. He was too weary to try and explain. 'It's just something we do. Now forget it,' he said.

The Leelee's attention had now been taken by the ornament beside Claude's console. It picked the thing up and again exhibited signs of shock and dismay.

'What is it this time?' Claude asked, trying to take the glass away from it.

The Leelee stepped backwards, clutching the ornament firmly. It had gone very pale. 'No glow, no glow at all!' it said and held the glass up to the light, shaking its head in disbelief. 'You haven't used it!' it cried accusingly. 'No wonder you don't glow!'

'Used it? Give it to me, Vava. What do you mean?'

The waft put the ornament into Claude's hand and leaned close to him, staring into it. The smell and aura of the creature in such close proximity caused Claude to break out into a sweat. He lifted the ornament up and gazed through it; an amorphous lump of cloudy glass.

'We give them to all new humans,' Vava said. 'We thought they helped you. Hasn't anyone taught you how to use it?'

'No. I don't think anyone here knows how, Vava. Perhaps you people didn't explain properly how we should. What is it? I thought it was just an ornament.'

Vava twittered in what Claude took to be amusement. 'Not very ornamental at the moment is it? It's an eeookha, suzerain.'

'Eeookha?' Claude repeated slowly. 'And what's that?'

'It stores your glow so you can use it in darker times. We all have one. Eeookhas are things that go back a long long way.'

'And how does it store one's glow exactly?' There was no evidence of even slight luminosity in the glass at present.

'I could show you,' Vava said, hesitating, 'But, because it's your eeookha, I really shouldn't. It would be... intrusive, like... like....' It held up the empty cup. '...like spitting in your drink. See?'

Claude laughed. 'I don't mind. Here, show me.'

'Very well, then. I'll fill it for you and then you try to take it, but you might not be able to use my glow... you're so different.'

Watching with perplexed interest, Claude handed the waft his ornament. It screwed up its eyes, grimaced, leered, twitched and then calmed. There was a new smell in the room, that Claude could never have described, and a weird feeling as of electricity brushing the skin. Then the waft smiled and Claude looked away from its face to the ornament sitting in its hands.

'Satan's teeth!' he said, almost in a whisper. The glass was glowing with a thousand turning motes of brightness and colour. 'How did you do that?'

'Simple. Try taking some. I don't think it will harm you.'

'How?'

The waft twitched. 'Think it in. I've made it loose. It shouldn't be hard.'

'OK.' Claude laughed nervously and took the glass in his hands. It felt neither warm nor cold. After staring at it for a moment, he looked up and shrugged. 'Nothing,' he said, sneakily relieved.

The waft grimaced and shook its head. 'Not trying,' it said. 'Make your head empty. Think it in.'

'Like a kind of meditation?'

'What?'

'Nothing. I think I get it.' He cleared his throat, settled himself and stared once more into the sparkling glass. Attempting to dismiss any misgivings, he calmed his mind. For a while, nothing happened, other than the feel of the glass weight in his hands; the shifting glow, became soothing, almost hypnotic. Then, as true relaxation spread through Claude's body, an alarming heat suffused his face, which he realised was coming from the glass. Suddenly the whole room was blotted from his sight by a flash of brightness as if he'd been smacked sharply in both eyes. He cried out and dropped the ornament, flopping back in his chair, then forwards, clutching his face. Gripped by confusion but not pain, he did not think about how it had been rather stupid to do what Vava had asked.

'You alright?' the waft said, pawing his shoulder in quick, birdlike gestures.

Claude shook his head. His vision was clearing. Alright? Am I? What happened? Suddenly, he began to laugh. 'Alright? I feel wonderful!' he cried.

The waft clapped its hands and skipped on the spot. 'Yes

you do. You're glowing, glowing. You're not dark anymore.'

Again Claude looked briefly at his hands. No change. He laughed once more. 'Vava, I don't think you meant the colour of my skin when you said I was dark, did you?'

The waft shook its head, uncomprehending. 'You're glowing now anyway,' it said.

'And glowing is... is happiness, right? And contentment and well-being and all that?'

The waft wrinkled its nose. 'If that's how you feel it, then it is,' it said.

'That's how I feel!' Claude said.

'You're not so sorry you came here now,' Vava told him. 'You're saying it. With your glow. I'm glad, and Zozozo will be pleased with me. We didn't realise you weren't using your eeookhas. No wonder your faces are so quiet.'

Claude, who currently felt like skipping, dancing and being utterly childlike for a while, realised that Guldron probably wouldn't want to encourage the use of eeookhas within the complex, even if she knew what they could do. Exuberance might interfere with the work schedules and that would never do for Ms. Guldron. He was pleased he'd proved her wrong about never being able to communicate properly with the Leelees. Pure joy for living was a sentiment that must be the same the universe over.

Vava leaned over Claude's shoulder and deftly turned off his console. Clearly, it had been watching him work far more closely than he'd thought. 'Time for that later,' it said. 'Let's celebrate for a while' It held out its hands. Before taking hold of them, Claude dimmed the windows and locked the doors. Somehow he thought it more prudent not to share his new-found source of enjoyment with Guldron and her like just yet. It would not be approved of, and certainly not understood. Therefore, subtle handling of the subject was called for.

Such matters were indeed for later perusal, however. For now, bathing in a delightful intoxication, Claude allowed the Leelee to lead him in a wild, crazy dance. It seemed, if he listened hard enough, there was music to dance to, music from outside; the call of birds, the pulse of wind, even the mechanical thump of the complex's machinery. Spinning in circles around the spacious office, they shared the warmth of Vava's glow which seemed to hang between them like a luminous ball. Claude was conscious of the vastness of Sheller's Brake beyond the complex walls; a place he wanted to explore and be part of. Almost drunk with the explosion of joy inside him, he saw himself as a benevolent mind from beyond the dancing moons with whom the Leelees could share new sensations, experiencing through him the variety of other worlds. From them, he could learn to understand the world that had become his home. The strange calls of the flyers would speak to him too and the wriggling of waftish features would become a language he could speak. The humans of Leeleefam had ignored the richness of the planet they were occupying for too long, so obsessed were they with their desire for commercial success. It occurred to Claude that maybe, just maybe, someone high-up on Abbey Five had thought about this. Could it be possible that it was why the gregarious Claude Enquito had been offered the position in the first place? Guldron could get on with juggling her precious figures and sending out the shipments on time; Claude felt there was far more important work on Sheller's Brake for him to do.

Eventually, he and Vava exhausted themselves and sat on the floor together in the underwater gloom of the shuttered office.

'Tomorrow, I shall begin showing you how to fill the eeookha yourself,' Vava said. 'Then you need never be dark again. And you will stay here, won't you?' Its voice was eager and its slim hands reached for his. 'Zozozo saw the glow inside you all trodden on and spoken sharply to and not allowed out. She saw this and knew you'd be the best person who'd ever come here from the other places in the sky. We want to be friends, Claude, but nobody will speak to us. Not until you, and we all know you will.'

Claude picked up the ornament from where it had rolled

under a chair. It still emitted a soft radiance and he could see within it the vague form of a tall man in ceremonial robes. A flaw in the glass? Imagination? Perhaps. He reached out and patted Vava's face, who chittered and rubbed against his hand, kitten-like.

The point of contact is joy, he thought, *not smug tolerance, or even a patronising attempt at understanding, just utter, child-like joy.*

'We'll learn to talk,' he said and, for a moment, the eeookha glowed brighter with the faintest shade of purest blue.

The Rust Islands

I found it on my second dig, in the catacombs near Samedi Lake. It was the colour that caught my eye: a small green thing.

I lifted it from the rubble; a cylinder that left a verdigris powder on my gloves. For just a moment, I experienced a sense of déjà vu that vanished even before I could attempt to fix a memory on it. At first, I thought the little artefact was just another holovid chip: more dim, fragmented nostalgia that would depress rather than entertain; wrinkled memories of the past, when this world had been more than just a graveyard rubbish heap.

I tucked the cylinder into my belt-pouch and then forgot about it.

I was delving around on my own, beneath the harsh glare of porta-lites. There were no skull faces watching me, no bones in the darkness. We called that place the catacombs, but it had once been a city, now buried under mountains of refuse and hastily constructed buildings that had fallen during the last Great Ecological War. Abos scuttled on its surface like cock-roaches. Anything of interest and value had been plundered centuries ago.

Recently, public interest had been rekindled in old Earth, and a team from the Historical Facility on the Organic had, after a struggle, secured funding to make a journey through space to come and sift over the remains. I was a member of that team. But what we'd found was just like the great pyramids of legend; empty plundered tombs. We could learn only from the shadows that civilisation had left behind in the sand.

Around our camp, from horizon to horizon, stretched the rusting hulks of the long-dead city. We found the climate far too hot. Little grew on the rubble, although it was teeming with hundreds of tiny grey cats. The abos worshipped them and, for food, hunted goliath spiders, mice and rats. The natives looked like zombies - ash-covered and dead-eyed - and they had little interest in us. We had not been greeted as gods, which I think disappointed Elenov, our team leader, a little. When we told them we'd come from a country, far up in the sky, they simply shrugged and said they thought many people lived that way. They could not understand our eagerness about the past and gave crazy answers to our questions. There was no curiosity in them, whatsoever. They seemed dull creatures - not at all how we'd expected - and it was hard for some of us to accept we shared a common heritage with these people.

Avoiding everyone, I went back to the compound at sunset and sneaked into my cabin. Our camp consisted of a row of rover trucks, which doubled as caravans - the living space was incredibly cramped. We had a power generator and a canteen hut. The showers didn't always work and there were insects and monstrous arachnids forever scuttling round them.

We'd been working on the site for months and I'd started to get home-sick for the Organic; it seemed so far away, it might not exist. I wanted to walk beneath the stars amid the lush fern-trees. I wanted to feel the universe spin around me. I didn't need dirty heat and the threat of disease. I'm an archaeologist, used to working on many different colonised worlds. Some I'd seen had been more hostile than old Earth, yet here, the weight of history pressed down upon me. Would all our worlds eventually come to this? My only comfort was the knowledge that the retrieval bus was already on its way through sub-space to pick us up. Our sojourn was nearly over.

I needed a shower, and as I tossed my trousers onto the fold-out chair beneath the tiny window, the little cylinder fell out and rolled across the floor. I looked at it lying there in the red rays of the sinking sun. It seemed somehow significant. The moment was silence itself, but for the hum of the cooling unit, and the faint call of one of my team-workers through the thick lens of my window.

I left the cylinder on the floor, while I indulged myself with a welcome cooling shower. Then, naked and wet, I sidled to my desk where my jacket was lying, and took my AI, Lucrezia, out of the deepest pocket. Once I'd set her on the table, she took form by steadying herself on limbs that spidered out from her belly, then flipping out her monitor and shaking it until it became firm.

I showed her the cylinder. 'Can you read this?'

Delicately, she extended two arms that were feathered with dainty, clawed clamps, and took the cylinder from my hand. Inquisitive antennae snaked out and quivered over the object's surface. She pulled it towards her mandibles to taste its atomic structure.

'What is it?' I asked her, walking to the cooling unit behind the door, to find myself a carton of guava juice.

Lucrezia hummed a little. It's a quirk she has, evidence of her personality. 'It's a recording built into a playback system. Special recording, for direct neural experience. There are minute sockets set into either end.'

'More yesteryears pleasureware,' I said, slamming the cool-unit's door. It had a tendency to swing open again.

'I don't believe so.' Lucrezia gently turned the cylinder in her mandibles.

'Then what?'

Lucrezia extended an arm towards me. 'That is for us to find out.'

I sat on the chair by the desk, plonked the carton of juice down next to Lucrezia, and took the cylinder from her. I turned it in my fingers. It looked corroded, dead. 'Could it be an historical archive?' The possibility was exciting. So far, we'd found nothing that had really told us anything about the civilisation that had once thrived in this place. The abos had scavenged everything, twisted it into something new, or else destroyed it.

Lucrezia hummed. 'I estimate that is very likely.'

'Then can we jack into it? It looks damaged.'

'The outer casing is marred, but I estimate the chip itself is mostly intact.'

I shrugged. 'OK, let's see, shall we?' My heart had increased its pace. I don't know what I was expecting.

Lucrezia took a few moments to decide how best to extract the information in the chip. She scanned it with light, inserted probes into the minuscule sockets, laved it with a chemical bath. Then, satisfied, she extended an arm to the socket behind my ear and we conjoined.

Information hit me in a blizzard and I pulled away, yelping as we disengaged. 'It's blistered! White noise!'

'The sensoria do seem to slip,' Lucrezia agreed. 'Some of them are corrupted.'

'Try to find a clean section,' I said.

'No, I think we should wait,' Lucrezia said. 'Allow me to work on it first.'

I made a decision not to mention my find to anyone else on the team. Not yet. I had a feeling it would be taken from me, appropriated by Elenov, who was the senior historian. I wanted to keep this artefact to myself. Would it be like opening a tomb? I'd done plenty of that in my time and what I'd found inside them had only been rags of old lives. I could tell you what the owners of those bones had eaten for breakfast the day they died, but no way could I tell you what their long-shrivelled eyes had once seen, nor what they had perceived once they'd translated those images into thought.

By midnight, Lucrezia told me she had the problem sorted out, although she seemed reluctant to proceed with our joint investigation. 'I could process this information myself, then play it back to you. In my opinion, the data is unstable.'

'So what's on it?'

'A personal recording, an electronic journal perhaps. A

note-book... It's fragmented, and beyond my ability to repair completely. Allow me to extract the existing data.'

I shook my head. 'No, Luce. I know my hardware is less sturdy than yours, and my software more likely to crash - irreparably - but whoever made that recording is a kind of ancestor of mine. We need feedback, human feedback. I'm sure it will be of more value.'

Lucrezia cannot sigh, but her retinue of hums are most eloquent. She hummed. 'I trust I am absolved from blame should this experiment prove unwise?'

'Of course.' I waved her caution away. 'Let's jack in! Let's ride!'

The first seconds were fried. Gone. All I got was white noise and snow. My excitement plummeted. Maybe the whole chip was dead, despite the promising results of Lucrezia's initial tests. Maybe whatever was left could only be accessed by her. The boiling spectrum of random visual noise would give me a serious headache.

'It's no good, Luce,' I said, readying myself for disengagement. Then, unexpectedly and abruptly, it all bloomed in my mind. Pixels converged into perspective, and a sense of remote time formed around my inner eye. A virtual world shivered into focus.

The data was empathic. Whoever had recorded it had wanted to share it utterly. This was more than a mere archive document, much more.

I sensed myself as female, slim, and in perfect health. I was striding along a swaying bridge, which was suspended from diamond fibre cables, between two bamboo cage towers. I glanced to the side, but the world below was wreathed in mist. Still, from the vague, shadowy shapes I could see, I estimated I was about a thousand metres up in the air.

I was aware of myself, but she too was aware of herself. We shared her body, or her non-local soul. It was difficult to determine, but the experience was at once euphoric and terrifying. She was aware of me, perhaps, only as a possible future audience. Disorientating. I could recall information about her, as if I'd known it a long time. She was eighteen years old, with dark skin and a mass of braided hair. Her name was Shade. She wore a leather jacket, lacquer-dyed with multi-coloured spiral patterns. Beneath it she wore old trousers and a cotton T-shirt, their colours bleached and faded. A string of shells hung around her neck. As I became aware of this necklace, a memory formed: water-hiss, foam. The trinket had come from a souvenir booth by the beachwalk. Gradually, I became aware of the device that linked us. She was not using it as an implant via a neural socket, but it clung to the crevice behind her ear, extending a web of microscopic, bio-plastic filaments over her scalp. Somehow, these filaments interfaced with her mind. I was not familiar with this technology, but because I was able to use a more conventional method to extract this information, the device clearly had an array of methods to link with a human brain.

There was a strange clarity of sound around us; multi-coloured noise of natural acoustics, voices remixed by wind. The girl was walking, walking, salt wind grazing her skin as she talked aloud, recording.

'This account will be of my life and my work - my mother's work too, although she's dead now. There are enigmas about the past, and my mother's love of history and mystery have been passed on to me. I want answers. I want to know what happened here, why everything changed.

'The legends say that people came down from the sky, and sometimes I think they're just stories. Other times, I get a feeling that the truth has been wrapped up in myths, to hide it. Anyway, now I have this device, and it will help me. And I'm passing the information on to you, future-souls.

'Heat - she was my mother - said my father came from one of the rust islands out in the ocean. He was called Alchemist. I reckon I inherited all my tech-know from him. Long before I was born, Heat worked on trying to discover the truth about history, the history of this place, and the rust islands. I never knew my father, never saw him. Heat wouldn't tell me why they parted, or even whether he was dead or still alive.

'This device I'm using now was his. When he met my mother, it had been in his family a long time, a kind of relic. No-one used it any more, although he would show it to my mother and talk about what it could do, if only someone could work out its secrets. It's like a psychic probe, and it can look into minds, but the mind it reaches most efficiently is that of the land itself. It reads memories, picking up traces of information that float around; thoughts, residue of events. My mother tried to get it to work, but couldn't, so she just wore it around her neck on a thong, a keepsake of her love affair with Alchemist. It came to me when she died. And, you know, I think it was waiting for me. I didn't bother trying to fix it with any of the tools he left at my mother's house. Half of them are arcane to me - I don't know their function. Heat used some of them as ornaments.

'Anyway, I cleaned the device as best I could, bathed it in moonlit water, hung it out beneath the sun, buried it in quartz for twenty-eight days. And it came alive for me. I put it behind my ear and it took a hold. With my thoughts, I ask it to record, and it does. It's the same for receiving data.'

Shade's voice fell to silence, although I could still detect some sweet echo of her thoughts. Wistfulness, questions. She stood gripping the segmented bamboo rail of the bridge, and through her, I could feel its warm smoothness. She peered down the estuary, towards the ocean, but it was hidden now by a low-skirt mist. She narrowed her eyes, looking for silhouettes in the fog. It was as if she was talking to me, yet at the same time, it was me who was talking.

'If you look really hard, you can still see the rust islands at night from here... I want to go out there, but whenever I make the preparations to hire a scudder, I just change my mind. Feel uneasy about it. Perhaps all that talk of ghosts when I was kid somehow stuck in my head.' She laughed aloud, then sobered. 'It's dangerous though, lots of ways to die out there: stray viruses, rusting hulks, blow holes, whirlpools, poisonous flotsam, you name it.'

Grey out, shadow out, migraine fuzz. Pain!
I couldn't disengage fast enough. It was like an electric shock.
'Shut if off, Luce, shut it off!'
Ghosts of sea-air currents; my breath. For a moment, I was dreaming in between the two worlds; micro-circuits and myths. Deep disorientation.
Lucrezia checked my vital signs. I checked out normal. 'Enough for one day?' suggested my AI with concern.
I slept for a few hours, hot and uncomfortable on my narrow bed, despite the air conditioning. Then, I stumbled out of the cabin into the blinding, white sunlight of morning.
My friend, Truce, was hunkered down in the grey dust next to the truck, sorting samples, his naked back plastered with unattractive UV filter. He turned round as I shambled towards him.
'Hi there, Serami!' He frowned. 'What you been up to in there? You look ragged.'
I decided not to tell him. 'Was sleeping,' I said, elaborating a yawn.
Truce stared at me for a moment, his nose wrinkled up. 'Have you heard that Lena can't make contact with the retrieval bus?'
I shrugged. 'No. What's the problem? Interference?'
'Maybe. She's been getting weird responses from the Facility too. Can't get direct access, but just receives recordings.'
'There could be any reason for that,' I said.
He nodded. 'I know.'
Our stares locked, though neither of us voiced our thoughts. We'd had problems getting the licence, never mind the funding, for this dig. The most paranoid of us thought there was a cover up going on, that certain individuals high up in the Historical Facility didn't want to risk us upsetting any

of their air-tight little theories about the past.

Before we'd left the Organic, Elenov had tried to requisition a craft of our own, but had been denied. We were out on our own, an unimaginably long way from the nearest inhabited world or station. Until the retrieval bus came, we were stranded. I didn't want to think about the implications of that just yet.

Truce made an effort to brighten up. 'It's no problem. Lena will make contact with someone eventually.' He jerked his head at the sky. 'There are a lot of people out there.'

I had visions of us being rescued by some rusting old merchant freighter, having to spend several lifetimes in cold storage to get back home. I smiled. 'Yeah, course there are.'

On the second day, as Lucrezia and I progressed with our study of Shade's recording, we discovered that the visuals or the sound would quite often muzz out completely, leaving a forlorn static that sounded like some long-distance alert beacon. By dusk, I was beginning to wonder whether the remainder of the chip was unreadable. Then Lucrezia found another clean space.

In the red evening light, I climbed the lookout tower on the left bank of the estuary and went to sprawl in the late light. Tilted on my foam-bed, I could look into the horizon where the sea skies swallowed another sunset, stubbing out the day. Sometimes, there's a mist out there and the island lights seem webbed and smeared, like a dream receding, losing clarity, becoming opaque.

I took Lucrezia from my pocket and we plugged into the next place in the old recording where the degeneration decreased.

Immediately, I was on-line.

I could see a city: ziggurats within transparent ziggurats, shattered in places to create yawning canyons. The elements had carved a chaotic expression from the city remains. Strange mosses grew on the metals. The landscape was a camera obscura of the sequinned night-sky: blue-white and acid yellow glows of chemical light, and the shivering pulsations of firelight; illuminations that signalled human life.

I saw skeletal towers of bamboo and crystal fibre and massive domes that looked partly vegetable, partly manufactured. Ribbons of aerial walkways intersected high overhead, and below them lay a labyrinth of wider, silvery trails: canals. The city was beautiful in its chaos, but was this a culture emerging from destruction or sinking into it?

Shade climbed down from the walkway but, for a while, only static filled my head. I felt impatient, angry. *No, don't go!* Shade's senses had degenerated into noise, but for audio.

Then, a new voice filtered in: male. The words he spoke were disembodied and at first, I could make no sense of them. I recognised, in Shade's mind, a frisson of interest. She desired this man, but she planned to hide the fact. He was the subject of study, and she must remain objective.

Abruptly, the visuals were restored, and I saw him through her eyes. Dark, thin, with penetrating black eyes. His hair hung to his waist, and his face was scored with ritual scars.

They were sitting on either side of a table, with rough cups set before them. The sweet taste of a fruity liquor was in Shade's mouth. From her mind, I picked up the man's name, which she was repeating silently like a mantra, throughout their conversation. Firetongue. He was renowned for his forthright speech; an Earthwalker, a member of a secretive clan who claimed to guard ancient knowledge. She was unsure how much he'd tell her, but was reassured by the fact he'd agreed to speak to her at all. Perhaps she fascinated him.

He took a sip of his liquor, gazing at her with amusement. 'You must know, that among my clan, only shamans may use the earth-ways,' he said.

Shade knew she must be careful, delicate with her words. 'This is not the earth-ways, Fire. I'm following my mother's tradition. She was a historian.'

Firetongue wrinkled up his nose. 'Yet you want to know

what you think I know.' He smiled. 'Why does an historian want to learn the secret language of the earth?'

I could feel Shade's heart racing, yet her voice was serene. 'Well, it's not exactly that. History leaves traces - all around us, and I use a special device to pick these traces up.' She lifted her hair to show him where the device nestled around her ear.

'Sounds like stealing to me.'

Shade shook her head. 'Really, it's not. Let me explain about it. Whenever an event occurs, it leaves a kind of energy behind it; a memory, like a photograph. The device I use searches everywhere for transmissions, but it's easier to catch things at night, because then I can relax and concentrate.' She leaned back and smiled. 'I am the aqueduct that meanders from one mountain-top to another.'

He grinned back at her. 'It still sounds like stealing to me. An easy way to take the thoughts of the earth. You should work to earn that knowledge.'

Shade lifted her hands to him. 'OK, I know your people use psychotropics and starve their bodies and have weird spiritual experiences. But they're not historians. My method might seem too easy to you, but I want the information for a different reason.'

'Which is?'

'I think we need to know the truth now. People conjecture about the past, and make up myths about it. Everything's got wrapped up in stories.'

Firetongue laughed. 'If your device is so powerful, what do you need me for?'

Shade shook her head. 'Some things have been... I don't know... *protected,* perhaps. I think your people, the Earthwalkers, have retained a lost and forbidden knowledge.'

'And you want me to share these secrets with you?'

She shrugged, wondering whether she'd spoken too plainly, perhaps offended him. 'Not all your secrets, no. I respect your traditions. But all I need is one clue, just one, and then me and my device can work out the rest. I don't want to strip your gods of divinity, Fire. No matter what I discover, your beliefs are still valid.' She felt, too late, her last remark was patronising.

Firetongue studied her for a moment. 'What *are* your thoughts on gods, then?' He seemed to be testing her. What were the answers he wanted to hear?

Shade cleared her throat, snatching time to compose her answer. 'I'm not saying I think they were human, but...' She paused. 'The legends speak of a primitive race who lived here, who had no knowledge of their own. Then the gods came from the sky, cast out by their own kind, and they owned forbidden knowledge. This, they passed to the people, who began to worship water, who built their temples and their cities around networks of canals, designed in specific patterns. It all *means* something, Fire. There's a secret in the patterns. Something...' She raised her shoulders in a shrug, daring to glance into his eyes. His expression was bland. She couldn't tell what he was thinking.

The intensity of her desire to learn his secrets, and the certainty that he *could* help her, flooded my awareness in a dull, unassuageable ache. I observed her feeling of need, that she must convince him to speak with her, trust her, and, finally, share his mind with her. It was all so real. I was *there*, with her, a discarnate entity within her brain, afraid she'd sense my presence, that I'd distract her. I wanted to advise her how to proceed, how to coax Firetongue to co-operate, sure that simply by thinking the words, she would hear them. *Ask to share his mysteries. Ask him to show you his way...*

Then Lucrezia buzzed in, to remind me this was just a recording and would I like her to stop the show for now?

I decided to give it a rest for the night. Lucrezia had bitched about me experiencing the recording twice in one day, and she was right to complain. Her welfare relied upon my well-being, and I couldn't blame her for her acts of self-preservation. Nobody wants a second-hand, empathic AI.

My body ached and tickled as it recovered from the sensory-noise effects. I found it hard to co-ordinate mind and body for a while. As I stood up, flashback images pulsed behind my eyes and I wondered whether I was steady enough to brave the ladder to the ground.

Lucrezia discreetly expanded flight vanes and noiselessly rose to a hover. She obviously did not trust my balance enough to snuggle back into my pocket.

I was OK until I reached the bottom when, suddenly, a city manifested around me. I saw steel and plastic cables, interwoven with vines and twisted tree-limbs; gantries of bamboo and wood; rope-nets and metal sheets; habitation platforms and a canal aqueduct that meandered overhead, from one mountain-top to another.

This must be a memory, I reasoned bravely, trying not to panic. I observed objectively as the images shivered slowly from a scattering of pre-thought into linear recall. Then it was gone, and the rubbish heap extended all around me, filled with the ghosts of a lost age. Only the estuary was beautiful with its firefly lights. I felt depressed again.

'Luce!' She alighted on my shoulder. 'I got flashback then.'

'Not unexpected.'

Lucrezia buzzed around my head as I walked back to the settlement. 'Tell me what you experienced this time,' she said.

I related all that I could recall. 'Our dead friend is poking around in the past, I think, like we are. But it was getting a bit creepy. I was assimilating too much, making it part of my reality. Not good.'

'I did warn you.

'Yes, you did. But you know I'll have to go on.'

'That too is expected. I must monitor you carefully for psychosis.'

'Naturally. Luce, I think this is really big. I get the feeling, well, this girl's going to show us all we wanted to know coming here. We must make hard copy of this material as we go along.'

Even though I was wary of what Shade might do to me, scared she'd make some kind of possession attempt, albeit unwittingly, I couldn't wait to get back at the recording and discover more. I knew that, before I progressed any further, I should tell Elenov about my research, but I was enjoying the privacy, and even after two meetings was becoming possessive enough about my ghost-girl not to want to share her. Elenov would probably decide that our resident psych, Bralle, should examine the chip. His training was more suitable for the task, and his personality profile adapted for it. I knew what I was doing was dangerous, but the danger had hooked me, and I could not surrender the thrill.

Also, Elenov had other problems to attend to. Lena had still not made contact with either the Organic or the retrieval bus. Much as no-one wanted to admit it, it was looking increasingly as if we'd been abandoned. I was aware of the mounting hysteria in my colleagues, but since I'd discovered Shade, the need to return home was not quite so desperate. I felt I had work to do here, and the retrieval bus' arrival in two days' time might curtail that. By now, no-one believed the bus would turn up at all. While everyone else began to panic, I remembered my talk with Truce. Someone would find us eventually.

The next time I accessed the chip, Lucrezia had to spin forward past a ravel of degraded data, more static, until we reached a section of pure thought and unblemished recording. I zapped on line and...

...fell into a rain storm of awareness. Energy sizzled through me, and cells of information whirled around me. I nearly disengaged. What had she done? What had she been doing while I wasn't there? I blinked, and it was a bizarre aural-visual experience, a slick sound that matched the sensation, a flickering of sight, retinas retaining the image of an inverted silhouette.

I heard and felt a subsonic, rushing noise throughout my mind and body. I saw, with more than my eyes, wild, shivering patterns evolving in and out of chaos. Fractal growth.

My breathing was tidal, a soothing motion, with the

backbeat of a rhythmic heart. I was no longer simply She/I, but She/*he*/I: a neurosomatic melding.

As my body shuddered into being in that world, I realised that she was making love with Firetongue. I could smell him, taste him, hear his grunting breath. His cheek was pressed to her cheek, and violating tendrils of her recording device had crept into his hair, his thoughts.

Now, cresting ecstasy, Shade travelled his mind and observed his memories. He did not know what she was doing. She had seduced him, clearly, and was now stealing his secrets.

This was not the kind of party I wanted to gatecrash unawares, but before I could disengage, I descended into pure experience.

Sparkling air; his nerve-endings, a blanket of sensual motion. She drew in breath, clenched her muscles, experienced the sensation in his loins. The ignition swirled and clustered into a viscous electric charge that, via her spinal column, rushed smooth and snaky into her mind. Real-time vision roared on a monochrome flight path through our brain.

And there was the image of the aqueduct, revolving like a gargantuan DNA spiral.

'They *were* *h*uman!' The words formed in her mind in time to an orgasmic tremor.

I felt my body spasm. My eyes rolled backwards into their sockets.

Then, the recording ran into a cascade of disjointed image segments; landscapes, sounds, scents - split seconds of random, sweet, semi-corrupted fragments, shattering like a waterfall in her mind. If this was information exchange, we did not have sex as good nowadays.

When the recording degraded into white noise, I was almost hysterical. I needed to know more, experience more.

Obligingly, Lucrezia fastforwarded and I got deep into the rush of noise and prickly touch. I knew I should disengage until we found a clean track again, but was too impatient. If the experience damaged me, I was beyond caring.

Then the world bloomed around my senses once more, and I exhaled deeply in relief. We were strolling along the beachwalk with Firetongue beside us. Foliage to either side of the creaking boards exuded a pungent, evening scent. The sky was scarlet and orange, fading to deepest purple up where the stars began.

Shade and I did not hold hands with our lover, although it seemed as if our bodies were touching. If he'd realised we'd eavesdropped on his thoughts, he held no grudge. We were easy with one another, walking through the fiery dusk.

We wandered out along the stubs of long-eroded sea cliffs, comfortable in silence. Firetongue lit a pipe and we shared a smoke as we walked. To the right, placid ocean reflected the lurid sky, while to the left, the land sloped gently downwards, jungled by city and biomass. We paused and looked down upon the silver arteries of the canals, the terraces of lock-gates.

'Tell me about the water,' we said.

Firetongue leaned down and kissed our hair. 'Do I need to tell you anything now?'

We could tell he believed our invasion of his mindsoul was based on purely carnal urges. 'Yes. Tell me what you know.' We reached for one of his long hands, squeezed his fingers.

'OK. Let's talk.' His voice was amused, but now, because feeling had ignited within him, he was also curious about us.

We sat down upon the damp evening grass and watched the glint of the water below. 'Fire, the myths tell us that, in the past, there was no fresh water here, but that cannot be true. Without water, there could not have been people. So there was water, and there were people, but they must have been... primitive, disorganised. The gods, whoever they were, came and built the canals, and from there on, civilisation was born. But the strangers must have given far more than just the instructions on how to build an irrigation system. Even now, the waterways are regarded as mystical. Everybody knows there's some kind of secret attached to them, but no-one questions it or speaks about it. It's like historical amnesia. We've forgotten something important about our own past.'

Firetongue looked down at us indulgently, reached to stroke our hair. 'Why is it so important to you, Shade? You're obsessed. Can't you just accept what is?'

We shook our head. 'No. As a historian, I am fascinated by discrepancies. A long time ago, some great change happened here, a massive technological advance. Almost overnight, an extremely primitive culture acquired science and technology. The gods came. I have my theories about it. We have to know what really happened in order to know ourselves.'

Firetongue sighed. 'Have you ever considered that the gods might just be a representation of our own evolution? We learned how to advance because we discovered the spirit of the earth. The gods are the spirits of nature. From them, we can learn all we need to know, and if we listen properly, with open ears, we can hear the whisper of their wisdom.'

We turned to look up at him. 'No, Fire. People came here from... from somewhere else. People with more knowledge. From the sky. Isn't that what the myths tell us?' And in our mind, the furtive thought: *Isn't that what your memory tells us?*

He laughed. 'You're crazy, romantic, a dreamer!'

We laughed too, to humour him. 'Perhaps I am. But think about my idea. Isn't there anything in your clan tradition that might back up my theory?'

He exhaled slowly. 'The rust islands,' he said.

'Yes?'

'That was where the gods built their city. They abandoned it after so many years. They vanished. But they left the legacy of their knowledge behind.'

We sighed, eyes closed. 'Why did they leave?'

He touched our shoulder, the hollow of our spine, with his long fingers. 'They told only the wisest of the ancient people. The knowledge was forbidden. I can't tell you more, Shade. These are secret memories. The shamans know them and relive them through the earth. Go out to the rust islands with your clever little device. Maybe the gods will speak to you there.'

We leaned against him. 'Thank you, Fire. Thank you.'

Like the closing scene of a romantic film, the image faded out, gently, with beautiful flares of colour. The chip died on me.

The retrieval bus had not arrived. Neither had Lena been able to make contact with the facility on the Organic. Elenov had kept her cool and quoted the usual platitudes about interference, sun-spots and transatmospheric storms. Only the most stupid were mollified by that. I wasn't bothered about it. Something was taking form in my head, something so momentous, I dared not even believe it. Was Shade's discovery somehow linked with us? Like Firetongue's gods, we had come down from the sky and been stranded here. Were we re-living some ancient event? Perhaps that was why the authorities had been so touchy about granting us a licence for this expedition. There was a secret here.

When I looked around the shanty towns of the abos, I was filled with despair. There was nothing there to remind me of the green, the people, the inland waterways thronged with coloured barges. I was suffering withdrawal, because Luce had hit a problem with the recording, and was taking her time smoothing it out. I knew she thought I needed a rest and was probably dragging her circuits on purpose. I pined for my Shade and her lover, who seemed to be my lover too. I wondered what conversations they were having, what Shade was thinking and whether she had learned the things she wanted to know. Had she visited the rust islands yet? I felt strongly that it was all continuing without me, and that rather than containing a fragment of Shade's world, the recording chip was a doorway, an interface, right into it.

Truce came up to me outside my cabin and complained I wasn't spending much time with the team nowadays. 'You mustn't be depressed,' he said. 'We've got to live with this.'

'With what?'

He shrugged. 'Staying here. If we're stuck, we've got to think about making this place habitable.'

I shook my head. 'Someone will come. It's too far-fetched to think we're stranded here, attractive though the thought may be at times!'

'I thought you were pining for the Organic.'

I glanced at him. 'I don't know what I'm pining for, actually.'

He laughed good-naturedly. 'Come back to us, Serami. Stop wandering. Nobody knows where your head is nowadays.'

I smiled in what I hoped was a convincing manner.

'You're missing so much,' he told me. 'We need to think about how we can sustain ourselves, perhaps indefinitely. Lem thinks that some of our bio-analysis equipment could be converted to help with agriculture and...'

'Woah! We're not supposed to give primitive cultures knowledge of our technology!'

'Neither are we supposed to get abandoned!' Truce rolled his eyes. 'Think about it. These people are the descendants of our ancestors. They had it all once, anyway.'

'Not exactly. Anyone with a gram of sense, incentive and nous about them abandoned planet and ran for the colonies. What was left behind...' I gestured around me. '...was rubbish. It might be dangerous to give these people any of our knowledge.' I don't know why I argued that way. Why should I care? I wanted warmth, comfort and good food, just like anyone else.

'We could do with your help,' Truce said hopefully.

I sighed. 'OK.'

He brightened. 'Good. Come along to the canteen with me and take a look at the plans Lem's created. Interesting design. We need an efficient water system, and the existing wells are certainly not that. Lem thinks they should be excavated, cleaned up. The town would be built around a canal system...'

'What?' Presentiment furred my skin. 'He's made plans?'

'Well, yes... What's up?'

I grabbed his arm. 'I want to see them. Now.'

There it was. A beautiful hologram created by Lem's AI. He'd put a lot of imagination into the design, and a lot of wishful-thinking. The rubbish tips were blanketed with green, with foliage and with crops. A mandala of canals circled and bisected the greenery. And there was the aqueduct, a graceful serpent linking the mountain-tops, carrying water down into Samedi Lake. 'I based it on my personal mandala,' Lem said, waving at the image. 'The one my analyst gave me back home.' He laughed. 'Now I'll turn it into a town. Pretty spiritual, huh?'

I nodded. 'Yeah, great. How do you propose we build all this?'

'We've found a form of bamboo growing a few clicks north of here,' Truce said. 'Should be able to cultivate it, use it for building materials.'

'Bamboo?'

'Yes. Are you OK, Serami?'

The bridges were strung from hill-top to hill top, daring aerial walkways. Lem's hologram even had little people walking across their swaying expanses. If I looked close enough, would one of them be Shade? I felt dizzy; sick, but elated.

I fled back to Lucrezia. 'Plug me in, Luce! I need to experience the last segments. Now!'

We must be on the brink of some great discovery that would blow our theories about the past into infinity. Lucrezia urged me to speak to Elenov about this, but I was still reluctant. One more time, I said, just one more time. I must communicate with her again. This time I intended to try and make her aware of my presence.

Shade had been in the rust islands for several days. Her skin was itching from the spores puffed from the lichens that grew on the rotting metal. She was surrounded by a surreal vista of what looked like skeletal scaffolding. There was little metal to be seen; everything was furred by the lichens - fire-red, luminous green, dull yellow.

She hadn't found anything. Others had been there, hundreds of years before, and picked the place clean. Every day, she came across timid mud-larks scavenging for any last morsels, who fled like ragged birds from the sight of her.

She looked at the strange ruins and wondered what kind of beings the gods had been. It was hard to imagine any human body feeling comfortable in these surroundings. Her device had been unable to pick up any information of use. She was squatting down on a wide deck that was filigreed with rot holes, staring out over the ocean. Was this the end of her quest? I sensed her despondency.

Don't give up, Shade.

It was then that she sensed me. Her spine stiffened. She became alert. Her hand fluttered to behind her ear. 'I know you're there,' she whispered. '*Speak to me!*

Keep looking!

Lucrezia's voice intruded. 'She can't hear you, Serami. It's something else she senses, perhaps something she wants to believe in.'

All the time I'd spent with Shade, she'd used her device for recording. Now, she was receiving. She closed her eyes and the world went black for me too. But even as she received, the device recorded the information. I felt her mind straining to translate the faint, gritty images that flickered like grey static across her inner eye. It was like watching a badly tuned transmission. Earth memories.

She got to her feet, with her eyes still closed. Carefully, using only a kind of sixth sense, she began to walk across the treacherous, fragile deck, letting the ancient messages guide her. For a moment, too brief, it all came back: images like old movie frames.

I could see now what the rust islands were: a hastily-constructed factory plant.

Then, through Shade, I saw the people. They were standing outside a facility of some kind, laughing together as if posing for a photograph. Their skins were brown, and their clothes, which looked vaguely like uniforms, were dusty and well-worn. Some wore necklaces and bangles fashioned from shells and driftwood. The gods.

One woman stood slightly apart from the rest, her hands deep in her trouser pockets. She had a strong face, with a wry, crooked smile. Her dark hair was cut square around her shoulders, although her thick fringe was pushed back with a bandanna. I recognised her, even though for a few moments I didn't realise exactly who she was. Then, a shock of adrenaline coursed through my muscles, made my legs twitch with a primitive urge to flee. I was looking at an image of myself, and there was Truce and Lena standing beside me, with other members of the team grouped behind; Elenov hunkered down in front of us, clearly in command. It seemed like a weird joke that had come back on me. I couldn't grasp the implications. The image of myself seemed to stare right into me, as if I were the camera's eye. Then, perspective shifted.

Now Shade looked back towards land, up the estuary. Her city did not exist yet. What lay there was a strange, colourless sprawl, but with localised areas of green. Building must have begun on the canals already.

'What happened to you?' Shade cried aloud. 'What happened?' Her voice seemed to scare the ghosts away, for the images broke up into grey muzziness once more. She opened her eyes, gasping, and saw a flapping curtain of sea-birds lift off the estuary.

'Damn!' she said. 'Damn!'

Shade, it's me! I'm here... She could not hear me.

She began to march back the way she'd come and in her anger was not quite so careful with her feet. Perhaps she really had invoked the gods. One moment, I was with her out in the sea air, the next there was a splintering, groaning sound and the visuals went hay-wire. I thought the chip had gone strange on me again, but then realised that Shade had fallen through the deck. My skin broke out in a cold sweat.

Was she injured? Dead?

Shade! Get up!

I heard her groan, experienced her anxiety as she tested her limbs for breaks. Nothing more than a few scrapes. She had landed on something yielding. The walls of the place she'd dropped into were laced with corrosion; ragged holes let in the light. But in the dimness, she could see that something had been etched deeply into the disintegrating metal. It looked like some kind of ancient wall painting, a picture found in the recesses of a tomb. Shade stood up, went to examine it. She took out a small torch from her belt and ran its beam over the pocked lines. A message from the gods?

Here, where the aqueduct meanders from hill-top to hill-top, here where the cluttered shores of Samedi Lake hides in its valley. A cave. A tomb. Where treasures lie. The sky woman sits in the cave and holds before her a strange device; a weapon, a magic artefact, a talking mirror. Through Shade, I saw myself discover the cylinder at the dig. It was so clear now. Shade was the future, not the past.

I wanted to communicate with her so badly, sure that somehow, through some weird glitch of time, we had made brief contact. None of this was coincidence. We were mixed up in each other, close yet distant. I could not begin to understand why or how this had occurred. Maybe it was a phenomenon conjured by this ancient planet, where the weight of time hung heavily over the seas and mountains; where so much had happened, and the land remembered it all.

Shade examined the picture on the wall, a picture I myself at some future time must leave for her. Then, she was turning away, leaping up for the hole she had made in the ceiling of the chamber, pulling herself out, hurrying, almost frantically back to where her scudder was moored.

She would go to the cave for the secret waited for her there. It must still lie hidden, awaiting the light her entrance would thrust upon it. It had to be there. Some evidence of what had happened to us.

Ultimately, I could not speak to her with my living voice or my mind, but only with my memory. And yet she had seen me; the woman with the bandanna, smiling with her long-dead friends.

Long dead.

Night was grey and silver across the landscape. Outside my cabin, I heard the sound of merriment coming from the canteen. They were all so excited making their plans for a permanent settlement. A pioneer spirit had awoken within them. It seemed bizarre to me; only days ago everyone had been panicking about abandonment.

I stumbled away from the camp, heading out to Samedi Lake. Lucrezia came too, buzzing around me, but not communicating.

A group of abos were sitting around a fire on the diminished shores of the Lake. As I passed them, they looked up at me with curious eyes, as if I was some kind of apparition. Once they were behind me, I heard one of them begin to sing; a monotonous chant. The voice resonated in my head, made me feel dizzy and slightly nauseous. I felt as if I was having to push my body through the resistant air.

The entrance to the shaft had been covered with plasti-sheet and, as I approached, I was sure I heard it flapping in the lake breeze. But once I crested the slope of rubble that led down to the shaft, I saw only a gaping black hole. The sheeting must have blown away. A long time ago.

The landscape was different. Nothing had been built here, but neither did it seem so desolate. To my left, the lake looked healthy and there were numerous little jetties along its shores, where boats were tethered in the darkness. I could hear the sound of wood rubbing on wood, the plashing of wavelets against their hulls. Then, a spectral image of how the lake appeared in my time superimposed itself over the landscape, only to surrender seconds later to the scene of Shade's time. I guessed that if I looked behind me, I would not see the lights of our camp; when I did glance over my shoulder, there was only a grey murkiness like a veil.

This was neither my time nor Shade's, but a strange interface of both. I accepted it fully, as if this was something that happened to me every day. It didn't feel strange, but somehow familiar. What or whose memories was I tapping into though? Landscape dreams?

I went towards the shaft entrance, my heart beating fast. Just as I was about to enter the darkness, someone came out of it in a hurry. We both yelped and jumped back. I looked into a startled face, lit by a greenish light from a lumi-cell.

'Shade!' I said. She would vanish. I was sure she would vanish. Or maybe I would. Was I the ghost or she?

Shade stared at me in what could have been horror or simple disbelief. 'You,' she whispered, and then glanced around herself quickly. I could tell she was shocked, slightly afraid, and wondering whether to run for it.

To reassure her, I reached out and took hold of her hands that were both gripping the lumi-cell. 'It's OK. I'm here. I'm really here.'

She did not flinch away from me. She was warm, alive. If I leaned closer, I knew I'd be able to smell her. Her startled expression was comical. I had to laugh. 'This is incredible. I feel I know you... The rust islands... the device... Listen to me, Shade. You were right: there were no gods, only stranded people, castaways.'

She narrowed her eyes. 'Have *I* made you appear here now?'

I shrugged. 'I don't know. Time is looping around us. We're connected somehow; perhaps like calls to like, even across time.'

Shade managed a smile. 'I've felt your presence,' she murmured. 'I thought it was my imagination, creating an audience for what I was doing.' She reached up behind her ear. 'It must be the device... some weird function everyone had forgotten...'

Suddenly, I was afraid she was going to remove the device and show it to me. My stomach churned, and a white-hot pain shot behind my eyes. I turned away from her. 'No, don't remove it, Shade. It already exists in this time... if this *is* my time. And I think you wearing it is one of the things that's making this possible, if not the *only* thing.'

'OK.'

I turned back to her. She was frowning.

'This is the past... isn't it?'

I shook my head. 'Not exactly. I think we're outside of both times, or somehow hovering between the two. All I know is that I found your recording in this place a while back and I've been interacting with it. You thought you were talking to the future, Shade, but you weren't.'

'So, I was talking to the gods themselves!' She walked past me, and her image seemed to shiver before me. I reached out and held on to her, although she ignored my presumptuous move. 'It's so different,' she said, in wonder, indicating the shifting landscape. Perhaps she saw more of my time than I did. 'So desolate... empty.' She glanced at me. 'You made this place live?'

'Not yet, but I think we will.'

'But how did the device get here? Can I get back?'

I looked behind us, at the entrance to the shaft. Weeds grew around it and some were in flower. I nodded. 'I think you can.'

She rubbed her face. 'I have to ask you things. Quickly. What happened? Where did you go?'

I laughed. 'I don't know. We haven't gone yet, have we!' I told her about the team, how we were stranded and then how I'd found the cylinder and all that had happened since. She was interested in Lem's plans; his realisation of his personal mandala.

'Is that the only the only thing that makes the canals sacred? An engineer's private joke?' She shook her head in bewilderment.

'Perhaps legends will grow up around it. I think, because of what Firetongue told you, that we must leave here eventually. Us, or our descendants. Some freighter will find us, or perhaps things will change on the Organic.'

Shade hunkered down beside me in the rubble, picked up a handful of ashy earth and let it sift through her fingers. Then she let her hands dangle between her knees, staring out over the lake. 'Why did they abandon you here? Was it because your people destroyed this world, used it up? What is it they don't want you to find?'

I sighed. 'I don't know. Whatever it is, I think it's long gone; buried, corroded or stolen. Perhaps we'll never know.'

Shade shook her head. I can't believe I've been given this.' She squinted up at me. 'Hey, what's your name?'

'Serami.'

'Serami the goddess.' She grinned. 'Perhaps I should start a cult!' Then she frowned. 'But how will my recording get back to you. It doesn't make sense.'

'Leave it here,' I said.

She raised an eyebrow at me. 'But you've already discovered it in this time.'

I raised my hands. 'So. We don't know what's going on, other than that time is weird. It's the only thing you can do. Don't show the recording device to me. Just leave it back in there somewhere.' I flapped my hand at the dark entrance to the shaft.

'In the old shrine?'

'Is that what it is?'

She nodded. 'I suppose I could... bury it or something.' She did not sound convinced.

'Just do it, Shade.' I was finding it hard to keep her image before me now. It was as if I was only wishing her to be there, visualising her. 'Do it now! Go!'

She stood up, reached out to me with one hand, but I felt only a shiver against my skin. Whatever fracture of time had allowed our meeting was closing up; I could sense it. Perhaps she could too. With one final glance behind her, and a grim smile, she walked back into the entrance of the shaft.

I filled up with emotion that spilled out of my eyes. It was over now. I knew we would not meet again. I sensed grief within me, but also a kind of awakening, as if I'd found something I could never lose.

It was only when I heard Lucrezia's soft buzzing whine at my shoulder that I realised I had put my hands over my face. 'Serami?' Lucrezia hovered in front of my face.

'She was here,' I said. 'Shade. We talked.'

Lucrezia was silent for a moment, a most human reaction I thought, but she was probably just scanning the surroundings for some kind of evidence. 'That is impossible,' she said at last.

I shook my head. 'No. I'm not crazy, Luce. I know what I saw and heard.' Around me, the lake was as it always was; a vast shallow puddle, devoid of life. Only irrigation would change that. It hadn't happened yet.

'Time to go,' Lucrezia said sternly. 'I think you've experimented enough.'

We went back to my cabin, because I didn't want to face anybody yet. Already the experience at the lake was contracting in my memory. I knew that, eventually, it would seem like nothing more than a dream.

Lucrezia would not accept I'd witnessed a real event. She told me it was impossible because she had been with me the whole time, that I'd simply stopped walking, let out a yelp and put my head in my hands. She'd seen and sensed nothing. Had I been hallucinating? Now, I couldn't be sure.

The following day I went out to the lake again, and after hesitating at the entrance to the shaft for a while, I went inside. What I expected to find was some evidence of Shade's visit, but of course there was none. The cylinder was in my pocket, and there was no eerie duplicate lying where I'd first found it.

Lucrezia has theories for what happened - some kind of hallucinatory displacement, brought on my interface with the recording. After analysing the situation, she suggested that the information we'd received from the cylinder had somehow been created as we'd accessed it, that the device might have been something other than a journal chip; perhaps some sort of leisure VR device that stimulated the imagination.

I didn't want to believe that and thought we should attempt to recreate the whole experience. Maybe I could even meet Shade again that way. But when we tried to access the data once more, we discovered that it had degenerated completely. Lucrezia said that the corrosion must have accelerated, damaging the cylinder irreparably.

Still, I sit every evening beside the estuary and gaze out to the place where the rust islands will be. Boats bob upon the placid waters; firefly fishermen trawl for shining treasures. I know that in some future time, Shade's life continues, only now the memory of her meeting with me is lodged firmly in her mind. I speak aloud to her sometimes, wondering whether some dream-shred of my consciousness can somehow leak through my time into hers. This old world: it stirs in its sleep and dreams. We are simply part of the dreaming, I think.

The sky is infinite above me, and I think about how the universe buzzes with unseen life. Here I am: so small upon this spinning ball. How young we are. How little we know.

Built on Blood

The morning of the Carnival of Day. Long Green Meadows estate waking up again. The grey is kissed by dawn, a red light stains the windscreens of the auto wrecks sagging along the kerbs. Even the two burnups, a derelict pub and a deserted grocer's shop, crooked black relics of last week's riot, are lent a certain gothic grandeur by this innocent radiance. Scrawny animals – cats or rats or some weird estate-bred hybrid of both – slink along the walls of the alleys. Somewhere a child begins to cry, then another and another. The dawn chorus; infant human despair.

Sallyann wakes up from a dream. The moment she opens her eyes the image fades, but she is sure it was terrifying. There is the beginning of a shout in her throat. She stretches out her arms from the bed and touches both sides of her small room. It is a morning ritual with her. She doesn't know why she does it, but she can't stop. The day can't begin without it. She rolls onto her side in the narrow bed, shrugging back the new Community Care-supplied sleeping bag (courtesy of registered charity number 5,000,123). Everyone in Long Green Meadows has been given these recently. Sallyann has to admit they're warm, but she doesn't like the flowers on them. It seems cynical somehow, because there are never any flowers in Long Green Meadows, unless you count the ones in those big tubs at the shopping mall, but they're always being burned by the kids and, anyway, they're artificial. Sallyann's clothes cover the small space between bed and wall, and it takes her a few minutes' rummaging to dig out the two precious roll-ups her friend Danny gave her last night. Danny lives in the fortress three streets away; two houses knocked into one and windowed by iron. Motorbikes are parked in the yard behind the house; one of them is Danny's. She'd met him in the vaccination clinic of all places.

He'd been sitting across the waiting room frowning at the muzak speaker overhead; a fierce, forlorn warrior, constrained, with embarrassment, in an inappropriate setting. His head was shaven, but for the tangle of dreads at the back, his scalp covered with curling blue Celtic tattoos. Sallyann, pretending to read a pamphlet on sexual hygiene, had covertly admired his facial bone structure with its thin fringe of Lucifer beard, until he'd asked her what she was staring at. They'd started sparring then, a ritual of mutual circling and snarling. She'd thought he didn't like her and had covered her disappointment with expletive gusto, but he'd been waiting for Sallyann after she'd come out of the nurse's booth. They'd ended up going to Elli's Drop In together to drink de-caf and share complaints about life, their right arms aching from the needle and beginning to swell. They were friends; nothing else. Neither of them felt the need for anything else.

Last night, Danny and Sallyann had climbed out onto the roof of the biker house to watch the sky. They were looking for stars because earlier Sallyann had heard on TV that shooting stars would be visible at 11 p.m. All they'd seen however, was the orange sicklight of the town and the ghost of the moon, but somehow the air had seemed sweeter up there. There'd been a breeze to muss their hair. The rotors from uptown had provided a lightshow of sorts. They carried cautious police units, who never set foot in Long Green Meadows, or else inner city rich kids, raving out in the sky, hovering over the sickpit for a perilous thrill. Somewhere sirens howled and at midnight, a Health Company flyer had winged silently over the estate, distributing Dominic Blair photopics, with the lyrics to his latest song on the back. 'Dominic Blair is King!' declared the slogans. 'See him live at the Carnival!'

Danny had read the lyrics aloud and said, 'Lucky world. Tomorrow, there's Carnival.' And he and Sallyann had laughed together, sharing a thin, bitter cigarette Danny had rolled earlier.

'Are you going uptown to watch it?' Sallyann had asked.

Danny shrugged and gave her one of those weird, thinking looks, perhaps the thing she liked best about him. He screwed up his nose. 'Nah...' Like her, he was intrigued by the prospect of the Carnival, but felt he'd be betraying some inner code by attending it.

'I am,' Sallyann had said defiantly.

'Why bother, Sal? It'll just remind you of all the things you hate about this country. Why bother?'

'I dunno.' She hugged her knees and peered through narrowed eyes across the estate. Parts of it were completely without light. In a couple of places, dull fires were burning, indistinct figures dancing against the flames. She could see a gang of kids on the rooftops a few streets away, leaping from roof to roof.

Danny, in comparison to Sallyann, is a very rich man. He has the protection of his tribe and the tribe are wolf-hungry and wolf-canny. They always have money, but Sallyann knows better than to ask how they get it. There are no police in Long Green Meadows; the bikers are the nearest there is to such a force. They kill rapists, child molesters and psycho murderers, but are generally involved themselves in most other criminal activities, which they prefer to conduct off their own territory. Sometimes there are terrible battles with biker tribes of other estates; people are killed. And yet, Sallyann knows it's the only way to survive, and she appreciates the little luxuries Danny can provide for her: rolling tobacco, fiery alcohol, pure drugs. Still, she'd be Danny's friend whether he was rich or not, because he can think, and sometimes she needs someone around her who can do that, just to remind her she can think as well.

Sallyann lives in Honeysuckle Crescent with her mother. All the tower blocks and tenements of the previous century are long gone, but the new houses, which were erected hurriedly in the first few years of the new century in an attempt to control public unrest, are tiny and drab. So, they'd had fitted kitchenettes and economy heating, and a government minister had even come to open the estate, but now, ten years on, the houses are beginning to fall apart. The boom had been brief and had burnt itself out quickly. Now, urban decay has reverted to conditions last seen in the 90s – and worse. There is mould everywhere and big shadowy insects. The little gardens are full of tall, yellow weeds and garbage. The road surfaces have broken up; the only cars in Long Green Meadows are stolen ones, used up quickly and trashed. All the patches of community lawn have worn away to dry, dry dust, where the gangs of feral children play. The place is cancerous and dying. Danny had once said this might be because Long Green Meadows had been built on the site of an old plague pit.

'Is it *really?*' Sallyann had asked, quite perturbed.

Danny had shaken his head. 'Doubt it. I saw something like that in an old movie once though.'

He'd watched one of the riots from the top of the biker house and apparently that had been like the old movie too, when the ghosts of the angry dead had gone crazy and destroyed the estate that had scabbed their resting ground. Since then, Sallyann and Danny had made up an alternative history for Long Green Meadows. It passed the time.

'We could get someone to make a film of it!' Sallyann had said, daring to fantasise optimistically.

It cued a look from Danny. 'Lovey, this already *is* a film.'

Sallyann had laughed then, but he hadn't.

Downstairs, Sallyann's mother is boiling the kettle. Sallyann can hear every detail of her mother's movement; she clears her throat, her hip brushes the edge of the table as she sidles towards the sink. The house might as well be one big room, Sallyann thinks, and then wonders whether, if it was, they might have more space.

Her mother is a young woman. She had Sallyann when

she was fifteen. Now, she's thirty-two and her daughter is a woman too. She's called Mel. Even though Mel won't discuss her past with anyone, Sallyann knows her mother came from somewhere quite different to Long Green Meadows. She suspects that, contrary to most people's situations, Mel lives on the estate by choice. She is a survivor; lean and lined maybe, but strong as a rope. Sallyann has never seen her depressed. The pair of them live on welfare from the local community care charity, and consequently have to spend a lot of time at the work centre putting useless information into computers, but Mel makes a bit of extra money for them, when she can, by dealing in speed and hash. Mel and Sallyann, like the majority of the people on the estate, are not without money. It's just that there isn't much to spend it on. Mel seems to know everyone in Long Green Meadows. She is called out to attend to would-be suicides, accidental overdoses, marital aggression and has even delivered babies, although the local Health Company fined her for that. Everyone hates the Health Company. The vaccination clinic is covered in graffiti and scorch marks. The windows are heavily wired over. Mel also runs a women's group, which is a phenomenon in itself in such an environment. She believes strongly in female power, and has a planet-sized patience.

Some time ago a woman had come to Mel's house who was dressed in a smart black suit. Sallyann believed her to be a Health Company woman. The woman had stayed for an hour, during which time the two women had talked continuously. Sallyann had been sitting upstairs, confident she'd be able to hear every word, but Mel had turned up the TV, which drowned out the conversation. Sallyann was sure the woman must have come to offer Mel a job, perhaps working for the Health Company itself, for that was surely the direction in which Mel's talents lay. Also, people on the estate trusted her. Mel, however, refused to discuss the matter afterwards. She must have turned down the job.

Sallyann doesn't know whether Mel will want to go to the Carnival or not. On those occasions when they've gone uptown together, Sallyann has always been alert for people in the crowds who might display some sign of recognition for Mel. So far, she has always been disappointed. Mel doesn't like going uptown. Is this because she envies Those That Have, the people who inhabit the dockside complexes, the Japanese garden condos, the air studios? Sallyann doesn't think so.

She pulls on her clothes; ex-patrol trousers Mel bought from an emergency sale, and a thin black t-shirt with a death's-head design on the front. The bikers had given these shirts out to everyone who attended the funeral last time one of their tribe was killed. Sallyann always attends the funerals. Not just because of respect for Danny, although that is one of the reasons, but because there is always plenty to eat and drink. Sallyann pulls on her boots. She doesn't wear underwear, scorning the disposable stretch-paper knickers and bra supplied by the Health Clinic. Her hair is a dark red colour, dyed by the vitamin juice that comes with the welfare cheque. A lot of girls on the estate use the stuff that way. Her face is strong and square and, although pale, surprisingly clear-skinned.

Downstairs, Mel is reconstituting eggs using bottled water. Both Mel and Sallyann prefer the dried eggs, which come from the TruGen labs to the fishy, watery 'real' eggs that they can buy at the mall.

'Coming uptown today?' Sallyann asks. She wants Mel to come with her.

Her mother gives her a sharp look. 'Things to do,' she says. 'Sorry.'

Sallyann shrugs. 'Oh well.'

'Do you want to go?' Mel asks.

Sallyann senses this is a testing question, perhaps to prompt a *talk*. Mel never tries to tell her daughter what to do, but sometimes can't resist criticising her decisions in oratory. 'Yeah, I think so.'

Mel nods. 'Going alone?'

'Dunno. 'Spect someone else will be going.'

'Then keep your eyes open.

'I always do.' Sallyann thinks Mel is trying to imply there's something sinister about the Carnival. It's been a media event for weeks. There will be performance art, circus acts, music, novelty stalls, and fortune tellers. Dominic Blair will appear in public. He's king of the show, a divinely beautiful youth whose face appears everywhere. Teenage girls lust after him in their millions. Mel says he was grown in a vat. There are certain areas of the city where the estate dwellers can attend the carnival. Certain food companies have promised to donate free refreshments. The event is supposed to be a celebration to mark the latest scientific breakthrough; a discovery which means that poverty will soon be a thing of the past. Using the revolutionary method of molecular computers, old land will be reclaimed, machines will be built without human labour in a few seconds, food will be synthesised in any quantity. Sallyann and Mel had watched the cheery documentaries on TV, in between the feminist broadcasts, which claimed the world was in such a state because men were incompetent carers.

'This is a new day for humankind,' the government had announced with misty eyes.

'For us?' Sallyann had asked her mother, turning away from the TV.

Mel had been tatting lace from paper fibre; another subsidiary income. 'I don't believe they've done it,' she'd said. 'I don't believe anything I hear coming out of that thing.' Yet, despite this claim, she watches TV quite a lot.

At first, Sallyann had wanted to believe it, but she found that nearly everyone on the estate, who held an opinion on the subject, agreed with Mel. Including Danny. Even if the breakthrough had happened, it couldn't possibly mean life would improve. The people dared not think otherwise. Hope was a thing of the past.

The dividing line between the estates that ring the city and Long Green Meadows is only one of many, and the inner city itself constitutes an arid expressway, a place where human feet never walk. Sallyann always expects to see dead animals lying on it, but there is never any sign of life or death. Discarded rubber tyres lie in the emergency stop lane. Nobody ever stops there. She is riding the Sprintertram, along with a few other young people from Long Green Meadows, who have also decided to sample the delights of the Carnival. All of them are making sarcastic remarks about it, because really they are embarrassed about wanting to go there. The tram slips down into sodium-lit tunnels, where eerie black cars slither past with hardly any sound. Soon, they will emerge from the comparative emptiness of estate-hugging roadways into the chaotic traffic jam of the city itself. It is eight o'clock in the morning. The journey will take two and a half hours. If someone were to walk on foot, they could make the trip in half an hour, but no one can walk across the expressway. If anyone tried, they'd be quickly picked up by surveillance monitors and arrested for jaywalking. That could mean a revocation of their city pass.

On the tram, there is a terminal where people can convert local currency into that of one of the city banks. It is possible to use estate currency in the city, in certain areas, but generally it is better to use one of the other banks, because it attracts less attention. Naturally, there is a charge for this transaction, but at least today, the exchange rate is favourable. Sallyann is only three shillings down on her original money. In city currency, the shilling is the standard unit.

The air inside the tram heats up as it eases its way into the city concourses. It is as if the vehicle itself is becoming steamed up with impatience. Hawkers jump on board selling tickets for city restaurants, distributing flyers for night-club venues and commercial whore-palaces. The tram crawls past gigantic hoardings: 'The Temple is Built on Blood!' declares one advertisement. It is for a loan company. Gold lettering, ten feet high, superimposed over a photograph of a sunset, against which the stark, black silhouette of an ancient ruin stands. Sallyann cannot remember having seen it before. For a few moments, she ponders the meaning of it, before her friend, a fierce black girl called Terror (loved by many, a femme fatale of cruelty and claws) distracts her by biting her arm. Terror is very excited about the Carnival.

Finally, with the unseasonal heat scorching the polarised windows, the tram eases its way gratefully into one of main city terminals. Sallyann and the others disembark, throwing themselves into the tide of humanity that is milling, in apparent confusion, among the tram stalls. An undeniable sense of celebration pervades the air. Brightly coloured balloons are bobbing against the green glass roof of the terminal. Streamers flutter from the fast food booths, magazines and posters are on sale everywhere, telling people the best spots to visit, what they can find there. A few enterprising street entertainers jostle for space among the crowds, attempting to perform mime plays or juggle knives. A group of Dominic Blair fan club operatives, dressed in white with artificial poppies pinned in their hair, are distributing leaflets offering cheap rates for club membership. Terror takes one, making the remark that she'd only join the club if her membership fee included a night with the King. The girl in white smiles, nods, and makes an escape. Terror laughs greedily.

Against the wall, by the passenger exit doorway, a row of maimed professional beggars are sitting in an untidy line. As Sallyann and her companions shuffle through, Sallyann notices that three or four of the beggars are listlessly beating another, who is lying prone, with their aluminium crutches. People are throwing them coins, smiling.

Outside, Sallyann and Terror link arms and decide to leave their companions behind and venture off alone. Terror thinks the other estate kids are too obvious about where they come from. Sallyann, on the other hand, is considered cool. The main street outside the terminal has been closed to traffic, although a number of cabs are parked along the kerb. Terror buys a photocopied pamphlet off a couple of kids in fancy dress that explains where the main Carnival events are taking place, and to which ones their passes will permit them entrance. Most of the people around them are from other estates, although a few daring inner city kids are there, in blue and green makeup. The hippest of that tribe will attend only the 'alternative' carnival, hoping for a little excitement with the have-nots.

Terror wants to go and see Dominic Blair. His float is due to go down Government Drive at five o'clock. 'We won't be able to see anything,' Sallyann says, who had been hoping they'd be wildly drunk at the reggae festival by then, physically unable to go anywhere.

'Course we will,' Terror insists, prodding the pamphlet in illustration. 'See, we can follow the float to Ecstasy Common. There'll be a concert there. Dominic's ending the Carnival – with us, the scummers.' She flutters her eyelids. 'Aren't we lucky! Look, there's free food and drink. We can't miss it.'

'But the reggae...'

Terror pulls a face. 'Oh come on! It'll be much better at the Blair gig. More for us to help ourselves to, anyway.'

Sallyann can't contain her irritation. 'Hmmph! You should like the reggae better. Isn't it your cultural music or something? Why go to this pathetic commercial shit?'

'We can go to the reggae afterwards,' Terror continues, unperturbed. 'The Blair gig finishes at ten. That leaves hours until the last tram and look, the two sites aren't that far apart.' She then proceeds to indulge in some heavy duty pleading and begging, which Sallyann can't resist.

They walk up to Harmony Mall, caged by the crowds. Here, a street market has been set up and everyone is wearing period costume from the 1990s. Memorabilia is on sale; magazines, clothes accessories, half-used plastic cases of makeup that are dim with age and smell of old women. Sallyann wants to spend her money carefully; preferably on some gold standard hash at the reggae festival, good beer and a few luxury foods she wouldn't normally eat. Terror, however, spends her funds lavishly on tat.

A public address system fills the air with the sound of

joyous songs celebrating the Breakthrough. Video monitors are strung across the streets, displaying promos for all the new products that will soon be available. Terror and Sallyann pause to watch one about cosmetic surgery. There is a foul scene of cutting and slicing, depicting the past, followed by that of an already beautiful woman sitting up in a health centre bed, being given a pill that contains the scientific magick that will transform her shape while she sleeps. And all this will be so cheap! declares a honey-soft voice as the woman sinks back gratefully into her bed and a uniformed nurse draws a gauzy curtain over the window, smiling gently over her shoulder at the patient.

'Man, it's so neat!' Terror says. 'Come on, Sal. What'd you change if you got the chance?'

'My friends,' Sallyann replies dryly.

At two o'clock, they drift into a plaza where a play is being enacted. The play is a musical. It depicts an historical event, the downfall of Christianity, when a huge conspiracy had been discovered by the media. The headlines had screamed that, in fact, all priests and nuns were really Satanists and had been running the paedophile network for centuries. Even though everyone read the daily reports hungrily, they were aware the whole thing was a crazy invention, just like all the other wild *exposes*. But too much damage had been done by the time the media noticed the momentum of the event was slowing down, and decided to unmask as liars the children who'd first informed on the Church.

A woman is standing on the stage, wearing a nun's costume, sweating in the hot smog. 'I am a Bride of Christ!' she sings. To the side, child actors in the roles of lying protagonists, stand in an impish line. Terror is tapping her foot to the tune, because the video's been on TV a lot recently.

'This is boring,' Sallyann announces. 'I want to go to the funfair.'

Reluctantly, Terror allows herself to be dragged away.

Unfortunately, by the time they reach the funfair, the rides have all been temporarily closed. An accident with the Shooting Star has put eight people in hospital. Funfair employees wearing stifling furry animal suits are still hosing down the blood. The broken Shooting Star is a sprawl of huge metal limbs, crumpled over the fast food booths, other rides, the ground. Loudspeakers are churning out the sound of a women's choir singing-in the New Age. 'Sisters, sisters! It is up to us now!' It is a sibilant exhortation, somehow urgent.

Sallyann, eating a pink floss of spun sugar, catches sight of a giant hoarding behind the spines of the Heavenly Spiral ride: 'The Temple is Built on Blood!' She can see now that, in the photograph, the steps of the ruin are crowded with pale figures. Then, a troupe of aerial dancers, borne aloft by rotor suits, swarm across the hoarding in a blitz of red and yellow and neon purple. Sallyann watches them for a moment, then turns away. Daytime firecrackers, thrown by the aerial dancers, explode in unbearable brilliance overhead.

'So where now?' Sallyann asks, throwing away the stick of her spun sugar. She peers over Terror's shoulder, who is busy consulting the pamphlet again.

'There's another fair a few streets away,' Terror says, 'and there should be a parade along soon.'

'What of?'

Terror laughs. 'Working people through the ages!'

'How colourful! Where's the music? I want music.' Sallyann wriggles. 'I wanna dance!'

In the next street, the crowds surge aside from a battalion of waste consumption machines that are humming down the middle of the road eating garbage. 'Mind your children! Mind your children!' yells the consensual artificial voice of the machines.

Terror shouts abuse at a bunch of drunken city boys. 'You want fucking? I'll tell you how to fuck!' she yells. 'C'mere and say that.'

The youths are not aware of Terror's fighting prowess. Sallyann, however, certainly is, and welcomes the prospect of a new diversion. Disappointingly, the youths only slink off uncertainly down the street, drawn by the more passive prey of a couple of younger girls in less aggressive costume further along.

'Shits!' Terror declares.

A few months ago, gangs of inner city youths had been making drunken forays into estate territory, in order to rape women. The biker tribes had stepped up their vigilante patrols and sometimes there'd been bloody fights. Since then, the craze appeared to be dying out.

'I'm gonna come uptown one night with the girls,' Terror growls. 'We're gonna kill some of them.'

Sallyann laughs. 'Here? How? You'd never manage it before you were arrested.'

Terror snarls sideways at her companion. 'You know nothing, lady! It happens. I heard about it. The Razor Bitches came into town from Sweet Pastures a few weeks ago. Killed ten. I heard it.'

'Wasn't on the news,' Sallyann says, aware even before she's finished speaking how naive that sounds. She laughs to compensate. 'But of course it wasn't!'

Terror smirks back. 'Well? Fancy some of that action?'

'Nah.' Sallyann would rather just keep away, or hide behind the protection of Danny and his tribe.

In the humid heat of a giant marquee, Terror and Sallyann drink away the afternoon. At least the beer is kept in refrigerators. This is a luxury Sallyann can't resist. It has been worth coming, she decides, if only for this. Never mind the sleek uptowners swanking their fashions, their accessories and their money before her eyes. Never mind the clean streets and well-stocked shops. She closes her eyes and drinks deep. This is good! Music pounds through the fibres of her body and she sways to its rhythm.

Someone offers her a happiness pill, which she takes and swallows with a mouthful of beer. The pill is large. She can feel it lodged in her throat and swallows and swallows to shift it. Shortly, a pink and green ambience slides over her sight.

She feels completely relaxed and content. Her whole world consists of music and movement. She dances with a girl who has waist length hair, squeezing her hard, only to discover it is a boy. He grimaces and pulls away, having thought she was a boy as well.

'Come on!' Terror is yelling in her ear.

'Come where?'

'Dominic Blair!'

'Oh no! Terror, do we have to? I can't walk!'

Sallyann's protests are ignored. Terror drags her, protesting feebly, out into the daylight. She giggles at passers-by as Terror hauls her along the street.

'What did you take in there?'

'Happiness!'

'Sal, you are a bitch. You wanna spoil my day for me? Is that it? Why couldn't you wait until later, huh? You're so selfish!'

'I love you!' Sallyann sings joyously.

'Oh fuck off!' Terror growls, tossing her head, and smacking Sallyann across the face with her long, beaded braids.

They jump on a tram, which will take them to Government Drive. Hundreds of other revellers are crammed on board. Feeling at one with the whole population at that moment, Sallyann sings and shouts, accepting kisses and caresses. Terror grumbles with her arms folded, her scowl as black as her skin.

The passengers alight in a colourful, sweating tumble at the north end of the Drive, in Eternity Circus. A company of fetishists are providing a pre-Blair display, led by a band of hand-drummers, who are being whipped by shaved youths in leather loin-bands. Towering dominatrices, in different skin-tight costumes of red PVC, march along like robots behind on six inch spike heels, their faces white, their lips a raw scarlet, their eyes concealed behind wrap-around shades. Men crawling on all fours in furry dog suits are being choked by tight leashes, wielded by women wearing rubber. One man squats to defecate, whimpering as the chain-link lead strikes home.

Terror is entranced. 'Oooh! Lookit that! Lookit that!'

Eternity Circus, in the late afternoon, is already berserk with flashing hoardings. Alone in the centre, a stark purity: 'The Temple is Built on Blood!' Sallyann is beginning to wonder whether she's hallucinating that particular slogan. It seems to her as if the figures on the steps of the ruin are dancing. Her earlier euphoria is beginning to cloy. A headache is coming on. At the corner of her vision, zigzag patterns flutter and spark.

Terror bites and scratches a path for them to the front of the crowd. They step over an unconscious girl, whose dress appears to have ripped off. The tail end of the fetishist parade scampers by, running close to the crowd, holding out their spike-dappled arms. Most people are ducking, squealing, away from the spikes, but others don't: they aren't squealing at all. Sallyann can feel an urge to go home stealing over her. She feels a little sick. A man standing next to her is thoughtfully rubbing a ragged cut on his chest, painting himself with blood. She yearns for the carefree intimacy of the music marquee. She doesn't like the sight of blood.

Terror grips Sallyann's arm hard. 'Listen, listen,' she says.

'To what?' The sound of the day is an incomprehensible whirl around Sallyann's mind. It means nothing, but it smells of blood. 'What?'

'He's coming!' Terror hisses.

Blinking, Sallyann tries to peer up the Mall. Thousands of young girls, uptowners and estate kids alike, have muscled their way forward to the front ranks of the bobbing crowd. Every female body is strained to the right, rising and falling like dancing snakes, trying to catch the first glimpse of the King of the Carnival. Silver balloons are released in a hectic cloud from the windows of a building opposite. Each one bears the grinning semblance of Dominic Blair. A sound comes down the Mall, passing along like a plague; the sound of female voices raised in adoring hysteria. The scream passes over and around Sallyann's body. She doesn't know if it is real or not, but is sure she can feel it slithering over her skin like electricity or a phantom cold.

First come the dancers. They are dressed in transparent body suits of a dark green colour, covered with fluttering rags of greeny grey and black. They whirl with tambourines, a soundtrack issuing from the tiny yet powerful speakers adhering to their bodies. Samples of African drums are sequenced through; it seems to shake the atoms of Sallyann's body. Next come a group of running children. Every race of the globe is represented. The children wear t-shirts advertising various soft and alcoholic drinks; adverts placed by the sponsors of Dominic Blair. They hand out glossy holographic pictures of Blair to anyone whose reaching hands they can thrust them into. Then comes a choir of neo-pagan singers, dressed in white robes, carrying palm leaves and crowned with ivy. They are singing about a king. The crowd seems to know the words; soon, they are chanting too. And finally, the great float of the King himself comes into view. It is high; a great leviathan of a vehicle, its wheels concealed by yards and yards of pale floating material, so that it appears to glide rather than roll its way slowly down the Drive. It is covered with dancers and singers, fire-eaters, jugglers, and mime artists. From their midst rises a dais, and upon the dais reposes the King of Carnival: Dominic Blair in person.

As the float crawls forward, the crowds close in behind it, following it in a great shambling mass. Just before the vehicle passes the place where Sallyann and Terror are standing, a great flock of black and white doves is released from behind Blair's throne. The youth stands up, raises both hands, salutes the crowd. Around him, the air is full of the sound of wings. Jets of perfume and dry ice are expelled from behind the wheels of the float.

He *is* beautiful, Sallyann thinks. Blair's body is lithe and slim. He is naked to the waist but garlanded with flowers. His honey blond hair cascades over his shoulders, his perfect face reposes in a blissful smile. That smile encompasses the whole world. For a moment, Sallyann understands why people love him. Then Mel's voice grates into her consciousness: 'He was grown in a vat. No one's that perfect. If they've made the breakthrough they claim they have, then they've used it grow Dominic Blair!'

Is that possible?

Against her will, Sallyann is gathered up into the enormous crowd that is now following the float down to Ecstasy Common. She couldn't escape if she tried. She can't even move her arms. The crowd carries her forward. She tries to look for Terror and one of the huge hoardings at the side of the mall catches her eyes: 'The Temple is Built on Blood!' Terror is nowhere to be seen.

At the Common, a fleet of ambulances, supplied by various Health companies, attend to those girls who have fainted and who can afford the fee. Others lie discarded like abused whores around the edge of the boundary wire.

Once she has been disgorged through the gates of the Common, Sallyann is free to move around a little. The crowd disperses into the wide space of green, while the float is now a distant speck, travelling towards the gigantic sound stage further down the field. Numbly, Sallyann follows the movement of the crowd. She is tired. She is beyond caring that her friend has brought her to this. She cannot be angry, or even annoyed. The estate, the roof of the biker house, Danny, all seem unreal to her. She can't imagine how she'll ever find her way back.

There are far too many people present, all of them girls, for Sallyann to get too close to the stage. Looking round herself, she can't see a single male in the crowd. She helps herself to a free drink from one of the gratuity stalls. It is thin, sour wine that stings her stomach immediately. As she drinks, a paper flyer blows along the ground and sticks to her leg. She bends to remove it, reads it in doing so. 'The Temple is Built on Blood.'

'What is happening to me?' she asks aloud.

Then the PA howls into life and a thirty foot video screen fizzes into action at the back of the stage. At first it plays popular commercials, the top ten; best-selling confectionery, clothes, beers and footwear. Company anthems are echoed by the crowd; bodies swaying, arms held high. A black-skinned girl dances past and waves her arms at Sallyann.

'How are ya?' she yells.

Sallyann can't remember if she knows the girl or not. 'The Temple is Built on Blood!' she says.

'Go with it!' advises the girl and whirls away.

On stage, the music has changed; throbbing New Age afro-jive. The crowd of women rocks to its rhythm. Sallyann drinks her wine, leaning against the booth. She says, 'It's crazy,' to the young woman dispensing the drinks. The woman pulls a sour face.

'Yeah.'

Sallyann grins. 'Ask me what I'm doing here!' she says.

The woman shakes her head. 'Kid, I know what you're doing here! You want another drink or are you going to knock my booth over? Move along, will ya!'

Sallyann sneers, gives the woman the finger and strolls away. 'Fuck you!' she adds, turning back for a moment.

Night has come. It seems to Sallyann as if she has been walking through the crowd for hours. Everyone is wearing the same face. Lights blaze upon the stage, fireworks splinter the sky behind it, cupped by laser streams. Aerial dancers, neon-glowing, haunt the dark spaces between the sparks. Lesser acts cavort and cry out to the music, melding one into another as they pass across the stage. Sallyann feels she must have had one plastic tumbler of foul wine from every booth on the site. Thoughtfully, she vomits where she stands and finds her head feels better afterwards. She thinks she sees some girls from Long Green Meadows a few feet away and tries to push through the crowd to reach them. She finds only strangers. *I must go home*, she thinks. *How? How can I get home?* She cannot see the edge of the Common from here, but if she keeps walking in a straight line, keeps pushing through, she must surely reach it. The crowd is getting tighter, a tense euphoria is building up. It is nearly time.

And then the stage goes black. Sallyann is caught in a knot of straining bodies, held upright, held motionless. She finds she can relax utterly, make no effort to stand, and not fall over. That, in itself, is almost comforting. Her head rests upon the shoulder of the girl next to her. She can actually see the stage from here. Gradually footlights flower to reveal a line of white-clad singers. A woman steps forward from the line to exhort the crowd. She appears uncannily like the woman who came to visit Mel from the Health Company, but now she is dressed in a long flowing gown, her red hair loose around her shoulders.

'Is this the new beginning?' she asks.

'Yes!' howl the crowd. 'Yes!'

'Then sing it with me!' She shakes a jubilant fist, gesturing with her mike.

'And we have it now
The new day, the new day.
It's dawn for all of us again.
Sing it sisters, for ours is the power
We are building the temple here
Where the new age begins,
And the temple is...'

'Built on blood,' Sallyann says. She doesn't hear the real words.

As the music swells to a deafening crescendo, Dominic Blair appears on a dais that rises through the floor of the stage. The crowd goes berserk. The night becomes the sound of female baying, nothing more. Sallyann finds her own throat is making a noise, low and desperate. Dominic Blair steps off the dais. He is clad only in a skirt of leaves, or feathers; perhaps both. His image fills the video screen at the back of the stage; his beatific smile, his gentle blue eyes. One of the singers hands him a mic and his voice too is beautiful.

'I am just for you,' he says and a despairing wail rises from the crowd. 'Yours alone,' he says, and blows kisses out into the night. 'We are lucky to be alive this day, for we are the future.'

Maybe you *are*, Sallyann thinks. *Maybe. But I'm not. How can I be? What will I ever have?* She wishes she could raise her voice to proclaim this undeniable truth, but even if she screamed until her throat bled she would be unable to make herself heard over the din of the crowd. Only Blair can do that, because he has the p.a. behind him.

Blair begins to sing. It is a facile love song that every girl in the crowd will believe is addressed to her alone. The words wash over Sallyann's mind: love, eyes, kisses, tenderness, baby, darling, angel. She begins to giggle. 'This is *unreal*,' she says. No one hears her.

On the screen, real tears have gathered in Blair's eyes as he approaches the climax of his song. His baby eyes beseech the crowd: *love me, I am yours*. As the final bars of music play, the crowd roars and screams. Blair throws back his head, arms outspread. He holds this pose for a moment and then shudders in a strange manner.

Sallyann blinks. She realises, with drunken slowness, that Dominic Blair has just exploded. She wants to laugh. It is quite true. Her eyes are not deceiving her. His chest has exploded outwards in a splendid arc of brilliant red. Is this part of the act? The crowd, strangely, do not react at first. They are still swaying and crooning, arms above their heads.

He's been shot, Sallyann thinks. *He's been...*

Instinctively, she forces her head around, seeking the place where the shot could have come from. Behind her, the skeletal form of the mixing desk gantry rears against the sky. It is utterly dark, but for the canvas-shielded cabin where the engineer is sitting. Too far away to see and yet... It seems to her that a lithe female figure is clinging to the scaffolding, and even as she looks the figure becomes more distinct. Light reflects off the chrome embellishments of an electronic cross bow, which the woman is holding in one hand. Sallyann's mind clears with realisation.

She used an explosive bolt! Yes, of course! But why?

The woman's face is wrapped in a dark-coloured scarf, but her hair is whipping free. There is something so familiar about her. Slowly, she turns her head towards Sallyann, unwraps the scarf from around her face. It is as if she is only a few feet away, her face large and pale. 'The Temple is Built on Blood,' she says to Sallyann. It is the voice of her mother.

Around Sallyann, the crowd is beginning to stir. Dominic Blair has fallen to the floor of the stage, nearly cut in two. His singers stand motionless behind him, their white robes splashed with red, as if they are only robots and someone has turned off their power. Then, a helicopter shudders its way through the night, and from its side a rope uncoils downwards towards the woman on the gantry. Hooking the crossbow over her shoulder, she reaches for the rope, wraps herself around it, and the helicopter purrs upwards. Clinging to the rope with one arm and both legs, the woman is borne slowly across the heads of the crowd.

My mother? Is that my mother? No! Someone will have a gun. They'll kill her for this!

But there are no guns. Arms are raised, a crooning sound issues from every female throat. The woman on the rope waves to them. They scream. Then, they storm the stage.

On the video screen, spattered with blood, is a freeze frame of a commercial. 'The Temple is Built on Blood!' The figures on the steps of the ruin are Maenads. They are killing a man. They are devouring him. Of course. *The King is dead. Long live the King.*

Sallyann does not remember too much of how she got home that night. She thinks Terror found her again and carried her onto the tram. In the morning, Mel brings her a cup of de-caf to drink in bed and Sallyann decides it is safer to believe she suffered a terrible hallucination the previous night. She says nothing to her mother about what she saw, although Mel does say, 'I did warn you about going, Sal.'

On TV, psychologists talk about catharsis and release. Sallyann just wants to forget. She is afraid to watch the programmes about the Breakthrough.

Now, she is sitting on the roof of the biker house, sharing a couple of cans of beer with Danny. He is polishing a gun, lovingly inspecting all the parts, dismantling and reconstructing. There hasn't been a riot for over a week, which Danny suggests, in an oblique way, might be something to do with what happened at the Carnival.

'Coincidence,' Sallyann says.

'Could be,' Danny replies. 'But don't you feel something different?'

'Something different where?'

He shrugs. 'Dunno. In the air maybe.'

Sallyann pauses with her can halfway to her mouth, sniffs. 'Nah.'

'How's your ma?' Danny asks.

Sallyann looks at him sharply. She hasn't told him everything. 'Fine. Why?'

He grins. 'Just wondered. She did business with Ziggy a few weeks back.'

Ziggy is the most terrifying of Danny's tribe. He usually deals in weapons. 'What kind of business?' Sallyann asks, needlessly.

Danny gives her a look, but doesn't answer. 'Reckon you'll stay here now?' he says.

'Of course! Nothing's changed. Where else can we go? We'll always be here. Mel likes it here.'

Danny shakes his head. 'Perhaps I shouldn't say this, but I reckon she'll send you out, Sal. She's always planned that. She'll send you out.'

'Fuck! I won't go!' Sallyann yells. 'Why would she do that? How can you know? I won't go.'

'Don't be an asshole, Sal. Take it when it comes,' He leans over to kiss her cheek. 'There are always sacrifices. It doesn't matter whether the gods are tripping out in skirts and thunderbolts somewhere in someone's heaven, or getting you to buy a can of beer on TV. There are gods, and they need blood to keep them sweet. We lost the way for a while, maybe. Don't you see? It's been a long time coming, but the show was well organised, down to the last detail.'

'This is just another of your stupid theories!' Sallyann says, but suddenly she feels cold and exposed sitting there on the roof. 'You're making it up!'

Danny shrugs, lovingly wipes a piece of gun with a piece of lint. 'The King of Carnival is dead,' he says, 'but there'll be another one soon, you see. There'll always be a king now. The people need it. We've got our New Age whether we like it or not, but, you know, it's not that new, not that new at all.'

Sallyann's heart has begun to beat quickly in her chest. 'I want to move in with you,' she says urgently. 'Let me live here.'

Danny raises one eyebrow. He is silent for a few moments, then says, 'Sleep on it,' and squints up at the sky.

Sallyann follows his gaze. 'Shooting star!' she cries, pointing.

'Falling satellite,' Danny says, 'but perhaps it's the same thing.'

God Be With You

You think I should talk about it? Why? It's gone hasn't it? Yeah, o.k., talk it out, spit it out, inner cleansing. I see. I suppose it all started just before my father walked out. That makes it sound like he was just sitting there one minute and packing up the next, but of course it took months overall for him to decide he had to leave. He left it so long because it only started with the small stuff, the problems, I mean. We never guessed it would get so bad, you see. We never guessed.

My mother was whacked out at the time, teetering between heavy neurosis stuff and hi-flying tranq heaven. She'd mope around the place, drinking rye nectar, and then stand staring out of the fisheye at the place where she said Gaia would be. She'd ramble on about a thing she called Life, but which my father intimated through shrugs and glances meant nothing of the kind, or at least that she'd got mixed up about it somewhere. I didn't know what was happening to her, though some people say some of us just never evolved properly to live off-world, out here in the Widebetween. We live on Africa Plate you see, the Experimental Autonomous Off-world Luxury Urban Complex, to give it its full title. It's a tumbling anemone structure, the size of a small planet, orbiting the sun somewhere between Gaia and Mars. Not just anybody was given a place here; it's bursting with bright sparks, scientists of all persuasions, mindtravellers and engineers, who bounce off each other and think up new ideas from the resulting fireworks. My father is a bioengineer. He invents plants; worktime, creating biomass that we can eat and use to regulate our atmosphere; hometime, perfecting his hobby of designing orchid-ferns. Our place was full of them which Mom forgot to look after. I had a good relationship with them though; one was clever enough to brew me nectar liquor in its bladder sacs. I used to take it along when I was gaming; the gang appreciated that.

So, the small stuff that got my father worried. I don't know how it got such a hold; no-one does, but it began as an interesting curiosity and escalated from there, spreading through the homekeep community like smoke. Not everybody has a high-responsibility lifepath on Africa Plate. My mother was one of those; bored looking out the fisheye and thinking of home. I was born on the Plate. It meant nothing to me.

Anyway, it started with a man called Graham Seeds, a biochem technician's boyfriend, telling everyone he was getting messages. Messages from an Alien. Of course. We were out here in space, weren't we? Exactly the right place to pick something like that up. Perhaps we'd find out at last why they'd been flitting around the home world for so long interfering with our evolution. Ha ha. Such sarcastic wit had no effect on the appeal of Seeds' disclosures. It burned like holy fire through the social meets of the uprooted husbands and wives associations. Something to latch onto. A purpose. Messages for the future. Life change interface. Everybody else thought it was a joke.

Me and the gaming gang even started bringing it into our scenarios, laughing about it. Alicia took the role of a woman who was tuned into it all. We made her a prophetess. Laughed. Alicia goofed along and camped it up. Her mother was compiling notes about the whole thing, so she had the research material. I was chipping in with the stuff I'd picked up from Mom about how certain foods were bad to eat. Apparently, the Alien was saying we shouldn't be tampering with genetics, whether of plant or animal, never mind the fact it was a necessity of life in a place like the Plate. My father is a patient sort. Perhaps he shouldn't have been. He said nothing when our mealtimes began to change. One night she gave us porridge for dinner. She wouldn't eat what Dad and I made when it was our turn to prepare meals, frugally laying out her apples and corn, saying nothing to us about what we ate, but the silence was crippling. One night, I just had to tell her corn itself had been mutated by people back on Gaia over thousands of years. She took no notice. Dad smiled at me encouragingly though and made me another fern. My room was getting so swamped I took a trayful over to Alicia's because she was hosting the game that night.

We were seriously into Kaoristica at the time, a fast, mind-development game, meeting three times a week, to travel the fractal paths of evolution, our game leader dreaming up reality conflicts to send us spinning into para-infinities. I'd reached Tripanic Experience and had started to compile my own scenarios at home, reckoning within a few months I'd be hosting my own game. I had a few surprises worked out already. Chevy nearly spoiled the game that night. He was in such a sulk. The rest of us were getting prickly and fouling our experiences because of it until Drina got him to tell us what was bugging him. Apparently, his father had got into this Alien business and had taken to barricading himself in their recreation room for two hours every night to commune with Him, moaning out all manner of mumbo-jumbo that drove Chevy and his mother mad with annoyance that was very nearly fear. In a low, embarrassed voice, Chevy told us his mother had confided in him about how she and his father no longer slept together. All that's just for making babies, she'd said. The Alien had told the father that. Suddenly, it seemed quite a few of us had tales to tell concerning the Alien 'transmissions'. There were ten people in our group, and only three of them hadn't been affected by it in one way or another. It was noticed straight away that those three people had parents who both worked for Plate Maintenance and Evolution. Gardner was the first to suggest that maybe this problem might get more serious than we thought. Perhaps it was a mistake to treat it as a joke. A sobering idea. When the conversation dwindled, we renewed the game with dampened vigour. Even my DNA Alchemist character was beginning to think more about the possible consequences of this madness than the reality manipulation in the Labyrinth beyond the Moon he was involved in. He was beginning to wonder if it might not be a good idea to investigate the Alien thing right away; perhaps there was some truth in it, after all. Neither I, nor the Alchemist, were particularly cheered by this conclusion, which is probably why I never followed it up.

Things got worse. Like Chevy's father, my mother drew away from her family, looking at us sourly as if we didn't smell right or something. Occasionally, she'd come out of her shell and corner me or my father, telling us the joys of embracing the Alien's words. She spoke of how her world had opened up, her heart was filled with love, but there was little of this for us to see. Dad told me he'd had a word with our section mindtraveller who was responsible for community well-being and that she'd just thrown up her hands in disgust when he'd suggested Mom ought to pop along to her office for a chat. 'O.k., o.k.,' she'd said bitterly. 'Your wife along with the hundred other people directed to me by their families!'

It seemed there was a waiting list in her department right now for consultations.

'They believe this junk!' the mindtraveller had said. 'I sit there asking their beaming faces questions and they're so happy, and nodding and smiling, that I'm beginning to wonder whether, in fact, it's not me that needs the therapy.'

The thing is, all these Alien lovers were not doing anything illegal or blatantly anti-social, so there wasn't much anyone could do. Everyone has a right to free choice. If it wasn't harming life on the Plate in any way, it had to be allowed to continue.

Then my mother married the Alien. Yes, really. Apparently, her contract with my father was invalid in her eyes because he was not a believer. She married a creature she had never seen (nor ever would in my opinion), in some kind of cerebral trysting ceremony presided over by Graham

Seeds, the self-appointed Alien mouth-piece. I remember my mother taking my hands in hers, my flesh crawling, as I looked in horror at her bland, smiling face. She asked me to understand. 'I'm so happy,' she'd said. 'I know I'm loved.'

'By what?' I'd asked, almost choked. 'Don't you know we love you, me and Dad?'

'I believe in Him,' she'd answered, eyes gazing upwards, beyond the multi-structures of the Plate into space itself. 'I really do believe.' Her face and neck flushed pink.

I pulled away, sensing the gulf, and a hint of something obscene.

My father moved into a singles block next day. Even though I begged him to choose a duapt and take me with him, he'd gravely shaken his head and asked me to stay with Mom. 'Just keep your eyes open,' he said as he packed his things to leave. 'Please do this for me, son.'

'Isn't there anything we can do?' I asked him, pleading, my comfortable image of Father Capable of Solving Anything dissolving to mist.

He shook his head. 'It's her choice,' he said. 'We can't force anyone to think in certain ways. You know that. We left all that behind a long time ago.'

Did we? Some scared part of me was beginning to wonder.

I took to visiting my Dad regularly, in between meeting the gang for gaming sessions. It got me away from home, which was a relief because my mother was beginning to spook me thoroughly. I cooked for myself all the time now, which at first hadn't bothered her, but lately she'd begun to whine about how I was perpetuating the sins of the people by my actions. It is not easy to eat a meal when someone's yelling that your food's evil down your neck. I was choking on her words as much as what was on my plate. Gradually, I was forced to take more of my meals in the canteen down the hall, just to get some peace and quiet for my digestion.

One day I got home from college to find she'd blanked all

the wall-screens in my room. I was furious. All my scenarios for the game I was creating had been mapped there. Mom looked triumphant as I raved my angry hurt at her.

Her eyes gleamed. 'Someone has to close the doors that let evil in,' she said.

'What are you talking about?' I cried. 'What evil?'

'The wall-screens. What you create there comes in and takes you. I know. He told us that. I won't have that in my home. I'm sorry, Lyle, but I'm going to have to do something about the wickedness you're involved in.'

My heart slopped into my stomach and I could feel the walls closing in on me, blank screens or not. 'What do you mean?' I asked.

Mom raised her arms, and stalked about, high on whatever was running in her veins to make her think this way. 'Screens, games, holo-films; all lies. They warp the truth and turn people into the walking dead. Lyle, I understand it all now, and it has to be stopped. We have a chance here, out on Africa Plate. I was wrong to want to go back to Gaia. It's here Salvation will find us. *He* found us here. The only thing we have to do is make the Plate a decent place to live. Then He'll come to us, but not before.'

She was waiting for her husband. The new one, without a name.

'The Ships will come,' my mother breathed, hands clasped, eyes all glassy, 'great shining, wonderful ships and they'll take us away from here, to the world of immortality and ultimate beauty.' She fixed me with a gimlet glance and added sharply, 'However, only the Believers will be given places on those ships.'

'And what about the rest of us?' I asked, just as meanly.

She hesitated. 'We have been told the Plate will destroy itself eventually. Those who insist on clinging to their ways of wickedness and ignorance will perish.' She put her hands on my shoulders, either ignoring or unaware of my flinching. 'You are my son,' she said. 'And I can save you. You'll see this for yourself eventually, I'm sure. I can wait.'

The mindtravellers were the first to get attacked. Oh, nothing physical. The Alien lovers were too smart for that. There were plasmaflyers in the air, adhering to walls, saying the mindtravellers were denizens of the black abyss beyond the universe disguised as men, whose sole purpose was to lead the people of Africa Plate towards dissolution. Apparently, these black denizens were lurking all over the place and hid in the subconscious mind. Trying to open up these areas, via normal personal development or with the mindtravellers, was a dark, disastrous mistake we were all making.

'We must get back to simple things,' my mother told me on one of the occasions I was trying to sneak out of the apartment to get to my father. 'If we trust in Him and turn away from the infernal meddling into our evolution, we will be Saved.'

I left her ranting.

Dad had a friend over when I reached his place. A mindtraveller named Selene, who I'd always liked, and who, it seemed, Dad has always liked as well, though perhaps not in quite the same way. She looked tired and harried, locks of hair falling into her eyes, which she kept having to brush away. We sat on Dad's cushions drinking orchid-fern nectar while Selene spoke in short, anxious sentences.

'Our department has been in touch with Gaian authorities over this,' she said. 'Left it too late, maybe. Wanting to prove we can manage without them. Shit!' She punched air and appealed to my father. 'I'm scared now, Lorin, really scared. These people spook me. We let it get too big. Laughing...' She shook her head. 'Yesterday, some maniac tried to throw something over me, saying the Alien had blessed it through him. Told me it would cast out the black denizen in me. He had no aura, Lorin, really, just nothing. Like he was dead or something. It sped me out.' She sipped her drink and looked at me. 'Lyle, you be careful.'

'Oh, I just ignore it,' I said, trying to cheer her up.

Selene shook her head. 'What I mean is, those games you're into. They're tuning into them now as the next Bad

Thing. Get it? Be careful.'

'How is your mother?' Dad asked tightly.

'I don't tell her anything,' I replied. 'She blanked my screens.'

'Maybe you should find yourself a place for you and the boy, Lorin,' Selene said.

It was what I wanted, but the mere fact it was necessary scared me rotten.

The skin round Alicia's eyes was purple when she came to the game-meet at Pieter's place. We were having to be more careful about where we met, and had naturally narrowed it down to the three members' homes whose parents were both still OK. Pieter's Mom really sped out when she came to sit and chat with us for a while and saw Alicia's face. We were all feeling a bit sick because bad bruises - that's what the purple skin was - wasn't something we saw too often. OK, people have accidents, but Alicia began to cry, thick tears running down her face, and told us her Mom had hit her. Not once, but four times.

Pieter's mother went green. 'What the 'Form's sake for?' she asked, swallowing deeply.

Alicia rubbed at her face, leaning against Chevy who'd lent a comforting arm. 'Because I told her yesterday I was coming here,' she said. 'Mom said it was evil, that I was letting the black denizen in my head take control. I tried to tell her she was wrong, that we didn't do anything bad, but she wouldn't listen. I told her she could think what she liked, that was her right, but that I didn't agree with her and I was coming here anyway. That's when she began to... that's when she began to hit me.'

'What did your father do?' Pieter's mother asked, her hand pinching the flesh of her throat.

Alicia blinked. 'He's not there anymore. She told him to go. She married the Alien. That's what she said. And she thinks she can save me. She says it's a war she's fighting, a truth war. I think that makes it OK for her to hit me.'

Pieter's mother had gone from green to white. She stood up. 'You guys carry on,' she said. 'I have to... I have to speak to someone. Anyone!'

After she'd gone, Alicia said in a small voice, 'This is violence, isn't it? This is what we've read about, isn't it? People hurting each other. I never really believed it. In-forms! It's real now.'

It was too late to speak to anyone. An angry wind was sweeping through the halls, tunnels, chambers and walkways of the Plate. It reached right down to the innermost levels where the core of our little artificial world burned hard and hot. It rushed over the yawning solar panels stretching out like hands from the spiralling limbs outside. It was a cold wind, full of fury and frustrated bitterness. The mindtravellers were beginning to recognise it for what it was, but naming this demon could not dispel it. It was more than a wind; it was an infection. One that we'd unwittingly carried with us from Gaia, something everyone had overlooked, being too pleased with themselves, too confident, to wonder whether the debilitating soul diseases might be more difficult to eradicate than they'd thought. The society that came to inhabit Africa Plate had been groomed for its role; outworn conceptions cast off and left behind, old mistakes accepted and shed. We were supposed to be an enlightened society, free from the repressive hierarchical structures of the past, free from the restrictions of primitive fears and guilt. The scientists, the engineers, the mindtravellers, had all been training themselves; they had been hand-picked. Their lovers, husbands and wives had been given the choice to accompany them to this new horizon. This had seemed only humane and right. Hardly any refused the offer. After all, they were loyal to those they loved. Perhaps their training hadn't been as meticulous. They were not hand-picked. An oversight. A vestige of patriarchal thinking. These people were not important. They would be carried by the bright stars who had married them and loved them. Wrong. Those bright stars misunderstood the responsibility, didn't even recognise it. Some people are too frightened to live without external gods. So they created one, and called it an Alien.

It was stupid of me. I can see that now. But she was out for the evening, you see. Said she'd be out for a long time. A meeting she said. More messages. I'd been clever enough to play down my leisure activities in her company, pretending to listen to whatever she came out with, asking questions. That satisfied her. So I asked the gang over to my place for a game. I wanted so badly to treat them to my scenarios - I'd secretly recreated them on the wallscreens when my mother was out, filing them and blanking the screens so she wouldn't know. I thought it would be safe. The group was depleted, not because anyone had dropped out exactly, but it was sometimes difficult for some of them to get away from home for the evening. We were being careful, all of us certain something would happen soon to make things better. We knew about the contact with Gaia and it was rumoured some people were coming out to help us. How, we could not, dare not, guess. The Alien lovers were becoming increasingly violent and no-one else could handle it. We lacked the desire to fight back, even to save ourselves. We believed the key to survival was to make ourselves invisible, but that was difficult in the enclosed environment of the Plate. We could only wait for help. Perhaps the people from Gaia would take all the Alien lovers away. We were all so sad. We'd lost so much. It hurt. Anyway, I had this subdued gang over and got them tuned into an uplifting experience chain so we could all forget our troubles for a while. I led them dancing and spinning into ecstasy spirals, parting layers of the multiverse and letting the lightseeds spill out and over us. My mindmaps gushed over the walls, wrapping us in colours and unimaginable vistas; I really had excelled myself.

We were all so high, it took a moment or two to come back to reality when the door to my room slid open, letting in harsh blue-white light from the hall outside and revealing the black, black silhouette of my mother standing there in the doorway, looking like one of those dark denizens she was always talking about. She let out a screech, half anger, half fear before leaping into the room amongst us. She started kicking out, kicking the walls, screaming about evil and denizens and lost souls and retribution and all manner of crazy things. The group was sitting around dazed and frightened of being kicked. I pulled myself together and told them to get out quickly. Alicia tried to pull me along with them, but I knew I had to face this thing out. I wouldn't hit back, but I certainly wasn't going to run. Not anymore.

When everyone had gone, I damped the walls and turned on the softlights.

Mom had started crying, kneeling on the floor, wringing her hands in her lap. 'How could you Lyle?' she whimpered, as if she'd caught me perforating the Plate skin or something.

'How could you?' I replied. 'You had no right to do that. You know that.'

She looked up at me with red eyes. 'But I have,' she insisted. 'Don't you see? It's for your own good, Lyle. You're my son. I have to do what's right for you. I have to help you. Please, let me help you.'

I shuddered. She looked pathetic huddled there, skinny and unhealthy. If anyone needed help, it was her. I could no longer be angry and squatted down beside her. 'It's just a game, Mom, remember? A learning game. It's something all kids do. It's how we learn about ourselves, how we face the things inside.'

She snorted thickly and swallowed, wiped her face. 'No, Lyle. That's the lie they told you. It's a conditioning programme. It lets the denizens take you over. You must believe me.'

'If there are any such things as denizens, then I've faced them out,' I said gently. 'I vaporised them, made them disappear. That's the point of playing the games. It makes us strong.' I tried to make her remember, but it was as if some part of her brain had shut down. She wasn't really listening, caught on her own reality loop. A very narrow one.

She sniffed again and reached for my arms with wet hands. 'Lyle,' she said, very carefully. 'I want you to come with me. Now. I think you'll be able to speak to Him yourself if I'm with you. Let me prove to you that what I say is right.'

My first instinct was to pull away. Did she think me so stupid? Of course people had checked the whole thing out. Mindtravellers had not overlooked the fact there might be something in this Alien business. They'd found nothing. There was no evidence other than that existing within the imagination of the converts. An idea entered my head. Perhaps if I went along with her, I could show her how wrong she was, make the real Mom come back. Other people must have tried it, but I had to attempt it myself. 'Where do you want me to go?' I asked.

Her face lit up, banishing the pallor of ill-health and fatigue. She squeezed my hands. 'Baby!' she said, embracing me so I could feel all her ribs. She kissed my cheek. 'To the Receiving Room. It's not far.' She drew me to my feet. I followed her.

The Receiving Room was a small recreation facility two halls down, annexed to one of the social meet apartments. She took me inside, to a place looking as if a freighter-load of insane primates had been let loose to mark it as their territory. Untidy slogans were daubed upon the walls, console monitors ripped out and disembowelled on the floor, a crude sculpture that looked like a manic foetus enshrined upon the top tier of a monitor rack, draped in circuitry. Anybody could tell that place was a temple to these people. There were a few others sitting down in there, rocking on the floor, singing little repetitive dumb lines to themselves, which would have looked like simple meditation but for their glazed, staring expressions and self-clutching hands. These were the Chosen Ones awaiting their vast, polygamous, alien partner and the doom of Africa Plate. It was a sobering sight. I wished my Dad was with me. Anyone. 'Sit down,' my mother whispered eagerly, patting the floor. I sank down warily beside her.

'So what do I do?' I asked.

'Sshh!' she cautioned, finger to lips. 'You have to tell Him you believe in Him. Keep telling Him that. Say you know He's so far above us, that we're nothing. Say you're His child and will obey.'

'All that?' I hissed, trying not to sound cynical. She gave me a glance

'That's just some of it,' she said.

I sighed. There was only one way to check this thing out. Open up the higher neurocircuits like a receiver (this was a receiving room after all!) and see if I could pick anything up. I knew it could be dangerous because of any negative energy flying around. I know my limitations. In my own scenarios, I call the shots, but I have to be honest with myself, I'm only a kid and this was Big Stuff. I might not be able to handle it. These freaks could get into my head and cripple me. Make me like them. Could I take such a risk? I suppose, deep inside, there was a tiny suspicion it might all be legitimate, no matter what the mindtravellers said they'd deduced. We are encouraged to question things from the time we utter our first squawk in this reality. I had to find out for myself. I started the Breathing, and heard my mother say, 'Don't do that', in a sharp undertone. 'That's not the way, Lyle.'

I can Breathe silently too. I did it that way.

There is blackness before my inner eye and then the central spark of my personal consciousness. I make it bloom. Enter it. Grow. Anything out there? Hello? Alien, are you there? Tune in. Forget the creepy humming outside of yourself. See with the inner eye. Learn.

I just enjoy myself for a few minutes tumbling around my personal playground, before getting down to business. Oh yes, yes, there is a black hole out there somewhere, and I have to go into that and find out what's inside. I become DNA Alchemist because he's older than me and less scared of things. He sweeps strongly up to the scary place and pops right through it. Now I can see. There is something in there; a massive, crawling thing. It's lived there for a long time and it's very hungry. It says, 'You are mine!' to everything, so jealous and grasping.

I say, 'What will you give me?'

And it replies, 'Freedom'

And I say 'What's the price?'

And it says, 'Obedience.'

'That's not freedom,' I say. 'Why should I obey you?'

'Because you're dead if you don't!' the thing answers. 'Get in line, kid. I run things around here. I made you.'

'No. We made you,' I say.

The thing ripples. It's a cosmic shrug. 'Whatever. If you insist. It's still the same. I got the power around here. You're nothing. I'll never die.' It begins to laugh and that's when I know I have to get out quickly.

DNA Alchemist pulls himself out of that black hole. The thing in there doesn't know what it is or why it was created. It'll just keep gobbling up frightened souls forever. I realise it's a necessary thing in a way, at least part of the natural disorder of our multiverse. That's a fine deduction. It doesn't help the situation on Africa Plate.

I opened my eyes to the Receiving Room and my mother was sitting there all breathless and clutching. 'Did you hear?' she whispered.

I stood up. 'Yes,' I said.

Her face fell when she saw my expression. 'Well, why aren't you happy then?' she asked, confused.

I knew I could not reach her. She had helped revive that old god in there. She wanted what it could give. We were worlds apart. It was sad, but at least I understood more now. 'I think,' I said, 'you should leave here soon, all of you. Find your paradise world and live there. If that's what you want.'

I knew there'd be no shining ships coming to take them away, that it was all a delusion, but it was the waiting that was important to them. Only they couldn't wait here. I didn't know where they could wait. I'm only a kid. Like I said, some things are Big Stuff.

The people from Gaia came in their lumpy ships and Alicia and I watched them from the fisheye in my Dad's apartment; lumpy ships limned against the sundisc. There was a predictable flurry of jubilant panic from the Alien lovers who believed for several hours that their saviour and potential mate had come to whisk them away. It was a fantasy dispelled only when the Gaian people docked and came inside.

Dad came and hugged me, telling us not to go outside his apartment until he came back. Selene came to call for him. They went away, tight-lipped and pale.

Alicia took my hand. 'Lyle, I have to see,' she said quietly. 'My Mom's out there. It'll only happen once. I have to see.'

'OK, come on.'

We went out into the hall where the lichen-trees breathed softly and filled the air with vapour. I breathed deeply, resonating with the plants. They knew something was wrong too. Alicia and I followed our senses to where the trouble was. I don't think my Dad really believed I'd stay put. That's how I comforted myself.

It was sort of right and pre-ordained that the rest of our group should drift into our path. After all we lived inside each other's heads three nights a week. We all linked arms and kept walking, not saying much but drawing strength from each other's presence. We'd walked this path a hundred times in games. Now it was real and our experiences had prepared us for it. I did not have to be DNA Alchemist now, just myself. I realised I could integrate that aspect of my personality whenever I wanted to. It made me feel older and strong. I think all the others felt that way too.

We went to the Solarium near the main docking chambers. Everything was happening there. The Gaians stood looking uneasy in dark uniforms, arranged in lines. All of them carried weapons. It made us feel as cold as the metal they were made of. They looked like death. No wonder my Dad hadn't wanted me to see that.

Then, the Alien lovers came yelling down corridors, running and waving their arms. They had decided, ultimately, that the black denizens had come for them and not their saviour after all. It was a chilling sight. They'd torn off piping to use as weapons. They brandished household knives. They sang the song of war.

We, the children crouched at the edge and watched, frozen, but not terrified. We were sad. We held onto each other and sang the song of wistful innocence.

The Gaians protected themselves with shields, and fired tranquillising sprays into the melee. They amplified their voices, calling for moderation. It had no effect. The Alien lovers, their rage dampened by the spray, milled in confusion, calling on their new god to aid them. Nothing happened. No flash of light. No divine protective aura.

Graham Seeds took control. We heard him shout. 'Have faith! The cause is not lost! I'm getting a message! He will come for us outside. Not here. Not this pit of sin! Outside! We will be saved!' He launched himself towards the docking airlocks, his comrades swarming behind him, singing out an eerie ululation of salvation. I'm glad I did not see my mother there.

It was all over very quickly after that. I can't help feeling our people and the Gaians sort of let it happen that way for convenience's sake. Perhaps I'm wrong. All the Alien lovers piled ecstatically into the great docking chamber and barricaded the door. Some were left on this side of it, clawing and screaming, but none of our relatives were among them. On the other side, Graham Seeds opened the airlock and all of them exploded out into airless space, like scraps of cloth filled with blood, into the waiting blackness of the Widebetween. It was horrible. We saw the debris tumbling past the Solarium windows. No Alien came to save them. They were not immune to the effects of the void. They just spun out and out, dead. I hope they did not suffer...

There, I've told you. It's all past. The alien lovers who survived were taken back to Gaia. Nobody wanted to stop them. Oh, did you know? Selene is my stepmother now. Yes, I'm very happy. We're all OK. It's kind of quiet though, isn't it? It's left such a hole in our society with all those people gone. Grief? Yes, we had that. I absorbed it. Worries? No, none. Honestly.... Well, perhaps just one thing. You remember I told you about what was inside the black hole? Well, I know it's still there. Waiting. I don't think it's true that once a god is no longer worshipped it disappears. Just a hunch. It knows we're here now. Oh, yes, yes, I know it's just a creation of our own brains, mankind's own brains, but... We *are* safe, aren't we?

So What's Forever

'So, what's so different about it, huh? A game is a game is a game!' Tally Ritter was in provocative mood. She shook out her long, golden hair, and waved the paper flyer under Brewster Corley's nose, attempting to sparkle coyly.

Brewster sensed merely tawdriness. He took the paper from her purple-glazed claws with a fastidious finger and thumb.

'Beyond reality,' he read out loud.

'So it says, so it says.' Tally stretched, bored, scanning the club for familiar faces, finding none. 'I hate this dump. Let's go somewhere else.'

She and Brewsters had discovered the glo-color flyer on their table. Brewster had presumed some gamer had been distributing them around the club. Beyond Reality didn't come cheap; 200 credits per Experience, as the promo grandly explained. Still, it didn't stop him slipping the folded paper into his pocket as they left. He'd never been into that kind of thing really - dressing up, pretending to be something else - but had neatly fallen for the seductive wording of Beyond Reality's creators. It was a tease; saying merely enough to whet the appetite, with just a suggestion of something not normally part of play in your regular role-playing game.

They hailed a hire-car and headed up town, Tally complaining about her pinching, spike-heeled shoes, patting her hair, pausing to glance out of the window and squeal at something or someone recognisable occasionally. Her teased hair had effectively taken control of the available space above neck-level, causing Brewster to sneeze and snap at her in irritation. Tally wrinkled her nose and grinned, and began to hum a popular tune, beating out the rhythm on her spangled, tissue-gauzed thighs.

Brewster was not really in the mood for her and was even less in the mood for Seltzers, the latest craze-club, where they were currently bound. He folded his arms and leaned back, conscious of the personal cloud hovering lightlessly over his head.

'Oh, I want to dance!' Tally enthused, frothing with weightless euphoria.

'Wait until we get there, please.' Brewster was sick of being bounced around on the seat as Tally got in some practice wriggles.

'You're such a glumdog tonight,' she said to him, refusing to let his mood affect her.

Brewster sat alone at a side-table, morosely sipping expensive warm ale and peering into the laser-shot darkness. He could just make out Tally's gunmetal silver dress on the dance floor, where pink and blue lights reeled drunkenly on waving arms above the dancers in a mass of cosmetic, curly cable. The music was so loud Brewster could feel his internal organs mimicking the beat. A head-ache had started. Oh to be home, he thought mournfully. But Tally was enjoying herself. He had enough sense of chivalry in him not to walk out and leave her to find her own way back, but the prospect of staying at Seltzers until the small hours and Tally had exhausted herself was unpalatable to say the least. It seemed that nearly all of her cackling cronies were here tonight too. Brewster was surprised he hadn't been blinded by all the glitter and deafened by the din of their screamed greetings. They were politely referred to by the less demonstrative as a colourful bunch.

Brewster fumbled in his pocket for cigarettes and encountered the folded paper he'd picked up at the last club.

He couldn't even remember the name of the place now, but its entrance fee had stuck firmly in mind. Smiling humourlessly, he examined the flyer again. In this light, the paper looked stark white and the black letters leapt out at him with uncompromising vividness.

'Beyond Reality!'

These words were larger than the rest and struck Brewster as being weirdly innocent and ingenuous. He grimaced and read on.

'Live out your wildest fantasies! Your dreams come true! A game with a difference! You can be your ultimate hero/ine! Not just an ordinary role-playing game, Beyond Reality becomes reality! Escape! Escape! Escape!'

Then there was a cautious box-number for interested parties to write to.

Brewster chuckled and folded the paper again. Then unfolded it to squint once more at the smallest print at the bottom.

'Have you tried to have a Waking Dream yet?' it said; the swift, needle thrust that guaranteed to hook. This must surely be illegal or a hoax to attract members to the game-club, Brewster thought. Waking Dream was a legend, a myth - at present. It was a newly whispered-of drug, the ultimate hallucinogen, whose effects were supposedly so powerful, awesome and unpredictable that government departments were already shrieking with hysterics before the stuff even hit the streets. There had been one or two scare stories in the tabloids - the usual nonsense: 'Girl Eats Parent in Bizarre Drug Dream' sort of stuff.

I wonder... Brewster thought. He sent a letter off the very next day.

Tally, of course, had wanted to go with him. Now she was being difficult. Brewster, although still not sure whether the Waking Dream hint was real or not, had worried about Tally yacking indiscriminately to her friends, so had omitted to mention it until they had nearly reached their destination. She had demanded he stop the car. Outside, she stood tapping her foot on the tarmac, hands on hip, gazing sourly at the mist covered fields that stretched away on either side of the road, where occasional trees reared black, naked limbs like ancient hags stepping from a vast, hot bath. Brewster got out of the car and sighed.

'You're so childish!' Tally exclaimed. She was a thoroughbred of the new generation of party girls that liked to live it up while inflicting a rigidly sanitised existence on themselves. She had never smelled even vaguely human to Brewster, who had accustomed himself to her perfume counter synthetic aroma. Alcohol was the legal intoxicant, so that was what she used to get her high. Anything else was looked upon as dirty and therefore repugnant to her. Anything as gutter level as the legendary Waking Dream was guaranteed to offend her deeply. Brewster kicked himself. Why had he been so stupid as to let her nag him into bringing her with him? It was madness. With shame, he realised it was because he usually obeyed her every word. Behind the pretence of girlish sparkle beat a heart of shineless iron. In truth, she was his strength. 'Well?' she demanded.

'Well what?'

Tally rolled her eyes between long, dyed lashes. 'Idiot! I mean, are you going to take some of that filth or not? There was I, a fool if ever there was one, thinking you'd merely taken an interest in some kind of hobby! It was about time you took an interest in something! I wanted to share it with you. Now I find it's a front for some shifty drug-dealers to ply their wares. Your stupidity astounds me! Did you really think I'd be into that?'

'If you'll just be quiet for a moment!' Brewster interrupted her righteous flow. 'I've no proof of the Dream thing. It was just a hunch I had. I'm curious. Aren't you? They'll probably be a bunch of kids living out stale old fantasy writers' dramas, that's all. It should be a laugh.'

Tally sniffed. 'In answer to your question, no, I'm not curious.' She got back into the car, folding her pale, woollen coat over her immaculately clad legs. Brewster slumped in beside her. She clicked her fingers. 'Give me the letter you got.'

'Don't get so worked up!' Brewster burrowed in the untidy mound of papers between the front seats. 'It's just a game. I should have kept my mouth shut.' He handed her the letter. It was ringed with coffee mug stains.

'Well, it seems innocent enough,' Tally decided in pompous, maternal tone after she'd read it. 'Rather infantile, perhaps, but there's no mention of drugs in it. Where on earth did you get that idea, Brew?' Her furious boil had calmed to bubbling simmer.

'Just a comment on the flyer we picked up,' Brewster muttered, starting the car.

'The only dreams are in your sick head,' Tally said firmly.

If only your friends could see you now, Brewster thought, accelerating down the road. *Where's Miss Partypants now?*

The letter had thanked Brewster warmly for his interest and had given him the address and date of the next club meeting. It was to be held at a country estate known as Daxton Manor, which could obviously be hired for conferences and meetings. He had been told not to worry about costumes or props, as all that would be catered for. All that was demanded was a primary subscription fee to the club, which would be refunded after the first game if he decided not to continue with them, and the cost of two nights' bed and board at the Manor. There had been very little detail other than that. Brewster had had to fill in a brief questionnaire as to which other role-playing games he had participated in, where he lied glibly, and his general interests, which he'd glamorised and exaggerated. In the place where he had to name his profession or job, if he had one, he refrained from inscribing 'kept by rich parents' and put 'freelance consultant' instead.

That could mean anything. Rather shame-facedly, he'd had to leave blank the section requesting him to list the last three books he had read. He did not want to risk having to act out a scenario from something he'd never even seen the cover of. Of course, Beyond Reality might be nothing like that. He had no idea what to expect.

Tally cheered considerably as they swept up the wide, leaf-strewn drive to the enormous grey facade of Daxton Manor. Seemingly built by a madman, the ancient house sprawled like a weary dinosaur across the countryside. Complicated turrets and domes jutted abruptly from the saurian outline. It made Brewster's brain ache just to look at the place, but Tally was delighted. 'Now this really is a Dream!' she said. 'I'll leave you to go hiking off round the countryside pretending to be a hero and just relax in this gorgeous pile! All my fantasies will be realised just by walking inside! Look at that door!'

The baroque double front doors were thrown wide, revealing little of the gloomy interior. They were at least the height of three tall men.

'Must have had some big furniture to shift into this place!' Brewster said, carrying their cases up the front steps.

'Don't be so unappreciative,' Tally said. 'They knew about style in the old days, yes they did! I love it!' Tally skipped ahead of him through the door. It was now impossible to imagine such an artless, joyful creature ever being sulky or demanding, other than in the prettiest, most disarming way. Tally was either a born actress or a dangerous schizophrenic, Brewster decided.

Inside, he found her already chatting breathlessly about what she thought of the house with a person typical of what he'd thought to find; a slight, male figure of medium height with prematurely receding hair and a scrubby fringe of beard. Not many people still wore glasses nowadays, but this person did; either an affectation or a sign of severe poverty. He was dressed in an oversized jumper and faded jeans and carried a clip-board. 'Hi, you must be Brewster Corley. You two are the last to arrive' The beard held out a long-fingered hand, which looked suspiciously pale and damp. 'I'm Warren Blisley, registrar for this round.'

'How grand!' Brewster said enigmatically, briefly shaking the hand.

Tally shot him a warning glance. Somehow, enthusiasms had swapped around.

'Well, I'd better show you your room, hadn't I?' Warren Blisley said, laughing. Tally laughed too.

Brewster picked up the bags again. 'Lead on.'

'So what made you get in touch with us?' Blisley asked as they ascended a shockingly ornate staircase.

'Oh, we found a little paper thingummy in a night-club,' Tally answered, sounding like a gushing schoolgirl. Brewster winced.

'Really?' said Blisley, grinning. 'Not many people come to us that way. I hope we can fulfil your needs.'

Brewster was ready to take that as a slimy remark and then met Blisley's eyes. Now why had he thought the man a wimp? There was a surprising firmness around the eyes, a penetrating look. *Perhaps these guys are into some kind of weird occult thing,* Brewster thought. He began to take an interest again.

Their room was huge, and exquisitely panelled, but Tally was disappointed to find the furniture quite functional and modern. She had been expecting a four-poster bed and tapestries. Antique grandeur was clearly reserved for the main halls and staircases.

'We'll all meet at dinner,' Blisley said, not venturing into the room. 'The first game will begin immediately after the meal.'

'What shall we wear?' Tally asked. 'Do you have costumes?' It appeared that now she was all for participating.

At least the 200 credits Brewster had had to pay so she could come along wouldn't be wasted.

Blisley smiled - carefully, Brewster noted. 'Not necessary,' he said. 'Didn't you read your pamphlets? Beyond Reality is a game created solely by the imagination. See you both later.'

Brewster and Tally both raised brows at each other when he'd gone, unified, for an instant, in conjecture.

Brewster shrugged. 'We'll have to wait and see, I guess.'

The dining-room was lit by candles. Long windows were draped with floor-length curtains down one side of the room. Twenty-eight people were reflected in the oversized, glossy table as they sat talking, waiting for the meal. They were clearly all well acquainted with each other. Tally and Brewster found themselves nervously hovering in the doorway, before Warren Blisley looked up and saw them. 'Meet our prospective new members,' he said and introduced them.

The greetings were genuine enough. Tally and Brewster sat down. The Beyond Reality Club was a mixed bunch. There were five people who must have been over fifty at least, several gangling youths and the rest middle-twenties to middle-thirties. Every ethnic and cultural permutation in the country seemed to have been represented. Brewster sat next to a handsome, wicked-looking black man, in expensive casual clothes, who spoke like a lawyer, and opposite an overweight motherly woman, wearing a cotton dress in screaming colours, who resembled his last school teacher. Tally's neighbour was a pretty, coltish girl with cropped red hair. The possible lawyer introduced himself as Guy and proceeded to embarrass Brewster asking him what role-playing experience he'd had before.

'I have to admit, I'm a bit of a new-comer to the whole thing,' Brewster said, furiously examining his soup.

'Well in this game, that won't make any difference, so don't worry,' his neighbour replied, smiling.

As the meal progressed an insidious tension began to build up, flowering into unashamed excitement as Manor staff cleared away the remains of the cheese and biscuits. Brewster was reminded of a children's party. Perhaps a magic show would ensue or cartoons on an ancient projector. Coffee was brought out. The Beyonders (as they affectionately referred to themselves) were positively wriggling in their seats.

'So when does the game begin?' Brewster asked, turning to Guy at his side. The man was surely a magician. His smile was a voodoo song.

'Why, it already has, my friend,' he replied, and without warning, the air was full of doves.

'You are to follow me,' Guy said, and Brewster found they had already left the dining-room. There was faint noise behind them, voices, laughter, an excited whoop! The corridor was dimly-lit, the walls were stone and there was a smell of animals.

'Tally!' Brewster said and turned round to point at the door. He felt ineffectual and cringing.

'The girl will be escorted by another. Come!' Guy strode towards the paler oblong of the open front doors. Brewster could see the cloudy night sky. 'Not much longer!' Guy said. 'Shall we run?' He grabbed Brewster's hand and then Brewster's legs were pumping, and the walls of the house were flashing by, and they were leaping, leaping out of the front door, through a veil of scents and sounds into a daylight landscape of towering crags and leaning pine forests.

'What the...?' Brewster couldn't even finish the profanity.

'Yes, the Dream is in the food.' Guy laughed and slapped Brewster on the shoulder. They were both dressed in leather and Brewster appeared to have shrunk in size. For a brief moment, Brewster smiled, thinking of the gushing Tally and how she had consumed the drug without even knowing it. What was she thinking now?

'What happens? What do we do? Where the hell are we?' Brewster's voice rose to a squeak.

'We are Beyond Reality, naturally,' Guy said. 'And we are here to compete, outwit and, not least, enjoy our fantasy. Come along.' He was already marching off towards the forest. Brewster tried to march after him but could only manage an effete scamper.

'Why am I like this?' he asked, catching up with his companion.

'Like what?

'All... small and feeble.'

'It's your first round. You have to prove yourself, learn yourself, grow. Try it now. Grow.'

'What do you mean?'

'Fight your fear and stand up straight and think yourself grown.'

Brewster found himself shoulder to shoulder with Guy, taller than he'd ever been. He managed to laugh.

'Well... How do you get the stuff, the Dream, I mean?'

'We don't know that. We're only the players. Only the Games Master knows that and, as long as we get to play, I don't intend to pry. Neither should you.'

'OK, I take your point'

They travelled overland until the dark forest opened out onto a vast plain, dotted by towering, stone tables. Leathery-winged birds nested in the stone and Brewster saw human figures falling out of the sky. He made a comment.

'Not all dreams are the same,' Guy replied.

An hour later, they came suddenly upon a wooden shack that had appeared from nowhere. In front of it sat a woman Brewster vaguely recognised as one of the Beyonders, although she was now some twenty years younger than he remembered. She stood up and lifted her dress, making lewd offers.

'You won't catch me this time!' Guy said and the woman stuck out a long, reptilian tongue at them.

'Had me dead and back home in no time,' Guy confided,

grimacing as they walked by. 'But it was a marvellous way to go!'

Then a gesturing group of semi-human grotesques barred their way. Their posture was threatening.

'Swords!' Guy cried, holding his hands aloft, where they were obligingly filled from thin air with hard steel.

'Swords? Why not a flame-thrower?' Brewster asked, stepping backwards.

'Brewster, please!' Guy said, over his shoulder, shaking his head. 'This is a game. Be a sportsman!'

'OK. Steel! I've never fought this way before. I'm going to die.'

'So? Think you're a fighter and you will be. Don't be a pessimist.'

Guy roared delightedly and sprang forward, already hacking limbs. Brewster roared too. It seemed to work. His arm worked effortlessly as if he'd done this appalling thing a thousand times. As he swung and cut, he wondered if these were fellow Dreamers he was despatching. Guy caught the thought.

'No, too easy. These are just dream forms.'

Eventually, there weren't any left. Guy and Brewster walked on, without looking back. Maybe there was nothing left on the grass behind them.

'Can't we ride horses or something?' Brewster asked.

Guy shrugged and then they were cantering through the plains grass on spindly-legged, snorting thoroughbreds.

'Like the tassels, Brew. Good touch.' Guy held his ornamented reins aloft and laughed.

By day, they rode. They wished for food and it was there.

'You have taken control of your dreams,' Guy said. 'The Waking Dream does this for us.'

By night, they encountered brightly-lit towns and stayed in bordellos. Brewster bedded girls he was never sure were real or not. It didn't matter.

The days passed. The countryside changed. Brewster found his real life had become indistinct and without importance. 'Are we here forever?' he asked.

Guy laughed then. 'So what's forever?'

Sometimes, Brewster thought of Tally. Sometimes, he worried about her, but less and less as time passed. Although they didn't really need to, being able to dream their financial requirements into reality, they decided to become mercenaries for a while. A fat man with one arm and a family problem hired them to find his son, who'd been kidnapped. They journeyed overseas to a far land, where there was nothing but sand, and found the boy, castrated, and slave to a powerful lord who doubled their fee to forget their task and go on a quest for him. They were to retrieve his beautiful young mistress from a warlock of questionable character.

'Guy, this is a cliché,' Brewster said, as they rode through a deep, yellow canyon into yet another land. 'All this rescuing stuff. It's straight out of a sword and sorcery epic.'

Guy laughed good-humouredly. 'So? I like it this way. Next time, you do what you want. This time, you're a novice and I call the shots - most of them.'

Next time. Brewster hadn't wondered since the beginning when this would all end and he'd find himself back at Draxton Manor. He didn't like to think about it. 'Does this place have any...well, say in what happens to us, or is it all subject to our own will?'

'The place? Don't know. There are other players here though. They do.'

'Just Beyonders?'

'No. Of course not. Everybody dreams. Some people may have control without the drug. We have an advantage, that's all.'

'Wait a minute! Are you saying everyone in the world comes here when they dream.'

'Don't be stupid. Come here when they dream? We're here all the time, Brew, my friend. We just can't see it.'

For a shimmering moment, as he shuddered, Brewster caught a glimpse of English fields and a cloudy sky. He shook himself and the hot walls of the canyon glared once more beneath a torrid sun.

The beautiful young mistress turned out to be Tally. Brewster was angry. Not least because the questionable warlock was Warren Blisley and the odalisque Tally Ritter was plainly loath to leave him and his luxurious, if eerie, coastal tower, to return to her fantasy of the harem. This one was better, she'd found. At first, she didn't recognise Brewster at all and then started to rant and rave that he was evil and had imprisoned her against her will. Blisley threw a few effective spells at the would-be rescuers and it all got rather unpleasant.

Just as Blisley reared up to a staggering fifteen feet of riled wizard, screaming, 'I will damn you to hell, warrior whore!' at Brewster, the ground trembled and Guy and Brewster found themselves falling through space, peering up between the legs of a gargantuan female giant, picking her teeth with a torn-up tree trunk. It was the Floral Print woman.

'Wings Brewster!' Guy instructed in a no-nonsense voice and they were flying away over the sea.

'I'm tired, Guy,' Brewster said, and his voice sounded faint and far away.

'Float down,' Guy replied and they circled and circled, riding warm currents of air, into a pearly cloud where they spread out their wings in radiant shafts of light and drifted... and drifted...

Brewster woke up with a foul, sticky mouth. He felt nauseous, febrile and started to shake as soon as he opened his stinging eyes. Bright sunlight fell on his face where he lay on the floor of the entrance hall of Draxton Manor. Nearby, Guy snored contentedly... still Dreaming? Brewster sat up. He felt like weeping. Like laughing. There was no sign of anyone else around, but the dining-room door was open. Tally was sprawled across the table, her thumb in her mouth, smiling. Brewster suppressed irritation (it was only a dream after all) and shook her. She gulped and squeaked and opened her eyes, arms scrabbling on the polished surface.

'It's over Tally, welcome to reality,' Brewster said, his voice sour. Luckily, Warren Blisley was nowhere in sight.

A Manor maid appeared in the doorway and announced that breakfast would be brought in soon. 'If you'd be so kind as to collect your friends,' she said with a tolerant smile and disappeared with a brisk step.

Tally was rubbing her face. 'How long, Brew?' she asked wistfully. 'How long?'

Brewster shook his head. 'One night or two... I don't know. We're booked in for two nights remember.'

Tally stared at him carefully for a moment. 'I hope it's just been one, don't you? Because then...'

'I thought you didn't hold with drugs,' Brewster reminded her sharply.

Tally smiled and lay back on the table, arms spread, her hair flowing out in an abundant golden wave around her head. 'It's not a drug. It's not. Warren told me. It's only a thing that opens doors, that makes the doors visible to us that are there all the time.'

'Suit yourself,' Brewster said. He didn't want to listen to any of Warren Blisley's theories.

Tally sat up again, her face radiant. 'I want to go back. I want to improve, play the game. I feel like I was only spectating this time. I want to be powerful! A sorceress! A queen!'

'A nightclubber? Oh, come on, Tally, pull yourself together. It was a good trip, but don't get too subjective about it, OK?'

But even as he mocked her, Brewster knew that, like Tally, he yearned to go back, to escape the mundane, to be free, powerful, living in exotica. Because of what Waking Dream could offer, they would make this club their life, as had all the other Beyonders, and they would pay again and again to experience the wonder of the world of fantasy, whatever dangers it might put their real bodies in. How could they know what happened to them as they dreamed? Were they jerking around, mimicking the actions of the game? Who knows? Who cares? They were just beginning and both felt that they had to get back there quickly because they'd wasted so much time before, not doing enough. Waking Dream. Have you had a Waking Dream yet? Would others come to join them? Brewster panicked. What if the authorities got wind of it and somehow prevented them having the Dreams. Perhaps, if they learned enough, they could reach the land of fantasy without the drug. Perhaps he and Tally had been the only ones to take it anyway. Please, please let it be so.

Beyonders began to drift into the room, embracing each other as they met.

Warren Blisley came and put his arms around Brewster and Tally. 'With us?' he asked.

Brewster was surprised to find he had no hard feelings left for the man. He nodded for both himself and Tally, who had been overcome by emotion and was now weeping on Blisley's shoulder. 'We're with you,' he said. 'Beyond Reality.'

The Germ of Life

The advance sales force of Heinz-Sizoto Ethnic Syndication (Trade Element) had been on Kodiak for several weeks now. The indis were taking their time deciding whether to take advantage of Freezone's outrageously attractive trading deals (free holidays to other worlds included), perhaps concerned about who was actually going to be taking advantage of who.

The landing team was beginning to get restless, two members of which - Taskell, company liaison officer and Orgida Frame, analysis officer - virtually allowing their professional relationship to decay to combat level.

Orgida had trailed Taskell to the leisure module of the lander, temporary home and institution, and was annoying him intensely as he tried to study the incomprehensible glyphs of a Kodiakny storyball. Orgida made no secret of the fact that she did not particularly like the race native to this world. She was not exactly a veteran member of the company.

'Well, there's a danger of... *anthropomorphising*, isn't there,' Orgida was saying, 'a real danger.' She bit into one of the indi fruit, munching thoughtfully.

'These are people, Giddy, not animals,' Taskell reminded her abstractedly, the ball still held up to his nose.

Orgida hopped nimbly down from the console where she'd been sprawling and batted the ball with her hands.

'Hey,' Taskell snapped.

'I think you should listen, that's all.' Orgida said. 'Weren't you taught anything at the Academy? You empathise too much.'

Taskell showed his annoyance only by a repressed, nasal sigh. 'I'm here to work, Giddy. This isn't a party, or a zoo for that matter.' He grasped air unsuccessfully in an attempt to retrieve the ball that Orgida had whipped from his fingers.

'Don't tell me you understand any of this,' she said, turning the ball in her hands. 'It doesn't say anything. It's nonsense.'

'Get back to your video literature and shut up,' Taskell said. 'And give me the ball back.'

'OK.' Orgida tossed it through the air and it landed on Taskell's lap. He contained a cry of surprise. Most of her irritating behaviour was caused by boredom, Taskell knew that. The landing party had already seen, examined and AV-mo all the places of interest into which they were allowed. The Kodiaknies were wary of strangers; not hostile, or even impolite, but the landing team of Ecuador 501 knew when they were being kept at arm's length. It was not an unusual circumstance. After all, in the mythologies of most cultures, aliens dropping from the sky was an event presaging tyranny and conquest. Very few races fell down at their feet and called them gods. They were more likely to greet them with firepower and suspicion.

Orgida was new to the ranks of Freezone Cartel. Taskell suspected she'd been hoping for something more exotic than the work really was. All those recruitment ad promises of far worlds, unbelievable sights and experiences, and the ego-massaging hint of how responsible a position it would be. You Too Can Be An Envoy For the Human Race! The fantasies of centuries encouraged this exaggeration. Trying to convince people they would really benefit from allying themselves to a trading cartel like Freezone was, more often than not, difficult.

Taskell shook his head, sighing, as Orgida flounced off to find someone else to annoy. He tried to concentrate on the book. Perhaps the girl was right. Perhaps he was trying to anthropomorphise the Kodiaknies. They looked no different from human stock; they smiled, they frowned, used all that universal language, but, as Giddy had reminded him, one of the first things he'd learned on his Xenology Studycourse was that it was a big mistake to behave as if people of other worlds functioned and thought like humans did. A mistake learned the hard way, by many unsuccessful pioneers returned home in jars with taciturn, incomprehensible explanations attached. So, the salesmen trod softly nowadays and were trained in the ways of Patience. Such considerations still could not quell the heady lift of pleasure Taskell experienced when he thought about his next meeting with the Kodiakny, Argolk. This was the human pronunciation of the name. In Kodiakny, it sounded more like a hearty belch.

He met her in the evening, a time all Kodiaknies appeared to regard as propitious for conducting business, or it might just have been they'd put aside other more important matters then. Taskell strolled down from the lander through the warm, moist air to the small courtyard of peach-coloured stone just inside the circular wall of the Kodiakny settlement. The visitors called this place Ogoch. As he walked, he reflected on what a delicate world this seemed, from the pale shrinking pastel light to the sweeping, gently swelling hills, to the lacy trees fluttering drooping fronds like nervous fingers. Ecologically, the inhabitants, both animal and plant, lived together in harmony, without waste or ruin. It was almost as if some wry deity, in creating the world, had felt impelled to taint it with one small imperfection. The Kodiaknies, for all their fey daintiness, croaked like frogs.

Argolk was waiting placidly, the yellow plug of the translator Taskell had given her already in place inside her ear. She'd laid a sheaf of wafer pages on the warm stone bench beside her, delicately inscribed with precise, dead- black glyphs. 'I have news for you,' her voice murmured in his ear, so close it drowned out the gurgle of the sounds she was really making.

'Good news from your face,' Taskell said, smiling back.

Argolk screwed up her face, which appeared faintly oriental in caste, and made a peculiar shuddering gesture.

Taskell already knew this signified agreement and pleasure. He sat down beside her. She had a smell of milky vanilla; almost a cliché, he knew, but there was no other way to describe it.

'Indeed,' she said. 'After much deliberation, the Community Council has decided to give the project a trial.'

Taskell made a jubilant cry and punched the air delightedly. 'Wonderful! I was beginning to think we'd failed to impress you.' He smothered his enthusiasm with a business-like calm. 'So what convinced them?'

'Well, as you know, they've had your samples for some weeks now, and various members of the Council and the Home Guilds have been using them. Their only concern at present is whether the power packs will work out more expensive than the goods themselves.'

'There's no reason why the cartel can't help your people build their own plant to manufacture the packs here on Kodiak...' Here Taskell broke off with a sheepish grin. 'Dammit, it seems obscene to suggest such a thing on this world, Argolk. Somehow I just can't imagine your perfect skylines being blighted by industrial plants, no matter how fetchingly they're designed.'

Argolk croaked out a laugh which rang in his ears like bell charms. 'Taskell, we are not all innocent children, you know! We do have factories of our own. The only difference is that we like them to blend in with the rest of our buildings.' She frowned. 'Not like the pictures on the tape you lent me.' She jiggled her shoulders rapidly and executed quick stabbing motions with her arms to signify distaste.

'Some of those pictures were of mining concerns, Argolk, just asteroids and such. I won't say my people are the best at building design but we do care a lot about the worlds we work on. We learned a very hard lesson in our own history, believe me.'

Argolk smiled politely, but didn't ask him to expand upon that. 'Tomorrow evening, the Council will meet with your people to discuss details. It was proposed I tell you of this tonight so that you might prepare yourselves.' She stood up, and Taskell was surprised by the pang of alarm he felt.

'You're not going, yet, surely?' he said, too abruptly.

Argolk clutched the papers to her chest. 'Unfortunately, I have other things to do now. I am in training for promotion, as you know.'

'Yes, of course.' She'd already spoken briefly of this to him. Naturally, the translator chose the path of least resistance in converting her words to universal tongue, but he understood she was destined for a higher place within the council hierarchy. It made sense. Despite her apparent frailty, she gave off an air of quiet and ambitious determination. This attribute only added to her unquestionable allure. Taskell sighed and watched her pass through the tall gate on the other side of the yard, into the city itself. He lifted his eyes to gaze up at the spiralling hump of the place. Orgida had called it a termite hill when she'd first seen it. To Taskell, it looked like a benign stone goddess, but then he was known to be rather a romantic.

The landing party were so pleased when Taskell told them of their success they decided to hold an impromptu celebration. Their Captain, Scallion, unlocked his liquor supply with hardly a twinge of the miserly pain it usually caused him. The lander itself, even within the few weeks of being stationary, had evolved from space vehicle to sprawling bungalow, littered with the crew's personal possessions and souvenirs of Kodiak. Everyone gathered outside the main hatch, where Taskell bathed in the congratulations of his colleagues, allowing them to believe he was wholly responsible for the Kodiaknies' swift compliance. Privately, he thought the goods had merely spoken for themselves. They were high quality and more than adequate trade for the Kodiakny artefacts.

Orgida, living up to her image of sharp-tongued viper, said, 'Oh dear, Taskell. Your little tete a tetes with the Kodiakny morsel are destined to be curtailed, it seems.'

Taskell couldn't help bridling and defending himself. 'If you're referring to Argolk, which it's clear you are, you know very well that she was the representative chosen to deal with us for her people, just as I was.'

Orgida grinned cruelly. 'A convenient, indeed cosy, arrangement as I'm sure you found.'

'I wonder whether you'd be saying these things if it had been a man I'd dealt with?'

'A male amphibian, you mean.' Orgida yawned theatrically. 'I for one will not be sorry to leave this place. It's boring.'

'And you are culturally dead. Sometimes I wonder why you're in this business Orgida Frame, I really do.'

'It's good money.'

'Have you no sense of aesthetics?'

She was clearly going to make a sharp, witty reply, then thought better of it, shrugging carelessly instead. 'I find the primitive innocence of this world annoying, if you must know. So bloody nice. Sickening. It's like the smell of the place; cloying and sweet. I can't believe it's real. In fact, I don't. It gives me the creeps.'

'You're just a cynic used to human cynicism and deceit.'

'Maybe,' she answered, in a milder tone than Taskell had expected, 'but I'm also female, so I trust my instincts.'

Taskell repeated some of this conversation later to the medical officer, Cylya Grant, an older woman, whose common sense he trusted. 'Is Giddy right, do you think?' he asked. The remarks Orgida had made worried him just a little, because she'd spoken with such confidence.

Cylya Grant had laughed and slapped his shoulder. 'You are an oaf sometimes, Task, the woman fancies you. She's jealous of the Kodiakny girl, that's all.'

Taskell found this hard to believe, but perhaps it was the explanation.

The following day, Taskell sat on the lander ramp, drinking fruit juice and gazing at the pastel mound of Ogoch. Orgida was right, he supposed, for after the trading deal had been secured the Traveller crew would up landing struts and go. A melancholy thought. Although he had visited many worlds, some pleasant, some uncomfortable, none of them had had such a effect on his soul as Kodiak. He loved it. He was reluctant to leave. Also, after a long career of dealing dispassionately with other races, he had found a people who had touched his heart. Their inscrutability intrigued him, their gestures warmed him, their dainty loveliness pleased his eye. The Kodiaknies were not prey to violent passions; they rolled with the world, calm, inexorable, infinite. In comparison, human beings seemed like quickly moving blurs of anxiety and detachment. He remembered one of the early meetings he'd had with the Kodiaknies, their cautious yet probing questions about other worlds, other cultures. He remembered how they'd said, 'we have everything we need here' almost unable to comprehend the benefits of having access to off-world commodities. Likewise, they failed to understand that other races would appreciate greatly the merchandise of Kodiak, the functional graceful, purity of their domestic implements, their pale, wistful art, their simple yet eminently flattering couture. No, the Kodiaknies did not realise what they were; small miracles in the vastness of space. Wars, even competitiveness, were concepts absent from both their language and philosophy.

That evening, the lander crew went in a group down to the cream walls of Ogoch. Already, they talked about where they would go next. Taskell knew this particular team would be broken up now. First a holiday was in order. They'd cross back to the pastoral space station Africa Plate, where

Freezone had its administrative HQ, check out their credit balances, and take a well-earned rest, before being assigned to new ships, new destinations. It was unlikely they'd all be placed together again. It was not company policy to keep one team in existence for more than a few assignments. Romantic attachments were destined to ephemerality because of this. Taskell was glad he would soon be parting company with Orgida. Cylya Grant's revelation the previous evening made him uneasy.

A party of Kodiaknies was waiting for them at the gates, to conduct the visitors to the Council Chambers. This was a building set high in the heart of Ogoch. Taskell felt inclined to look upon the city as one vast building in itself. Everything was joined together, narrow streets curving between the clots of dwellings, shops and workshops. It was a long walk. Another surprising thing about the Kodiaknies was their apparent lack of transport. Argolk had professed they had no need for it. Their technology too seemed minimal yet they were clearly an advanced people. Orgida's sharp remark sprang to Taskell's mind. He must stop thinking of these people as human. They were not driven souls in the literal sense, ever searching to break new boundaries of conception and ability. He'd had so little opportunity to study their history, but it was likely they were an ancient culture who'd transgressed the adolescent yearnings still experienced by any other race Taskell had come in contact with. He had not really expected the Kodiaknies to agree to a trade deal.

When the human group reached the Council Chambers, there was no sign of Argolk, as Taskell had hoped for. The Councillors, all wearing sweet smiles and translator plugs, looked as charming and innocent as children dressed up in their parents' clothes. As the visitors were conducted into an airy, pleasant room set with a long polished table and chairs, Taskell asked where Argolk was. She was their spokesperson after all. 'She has been a great help,' he said, to qualify his obvious desire for her presence.

'Indeed,' replied the stately Councillor he'd addressed. 'She is a great asset to our people, greatly honoured. The experience she's gained through dealing with you will help her immensely, I'm sure. We all need experiences to look back on.' Her absence was not explained.

Before beginning business, the Kodiaknies served light refreshment. This consisted of a mild, alcoholic beverage that tasted like a flower wine and fried chunks of the mainstay of their diet, a kind of cheesy curd that was equally delicious whether cooked as sweet or savoury, accompanied by a crisp, bitter salad.

Cylya Grant, in her capacity as medical officer, had long been intrigued by the foodstuffs. Now she saw the opportunity to ask questions. 'We have something like this,' she said to a female Councillor sitting beside her as she waved a piece of the curd on a prong. 'We call it tofu, it's made from beans. How do you make this?'

The Councillor glanced at her superior at the head of the table. He said, 'We call it kha.' The word was almost spat. 'Food of the mothers.' The translator had clearly had a problem with this.

Clearly, Cylya wasn't sure it had grasped the right nuance. 'It's made from a grain then, or a seed?'

'You noticed the smooth building further down the path?' the Head Councillor asked.

'Smooth?' Cylya said. The councillor frowned.

'No, flat, ground sight. That is the re-process plant. It's where all the kha is refined. Feeding our people is perhaps our largest industry.'

Cylya shook her head quizzically, glanced at Taskell. Perhaps the translators hadn't been programmed too well by the survey team.

'Maybe you should think about exporting the kha too,' Scallion said.

The Head Councillor shook his head, made a guttural sound. 'Oh no, impossible. We were given the kha by the

Ground Spirits. It would be blasphemy to treat it like that. Anyway, we could never produce enough. It takes all our capabilities just to supply ourselves.'

'How fascinating,' Cylya said.

Orgida, who'd made sure she sat next to Taskell, pulled a face at him and disinterestedly nibbled on a piece of the kha.

Taskell repressed a surge of irritation and made no response. This did not repel her advances.

Leaning over confidentially, Orgida whispered in his ear, 'Probably make it from children, or criminals or...' she giggled, 'even visiting aliens!'

Taskell, who'd been a vegetarian for years, grimaced and said, 'You're disgusting, Giddy. Be quiet.'

After the food was finished, the platters removed and the wine pots replenished, the discussion moved sedately towards business. The Kodiaknies could either operate on a strict barter system with Freezone, or else open an account in the zone bank HQ. on Africa Plate, enabling them to canter into the arena of interstellar marketing. Taskell was surprised when the Kodiaknies chose the latter. Freezone would undertake to help build a serviceable port outside the city, and also offer advice and contacts concerning the construction of any new plants the Kodiaknies felt would be needed once their new profile in the trade-space took form. Scallion shook the Head Councillor's hand. 'Welcome to the partnership,' he said, grinning.

'Welcome to civilisation, he means,' Orgida whispered in Taskell's ear.

'And you're civilised?' Taskell hissed back. His annoyance was clear.

Orgida shrugged and moodily drank her wine.

Taskell was aware the entire crew harboured a certain antipathy towards the Kodiaknies, even if they were not consciously aware of feeling that way. He could not understand it. Was it because they hadn't been given the red carpet treatment they preferred? The Kodiaknies had never been impolite or hostile, but it had been made gently clear they did not want the aliens actually staying in the city. Taskell respected their desire for privacy, and their circumspection in dealing with an unknown race. Worlds whose inhabitants were more gregarious were the places where traders were most likely to get swindled.

The morning after the meal, Taskell decided to take a stroll down to Ogoch and request an interview with Argolk. After all, once the lander left Kodiak he would never see her again. The usual procedure was for him to enter the courtyard and ring a bell attached to the wall. Someone generally answered it in seconds. Today, possibly because he was earlier than usual, it took several rings to get a response. Eventually a young Kodiakny boy opened the hatch in the door. His bland face registered neither surprise nor annoyance at Taskell's unscheduled visit. The boy wrestled his head into a translator and Taskell made his request. The Kodiakny ducked away, closing the hatch behind him.

Taskell stood for a few moments, expecting it would take a while for them to fetch the girl. She may be working, he mused, or else studying her papers. He smiled to himself, visualising her glossy head bent over a desk, her gamine face frowning in concentration.

Minutes passed. Taskell sat down on one of the stone benches and watched the sun creep higher in the sky. Irritation set in. He paced a little. Then rang the bell again. It was opened promptly.

'I asked to see the Council representative, Argolk,' Taskell told the elderly female looking through the hatch. She wore a cockeyed translator. 'It was some time ago. Perhaps I should call back later?'

'A moment please!' The hatch slammed shut before Taskell could say more.

In a short while, the door itself opened and one of the Councillors walked into the courtyard, smiling. 'So sorry you have been kept waiting,' he said. 'What may I do for you?'

'I was hoping to see Argolk, actually,' Taskell said.

'Ah, unfortunately the young lady has now accepted her promotion,' the Councillor said. 'Perhaps you can deal with the Council directly now, for the remaining time you are here?'

Taskell wondered whether the translator had picked up correctly the hint of rebuttal. 'I hope you are satisfied with the arrangements,' he said.

The Councillor spread his hands. 'All was arranged to satisfaction last evening, I think. We of Ogoch look forward to doing business with your people. Now, if there is something else you wished to discuss, I must stress there is work I have to attend to...'

'Oh, it was nothing really. Just something Argolk and I were discussing. Is there no chance of seeing her at all now?'

The Councillor looked over his shoulder, so swiftly Taskell was not really sure whether he'd seen it. 'Mr. Taskell, it would be best if you did not ask for Argolk again. It would be embarrassing for her. It's not your fault, because you can't be expected to know our customs, but Argolk is really beyond trivial interaction. You see, her time came unexpectedly sudden. Now, she has been elected to the Mother Providers at the lake site. She is no longer here.'

'I had no idea she was in training for such an honour. What exactly are the Mother Providers?'

The Councillor drew himself erect. 'I regret that, as an Outsider you cannot be privy to our Religious Mysteries. I don't mean to sound rude, but if you were more familiar to us, it might be different.'

'A religious position, then?' Taskell was thinking, crestfallen, of nuns; shorn heads and celibate lifestyles.

'Of a kind. We look upon all aspects of our life as part of our religion. The girl Argolk is involved with a Higher Mystery of Life. I'm sure she is grateful for the experience of having met you and your people before her new phase began. I'm sure she will think of it warmly for as long as she can. I'm sorry your friendship with her was cut short in this way. I know she enjoyed speaking with you.'

'And I with her.'

The Councillor signified acknowledgement. 'Yes. It may, or may not, be a comfort, but you will not be alone in feeling wistful at Argolk's absence. Still, the young man concerned must come to terms with what he knew to be inevitable and you have your stars to comfort you.' The Councillor gestured to the sky. 'Perhaps, if things had been different, you could have copulated with Argolk before you left. Would that have pleased you?'

'Well...' Taskell was taken aback by this frank question. He had considered the Kodiaknies to be rather fastidious about such things. Argolk had never intimated otherwise.

'If that is where your curiosity lies, it would be no trouble to send another girl to the courtyard...'

Taskell raised his hands in an uncontrollable gesture of defence. He took a step back. 'No, thank you, but... that is not quite what I had in mind.' It had been, utterly, of course, but he'd never dreamed such a fantasy could have been realised. Certainly not in such a passionless way. He felt the glow begin to fall from his mental picture of Argolk. Perhaps it was best this way.

Expressing his thanks to the Councillor for his time, Taskell returned to the lander. He considered what he'd been told. Argolk's next phase? She'd think about him for as long as she could? Odd. Must be the translator fouling up again, he told himself, to banish any more sinister implications.

Shortly after sunset, an unannounced visitor arrived at the lander. Everyone was beginning to pack up. One of the company mother ships would be in orbit in a day and half Kodiak time and the lander would then take off and rejoin her. Taskell was helping to check service the outer hull; a routine, the lander had suffered no damage during the visit.

Scallion came round the side of the craft, wiping his hands on a rag. 'There's a Kodiakny lad to see you, Task,' he said. 'Had no translator so he was croaking away like a mad thing till we got him wired up!' The Captain laughed.

Taskell followed him to the hatchway. He saw the Kodiakny, not a person he was familiar with, young and handsome, also extremely nervous to go from his body language. There was a few moments' delay as Taskell hunted for a translator of his own. 'How can I help you?' he asked. The longer the boy was in human company, the more demented he looked. The translator had considerable trouble coping with his vocal farts.

'It wasn't what she wanted. She had no choice,' the boy garbled.

All the lander crew had gathered now to watched the proceedings, translators wired in.

'What are you talking about, slow down,' Taskell said calmly.

'Argolk. They took her. It was wrong. We could have petitioned. A marriage could have repealed the injunction but they took her before we had chance. Mother Providers never marry. They can't. They only mate.'

'I don't understand why you're telling me this.' Taskell had a tight edge to his voice. He was acutely conscious of Orgida standing behind him, and sensed she was fighting an intense urge to put her hand on his shoulder.

The boy pointed at the sky. 'You have up there. All of it. Take her with you. Get her back before it is too late. She won't disobey the calling herself. She respects it too much. But I know she doesn't want it. Not really. She's too good for that. It was a mistake. She was a third child. Her parents had no way of knowing she'd turn out so bright. Please help her. There's no-one else.'

A profound silence fell over the landing party. All eyes turned to Taskell, then to Scallion, who naturally stepped forward to display his command.

'Are you asking us to perform some kind of rescue?' His voice held a laugh, but then it generally did.

The boy spread his hands, pleading. 'Help her.' It was such a poignant appeal, not one of the party felt unmoved by it.

Scallion began to speak, cleared his throat, began again. 'Now look, boy. I'm sorry if you or the girl is in trouble, but we're only envoys, only doing a job. We can't get involved in local affairs, understand? We couldn't operate if we did. Could we, Taskell?' This last was spoken very firmly.

'No, we couldn't,' Taskell confirmed, painfully.

'You have the stars,' said the Kodiakny boy, but from his posture it was clear he knew he'd get no help here. He began to take off the translator.

'Where is she?' Taskell asked.

The boy met his eyes, perhaps seeking a message Taskell was not even sure was there. 'The lake. The mother cone.' He threw the translator on the ground and headed back towards Ogoch.

'No way, Taskell,' Scallion said and stomped into the lander, 'And that goes for all of you, so no wet eyes understand? It's none of our business. We got the job. We're leaving. End of story. Got it?'

'Yes, sir!' said Cylya Grant, fiercely.

Scallion poked his head out again. 'Don't give me that 'Captain's a Monster' tone, Grant. You know I'm right. We could be up to our necks in shit, diplomatic and otherwise.' He went inside.

At dawn, even before the sun, Triomides XI, had backlit the womanly curve of the East Ogoch hills, Orgida Frame floated one of the lander's two sleds silently out some way so as not to arouse any of the others. She had no particular plan in mind, certainly nothing heroic, but her natural curiosity, coupled with a niggling desire to please Taskell, urged her to partake in a little clandestine investigation concerning the

Kodiakny, Argolk. She had her own suspicions, and was somewhat impatient that Taskell hadn't come to the same conclusions she had. But he was a man, and perhaps lacked the gut feelings she was experiencing. Talking of guts, she knew Scallion would have hers if he found out what she was doing; the visiting party was under strict instructions not to nose around.

The sled surged forward, lifting towards the clouds and the dawn. Arrowing up towards thinner air, Orgida activated the atmosphere bubble of the sled. It eased over her, silencing the morning. A faint whine could be perceived as the air control supervised the micro-atmosphere within the bubble. From a high altitude, Orgida surveyed the pale, sparsely forested hills below. There was very little sign of habitation. The Kodiaknies had told the visitors the next city was two weeks' march away; communications was another undeveloped aspect of Kodiakny life. It seemed each community was autonomous. There was no central government and very little interaction, not even for trade. A strange, isolated race. She wondered why they had agreed to the trade deal. Were they so impressed with off-world trinkets?

That boy appearing last night like that had really spooked her. It seemed obvious to Orgida what was going on. Argolk was a Mother Provider; that meant she provided something, and something vital. She would not marry, only mate... *Oh, come on!* Orgida thought angrily. She swung her sled around to the east a little. There seemed little chance she'd be observed from the ground. Nobody was around. She took out her camera and snapped a few dozen pictures. Might as well do something.

The sled followed the undulations of the hills heading north east. After a few miles, Orgida registered the metallic glitter that presaged water. Perhaps this was where the Kodiakny farms would be. She activated the sled's viewer and cranked up the magnification. Sure enough, a spoked sprawl of low buildings radiated out from the lake ahead. Almost on the shore was a miniature version of Ogoch itself; a pale cone of a building. Orgida could see a spiral ramp winding round it. There didn't appear to be any sign of agriculture, but for a small group of sheep-like creatures grazing placidly beyond the compound. Perhaps other animals were kept inside the buildings.

Orgida shot a few more frames, skimming over the water. She took care to photograph the thick pipe issuing from the cone building's base that was, even at this early hour, exuding a peculiar foamy effluent into the lake. Nice. It took the edge off Kodiakny purity. Pollution was a vice humanity had wisely discarded centuries ago. Hoping for some kind of aural clarification, Orgida lowered the sled and opened up the bubble. In an instant, she was scrambling for the reseal button, her stomach retching. Gods, what a stench! With streaming eyes, she accelerated the sled skywards. What was that? Manure? Orgida was forced to wipe her nose on her sleeve, lacking either rag or tissue. The smell had been like a concentration of the sweet smell of Kodiak itself, nauseatingly strong. She decided it was time to head back to the lander.

Orgida asked Taskell to meet her in the rec cabin, and here showed him the photographs, which he leafed through with feigned disinterest. 'This was a waste of time,' he said. 'You know we can't do anything.'

'Aren't you curious, though?' Orgida asked him. She was crestfallen he didn't seem to appreciate her conciliatory gesture.

'Some part of me says I'd rather not know,' he replied, throwing the pictures down on a table. 'It all sounds rather sinister.'

'Not sounds,' Orgida said firmly. '*Is sinister!* Task, think about it...'

At that point, Cylya Grant marched into the rec. cabin,

clutching a sheaf of computer printouts. 'Aha, sinister!' she said with delight. 'What is?'

Taskell wordlessly handed her Orgida's photographs.

'The Kodiakny place at the lake,' Orgida supplied, sullenly. 'The so-called *farm*.'

Cylya flicked through the pictures. 'Interesting, though not as interesting as this.' She patted the printout with pride. 'Although they are certainly part of the same story, I'd say. I took the liberty of analysing some of the Kodiakny kha we ate last night. Brought a bit back with me in my pocket.'

Orgida correctly predicted the cause of Cylya's gleeful expression. 'Uh oh, something tells me I'm going to feel nauseous very shortly.'

'Don't tell me, it's made from processed baby,' Taskell said sourly.

Cylya laughed. 'You should not joke, my friend, although that description is rather an exaggeration.'

'What do you mean?' Orgida asked, trying to wrest Cylya's printout away from her.

'Well, the stuff was organic in content, as I suspected,' she said. 'A complex foodstuff; protein, carbohydrate and a high concentration of minerals and vitamins. Highly palatable too.'

'And?' Taskell enquired.

'Well, after my computer finished the analysis, it told me that, in view of certain substances that were present, the kha is very similar to what you'd end up with should you mince and process a, well I hate to this, but a pre- parturient form of life.'

'You mean a foetus?' Orgida cried in horror.

'Wait a minute,' Taskell interrupted. 'She said very similar. That's different from saying that's exactly what it is.'

Cylya nodded. 'True. The computer also said the stuff didn't appear to be totally mammalian in origin, but almost reptilian, like the goo you'd find in a crocodile egg, probably. That discounts the Kodiaknies, I would say. They don't appear reptilian to me. However, we have to bear in mind our knowledge of them as a race is scant.'

'I can't imagine why you'd even think they used their own people to make kha,' Taskell said. 'They obviously breed the animals that provide it in the place Orgida saw today. That's hardly a mystery, not even sinister.' He sounded relieved.

Orgida sighed. How could he be so blind?

'I would have agreed with you,' Cylya said, 'if it wasn't for what that boy said last night. Have to take that into account, don't we?' She smiled. 'But perhaps it *is* just my over-active imagination.'

Both Orgida and Taskell were silent.

'Not our concern anyway,' Cylya continued. 'We're off soon, thank the gods! I'll show this to Scallion. It might interest him. See you.'

Orgida and Taskell stared at each other. Orgida picked up a photograph of the dome by the lake. Was it possible? She found herself thinking of hen's eggs, and Argolk condemned to a life as some kind of battery chicken. Perhaps, once Kodiakny girls were chosen for the role of Mother Provider they even changed physically in some way. She remembered that awful scum on the lake, the eye-watering stench of manure. It would be kinder not to dwell on this aloud, she thought. Instead, she risked patting Taskell on the arm. 'She was a pretty girl, for all her frog croak,' she said. 'I know you really liked her. I'm sorry, Task.'

Taskell took the photograph off her. 'A pleasing diversion,' he said, with unconvincing carelessness.

'Yeah, well, I told you not to anthropomorphise,' Orgida reminded him, carefully.

Taskell grimaced and put the photograph down. 'I think I need a rest from this job,' he said.

Did You Like What You Read?

Paradoxine by Roberto Quaglia
978-1-904853-67-1/IP0091
$21.99/£12.99 paperback
The hilarious misadventures of James Vagabond and the mysteries of reality and the universe. Be amazed at how Japan takes up residence in central Europe. What is the real identity of Omar Khatib, also known as Mu'azib the Torturer, and why doesn't Omar Khatib know?

Mythangelus by Storm Constantine
ISBN 978-1-904853-59-6/IP0024
$21.99/£12.99 paperback
The second volume in the collected short stories of Storm Constantine – stories with an angelic theme.

Queenmagic, Kingmagic by Ian Watson
ISBN 978-1-904853-66-4 /IP0090
$19.99/£9.99 paperback
Two lands are locked in perpetual war, conducted by magic. A war may continue for centuries, until one side succeeds in killing the other side's king, at which point the whole world vanishes, only to reappear and have the cycle begin again.

A Dream and a Lie by Fiona McGavin
ISBN 978-1-904853-63-3/ IP0087
$25.99/£16.99 paperback
The omnibus edition of Fiona's highly praised fantasy trilogy: 'A Dark God Laughing', 'Dreams of Drowning' and 'The Fourth Cleansing'.

Find these and the rest of our current lineup at http://www.immanion-press.com